getting in

For
SID

"Life is what happens to you
while you're busy making other plans."

—JOHN LENNON

Life, for Nora, had become an endless SAT exam. At seven forty-five on a Saturday morning she stood in her closet in her underwear, paralyzed by a series of multiple-choice questions.

Question 1: It's really sunny but I felt a cool breeze when I opened the bedroom window. Should I wear:

    a. A thin turtleneck

    b. A light sweater

    c. A scarf

    d. All of the above

Question 2: I won't be home until after one. Should I eat:

    a. Egg whites and turkey bacon

    b. Flaxseed raisin bran with nonfat milk

    c. A carton of yogurt while I drive

    d. A glazed donut

Question 3: Given Lauren's stress level, should I say:

    a. "You know I love you no matter what happens, honey."

    b. "I just know this is going to go well."

    c. "How six hours of sleep is enough is beyond me, but hey."

    d. None of the above

Seven forty-seven. She put on a clean T-shirt, a crewneck sweater, and a pair of loose khakis, slid her feet into her work clogs, and reached for the closet door just as Lauren pushed it open from the outside.

"Hey, am I supposed to ace this on an empty stomach or what?"

⟡

They pulled into the school parking lot the prescribed half hour before the test was supposed to begin, and Nora drove aimlessly up one row and down the next, marveling at how many juniors seemed to own their own Priuses, and to believe that getting to the parking lot first would somehow give them an advantage. She was about to begin a second loop when Lauren grabbed her purse with her left hand and gestured toward the curb with her right.

"Mom. Just pull over," she said. "Here. Right here." Nora obeyed, and Lauren hopped out before her mother could say any of the things she had rehearsed, which was probably a good thing, as Lauren undoubtedly would have misinterpreted every one of them. Nora settled for rolling down the window to yell, "Call when you're done" at Lauren's back, and Lauren waved without breaking stride.

Nora sat with her hands clenched on the steering wheel.

Question 4: I have four hours to kill. Should I:

    a. Go shopping for something I don't need
    b. Drink too many cappuccinos
    c. See if there are movies this early
    d. Call Joel

She would have picked *d*, except that he was on an airplane. She had to find something to do, though, as it made no sense to drive a half hour home, and then back again, for no reason. Nora had seen that photograph of the polar bear perched, bewildered, on a melting platform of ice. She was not about to subsidize her own indecision with an hour's worth of exhaust fumes; not going to ask the poor bear to pay for her lack of planning.

She should have been thrilled to be stranded without an agenda for four hours, as her usual schedule involved a puff pastry of layered responsibilities, but this did not feel like freedom. Nora had the nagging sense that there were right answers and wrong answers to almost everything these days, and that God kept a running tally of how smart she was about her daily life. Unstructured time seemed like a punishable offense for which she anticipated dire consequences down the line; the lucid ambition that had fueled her twenties and thirties had given way, on the down slope of her forties, to the kind of vague superstition she had once ridiculed in her mother and grandmother and aunt. Her attempts to stick with a rational approach to life met with diminishing success, and she tried not to worry about the possibility that she was genetically predisposed to utter the word "portent" with a straight face, someday.

The right answer, or the least wrong answer, was *b*, so Nora drove the short block to a Starbucks in the lobby of an office building in the nearby neighborhood business district, a Starbucks that this weekend would owe most of its profits to the parents of the juniors who were filing through the gates of Crestview School. She strolled toward it with her best approximation of a carefree air, and when her feet hit the sensor the automatic door swung toward her with a slight pneumatic sigh, not unlike the sound that would soon be generated in the Crestview auditorium, library, and four history classrooms as four hundred hands, on cue from the clock-watching proctors, simultaneously opened their SAT test booklets.

Nora got stuck in line behind a woman with a written list of twelve custom coffees and a sweaty middle-aged couple reaching loud consensus about the biomechanical advantages of their new sneakers. She stared at her reflection in the dessert case and found fault with everything. On most days her tousled brown hair shot this way and that in two-inch bursts of energy, but this morning it fell on itself in deflated little parentheses. Her eyes, large and gray like her daughter's, looked as startled as they always did, a nice quality when she needed to feign attention, but not so much of a plus when she was striving for calm. Another customer might have admired her straight, sculpted nose, had plastic surgeons not eliminated all the excesses to which a nose with discretionary income could fall prey, making Nora's seem less remarkable by comparison. As for her mouth, it was so tight that Nora instinctively let out three little breaths—*whoo, whoo, whoo*—to force it to relax.

Joel liked to say that his wife was too energetic to be merely pretty, and too sexy to be considered handsome. Nora appreciated the effort on his part; he was trying to protect her from the prevailing belief that pretty was the exclusive province of women under thirty, while handsome belonged to women with an income in the high six figures. She did not look the way her mother had in the shadow of fifty, resigned, designed, with the muscle tone of a baked potato, and under normal circumstances that was good enough for her. This morning it was not. The face in the dessert case looked manic in a way peculiar to postmillennial mothers about to launch their daughters into a world that was larger than it had been when the moms were in college, but smaller, and less yielding, than the girls imagined it to be.

She forced herself to change focus. She flirted with the idea of ordering an apple fritter, but as she looked at the tray of knobbly, glazed pastries she suddenly imagined other SAT moms considering other, identical apple fritters at Starbucks from coast to coast, an infinitely replicating population of apprehensive moms rationalizing a 400-plus-calorie sugar rush by concentrating on the amount of fresh apple they were about to consume. The knowledge that she was not alone—that she was far from alone—failed to comfort her. Nora was not normally a Starbucks person, any more than she was a McDonald's person; she had a natural distrust of chains. She liked the local, the mom-and-pop, the neighborhood business, just as she liked short hair, the clogs she wore more and more outside of work, the baggy khakis that sat closer to her waist than to her crotch but were nothing like the dread mom jeans, and the same brand of T-shirt she had worn since before Lauren was born.

All of her choices were of a piece, as she saw it, and she told herself that the common denominator, the theme of her inner life, was a search for authenticity. Her friends admired her for the thoughtfulness required to find an alternative to the chain coffee boutiques, and for the important ideas that must be rattling around in her head in the space they consigned to losing five pounds and getting a weekly blow-dry, though privately they felt she could do a bit more with her hair. They considered her to be a valued friend. They used the word "genuine" when they spoke of her, and believed that they acquired a little spiritual heft by association.

The warier, more competitive moms at school considered Nora's stated preferences to be a quirk, if not an affectation—an artificial means of singling herself out when there really was not much she could claim as unique. What she saw as nonconformity and her friends prized as originality, they saw as a lack of standards. In the thin air on the west side of Los Angeles, where appraisal was a contact sport, everyone had an opinion.

Joel teased that her love of the individualist might evaporate if a conglomerate ever offered her millions for her little bakery, and he had a point. Still, she was suspicious of the scripted enthusiasm of the corporate coffee scene.

"Next guest in line," said the barista. The man behind Nora cleared his throat loudly so she would wake up and realize she was it.

The barista had dyed the tips of his brown hair blond, and when he spoke, Nora could see the stud in the center of his tongue. He wore those new earrings, not studs but half-inch plugs embedded in his earlobes, which she was sure would leave gaping holes that could not possibly close up completely, ending any chance of a career in politics or constitutional law or even medicine, because no one in their right mind would go to a brain surgeon with big holes in his ears. Then again, if you were seeing a brain surgeon, you were unfortunately not in your right mind, in which case he might have a future. For a moment Nora pitied him, this dead-end boy in a dead-end job, whose parents should have explained to him that certain mutilations might hamper his job search. Then she berated herself for being shortsighted, for assuming that he was lucky enough to have options and parents who pointed them out. Maybe his mom and dad did not care, maybe he lacked the grades for a decent college, or for any college, or even to graduate from high school. Maybe he was in rehab, or supporting a ruined brother who had been thrown out of rehab, stepping in to care for the boy because his parents had long since moved up to Mount Shasta, if indeed they had not split up weeks before he was born. Running the counter at Starbucks might be a good job for this kid.

She decided to like him. Nora made a point of pursuing instant and unexpected friendships, even if they lasted no longer than it took to order coffee. She loved to strike up conversations with strangers as much as she disliked it when strangers tried to initiate an exchange with her. She preferred to decide whether she felt like talking, which gave her the illusion of control.

"Let's see," she said. "I'd like—well, if it's a cappuccino is the Venti more milk or more espresso?"

"Than what? Than a Grande or a Tall?"

"No, I mean the proportion in the cup, is it—never mind. I'd like a nonfat Grande cappuccino," she said.

The boy turned toward the girl at the espresso machine and yelled, "Grande nonfat cappuccino."

There it was. Nora had failed to master Starbucks' ordering syntax on the very day that her daughter was taking the SAT exam for the first time. This was not a good omen.

"Your kid doing the SAT?"

"Oh. Yes, she is. She's a junior."

"She do All-Prep?"

"She did. Yes."

The boy reached into his apron pocket and handed a business card to Nora. "Sam's SAT Slam," it read, above a raft of email addresses and cell phone numbers.

"I work for All-Prep three nights a week," he said, "but the rest of the time I'm freelance. If she blows it this time. You know, if she needs any extra help."

Why would he say that? Everyone remembered the girl who had fried her circuits with too much prep, cried through much of the SAT she was supposed to ace, and was now at a local junior college, the educational equivalent of a halfway house—but everyone assumed that such things happened to other people's children. At Crestview, not sending a child to test-prep classes was considered negligent behavior.

"She did very well on the sample tests," Nora replied. "Very well. We just wanted her to learn the strategy. She did very well." She seemed unable to think of anything else to say.

"Great. If she wants to take 'em again right away in May, I've got some slots open."

"You did well on your SATs, then."

"I got 2380—1600 on the part you remember."

"That's very impressive. Good grief, 2380 out of 2400. May I ask where you went to college? Or are you still in school?"

"It's went. Yale. You got the Fiske yet?"

Nora might have started to cry, right then, if not for dollar bills and exact change to distract her. Fisk was a black university in the South. Was this some kind of slang, to *get the Fisk*? A moment earlier she had been merely anxious about Lauren's future, in the reassuringly linear and slightly giddy way of parents who had paid for the first round of test prep and considered this, the day of the first SAT exam for juniors, to be the official start of the college application season. She had been the Zen master of moms, relatively speaking, until a Yale graduate with holes in his ears as big as her espresso mini-truffles confronted her with her own ignorance. Suddenly Nora was alone in the universe with a new fear—that despite love and good intentions, she would fail to do what Lauren needed to help her get into the right college, fail even to figure out what she needed until it was too late.

She took a deep breath. For a woman who had spent most of her working life confirming fact and discarding fiction, there was nothing worse than an informational ambush. Nora had felt this way when one of her competitors beat her to the punch on red velvet cupcakes, and she had to revamp the whole fall product line at the last minute to feature mini–sticky buns topped with fruit. For that matter, she had felt this way when she got fired from her magazine research job the week after Lauren started high school, rendered obsolete by search engines that enabled anyone to find out anything without the help of a human being who required health benefits and a pension plan. She stared at the barista and reminded herself sternly that she knew how to cope with the unexpected, as long as there was not too much of it.

"Ah, the Fisk," she said, trying to sound like someone who had an assistant to run such errands, an assistant who might be fired on Monday for having forgotten such an important acquisition. "Not yet . . ."

"There's a BookWorld over on National," he said.

It was a book. Relieved, Nora resorted to a small fib to cover her momentary confusion. "The store near me was out."

"Yeah, it's time, it's more than time."

"What did you major in at Yale?"

"Comparative religion." He read the next question in the dove-tailed lines between her brows. "I'm writing a pilot. Sort of a Doctors Without Borders thing, but funny."

"Like *M*A*S*H*," she replied, on the happy upswing of the conversation. But the boy had already made eye contact with the man behind Nora, so she slid over to where her drink was waiting. Finally, she had a plan. She would drive to BookWorld, find the Fisk, come back to Starbucks, and read until the exam was over.

She watched the barista hand his business card to the man and wondered what she and Joel were doing, paying $150 an hour for tutors who came to the house to show Lauren how to get the great standardized test scores she needed if she wanted to get into a top college—so that she could graduate and end up like the barista, a tutor who showed kids how to get the great scores they needed if they wanted to get into a top college. The test-prep rep who had spoken at Crestview the previous fall had described the trajectory of students who nailed the SATs, but he had made it sound more like a bird in flight than a dog chasing its tail.

❧

The firing had come without warning, as the publisher viewed the editorial staff the way certain childless people regard children, as charming, peripheral nuisances. Not even Joel had known that he was about to lose 10 percent of his staff, including his wife. On that score, the publisher figured he was doing his executive editor a big favor.

At first, she had no idea how to cope. Lifers ran in Nora's family. Her father had worked at the local high school in ascending positions since before she was born. Her mother was Sheboygan's acknowledged queen of needlepoint. Her older brother taught introductory psychology classes at the University of Wisconsin and liked to mutter insufferable little asides—"Hmm, projecting?"—on the rare occasions when the whole family was together. If not for Nora's favorite journalism professor, whose career advice had amounted to "Get out of town," she might have stayed in Madison herself. Until she was told to clean out her desk at the magazine, Nora had assumed that she would run the research department forever.

For a month she alternated between elation and depression, with a few side trips to abject terror, and then she began to bake, a bit too compulsively for her mental health or her family's nutritional profile. Almost four years and a home equity line of credit later, she ran a small commercial bakery that supplied restaurants and a couple of gourmet food shops. The bulk of her fans, all of whom would be terribly upset to hear the word "bulk" used in reference to them, lived in a crescent of inflated real estate that started in Malibu and ran south along the ocean only as far as Marina del Rey, which lacked the cachet of the other beachfront neighborhoods, never having lived down its early reputation as a haven for desperate singles who refused to wear sunscreen. The customers who preferred the exclusivity of a private pool to a windblown beach lived only as far inland as Brentwood or Beverly Hills, neighborhoods where people hired a private chef and then banished her before the meal to perpetrate the fraud of a home-cooked dinner. These were the people who had made Nora a success. She preferred never to get closer to them than an order form, because they misunderstood her intent completely.

Nora made small desserts because she could never make up her mind about whether she wanted chocolate cake, strawberry short-cake, or a flavored pot au crème at any given meal. She meant them to be served three on a plate, one chocolate, one fruit, and one creamy dessert, a medley for the indecisive. Instead, adamantly svelte hosts ended their dinner parties with individual servings of a single two-inch Nora dessert, amidst appreciative murmurs about minimalist proportions. Restaurants featured a solitary little des-

sert shipwrecked on a huge service plate and called it style. Nora
retaliated with a line of standard-serving desserts, which the restaurants refused to order. The gourmet shops reported that people
occasionally bought them for more casual events—a picnic, a backyard barbecue—and cut them into fourths.

She might not be able to control her demographic, but she had
shown herself to be resourceful in a crisis. By the time Nora got to
BookWorld, she was back in charge. She rushed into the store as
though Lauren had been bitten by a snake and BookWorld had the
last vial of antidote, grabbed the store's one remaining copy of the
Fiske Guide to Colleges, and marched into the pharmacy next door
for a pack of multicolored paper clips. She found a short, fat plastic
jar with a twist lid in the travel aisle and dumped the clips into
the jar as soon as she had paid for them. Nora was never happier
than when she had the proper tools. It was time to get to work.

When she got back to Starbucks, almost every table was full. A
man with a laptop had commandeered the oversized handicapped-
access table, because apparently he defined handicap as any situation where people did not appreciate how important he was. The
two women at the next table were exclaiming loudly about the
very big purse one of them had just bought at an equally oversized
discount, oblivious, in their retail high, of the laptop man's occasional glare. A quartet of aggressively cool girls sat at a window table, having long since learned how to disguise their insecurity as
aloofness, but Nora was not good at guessing ages, so she could not
tell what they were hiding. They could be apprehensive sophomores
who were still six months away from taking the PSATs, let alone
the SATs, or they could be seniors faking their blasé way through
April college notifications.

So much for her feeling of mastery, which seemed today—
what section of the test were they on by now?—to be in a big hurry
to desert her. Nora got in line for another cappuccino, wondering
if she would be able to walk past a bunch of girls at Starbucks at

any point in the coming year without triggering a meteor storm of college nerves. When it was her turn to order, she held up the BookWorld bag so that Sam the barista could see that she had taken his advice. With the jazzy snap of a blackjack dealer, he flipped another business card at her, having forgotten their earlier conversation the moment it ended. Chastened, she paid for her drink, did not leave a tip, collected her cup, and took a seat at the end of the counter, away from prying eyes. She propped the *Fiske Guide* on her crossed knee, hidden behind a copy of *Food* magazine.

Nora was overwhelmed by the time she got to the G's—who knew there was a George Washington as well as a Georgetown? And who was George Mason? She decided to stop reading. She had started, that was what mattered, and she felt better about certain things, like Lauren's test scores so far, and worse about others, like the fact that obscenely expensive schools felt the need to describe the rescue services they offered when their incredibly intelligent underclassmen got stupid drunk just like anybody else.

She put the book in her bag just as a sea of kids spilled across the intersection and onto the sidewalk, shrieking and chattering away their accumulated nerves. A dozen of them jammed their way into Starbucks and scattered toward the two women shoppers, the laptop man, and the cool quartet of girls, and as they peeled off, Nora saw Lauren at the back of the pack. She had not even bothered to call when she got out; she was carried along on the tide of probability to Starbucks. Wordlessly, she plopped down in the chair next to Nora's, grabbed her drink, and took a long slurp. She twisted up her face.

"Sugar, it needs sugar. I'm so thirsty and I didn't bring anything. Where's your wallet?"

She started to dive for Nora's purse, but Nora threw a shoulder in her way and pulled the bag onto her lap. She had no idea how Lauren would react to her mom reading a college guide book, whether she would consider it a big help or meddling, and she did not want to find out five minutes after the SATs.

"What is wrong with you?"

"Nothing. Nothing. I'm getting money for you."

"I can do it myself."

"Yes, you could. But I'm closer."

"Only because you tackled me."

Nora held out a twenty and did not quite let go. All around her she heard a chorus of "great, great, it was great, just great," delivered with varying levels of conviction. She looked at her daughter. "So how did it go?"

"Great," said Lauren.

"Well, that's terrific," said Nora.

"Yeah, it was great. You want another of whatever that is?"

"No. Go ahead."

Lauren got in line to order a drink that involved far more whipped cream than coffee. Nora collected her bag and jacket, happy that the ordeal was over, happy that Lauren thought it was great. It was too soon for either of them to understand that great was what kids said to keep their terror, and their parents, at bay.

Lauren was asleep before they got to the freeway, asleep all the way home, asleep even after Nora pulled up in front of the house and turned off the ignition. Like most of their friends, Nora and Joel could fit only one car into their two-car garage. The rest of the space was occupied by two sets of grandparents' housewares waiting for a resurgence of interest in ornate silver platters and asparagus tongs, souvenirs from Nora's and Joel's childhoods, and a growing assortment of Lauren mementos. The fact that the older boxes remained sealed in no way discouraged Nora from packing up everything, from Lauren's favorite books to a large stuffed elephant. The first generation to move far from their parents did not travel light, after all: for Nora and her husband, half a garage of unused possessions provided welcome ballast, a movable sense of place.

There was no good reason to wake Lauren up, so Nora sat, grateful for an excuse to hold still, and watched her sleep. Lauren's long black hair tumbled over her face; what a peaceful face, Nora thought, no impatient glare, no pout, no scowl, just intersecting planes of pale skin and a rosebud mouth that looked like it was about to smile. Joel had called her Snow White when she was little, because of her coloring, but he stopped before she started preschool because he did not want anyone else to do it. No kid of mine, he told Nora, gets named for a girl who is dumb enough to take unwashed fruit from a stranger, wanton enough to live with seven little guys, passive enough to need a handsome man to straighten out her life. They adored Lauren with the abandon of two adults who had been raised in tailored households. They liked the idea that there was nothing they would not do for her.

When Lauren was a baby, Joel sometimes took her for a drive in the middle of the night to help her fall asleep, which worked fine until he pulled into the driveway and turned off the engine, and the sudden absence of noise and vibration woke her right up again. A pitying friend bought them a contraption that hooked onto the side of the crib and mimicked the hum and soft motion of a car, ending the late-night commute, but it was a story they told once too often, so Lauren made contradicting it an element of her growing autonomy. If her parents thought she always fell asleep in the car, she would make sure she never fell asleep in the car. Sometimes she stayed up so late doing homework that Nora begged her to sleep on the half-hour drive to school the following morning.

"I don't sleep in cars," Lauren said.

Nora considered waking her daughter up, considered letting

her sleep, and realized that it made no difference. Lauren would be embarrassed and defensive either way. Nora sank into the angle of her seat and the door, trapped, and quickly gave in to her own exhaustion. When Joel got out of the airport cab a half hour later, he found both his wife and his daughter asleep in the car. He put his bag and briefcase inside the house, grabbed the mail out of the box, and sat on the front stoop, sifting through the junk mail for anything that might require attention, wondering whether the driver's or the passenger window was the right one to knock on.

chapter 1

Crestview Academy lacked both a hillcrest location and a panoramic view. The school sat in the curve of a Culver City slough, on land that the Los Angeles River had carved out and then abandoned in its reconsidered meanderings down to the beach, and the vista from the school's west-facing windows was not of rolling hills but of the concrete swoop of a freeway on-ramp. Its founder had come up with the name Crestview when he moved west in the late 1960s, intending to put it on a plaque above the gated entrance to the hillside mansion he would purchase once he left Pittsburgh and high school English lit classes behind for a new life as a Hollywood screenwriter.

He had three speculative scripts and the name of a studio executive whose nephew had been in his advanced placement class, but the closest he ever got to the movies was a series of meetings with men who were far more interested in his educator's past than in his story pitches. They wanted to buy his expertise, to stake him to a new prep school, because they could not get their children into the city's old-guard private schools, where "entertainment money" was code for Jewish. Those men liked the name Crestview, despite the gully location they eventually found—but then, grandiose names were common in their line of work. The would-be screenwriter accepted his fate, deposited their checks, and built Crestview, which, like the hyperbolic Paramount and Universal, like Fox laying claim to an entire century, would have to live up to its advance billing.

After forty years and half a dozen capital campaigns, Crestview looked the part of a century-old East Coast private college preparatory school. A hulking set of earthquake-reinforced Tudor buildings nestled at the center of lush, landscaped grounds, a stand of climate-challenged sugar maples on either side of the entrance and a pool, tennis courts, and athletic fields behind the main buildings. The wood-paneled lobby featured at its center a bronze bust of the school's founder, its patina hastened chemically to enhance the notion that Crestview had been doing things right for a very long time. The students wore uniforms designed by an employee of the Fox costume department and ate lunch at massive oak tables trucked over from the Paramount lot after production had wrapped on a World War II drama set in London. Teachers were prohibited from wearing T-shirts, anything made of denim, and athletic shoes, and were encouraged to exploit their role-model appearance for a meaningful dialogue with any girl whose hemline was too high or any boy whose waistband was too low. Skeptics called the place a shark tank, but the number of new applicants rose every year along with the number of satisfied customers, those being families whose children went on to a handful of prestigious colleges and universities. They knew what the critics said, and they knew which of those critics had tried and failed to get their own children into Crestview. In response, the luckier families thought, "Sour grapes."

Ted Marshall and the four other college counselors on his team met with every one of Crestview's 120 senior-class families during the first two weeks of the new school year to reconsider the initial list of twenty schools they had created the previous spring, to review test scores accumulated since that meeting, to find out how the application essays were going, and to come up with a final, ranked list of ten target schools. Each counselor had his own distinctive style, but Ted, the head of the department for the last six years, was the counselor everyone wanted, the one with perfect pitch. Time after time, he came up with strategies that worked.

A year earlier he had orchestrated a letter-writing campaign for a boy who got turned down at Brown University for no apparent reason except that there were plenty of other boys just like him. At Ted's instruction, every single member of the senior class had written a heartfelt letter on the boy's behalf, yielding a last-minute acceptance accompanied by a handwritten note from a Brown admissions committee member who bemoaned the fate of so many highly qualified applicants. Deciding which families to assign to Ted was perhaps the hardest job the college counseling staff faced. If he took the strongest candidates, he could improve Crestview's college acceptance profile, a potent sales tool with incoming students. If he got the less than sterling candidates, he might be able to get them into a better school than they deserved, but it would not necessarily be a school that impressed prospective families.

He kept a private list of students he never took, which included any beautiful girl who might scream sexual harassment if she failed to get into her first-choice school, any overtly gay boy who might do the same even though Ted had had a fairly serious girlfriend until the year he was named director of the department, anyone with a recently divorced mom who might take a more than parental interest in him, anyone whose parents happened to send him a gift in the week before the department met to make assignments, and any but the most talented minority candidates, to avoid the subterranean accusations of partisanship that had accompanied the placement of a black tennis player at Princeton his second year on the job. Princeton had been chasing the girl ever since she made the national amateur playoffs in ninth grade, and was far more interested in a nationally ranked black female tennis player than in her Bs in science, but a trustee had been heard to mutter, "What is this guy, our minority priority counselor?" as he walked into a board meeting, and after that Ted had reeled it in. He was Crestview's first—and so far only—black college counselor. He had to make sure that the minority candidates on his roster were bullet-proof, as performance-perfect as their majority counterparts.

He stuck with the students who needed him the least, if he was going to be honest about it, a strategy that had its own unique rewards. Ted had just reached a milestone in his career that was all the more significant because he had never heard of it happening to anyone else. He had gone to the annual fall convention of the National Association for College Admission Counseling, as he always did, one of fifteen hundred high school counselors facing off with an equal number of college admissions representatives, surrounded by what he liked to call the sucker-fish industries: the test-prep companies, the guidebook publishers, the testing companies jockeying for national supremacy, and even *U.S. News & World Report*, which dispatched a team of researchers to maintain its rankings supremacy. He had visited the booths of the colleges and universities his students were interested in. He had slipped each rep a business card on which he had printed the name of a special candidate. One card for each candidate, and never more than four at any given school, to avoid seeming presumptuous about Crestview's standing in the general applicant pool.

On the second morning, it happened: for the first time in his twelve years as a college counselor, a handful of Ivy League admissions reps quietly slipped their cards to him, inscribed with the names of candidates they wanted to encourage, though not officially. Each one of them warned him not to say a word and cautioned him that this was in no way a commitment. Still, he came home with eight cards in his wallet, cards that he clipped together and put in his locked desk drawer. Eight kids on the fast track and he was hardly warmed up yet. Nine, if he was being honest. He had the equivalent of a card from Harvard, which was never going to stoop to such behavior. All he had to do was mention Brad's name to the rep and he got a chuckle and a smile, which was just as good.

He came home happy, and aware that only a fool would allow himself to feel secure. As far as Ted was concerned, there was no such thing as good news as early as September. He dismissed all the peripheral chatter about how the end of the college application madness was surely in sight, and any day now there would be less emphasis on standardized tests, more attention paid to the individual candidate, and a new commitment to more reasonable behavior from all the involved parties. He knew better. The forecasted easing of tensions was as likely to materialize on the college circuit as it was in the Middle East. Ted approached each application season anticipating that it would be more difficult than the years that had preceded it, not less, and so far life had met his expectations.

He was at the center of a perfect storm. The west side of Los Angeles was the applicant equivalent of the strawberry fields up the freeway in Oxnard, packed so tight with succulent fruit that it was almost impossible to reach for one gorgeous berry without bruising a couple of others. The luckier candidates attended a handful of prep schools that were proud to call themselves elite, and each one of those schools had a team of warrior counselors like Ted.

Most of the private school parents were wealthy, or serious enough about time management to reassign the budget for a non-existent, standard-issue second child to the enhanced education of a first—or both. Ted believed that there was no one more ambitious than the parents of an only child. It was simple math: If each parent represented one unit of ambition, and if they invested those two units, combined, in their offspring, then an only child demanded twice the payoff of two siblings, and three times the payoff of three.

The older moms and dads, who had protested the war in Vietnam or marched in Chicago, were fed up with the way life had dwindled from macro to micro and all too eager for a new cause. The younger ones, who had missed out on social protest because they needed a nap after kindergarten class, had convinced themselves that the right college for the right kid was going to make the synergistically large difference they had so far failed to make in the world. And those were the liberals. The more conservative ones, who had always chafed at their generational identity, focused on accruing accomplishments of enduring value. Either way, they all got to the same place, an obsession with their children's college choice as empirical and irrefutable proof of their own worth.

On those two counts—too many qualified candidates and too many heavily invested parents—Ted was under no more pressure than hundreds of counselors at dozens of urban prep schools all over the country. What set him apart, what made his victories uniquely sweet, was that he was dealing with a pack of gamblers, no matter what they did for a living. Crestview parents might pretend to admire the diligent dad who worked his way through Stanford Law and up the ladder at a prestigious firm, but in truth they found him boring, the equivalent of a big tropical storm you could track for days in advance on the Weather Channel. They were not impressed by the institutionalized risk of Wall Street, not when everyone knew someone who had made a fortune in a more surprising and nonlinear way. They preferred the stories of the ex-junkie who sold a screenplay, the gang member who became a rap star, the newspaper beat reporter who picked up the phone right before he got fired to find out that any one of a dozen buff young actors wanted to option the rights to his final, pre-layoff story and make him an associate producer as well.

They chose to live in a city where the defining weather disaster was the earthquake, which said something about their tolerance for, and infatuation with, the unexpected. Crestview parents went to bed each night knowing that they might wake up before dawn to find the bed in the backseat of their car—but if surprise could turn a two-story faux Georgian into a one-story ranch, surprise could just as quickly, just as randomly, turn a life around. The issue, for Ted, was that at some point millionaire ex-junkie screenwriters conflated with earthquakes to yield a dangerously why-not mentality. West side parents embraced the inevitable jolt. If fate was a matter of fluke and denial, it was all too easy for Mom and Dad to imagine a beloved but ever so slightly unqualified child catapulted into Harvard Yard. Stranger things had happened, and look at what Ted had done for that kid at Brown.

Nora sat down in one of the plaid club chairs that were supposed to make the college counseling lobby not feel like purgatory, while Joel studied the biggest piece of furniture in the room—a standing, revolving, six-foot-tall bookcase full of college literature, arranged by topic. Standardized testing and prep, college brochures, financial aid and planning, and, on the side that had been facing the wall until Joel nudged it into view, as though Ted and the others were trying to hide them, sheaves of articles on surviving the stress of the application process. One of them was about seniors who slipped in their second semester and had their acceptances revoked; another was about perfect students who went to perfect schools, only to fall apart once they got there. "Eggs," the admissions directors called them, or "teacups." They were too fragile; they tended to crack. He spun the bookcase back to its original position and hoped that Nora would not ask him what he was looking at. His role in the college drama, as far as he could tell, was to defend against this kind of peripheral information, to edit out any stressful data that did not directly pertain to Lauren.

Joel had designed his first magazine when he was eight, a single-issue, four-page, hand-colored and -lettered publication called

Pet, full of pictures and articles he had drawn and written about the dog he did not own but wanted his parents to acquire for him. He had worked on the student newspaper in high school and college, and, after a brief stint writing news items for a restaurant trade magazine, he had settled in at *Events*, where he had been ever since. He had been the west coast editor for ten years, which meant that he knew a small amount about a great number of subjects, information that had served him well until very recently; he could sit next to anyone at a dinner party and keep the conversation afloat through Nora's dessert course.

And then, for reasons he could not name, gradually, imperceptibly, Joel had shifted his focus from what he knew to the gaping maw of what he did not know, most of which had to do with his daughter. He had plenty of research at his fingertips—school rankings, acceptance rates, online slide shows of dorm rooms, average financial aid offers, all of his daughter's statistics—but it refused to congeal into anything resembling a point of view on what Lauren ought to do about college. He worried that the true curse of middle age was not thick yellow toenails or progressive bifocals or sore knees. It was not the creases in his long, thin face, because men could get away with craggy. It was not his salt-and-pepper hair, because George Clooney had single-handedly made gray desirable. No, Joel feared that middle age brought an absolute and terrible clarity: he understood, finally, that information was not the same thing as wisdom, no matter how much of it he compiled. He wanted Ted to help them create a plan almost as much as he wanted print media to survive until after he was dead. He could only hope that the odds of the former were better than the odds of the latter.

Ted's office door swung open.

"C'mon in," he beckoned, with a calibrated enthusiasm. "How's the master baker?"

"Oh God, I didn't think," said Nora. "I'm so sorry, and I had these little apple charlottes, how could I . . ."

"Hey, I could lose five pounds. Lauren will still get into college, I promise. Maybe not the college of your dreams . . ."

Joel saw an opening. "And if Nora delivers a chocolate cake by noon tomorrow?"

"Any school you want, early decision," laughed Ted. Lauren was not an Ivy League candidate, but he had plucked her off another counselor's list because he had a fairly good contact at Northwestern—she was going to need help—and because he was curious about Nora, or rather about Nora's midlife career change. Ted's current fantasy involved ditching his job someday for something better, though he had no good idea what that might be. He could write the insider novel to end all insider novels, but he worried that what he knew about college apps would only scare off potential readers. He worried that no one would make a movie out of his novel, so he would have to keep his job—except that parents would refuse to work with him out of fear of being ridiculed in the sequel. He could write an original screenplay instead, but one screenplay was not enough to subsidize his freedom, and he had no idea what the second screenplay would be about. Ted could not figure out how to turn desire into advantage, but Nora was proof that it could be done. She had switched over from magazines to baking. She knew something he did not know, which made her potentially as useful to him as he was to her.

"Tell me it doesn't work like that," laughed Nora, who had already decided on the dark chocolate cake with the espresso ganache.

"It doesn't work like that," said Ted. "You have to come up with much more than a cake. A wing of a building, maybe."

At that exact moment, Lauren blew into the room, all apologies and flying shirttails.

"Here she is," said Ted. "Now we can get to the important stuff. You have a list for me, young lady, I believe."

Lauren pawed through her backpack and extracted a sheet of paper, which she handed to Ted, while Joel quietly opened his briefcase and pulled out a copy for himself and one for Nora. Nora reached for it without taking her eyes from Ted's face.

Ted stared at the page for one of those long moments that seemed, to Nora, to define adulthood: the periodontist looking at the x-rays, the colorist looking at her roots, the associate publisher pretending to review her file before he followed his boss's order and fired her. Getting older meant handing over far too many fateful decisions to people who had no vested interest in the outcome, and Nora was never comfortable waiting for the verdict.

"Northwestern is a very popular school this year," said Ted. It was a very popular school every year, one of about twenty schools that sat high on the *U.S. News & World Report* rankings and were either near a major airport or ranked in the single digits, which compensated for the connecting flight or the rental car. It was one of the schools Crestview seniors thought about without thinking about it, which made for a crowded applicant field.

"Yeah," said Lauren, who liked the school because the proportions felt right—far enough away to prevent spontaneous visits but closer than the East Coast, selective enough to feel special but not as daunting as the Ivy League, big but not too big, a modulated choice for a girl who had yet to be seized by an extreme desire. "It would be so fun if a bunch of us ended up there together."

Nora watched Ted, who did not smile enough.

"Or are you saying it's too popular to get into?" she asked.

"Mom, will you stop?"

"No, she's right to ask. Their apps were up maybe, I don't know, fifteen, twenty percent last year. It's a big favorite."

"She's the news editor," said Nora. "Doesn't that help?"

"Mom. It's not like I'm the editor in chief."

"Well, if Mr. Nelson lived in this century . . ." Nora was convinced that the faculty sponsor had decidedly obsolete ideas about what women could and could not do.

"*Mom*. Could we not talk about this here?"

Ted smiled and waited. Lauren was right and Nora was right, but there was nothing to be gained from agreeing with either of them. He studied the list again and made a decisive mark with his pencil.

"I'd say it's a stretch unless you apply early, and early might get you even odds, but they don't defer, so if it's over, it's over."

"Hold on." Nora reached into her bag for a pen, despite the fact that Joel was already taking notes.

Lauren gave her a pulverizing stare. "You know what that means. I can apply early decision and have a better chance of getting in, but Northwestern doesn't defer you into the regular pool if you apply early. They accept or reject. No in between."

"Good job," said Ted. "You want to handle my ten thirty appointment?"

They made their way through the rest of the list that way. Ted alternated between tough love and humor, Nora asked questions she knew the answer to in case the response changed with repetition, Joel took more notes, and Lauren refused to hear anything but the optimism she needed to make it to the end of first semester. If Ted had polled each family member at the end of the half hour, Lauren would have said she was getting in everywhere but Stanford, Joel would have said she would get into more than half the schools on her list, and Nora would have wondered why her beloved and accomplished daughter was clinging by a hangnail to the bottom of the acceptance brackets at so many schools.

Still, they had a list, which Ted transferred to Crestview's printed form and embellished with underlining and brackets, arrows and margin notes. The point of this meeting was to evaluate the schools and divide them into three categories—Stretches,

Even Odds, and the newly renamed Best Chances, which he had called Safety Schools until last year, when a very contentious father complained to the head of school that safety meant safety, and what was Crestview going to do about the fact that his child had been rejected?

Ted made three copies and handed them out:

STRETCHES
Stanford
Williams/Wesleyan
Columbia
Northwestern, underlined, with an arrow pointing down toward the Even Odds category, with the notation, "Early?"

EVEN ODDS
University of Michigan (too big?)
Claremont (too small, too near?)
NYU (no campus), also underlined, with a smaller arrow and "Early?" pointing toward the Best Chance category. Ted knew of eight other students who planned to apply early, a bit of information he would not reveal unless asked.

BEST CHANCES
UC Santa Barbara
Skidmore

"So all you need is another best-chance school and I'll let you go," said Ted.

"But there's no place else I want to go," said Lauren. "I mean, I don't even want to go to some of these."

"You know the rule. Everybody comes up with three likely candidates and I get to sleep at night. We're just a bit top-heavy here. A bit top-heavy. We need to add a little more weight at the bottom."

Lauren's voice got smaller. "I'll think about it. Can't I make NYU a best chance?"

She had opened the door.

"Bad-mouth it to the other seniors," Ted said. "Your test scores are strong—"

"That's nice to hear," Nora interrupted. A score of 2200 in May might not beat Sam the barista, but with his help Lauren had improved on her April score, and she was going to try one more time in October.

"Mom."

"Well, they are, sweetheart. It's nice to hear Ted say so."

"The scores are strong," Ted continued, rowing for shore, "but I'd like the GPA up just a little, so no slacking this semester, no senioritis. It would be good if they didn't have the biggest increase in apps of anybody last year, which makes them even hotter this year, but there's not much you can do about that. Except convince your friends they'd hate it."

"Wait a minute," said Nora, trying for a light tone. "I've got it. Tell us a great school nobody wants to apply to and Lauren can go there."

"Macalester," said Ted, without hesitation.

"Where's that?" said Joel.

"Minnesota," said Ted. "St. Paul, either of you been there? Really a great city, great food . . ."

"I am not going to school in Minnesota," said Lauren, a pinched note of fear in her voice.

That was Ted's cue: logic and strategy were about to give way to emotion, and to preserve his sanity he had to get them out of his office, fast. "Anyhow, let me know by Friday and we're good." He stood up and shook hands all around, and before the Chaikens quite knew what had happened they were standing outside the counseling offices. Lauren put on her best harried face. The bell was not going to ring for another ten minutes, but her parents did not know that.

"Listen, Chloe wants me to come by after school, so can you go home together and I'll take Mom's car?"

She waited while her parents got flustered, compared their schedules, and worked out a new plan. Other girls' parents acted as though they had it down cold, whether they did or not. Lauren's parents were in what her dad called a suspended state of constant revision, which was not as unnerving as it sounded. Lauren knew they were going to let her use the car because they missed Chloe, too, so there was nothing at stake. She could stand there, safe in the outcome, and appreciate the effort they made on her behalf.

Nora handed her the keys. "You're going to pick her up at school?"

"Right."

"And then?"

Lauren shrugged. "Probably Coffee Bean."

"You have anything tomorrow?" Joel was double-teaming her.

"You guys. I'm not going to flunk the calc test." She rolled her eyes. "If I get a B, Ted will make all my Best Chances into Even Odds. Oh no! My life will be over." She pocketed the keys, kissed them both, and ran off down the hall.

"Home in time for dinner," said Nora in a stage whisper.

She and Joel were huddled over their respective PDAs, arranging their new mutual commute after work, when Dan and Joy and Katie glided up for their meeting, all smiles and twelve-ply cashmere. They waved without breaking stride and headed for Ted's office. Joel, wondering why Dan's perfunctory greetings always felt slightly like a snub, turned with what he hoped would be interpreted as urgency and strode toward the parking lot. Nora skittered alongside, glancing over her shoulder, wishing that she could be a fly on the wall for the sake of comparison. It was so hard to evaluate Ted's comments in a vacuum.

"Now that's going to be a meeting," said Joel.

Nora slumped onto the passenger seat, in a deep adrenaline deficit.

"Here's what I don't understand," she said, hoping to keep the quaver out of her voice. "We weren't going to force her to take AP biology, what was the point. Okay, maybe she pays for that at someplace like Wesleyan. But still, she's got, you saw the list, APs and good grades and awfully good scores."

"Yes, she does," said Joel.

"But you know what Ted says," Nora continued. " 'Take the AP and get the A.' And she did, some. You can't always . . ."

"You don't have to defend her to me," said Joel. "I'd take her in a minute if I ran an admissions department. Since I don't, she took some APs but not all of them, and she got some As but not all of them, and that's where we are."

"Please, a B plus in AP English with that teacher?" Nora snorted. "She wouldn't recognize imagination if it wore a name tag."

Joel grinned. "I think you ought to send a letter in with Lauren's transcript—you know, kind of an annotated explanation of what the grades really mean."

"You think this is funny? The other teacher would've given her a better grade."

"Nora, stop. If you get this worked up now you're not going to make it to the end in one piece."

"And besides, what use is a likely school if she has no desire to go there? We might as well put down, I don't know, South Dakota University, if there is such a place."

"She's not going to South Dakota. Ted said he's going to go to bat for her at all the schools she likes. Remember, he said, and I quote, 'I'm going to fill in all the blanks for the admissions people so they know how special Lauren is.' I took that down verbatim. Don't mess with me."

"What blanks?" said Nora.

She had him there. Joel had tried very hard, and with success until this exact moment, to focus on the positive aspects of the meeting. Ted was ready to do battle, which was a good thing— except that it implied that Lauren needed to be fought for, which was not such a good thing.

"I thought she took AP bio," he said, quietly. "Didn't she take AP bio?"

"No. She took physics last year. She's taking bio now."

"There. AP physics, are you kidding? I couldn't handle AP physics, I know that much."

"Regular," said Nora. "She took regular physics, too. Why don't you know this?"

The silence in the car got very large.

"So how're the orders going?" Joel asked. "For the charlottes."

"I know what you meant."

"You want to keep worrying, go ahead," he said. "I thought I'd ask about the new star dessert. Shoot me."

Nora sighed. "I could hire two more people just to cut crusts off bread and peel apples, except I'd have to fire them after Thanksgiving. Never thought about crusts and peels. I only thought, Charlottes, cool, nobody's doing that. No follow-through."

Joel thought for a moment.

"We can go look at some other schools," he said.

"Top-heavy," sniffed Nora.

chapter 2

The Dodson family rolled up to Crestview in a perfect caravan of blended want and need. Dan refused to surrender his Mercedes to the possibility that generations he would never meet might find their beachfront properties eroded by a bloated ocean, but he encouraged Joy to trade the Navigator for a hybrid SUV, and Joy, in turn, had jumped the waiting list on Katie's new Prius because every three months she dispatched the jowls of a grateful Toyota dealer with a jolt of Botox. There was no carpooling in a family like this, not with everything they had to do, but they did their part to emulsify personal preference and global responsibility.

Katie drove around back to the student parking lot while her parents waited for her in front of the two-story wrought-iron security gates that Dan called the pearly gates, even though Katie no longer laughed when he did so. What a life he and Joy had made: two kids from Chicago public schools, the first in their respective families to attend college, to say nothing of law school and medical school, about to send their second child to the best small liberal arts college in the country. Dan was not being cocky about Katie's chances—merely reasonable. Early in Katie's junior year, he had drawn up a comparative tally of his two children's accomplishments: Ron had better reading scores, but Katie had him beat in math, which was nice for a girl; neither of them had ever gotten a B; Ron had compensated for a profound lack of coordination by getting up at five every morning to be the rowing team's coxswain, while Katie got up almost as early for the swim team; he was class treasurer and she was vice president of school council; they dabbled in community service enough to get credit for being humanitarians. No matter that Ron seemed to be majoring in disdain at Williams, or that Katie sometimes treated Dan like her personal ATM machine. He doubted that community college students were any nicer to their parents.

During the spring of Katie's junior year, after a short and efficient family tour of the Ivy League and a handful of small East Coast schools, each one of them read through their own copy of the Fiske—to avoid influencing each other—and flagged any school that appealed to them. Dan handed over all three annotated copies to the most sycophantic of the paralegals in his firm, with instructions to turn the flags into an Excel spreadsheet arranged in order of the schools' decreasing popularity, with columns for contact information, mailing and web addresses, and application deadlines. When he first saw the list, he reminded the young woman that he had asked for the schools to be listed by combined preference, not solely his own, but that was the beauty of the exercise. Without once consulting each other, he and Joy and Katie had all agreed on their top ten choices: Williams, the Ivy League eight, and, to avoid accusations of hubris, one of the University of California campuses. It hardly mattered which one, as Katie would not be going there, but as it turned out, they all chose Berkeley.

There was no point in coming up with the twenty schools Crestview requested for the junior-year list, because these ten were the only ones they wanted to consider. They returned for their first senior-year appointment without having added or subtracted a single name.

Dan smiled at his wife as Katie walked toward them.

"I'm actually looking forward to this meeting," he said.

Joy smiled back, big, confirming that the new cosmetic dentist really had a way with veneers. "Not a whole lot of people who can say that," she replied.

When Katie caught up with them, they strode across the courtyard together, floated past Nora and Joel, and walked into the college counseling lobby, where Ted was already waiting. Ted enjoyed a Dodson family entrance. He thought they wore success better than almost any other family at school, even more so now that Ron had graduated. Not that they were humble about their accomplishments. In fact, just the opposite: they lived in every inch of their lives; they were bursting at the seams of their existence. It did not matter that Ted had known them for almost six years. The impression they made did not dull with time.

Privately, he assumed that Dan and Joy must have been drawn to each other by vanity. They looked far too much alike for a husband and wife—both of them tall and big-boned, with thick, wavy hair in a tawny shade that was striking enough to make people wonder if they shared a colorist, a hue they showed off by never wearing any color brighter than navy blue. They had shoulders that made shoulder pads redundant, and, best of all, they shared the one attribute that no one in Los Angeles had yet figured out how to duplicate surgically—long legs. Anyone with the price of admission could have new hair, new skin, a new nose or eyelids or lips or ears, new teeth, and new breasts; people could alter their tummies, their thighs, their hips, their rear ends. No one could have long legs unless they were born with them. A self-made couple with new money and two sets of long legs—three, if you counted Katie's, in whom their combined DNA had found a perfect vessel, and dismissed Ron, who at a fidgety five-foot-ten was a throwback to his paternal grandfather's double helix. The Dodsons were confidence incarnate, as long as Ron was out of town.

Ted allowed himself to relax a bit. The Dodsons and Brad's parents were this year's anchor parents, another secret category

Ted had devised for himself, this one designed to compensate for the more high-maintenance families. He made sure always to include on his list a couple of families who knew what they wanted and looked good enough on paper to have better-than-average odds. As much fun as Nora and Joel might be, he needed a few families who never even joked about a causal link between cake and outcome.

Fifteen minutes after the Dodsons sat down in Ted's office, each one of them had a photocopy of the family's list transposed onto Crestview's template, which Ted had already prepared with Katie's near-perfect GPA, a list of the awards she had won, her extracurricular activities, and the names of five teachers who had offered to write one of her two letters of recommendation.

Ted quickly reviewed the list in his head, taking into consideration the eight business cards in his desk drawer: Columbia wanted the speech-and-debate kid who interned for the congresswoman. Cornell would not be Katie's favorite because people out here forgot it was in the Ivy League, so much for bragging rights, and Brad stood between everyone else and Harvard. Yale was the flavor of the month for some reason, and Ted could think of at least four other seniors who swore it was their first choice. The Dodsons were not serious about Berkeley. But one of his eight business cards had the Williams seal on the front and Katie's name scrawled on the back. The solution was obvious. Katie was a legacy at Williams, and he knew of only one other girl who planned to apply there. If Katie applied early decision, she would get good news in December, and he could take her off his to-do list. Better still, getting her out of the way improved the odds for the other Yale applicants. It made all the sense in the world.

"Okay, we'll pretty much ignore the UCs. On the others, I think you've got a really good shot with at least one of these schools." The first rule of influence, Ted knew, was to nudge, not shove.

"Her brother's at Williams," Joy said firmly, discomfited by "really good shot," and "at least one." She felt that Katie was a stronger candidate than Ron had been, and she had told her daughter as much, as had Dan. It was hard for both of them not to feel that their son was a rehearsal for their daughter.

"And her math scores are higher than his," said Dan, studying the page he held in his hand. "It's the A in art, isn't it. Shouldn't have taken ceramics. Not a weighted grade."

"I liked ceramics," said Katie wistfully, the way a vegan might confess to having once enjoyed a quarter-pounder.

"Dan, the other seniors would kill for this GPA," said Ted.

"Ceramics shows she's well-rounded," said Joy, who almost believed it. "And I hope someone's going to point out that Katie should have been captain of the swim team. I mean, any other year there wouldn't have been a girl on the team who was training for the Olympics. Who saw that coming?"

"I really want to go to Yale," said Katie. "I thought about it, and I don't want to go to Williams after all. I'm going to apply early."

Ted took too long underlining Yale in red on his chart. He glanced up to see if Katie's parents were going to say anything, but they looked as startled as he felt. Kids sprang surprises like this all the time in his office—they saved up news they thought their parents would not want to hear, relying on Ted's shielding presence to blunt Mom and Dad's response. It was not his favorite maneuver, not by a long shot—there would be emails or phone calls from the parents later this afternoon, he knew it—but Ted was not about to be thrown off his game by Katie's experiment in independence. He had his moves, too.

"No family dynasty? How come?"

Katie thought and did not say: Because I am not going to be Ron's little sister ever again if I can help it. Because I would like to do one thing that isn't because it works so well for my folks and just think how much easier it will be to visit if both of you are in the same place. Because I don't need a reason. Because I'm tired of coming up with them.

"I like the courses at Yale," she said, though she had yet to open the course catalog the school had sent her.

"Ron's been very happy at Williams," said Dan. He addressed Ted directly. "We're going to talk about this some more, of course. It's early in the game to be . . ."

At that, Katie stood up and slung her backpack over one shoulder.

"I have a test," she said. "I have to go. Sorry. I've got a draft essay and I think I'll ask Madame Marie and Dr. Wright for letters. I want to file by the end of the month. Don't you think that's good, to get it in really early?"

"Let me think it over," said Ted feebly.

"Okay, then." She walked out the door.

Ted pretended to jot down some more notes on his copy of the master plan, which he ceremoniously placed inside Katie's folder. He inserted the folder in the very first segment of the stand-up metal file on the cabinet behind his desk, which was his way of saying that Katie's future was extremely important to him. Only then did he make eye contact with her parents.

"Sometimes it can be good for them to strike out on their own," he began. "Katie and Ron, two different people, two different sets of needs. She needs to feel this is all about her. If she sticks to it, at least they're on the same coast. Be grateful she didn't fall in love with Stanford." He got a wan smile from Joy and the smallest belligerent grunt from Dan, but anything was better than silence.

A seductive, conspiratorial tone crept into his voice. "Besides, a month of feeling like it's her decision and she might be willing to reconsider. Let me get her in here again and we'll talk about Williams for her, not for her brother, not for anything but what's best for her. And trust me: she'll start talking to the other kids and the legacy advantage'll start to sound very appealing."

"I can't see why she'd think of anyplace else," said Dan.

"Well, she's a terrific student," said Ted, with an eye on the clock on the wall behind Katie's parents. "And you have to expect this a little bit. I mean, she's got parents who really struck out on their own in a big way, am I right? So it's in her makeup. And for six years we've been telling her the sky's the limit as long as she excels, so she excels and maybe she wants to fly just a bit too close to the sun. We'll talk about it. If she sticks with Yale, I'll have to get them to fall in love with her."

He shook Dan's hand and gave Joy the thin sort of hug that two people not prone to embracing settle for, and after they left he moved Katie's folder to the back, to leave the first slot vacant for the next student's folder. If Ted had been greedier he might have become an agent; if he had been more self-effacing, he could have been a personal assistant. He would sell Katie on Williams without ever divulging all the variables that informed his recommendation. Katie would come around. Ted was very good at getting people to think they wanted what they got.

❦

Joy pulled into the medical building's underground parking garage without quite remembering how she got there, threw the keys at the valet, and kept jamming the elevator call button until it arrived. She had ten minutes before her first peel, but it was going to take her at least that long to collect herself. She held up five fingers twice as she passed her nurse in the hall, shut her office door behind her, and fell into her posturally correct but unsympathetic Aeron chair.

She did not like surprises. Joy picked medicine because new customers were born every day, and dermatology because the likelihood of an off-hours emergency call was low. It was a clean, finite specialty, which appealed to a woman who equated creativity with disorder and disorder with stress, a specialty that spared her having to see anything more gruesome than a suspicious mole or a fungus. She improved her odds even further by opening an office in Beverly Hills, where she could fill a practice to the brim with people who had nothing wrong with them beyond the perceived ravages of time. Word of her finesse quickly got around, and over the summer she had informed her staff that from now on she would see noncosmetic patients only on Thursday afternoons. If a patient slipped in with a problem she did not want to treat, all she had to do was feign concern, say that she was worried about scarring, and recommend a plastic surgeon. She intended to retire in two years, when she was fifty, whether or not her television-producer client was right about the demand for a skin-care reality show for Lifetime, if not Bravo. Having expended a great deal of energy getting from Wheaton, Illinois, to here, she was slightly more willing than Dan to take what they had as more than enough. She was satisfied a moment before he was in all things except sex, where she was the appreciative recipient of the same attention to detail that he lavished on his work.

In a life where nothing was left to chance, the business about Katie wanting to go to Yale threw Joy more than it should have. She dug the Fiske out of her briefcase, found the pages for Yale and for Williams, and ripped them out so that she could study them side by side. What was Katie's problem? Williams was smaller and lovelier and equally rigorous; Dan had taken to saying that it out-Ivied the Ivies. Joy was mystified and irritated by Katie's behavior, and she was out of time. The light above her office door blinked on, signaling that the divorcée who thought that fewer facial lines would compensate for her sniping personality was waiting in exam room 3.

It was only when Joy stopped thinking about Yale and started thinking about her patient that her brain relaxed enough to allow a new thought: Yale was not the problem; or, rather, it was the manifestation of a more serious concern. Katie had changed her mind without consulting either Joy or Dan, and she had known what she intended to say to Ted for days, maybe even weeks. Katie had kept a secret, and that, not the specific content of the secret, was what rattled Joy. Besides, as far as Joy was concerned she was simply wrong.

Joy hung her twin-set cardigan in the closet, slipped into her white lab coat, grabbed the Fiske, minus two pages, and headed for exam room 3. Yoonie was standing outside the door, waiting, and Joy held out the book to her.

"Your daughter's a senior, right?"

"Yes," said the nurse.

"Well, you'll need this. We have an extra. Go ahead."

The nurse reached for the book and tapped at the Post-it tags with her thumb.

"I should take these off for you?"

"Ignore them. Don't worry. Don't give it back. Your daughter might see a school she likes in here. Quick, go put it with your stuff."

Joy took the patient's folder out of the Lucite holder that was mounted on the outside of the exam room door and stood quietly, her hand on the doorknob, her eyes closed, while she located her professional demeanor. A moment later, she swung the door open, exclaimed, "Now there's a face that doesn't look like it needs me," and sat down next to Marsha for the requisite chat that preceded every peel or injection. Yoonie was quick. Joy could depend on her to put the guidebook away and be back in room 3, poised to assist, before Marsha had finished describing her disastrous blind date.

⋅⋆⋅

Yoonie told a very small lie when she first came to work for Dr. Joy: she said that she had to leave at two thirty on Wednesday afternoons. It was not a premeditated lie but a sudden, spontaneous, self-indulgent one, unusual for a woman whose idea of a big treat was a single mini-Snickers in the evening, after the dishes were done, no more than once or twice a week. She had no need of time for herself, not with a job that required her to wear surgical scrubs, white sneakers, tidy hair, no nail polish, not that Yoonie would have used it, and less makeup than the patients wore. When she got home after work she changed into sweats, and if they visited friends on a Saturday night she had a rotation of three interchangeable outfits that yielded nine agreeable combinations. There was no real reason to leave early, but she said it on the off chance that someday there might be, and she picked a weekday afternoon in the hope that whatever it was would involve her daughter.

When Elizabeth was younger, Yoonie had picked her up at school every Wednesday afternoon, but lately there were more and more reasons to break their date, meetings with teachers, meetings of the film club, orchestra rehearsals for the fall musical, days when Elizabeth chose to do her homework at school for no reason Yoonie could fathom. Most Wednesdays, Yoonie drove straight home and took a brisk walk down to the ocean and back, focused on maintaining her pace, hopeful that the following week she would not have the chance.

On the rare occasion when Elizabeth had nothing else to do, Yoonie made sure to be first in the pickup line, rather than waste twenty precious minutes edging forward behind a row of other cars. The daily drama was always the same. The security guard walked the perimeter of Ocean Heights High, stopping only to glower at the neighborhood drug dealer, who glowered back from the sanctity of the public sidewalk in front of his conveniently lo-cated apartment building. His circuit complete, the guard unlocked the main gate and the driveway gate, waited for the bell, and nod-ded to three custodians, who opened three sets of double doors with the precision of synchronized swimmers. At the start of each year, the three-story concrete slab that was Santa Monica's contribution to blockhouse architecture spewed forth almost four thousand students every afternoon, though that number would dwindle by hundreds by spring, as a predictable percentage of the seniors made life choices that did not require a diploma, one or two of them always drafted by the freelance pharmaceuticals rep across the street. Even so, it was a great wave of teenagers. Yoonie had the chance, on increasingly intermittent Wednesdays, to watch them grow up, to be reminded—not that she ever forgot, not even for an instant— that in three years, in two years, next year, she would be able to walk on the beach every week. She opened her checkbook register to the little calendar printed on the back, to get an idea of how many Wednesdays there were between now and college, but Elizabeth swung open the passenger door and plopped onto the seat before she could finish counting.

Liz. Yoonie corrected herself. On the first day of senior year, Elizabeth had informed her mother that she preferred to be called Liz.

"You have anything left to eat?"

"No. I'm sorry."

Liz settled into the passenger seat, carefully set her water bottle into the cup holder her father had built for her out of a beheaded Big Gulp cup and some duct tape, and reached down at her feet for her mother's new book bag, which sported the logo of the wrinkle filler whose manufacturer was courting Dr. Joy. She pulled a Sharpie out of her own backpack and began to color over the pharmaceutical logo with black ink.

"You're not a billboard," she told her mom, as she had when she had blacked out the logo on the previous book bag, "and you really ought to carry a regular purse separate from lunch. What if something spills?" Yoonie watched her daughter with frustration. She was proud to carry the bags from the pharmaceutical companies, just as she enjoyed wearing the pastel scrubs that Dr. Joy liked the nurses to wear instead of plain white, but Liz always marked out the logos anyhow. As she turned the bag over to start on the other side, the flagged Fiske guide slid out of the bag onto her lap. She riffled through to see what schools were marked.

"Where'd you get this?" she asked. "Why did you flag all these?" She picked a page with a blue flag and held it up for her mother to see. "Duke? You're not serious."

"Dr. Joy gave it to me," Yoonie said.

"But we're not interested in any of these schools."

"I know," said her mother. "When I read some of it I felt even more sure that we are not interested."

Yoonie pulled carefully into traffic and headed for home, a small stucco cottage in a corridor of rentals sandwiched between the Santa Monica freeway and the gentrified neighborhoods to the south. She and her husband and her daughter lived on a street where gang members still sprayed their initials on fences, where the neighborhood market stocked a dozen kinds of salsa but not a single jar of danmooji. Her second cousin, who lived in Koreatown, liked to remind her on a regular basis of exactly how crazy she was not to move, but Yoonie ignored her. She and Steve had moved here for the schools, because the district served the overpriced beachside communities as well as the few remaining blocks at their margins that had not yet been remodeled. They had endured thirteen years of kids smoking who knew what on their front lawn after school, of boys walking flat-headed, spike-collared dogs that growled at anything that moved, of sirens that screeched to a halt in their neighborhood, all so that Liz could attend a halfway decent public high school. In a year, she would go to Harvard, and then perhaps Yoonie and her husband would move onto her cousin's block, where people understood that Eun Hee was pronounced with a breath in the middle.

Liz flipped to another flagged page, read silently for a moment, and tossed the book onto the floor of the backseat. "Can we go to Coffee Bean?"

"Yes," said Yoonie, who had yet to develop a taste for even the most doctored of coffee drinks, but would never turn down such an invitation. "But look again in the bag and see what I got you."

She pulled into the left-turn lane so that she could double back toward school, and Liz dutifully rummaged around and extracted a half-dozen sample tubes of sunscreen in a range of intensity and formula: SPFs from 15 to 55, finishes from matte to all-sport waterproof. Liz muttered her thanks and put them in her purse, so that she could empty them into her bathroom drawer along with all the other sunscreen samples her mother had presented to her in the last year. Yoonie devoutly believed that the Los Angeles sun was her mortal enemy, and she kept her family in an oversupply of sunscreen, which she insisted they slather on every time they left the house. Her adopted home was a city full of terrors, from earthquakes to the subjunctive, and she was powerless to do anything about most of them. The blinding sun was a problem she could solve. Her daughter would go to Harvard with very healthy skin.

A generation earlier, an after-school snack meant a Coke and fries, or a milk shake and a burger, any carbocentric treat that pumped up the collective serotonin level for such slap-happy concerns as a pep rally or the annual disco night fundraiser. There might be a city somewhere where similar tastes still prevailed—a flyover state that no one from Crestview or Ocean Heights had ever visited—but for twenty-first-century urban teens, the snack of choice was caffeine. They knew the difference between a cappuccino and a macchiato before they were old enough to drive. They sneered at the hardcore users who chugged cans of Red Bull after an all-nighter and convinced themselves that four visits to Starbucks between breakfast and dinner was a sign of sophistication, not dependency. Between three and five on weekdays, the gourmet coffee outlet nearest a high school was this generation's hangout, and an

espresso-powered drink topped with whipped cream was its strawberry ice-cream soda.

One of the city's luckier franchisees ran the Coffee Bean across
the street from Ocean Heights, which was mobbed by the time
Yoonie and Liz arrived. They took their place in a slow, snaking
line, as one after another of Liz's classmates debated the relative merits of an extra shot, the addition of cocoa nibs, or the exact amount
of whipped cream required to avoid speculation that the consumer
was either an anorexic or a pig. Like any self-respecting teen, Liz
stood far enough away from her mother to allow people to mistake
them for strangers, but when she made the tactical error of waving
to a girl at one of the tables, her mother closed the gap.

"Who did you see?" Yoonie asked. Liz never brought friends
home, and if Yoonie and Steve had not been completely focused
on academics they might have worried, but Liz never seemed unhappy, and there was plenty of time for friends in college, so they
did not dwell on their daughter's nonexistent social life.

"Chloe," said Liz, nodding toward a girl who waved back from
one of the little round tables. "The kid I tutor."

Yoonie stepped out of the line so that she could get a look,
and she would have waved, too, if Chloe had not turned back to
the other girl at her table.

Liz pulled at her mother's elbow to get her attention. "Mom,
it's a terrible line and there aren't any tables. You want to wait on
the bench outside and I'll bring you yours?"

"Okay," said Yoonie, who would have much preferred to stay in
line. She found it increasingly hard to distinguish between compassion and embarrassment, to figure out if Liz was sending her outside
because she had Yoonie's best interests at heart or because she was
trying to choreograph a temporary escape from being a daughter.
Yoonie imagined that women like Dr. Joy had a private bank account of carefree memories from which they could withdraw a
happy story when they were asked to wait outside, or whatever the

dismissive equivalent was in their family. Yoonie had precious few such assets, for almost all of her memories had goals attached. She felt satisfied, surely, because Liz had accomplished more than she and Steve could ever have dreamed, but satisfied did not make the bench any more comfortable.

⚘

Chloe had just sat down with two iced blendeds when Lauren blew in the door, and she instinctively placed a protective hand over each drink as her friend dumped her purse and backpack on the floor and sank into the empty chair across from her, legs splayed, seams askew. Chloe thought that Lauren dealt with the stress of junior and senior year better than anyone else she knew. Some girls ate too much, others ate too little, and the fringe element dabbled in drink or drugs or random sex or all three. Chloe had tried each of the standard remedies right up to the point where she scared herself, and since then she had settled for dripping sarcasm, the refuge of the timid but angry. Lauren was smarter; she let stress seep right out of her pores. It untucked her uniform shirt and ripped her hem, derailed her center part and sent her hair cascading, kept her knee jiggling no matter how hard she tried to sit still.

She took a long slurp of her drink, sat back, and cupped her hands under her breasts, oblivious of the effect she was having on the Coffee Bean employee whose job it was to wipe down the tables and refill the napkin dispenser.

"Get this. Ted the Great says I am top-heavy. Top. Heavy." She waggled her fingers at Chloe, who laughed so hard she had to wave her hands at Lauren to get her to stop. If she tried to open her mouth to speak, she would have sprayed her drink all over her friend.

"I want too many schools that don't want me, is what he thinks. So my mom is in full fret mode, like, 'What're we going to do?' and my dad doesn't know what to say, and Ted wants me to go to, I don't know, maybe night school?" Lauren paused to take a breath, which became a sigh, which became a sullen weight at the back of her neck. "It was totally depressing. 'You're a terrific kid—except wait, now that we think it over, oh, sorry, you're a failure.'"

Chloe's mood turned appropriately somber. "He didn't really say that. You're not a failure."

"You're not a college counselor. Do you have a college counselor?"

"A college counselor. Well, almost. I of course got assigned to the loser one, basically she's the receptionist."

"Would you stop it?"

"Would *you* stop it?" Chloe had left Crestview at the end of her sophomore year, when, as she liked to put it, her parents had decided that it was more important to send their divorce lawyers' children to private school than it was to let her graduate with her friends. That was not fair, and she knew it—her father had moved into a vacant dingbat apartment in a building his brother owned, and her parents did most of their fighting outside of the lawyers' offices to keep costs down. Like any other overextended family with exploitable assets, Chloe's parents had available to them all the usual resources for creating cash: a house whose equity they could borrow against, credit cards they could max out at ever-inflating interest rates, investment accounts they could raid. All that really stood between Chloe and a Crestview diploma was the specter of monthly finance charges or a chunk of added income tax on the investment money, and her parents willingly would have paid the extra freight to assuage their mutual guilt. In fact, it had been Chloe's decision to switch to public school. In the spring of her sophomore year, her parents had gotten into a loud argument in the Crestview parking lot after the school play, in front of witnesses, and the next day Chloe had informed them that she would not be returning the following year.

GETTING IN

The problem with the truth, though, was that it was dire, and decidedly not funny. As Chloe had no interest in being the object of anyone's pity or sympathy, she made up the business about the divorce lawyers' children and stuck with it. The line always got a laugh, which was pretty much all Chloe cared about these days— that, and being able for the first time in her life to give her old friends a hard time for being sheltered and spoiled, which was what she tried to convince herself they were.

"You can't be suffering that bad," said Lauren. "Your mom doesn't even work. I mean, if one of my parents stopped working, I'd be at Cal State Wherever."

"My mom is going to work a couple of mornings to trade for free Pilates," said Chloe, and she began to giggle. "Big bread-winner."

"So what'd the counselor say?"

"Haven't seen her yet. Basically she answers the phone and alphabetizes brochures. I'm not holding out big hope for help there."

"But when do you pick?"

"Maybe I have," said Chloe. "Hampshire, Bard . . ."

"I've heard of Bard."

"Well, now I'm back with the cool crowd." Chloe regretted the jab immediately. "Never mind."

"Y'know, it's not my fault your life's a living hell."

"Right. I have my parents to thank for that. Anyhow, some-place where they don't expect me to take fundamentals of every-thing before I can have any fun. Oh, but there's Harvard right there. See that girl? Total perfection. She's the spoiler. Good thing I don't want to go to Harvard. Like that was ever going to happen."

Lauren glanced in the direction Chloe was pointing. There were two girls in line to order drinks, a tall blonde in her Ocean Heights High basketball uniform and an Asian girl who was trying to pretend that the woman standing behind her was not her mother.

"The jock or the nerd?"

"Nerd, also known as my math tutor. Jock's getting recruited at Stanford." She made a polite wave, as opposed to a beckoning one, and got the same wave in return.

"And Harvard?"

"She got 2300 on her SATs, I asked her, straight As, she takes APs they haven't even dreamed up yet." Chloe shook her head. "Not a normal childhood if you ask me."

"Has she cured cancer?"

"Next week. After the violin performance or the track meet, I'm not sure which, or tutoring five kids in South Central. Or saving me from failing calc. You're taking calc, aren't you?"

"Like I had a choice." Any girl who was halfway serious about college had to take more math classes than she could ever possibly need or want. It was the progressive choice. An A in AP calculus carried more weight for a girl than an A in AP American lit, no matter what anyone in the English department said.

"Too bad for you," said Chloe. "Reading is so yesterday."

Lauren got up suddenly. "I've got tons of homework. I'll drive you home." She had gotten out of bed that morning with a list of possibilities, and now all she had were downward arrows, stretch schools, and strategies designed to compensate for what Ted seemed to feel were her shortcomings. The airy feeling she recalled when she first composed the list had congealed into something heavier, an awareness that the future might end just shy of where she thought it would—that it was not quite as vast as she had imagined. She looked at the Asian girl and felt a jab of envy, even though she had no desire to play the violin, run track, or go to Harvard.

She never quite trusted girls who seemed to know exactly where they were headed. Chloe liked to tell people that she planned either to go into politics or to write fiction, though Lauren's dad said that choosing the former, given Chloe's lack of interest in current events, indicated her talent for the latter. Katie told everyone it was Yale and Yale Law, while Lauren had trouble hanging on to a version of herself for more than a couple of weeks at a time. Her parents always said she was not supposed to know if she wanted to be a chef or an architect or a teacher, and she might want to be a psychologist once she got to college and took a psychology class. That was the whole point of going to college, they said, to read and think and figure out who she wanted to be. Lauren watched Ms. Absolute Perfection inch toward the front of the line and wondered, for the first time, if they had any idea what they were talking about.

chapter 3

Chloe looked as though she had been drawn with a com-
pass, a source of infinite exasperation to her mother, who
had been laid out with a straightedge. Chloe was adamantly, irrevocably round, from her mink eyes to her soup-bowl belly to
hips that yearned for the demise of low-rise jeans. A fat halo of
russet curls framed her face, despite her mother's repeated offers
to pay for Japanese straightening. Her little cobalt blue toenails
were rounder than her mother's red brick rectangles; she was not so
much plump as circular, as unsubtle and unstable as a beach ball.
She knew from her mother's perpetually downturned mouth that
Deena resented the way she looked. As long as Chloe was in the
house, it was impossible, despite a folder full of legal documents,
for Deena to eliminate Dave from her life entirely.

In an intact household, Chloe told herself, she would have
channeled her energy into something big, an as yet unidentified
career that guaranteed her a closet full of the latest fashions and
public appearances where she would be photographed wearing
them. Ever since her parents' argument in the parking lot, Chloe
had a darker mission—to retaliate, to punish them for being so
selfish that they could not manage to stay married until she left
home.

If getting into a great college was going to be the one stellar
accomplishment her parents pointed to, to prove that they had
not irreparably harmed their only child, then college was going to
be the one thing Chloe blew off—just shy of not going, of course,

for she was not that brave. Chloe intended to find a decent school that her parents considered to be completely inappropriate, a private one that cost a lot of money, and to insist that it was the only place on earth where she could be truly happy.

Chloe had sustained damage in the breakup, she just knew it, though she figured it would be years before she understood its scope, and years more before she was willing to give it up as a convenient excuse for bad behavior. The right college might help her get her bearings, but of course losing those bearings in the first place probably guaranteed that the right college would not want her. Other kids might feel like rejects when a school turned them down. Chloe intended to occupy the much cushier berth of the emotional casualty.

If she were being honest, she would have admitted that life before her parents' split had not been much fun, either, and that in fact there was a certain relief to being able to get through a day without holding her breath. She preferred instead to remind her parents, whenever possible, that she had endured a wrenching detour, one that involved not just the logistical challenge of joint custody but the academic and social demands of a new school—a transition of a magnitude her parents failed to appreciate to this day.

There were so many adjustments to make. At Crestview, she had never carried a real purse, thanks to an informal competition that involved being the senior with the most beat-up but still serviceable six-year-old backpack. At Ocean Heights, girls started babysitting in eighth grade so that they'd have enough saved up for a Kooba or a Tylie Malibu by the time they started high school. They bought their shoes at Payless and their jeans at Target—at Tar-jay, merci—but the purse had to be an important one, even if it was last season's, even if they ignored their algebra homework to scour eBay and the online discount sites for markdowns.

By the time anyone remembered her name, Chloe was sporting a brand-new Tylie that the other girls would have to dream about until the after-Christmas sales. She banished to the back of her closet the $175 jeans favored by Crestview kids, with their frayed hems, strategic holes, and machine-aged denim, and replaced them with four pairs of pristine, perfectly pressed jeans and two pairs of Dickies khakis that cost the same amount, total, as a single pair of her discards. Private school girls, who saw nothing wrong with calling their tank tops "wifebeaters," wore them with push-up bras in a contrasting color, but public schoolers called them "tanks" and piled on two or three at a time over bras with transparent plastic straps, so Chloe had to buy some extras, along with the proper underwear. She needed a new cell phone; she switched to a different styling gel. Whenever Chloe felt like stabbing her parents in the heart she speculated, loudly, about how much better she might have done in the two high school years that really counted, if she had not had to navigate the educational equivalent of a move from France to Sri Lanka.

"Salad night, honey." Deena's voice from the kitchen interrupted her daughter's internal rant. "Ten minutes."

Chloe had made it a policy, since the breakup, never to respond to either of her parents the first time they called. Deena waited for a reply, got none, and blamed Dave for the silence, as she blamed him for everything. Dave, the only man in the known universe who managed not to get rich in advertising, the man who created what was widely considered one of the most offensive television campaigns ever made for an intestinal gas product. The executives who had approved the campaign pretended that they had not been involved and transferred Dave to media sales because they felt too guilty to fire him. Now he told people that he sold time and space for a living, a sure indication of how funny he was not, in case anyone needed proof beyond what Deena referred to as the singing fart commercials.

GETTING IN

When Deena had first confessed her dismay at his downward
mobility, he said she was being inflexible and lacked compassion.
As his income decreased and her spending did not, he complained
further that she was grasping, selfish, and unsupportive; he accused
her of everything short of having given him the original inspiration for the gas commercial. Deena replied that Dave had failed
to live up to his obligations as a husband and a father. Dave, having recently found sympathy incarnate in a twenty-nine-year-old
yoga instructor who frequented a deli he liked, agreed with his
wife. He had not done a good job. He was resigning his post in the
hope that he would do better as an ex-husband, another line he
found amusing.

If only it were that simple, if only leaving really meant gone.
Deena knew all too well that people did not disappear just because they were no longer around. Her mother, Nana Ree, was
getting the biggest laugh of anybody about Dave, and she had been
dead for four years, felled by an aneurysm in the porte-cochere at
Saks and buried in the navy blue two-piece St. John knit that she
had purchased mere moments before. She was sitting in a fitting
room in heaven shaking her head and muttering, "I told you so,"
because she had recognized in her son-in-law the same fool's
belief in change, not effort, that had drawn Deena's father away
from his wife and daughter for life with a North Beach bartender.

Deena was getting better at not thinking about any of this
during the day, but at dusk, with Chloe sequestered in her bedroom
and only fresh produce to keep her company, the kitchen filled
with unwanted ghosts.

"Stop it," she said, sawing at a hapless tomato with more force
than its pliant skin required. "Everybody out of my kitchen," she
muttered as she proceeded to dice the memory of her mother
and her ex-husband into an exceedingly fine chop. She mutilated
tomatoes, olives, avocados, and a takeout rosemary chicken breast,

dumped them into a big bowl already half-full of shredded let-tuce, and padded down the hallway to knock on Chloe's door.

"You can come out now," she said. "There's nothing left to get ready, so it's safe."

"Right," came Chloe's voice from behind the door. "Wouldn't want that lettuce to get cold."

Deena bit her lip, walked back into the kitchen, and drowned the salad with bottled no-calorie Italian dressing, knowing that Chloe often required a third call these days, knowing that Chloe hated soggy lettuce. Too bad. Salad night was Deena's thinly veiled attempt to get Chloe's weight down and make it seem like fun, with a different combination of veggies and protein each time, and all she got for her trouble was sarcasm and resentment. She was not about to sit here and wait until Chloe deigned to appear. Deena piled salad on her plate, poured herself a glass of iced tea, and tried to focus on the first delicious and virtuous bite even as she listened for the doorknob turning.

She took a second helping that she did not really want, to make it look as though she had a good reason for sitting with Chloe while she ate, and worked hard to ignore the melodramatic sigh as Chloe hoisted her first swampy forkful. Deena poked at her food until Chloe's plate was half-empty, to ensure that her daughter had a healthy meal even if she stormed out of the room once Deena said what she had to say.

"Your father and I had a talk," she began.

"That always works well," Chloe shot back.

"Do not use that tone of voice—"

"Any more olives?"

Deena got up to retrieve them from the fridge.

"I'm going to finish my sentence. Your father and I had a talk about these ten schools on your list . . ."

Chloe smiled, which Deena took as encouragement, though it was in fact amusement. Her parents had managed to have a conversation about the ten schools on her list without ever realizing that each one of them had a different list, that there were twenty schools, not ten, that so far her search for a school resembled nothing so much as a Saturday afternoon spent on random shoe-shopping sites. It included the top five private schools from the *U.S. News & World Report* list, on the off chance that one of them might consider an applicant with premillennial SAT scores; Berkeley and Michigan, because they were big enough to disappear in; five schools close to big cities from the book about schools that made a difference; six from the deep double digits on the *U.S. News* list, because who was she kidding; and two UCs, in case her parents' endless arguments about money caught fire.

In the single most profitable consequence of her parents' separation, she had a Jet Blue American Express card from her mom and an iTunes Visa card from her dad, so she could charge half the applications on each and perpetuate the illusion of thoroughness, not wantonness. Her mom shopped to fill the vacant space that was her life. Chloe shopped, in this case, to pave the road away from home. She saw this as a crucial distinction.

Deena reached over to pat Chloe's hand. "And we wondered why you're not applying early to some special school. If it's a reasonable choice you could get all of this over with before Christmas, and not have to spend time you don't have on all those essays."

Chloe stood up so suddenly that Deena flinched.

"That is so insulting," said Chloe. "What you really mean is why don't I pick someplace easy that no one else wants to go to. Why don't you just say so? Let's sign me up for City College and spare ourselves the disappointment. And spare you and Daddy all that money. I ought to bug the house, and then if you and Daddy ever decide to worry about my self-esteem, which I doubt, but if you ever do, you can just listen to the things you say to me. Then you'll know why I don't have any."

"Chloe. I was just asking. If we can't ask simple questions . . ."

"But they're not simple questions. I picked out ten schools because I thought they gave me a really good range of options." Suddenly she recalled something useful Ted had said at the one Crestview college workshop she had attended in her sophomore year. "Some of us aren't really ready to make a decision this early, and the six extra months gives us time we need to mature. I'm a different person today than I was last year, right?"

"Right," allowed Deena, wondering what trap she was stepping into.

"Then I'll be a different girl when the letters come out next April than when the early ones come out in December, right?"

"I guess so," said Deena, although she had no idea if she really believed it. At some point the apocalyptics of growing up steadied into a more manageable rhythm—in Dave's case, they had congealed into an infuriating sameness. Why not assume that Chloe would still essentially be Chloe next spring and go for early decision? Deena had no patience for the subtleties of a real college strategy, but she understood dating. Schools wanted to say yes to kids who definitely would say yes to them, not to kids who might have their heads turned by a more handsome suitor. That was what early decision was all about, at least at schools where an average student like Chloe might stand a chance.

"Excuse me?" said Chloe. "You guess so?"

"I'm thinking about what you said."

"Yeah, but while you're thinking I'm not getting my homework done."

Chloe retreated to her bedroom, closed the door, and sent Lauren an instant message to see if she was home. Before the parking-lot argument, Chloe had had friends over all the time, but once she moved to Ocean Heights she had started inviting herself to other people's houses. It made her parents feel bad, which never hurt, and it reminded her friends of how drastically Chloe's life had changed, which was always good for a little attention.

Lauren's parents only minded company during midterms and finals, and occasionally on the night before a big test or paper, which, happily for Chloe, this turned out not to be. As soon as Lauren messaged back, Chloe threw her laptop into her bag along with her calculus binder, cell phone, a twenty, and her driver's license. She ducked into the bathroom and rubbed her face with a dry towel until her cheeks and forehead colored up, and she ground a fist into each eye socket to make the whites redden, just a bit. She stood for a moment behind her bedroom door, as generations of actresses have stood in the wings before a big entrance, and then she rushed into the kitchen, looking suitably distressed.

"I can't believe it," she said to her mother. "My calc binder is at Dad's."

"How can that be?" said Deena. "Honey, you really have to—"

"It's not my fault. Daddy always double-checks, or he said he does, I don't know, oh, Mom, I have to go get it right now."

Deena dried her hands and tossed the dishtowel on the counter. "I'll drive you over. This has got to stop. I'm going to talk to him, sweetie, really, we'll figure this out for you . . ."

Chloe startled her mother by wrapping her in a hug. "Oh, Mommy, you are the best, but you don't have to drive me all the way to the Valley. I'll talk to Dad. Really. I have to learn how to take responsibility for myself."

"It's seven thirty," said Deena, thinking that it had been a while since Chloe had called her Mommy. "Really, I can take you."

"If I leave right now it's a half hour to Dad's, and maybe I'll study when I get there instead of waiting until I get back, and then a half hour back, so I'll be home by ten."

"What if he's not home?"

"Then I won't have to take any extra time talking to him. I can be the world's most efficient calculus student." She grabbed the car keys off the little hook by the kitchen door and sealed the deal with a kiss on Deena's cheek. "Love you, Mom. Bye."

Communications technology was kind to high school students: instant-messaging, texting, and the vibrate feature on cell phones made it impossible for a parent passing by the closed door of a child's room to distinguish between the keyboard clack of homework and the keyboard clack of chatting with friends. Outside Lauren's bedroom, her parents commented on how nice it was of her to help Chloe with her history paper rather than relax once her own homework was done. Inside Lauren's bedroom, the girls flitted from talk.collegeconfidential.com to a generalized Google search of "National Merit semifinalist cutoff scores." Lauren had waited for almost a year to find out whether good news was good enough; she had scored 215 on the PSAT in the fall of junior year, which was exactly the California cutoff score for the previous year's National Merit scholarship semifinalists, but National Merit issued new state-by-state cutoffs every year, which were almost always higher than the preceding year's scores. Short of a mysterious infusion of bad test takers into the California population, Lauren had next to no chance of becoming a semifinalist. Unless, of course, she did. There was no way to know until the mailing arrived, except at schools that broke ranks and notified seniors before the official announcement. Word had begun to leak out, so seniors across the country were trolling the Web, looking for clues.

As she and Chloe watched the screen, an Illinois girl set off a flurry of posts by reporting that she had made the cut with a 220. No one congratulated her. All the responses were from Illinois students and parents who demanded to know if 220 was the minimum or if the girl had qualified with 220 but the actual cutoff was lower. As the girl had no interest in what happened to anyone else, she had not thought to ask, which led ChiTown Teen to post, "I'm sitting here going crazy with a 214. HOW COULD YOU NOT ASK WHAT THE MINIMUM WAS????!!!!???? Selfish biatch. They say SAT scores move toward the middle, so I hope you get a 1900. Watch out if you're applying to Wash U is all I can say."

"Nice," said Chloe.

"Welcome to my world," said Lauren. "I say ten minutes tops before we hear from Katie." Lauren had intended to confide her PSAT score only to Chloe, but Katie had pried it out of her under the guise of comradely suffering, as though Katie's score of 220 was in any way as precarious as Lauren's 215. A moment later, her cell phone skittered across the bed. Chloe grabbed it and read the message. "She says did you see the 220 in Illinois, she just knows it'll be lower here and you shouldn't worry. Why did you tell her?"

The phone jittered again, and this time Lauren dove for it.

"Brad," she said. "His dad just got a call from Ted and did I get one." She felt an uncomfortable shudder work up her spine, as her default position of not caring wrestled with a younger, stronger adversary, the notion that all of this mattered tremendously.

A third text. "Katie just got a call from Ted and I have to let her know the minute I hear."

"Well, fuck," said Chloe, "what kind of friends are they? I mean, doesn't anybody the fuck think to ask what the cutoff is?"

"I can't ask Katie."

"Ask Brad. Or wait for the phone to ring."

Lauren sent a text to Brad and sat, immobilized, watching the screen, waiting, but not for long. She read the message and tossed the phone back toward Chloe.

"The cutoff was 216 and he wants to know did I make it. Can you believe it? I can't believe it."

A single point. This happened to Lauren far too often to be merely frustrating. If the teacher in the other section of AP calculus rounded an 89.5 up to a 90 and an A minus, the teacher in Lauren's section inevitably left it right where it was, as a B plus. *Esos* instead of *esas* on a Spanish translation was the point that would have meant an A, which would have canceled out the B plus, but instead the A minus faced off with the B plus, and lost.

One point and she got a letter of commendation instead of being a semifinalist. One point, and she found herself far more disappointed than she had expected she would be.

"Am I leaving?" Chloe started to gather up her things.

"Yeah, I have to tell my parents before somebody else does, that's for sure." Her phone moved again. "Katie's so very sorry. Not sorry, not very sorry, but so very sorry. She sounds like her mother."

"Hey, it's tough only being in the top, what are you? Two percent of all the seniors in the country?"

"One and a half percent," said Lauren, listlessly.

"Agony," said Chloe.

The Crestview computer lab was empty, so Katie slipped in right after AP French, retrieved a small dog-eared notebook from a zippered compartment in her purse, and entered the 98 from the first test of the year on the page devoted to AP French. She had kept this book since ninth grade, and while she could hardly go around asking people what their grades were, she always listened carefully and watched the looks on certain of her classmates' faces. She believed that Brad had an A minus in AP chemistry, and she knew from an overheard tantrum in the girls' bathroom that the science nerd did not do well enough in AP Latin to pose a threat. Katharine Dodson, National Merit semifinalist at the very least, was almost certainly going to be valedictorian of this year's Crestview senior class, even with the unweighted A in ceramics.

She tucked the notebook back in its hiding place and decided to take another look at talk.collegeconfidential.com, which was filling up with California posts.

"What's so funny?"

Instinctively, Katie clicked the site closed and put on her best sympathy smile for Lauren.

"Forever 21 has such slutty clothes, it's just amazing," said Katie. "Listen. How're you doing? It's crazy, you know, somebody gets semifinalist and a point away you just get a letter . . ."

"Katie, if you ever say 'just' gets a letter again I will hate you for the rest of my life."

"Can I join?" Brad came in just in time to hear the second half of Lauren's sentence. "Do we get club T-shirts? Just kidding, Katie."

She ignored him and glanced at the wall clock.

"Oberlin rep's coming at lunchtime. Want to go?"

"You're not applying there," said Lauren. "Neither am I."

"Exactly the point." Katie brushed past Brad and hooked her arm in Lauren's. "My dad says it's good practice and it doesn't matter. We should go pretend we're desperate to go to Oberlin and see what kinds of things the woman says. What kinds of questions she likes. What she thinks is stupid. C'mon. And they always bring in turkey wraps, so it's free lunch besides."

Lauren sighed and followed Katie down to the college counseling conference room, wondering about the potential advantage of having a dad who thought of going to a college rep visit to rehearse versus having parents who had never met a bureaucracy they liked. She and Katie took seats on either side of the Oberlin rep and took notes on how she responded to various questions, on what made her smile, on the way she gently demolished one applicant by pointing out that the answers to all of her questions were on the school's website. Four of the other attendees, for whom Oberlin was far and away a first choice, went home that afternoon in varying states of distress and announced to their parents that Katie and Lauren seemed interested in Oberlin, which undoubtedly wrecked their chances of acceptance. On the mere fact of their attendance at the meeting, one girl decided to switch her early application from Oberlin to Grinnell. No one of their caliber had shown up for the Grinnell lunch.

On their way out, Katie leaned in close to whisper, "You should ask Ted how many semifinalists there are, total."

"To make myself even more miserable?"

"How can you say that?" asked Katie. "I meant as news editor. I thought you might not be thinking about it right now, you know, but isn't there usually an article when the names come out?"

Ocean Heights High School was a vestige of an era when insulation was asbestos, paint was lead-based, and the only students who went to private schools on the West Coast were debutantes or discipline problems or devout Catholics. It was one of the better public high schools in Los Angeles, which was an accomplishment in a universe where no one used superlatives anymore, but every year budget cuts claimed another chunk of the curriculum. The custodians regularly mopped and buffed the floors of rooms that no one used—the dance studio, the little theater, the girls' gymnastics gym. If a senior tracked the fresh buffer marks on the linoleum floor, she could always find a pristine and empty room where she could hide to catch her breath.

When Liz needed to call her parents, she liked the privacy of the long, narrow locker room on the far side of the swimming pool. Now that swimming was no longer part of the physical education rotation, the locker room filled up twice a day at most, before school when the team practiced and after school during the competition season. Sometimes it was empty for weeks on end. She slipped in before lunch and left an identical voice-mail message for her mother and her father.

"I got National Merit," she said. "I am a semifinalist. They gave me the letter today so I wanted to let you know. Not a surprise, but it feels very nice."

Chloe, who often hid out in the deeper recesses of the locker room to sketch without anyone seeing her, waited until she heard the swinging doors swoosh a second time and counted ten fading footsteps before she closed her pad and took out her phone.

She texted Lauren. "Math tutor scores on NMerit. Let's fix her up w Brad."

Lauren read the message and flipped her phone shut, fast, before Brad could see what Chloe had written. She took a pair of latex gloves out of the lab station drawer and reminded herself sternly that her fetal pig dissection was not merely a lab exercise but a brick in the foundation of her future. That was one of the phrases Ted liked to use. Another of his favorites: first-quarter grades are the swing states of the college application process, and they can make the difference between acceptance and rejection for an early-decision candidate. Regular-decision kids had to hold it together for an entire semester, but the early applicants had nine weeks to make a good impression. As she made the first incision, she was sure that Ted's comment was the reason the biology teacher always scheduled the dissection for first quarter, and grateful that she had drawn Brad as a lab partner. He was getting AP credit because he had a scheduling conflict with AP bio and Ted had insisted that the regular-section teacher accommodate him, and Lauren depended on credibility by association.

Second quarter, she might have been tempted to say that she had a profound moral objection to the use of dead lab animals. By second semester, she happily would have threatened to throw up all over the lab station rather than do the dissection. First quarter, she would cut open a dead pig even if her family kept kosher.

"What do you think I should call myself next year?" asked Brad, who was kind enough to take over scalpel duties whenever the teacher turned his back.

"What?"

"Nobody gets to call me Four in college. I need a name."

"Nobody calls you Four but your dad. Just be Brad."

"But he thinks it'd be cool to be Four at Harvard, you know, because then people would ask and I could tell them about the other three."

"Say he has Alzheimer's when he comes to visit."

"Right. 'Listen, if my dad starts using numbers for people just ignore it, that's how he keeps track.'" He pushed aside a piece of porcine gristle and wrote a note down in his lab book, which he loaned to Lauren every weekend because she and Chloe were the only girls he knew who occasionally said what they meant to say. "My mom thinks I should switch to Preston."

Lauren glanced over and was amazed at how sad Brad looked, as though a fourth-generation Harvard legacy who was probably down to the wire with Katie for valedictorian had any reason to be upset.

"Call yourself Gene," she said.

"Why?"

"It's such a dumb name. You could use something dumb in your life."

❧

The dark secret of Brad's life was that he was a virgin, despite the legions of Crestview girls who swore, with a knowing smile and a sigh, that they had succumbed to his charms. It was all the fault of the girl who was in the same inner-city ecology program as Brad the summer before their junior year, and was assigned as his partner to drive around South Central and East L.A., instructing people on the dangers of all the things in their environment that they could not afford to repair or replace. In the morning, they pointed at flakes of lead-based paint and rattled off statistics about toddler brain damage, or suggested planting trees to absorb emissions. In the afternoon, having left behind parents plastered with a thick new layer of helpless rage, they fought their way back home, making their own contribution to the particulate layer. It was a long ride, made longer by the fact that rush hour began at two in the afternoon. The girl had since been sent to a boarding school where she had to get up at five in the morning to feed the chickens, but that summer she had devoted her excess energy to Brad, who in turn had worked very hard to fend her off.

He did not like her, and after weeks of being polite he finally had to tell her so—at which point she promptly told everyone she knew about their wild night of passion. Wild nights, actually; by the time the story got around, like a secret whispered around the table at a five-year-old's birthday party, it had mutated and grown into a summer's orgy of fun. To his horror, it spawned offspring. During junior year, a dozen other girls came up with stories of their mad fling with Brad. And then Katie joined their ranks, in retaliation for Brad informing her that a second month of dating was pointless because they really did not get along. He had never gotten north of the fabric-care tag on the side seam of her T-shirts, never wanted to, never tried, which enraged her. She chimed in to the chorus of conquered voices with stories that frightened him in their specificity, almost daring him to contradict her.

He did not have the energy to fight with her. Some of the other boys, intimidated by the scope of Brad's conquests, demanded to know the operational secret of his success and bitterly accused him of holding out when he tried to tell them the truth. They settled for honing their foreplay skills—which was fine with the girls, who, truth be told, were not as eager to lose their virginity as the headlines had their parents believe they were. They were perfectly happy—relieved, actually—to pretend that they had slept with Brad and to spend senior year pretending to get over him, while they devoted their real energies to college applications. Brad resigned himself to ending his Crestview career as an entertaining rumor, and consoled himself with the notion that he probably had kept at least a few of his friends from getting herpes.

Preston Bradley IV: safer than a condom. He doubted that calling himself Gene was going to help.

The world loved Brad to excess, more than he thought any one person deserved, and he was always looking for ways to put a scratch in the veneer of his life. It was the one thing he failed at, again and again. He ate between meals and never gained weight, he rolled through stop signs and waited for a cop who never appeared, he wrote a paper no smarter than Lauren's and got not just an A minus to her B plus, but an outright A. A dozen girls picked him as the costar of their fictional sex lives because of nothing that had anything to do with him.

He was old money, which in Los Angeles meant wealth that predated the advent of cable television. He was high society, which meant money derived from law or banking or real estate and membership in both a tennis or golf club and a non-Catholic church. And he was impossibly, unarguably handsome, in a way that defied category and appealed equally to girls who had previously defined their type as surfer boy, as metrosexual, as neo-Goth, as whatever type their parents disliked the most. Lauren, who was the only one who knew the truth, told him that some of his fake conquests had devised a ranking list, to see if the female members of the Crestview senior class could think of anyone famous under the age of thirty who was better looking than Brad, and so far the consensus was no. The blue of his eyes was deeper than this actor's, his wavy black hair more luxurious than that one's, and on and on, feature by feature, from his cheekbones to his shoulders to the very toes that all of those girls said they had seen, exposed, in bed.

He was a catalog of perfection, which was a terrible burden for a boy to bear. A beautiful girl at least had the support of feminists who encouraged her to develop her brain and sympathized when her looks kept people from taking her seriously. A handsome, wealthy, about-to-be fourth-generation Harvard boy had no such system to help him cope. Brad's life always rounded up. He could hardly have any complaints.

chapter 4

Final Draft
Preston Bradley

Man has yearned to fly ever since he realized that gravity prevented him from doing so—from doing anything more than envying the birds overhead. Knowing our limitations hasn't stopped us from trying, though, too often with disastrous results: from Icarus to Brewster McCloud, we get into trouble when we let ourselves think that we can defy the laws of nature.

Air is just not where we're supposed to be, I guess, which is why I get nervous every time there's turbulence when I'm flying. As long as the flight is smooth, I can deceive myself into thinking that it's reasonable for hundreds of people to be hurtling through the air in a metal ship. But as soon as there's the slightest shudder, or one of those sudden drops, my stomach flips over and my palms start to sweat. I remember what I try so hard to forget, that flying is an unnatural act.

There's one way to defy our limitations, though, and that's to rebel against the geometry that's defined us ever since we decided we needed something better than a cave to live in. For too long we thought we needed the stability of a ninety-degree angle to hold up the buildings we live and work in, and to be fair, if it wasn't for thousands of years of rectangles, Frank Gehry never would have had the nerve to try one of his tangled roofs. But now we know how to make metal and wood ripple, how to make shapes move, and the illusion of motion seems to me to be a pretty exciting step—and a whole lot safer than pasting feathers together with wax.

I saw the bandshell that Gehry designed in Chicago, when I was there with my dad last year, and I say it looks like Mozart's wig, curled back from the stage like that. It's not quite flying, but it's a good start. It feels like it defies gravity.

Although there isn't a wood shop at my high school— my mom says that went out of fashion with home economics classes, back in the 1960s—I've met a cabinetmaker who's let me spend time in his workshop, figuring out how to make wood bend and turn, and right now I'm trying to make a double helix out of balsa wood. I could say I've dreamt all my life of being an architect or an artist, and I imagine that might enhance my status in the applicant pool, but the truth is that I don't know yet where this is going to take me. Maybe I'll end up a math teacher who builds little wooden birds on the side, or maybe I'll build buildings that people make pilgrimages to visit. I might be able to make people feel that they're lighter than air.

It seems to me that that's what college is for—to find out how a personal passion might translate itself into an adult life.

Ted poured himself a glass of the Super Tuscan Dan had dropped off when he happened to be driving past school in the middle of the day, a wine intended to ensure that Ted read Katie's essay first, which he might have done if not for the conspiratorial smile on Dan's face when he handed over the bottle. It was not

really Ted's job to review college essays. The English teachers offered weekly workshops to help every senior develop at least one
serviceable essay, if not two, by the last week in September, so that
the ones who needed to take the SAT again could clear their heads
in time. But he always read his early-decision candidates' essays,
the prime contenders, the ones who made his reputation. He was
not about to leave their fate to a neofeminist literature teacher
who saw a connection between having a vagina and having a voice,
or to the lumberjack head of the department, a fan of Hemingway
and London who mistook short declarative sentences for power.
English teachers might know a dangling participle when they saw
one. Ted knew what the admissions readers wanted to hear.

Now that Harvard had abandoned its early-decision program,
Ted did not need to read Brad's essay for at least a month, but old
habits died hard, and he liked the idea of Brad filing early, regardless, to reinforce his commitment to going there. A good thing he
had decided to take a look: Ted was fairly sure that the story of an
aspiring math teacher who built little wooden birds was not going
to wow the Harvard admissions committee, and, worse, he figured that Brad knew it. What was the best boy at Crestview up
to? This batch of essays was supposed to be the final drafts of essays Ted had seen two weeks earlier, which in Brad's case had been
a fairly formal appraisal of Gehry's architecture and a reflection on
the immortality of a great building. All that stood between him
and the final draft was ditching the passive tense—what was it
with these lawyers' kids?—and Ted had fully expected to see a
more active version of the same essay this time around. Instead,
he got two new essays clipped together with a little Post-it note
on the front:

Dear Mr. Marshall: Maybe Brewster McCloud is
too weird a reference, but the first draft seemed
too stiff, and nothing else works as well. Have

you seen it? Thanks for reading two of these.
See you Tuesday. Brad.

He reached over to the stack of essays for Brad's second effort, hoping that it was a new version of the architecture essay,
knowing before he read the first line that it was not.

A college's policy of giving preference to legacy applicants might not seem fair to a deserving candidate who
happens to be the first in his or her family even to go to
college, but those of us who stand to benefit from it appreciate the powerful lure of being, in my case, the fourth
generation to attend Harvard.

It makes me part of the narrative that has defined our
family. My great-grandfather went to Harvard as an undergraduate and then to Harvard Law, and he worked for
many years at a large Manhattan law firm before moving
his family to San Francisco to open his own firm there.
My grandfather went to Stanford because he wanted to
be near his family, but then continued tradition by attending Harvard Law. My father, who grew up in San Francisco, was eager to experience the East Coast, so he went
to both Harvard and Harvard Law before returning to
California, where he is an estate lawyer.

The extent of my adolescent rebellion, I guess, is that
I may be the first man in my family in years (MR. MAR-
SHALL, I still have to figure out how many, sorry) not to
go to law school. But if I subtract that from the equation, I
see that my father, grandfather, and great-grandfather
are all hardworking, intelligent, well-educated men whose
Harvard education gave them a tremendous foundation
for what came next.

Maybe I'm going to start the next chapter in the family

legacy: three generations lured to Harvard and the law, and now a new set of legacies who might be drawn to Harvard and then to the arts. I'm very interested in architecture and sculpture. Who knows? Someday my great-grandson might decide to become the seventh generation of my family to attend Harvard because he feels it's the best possible place for a performance artist to get a great education.

Certainly that's not a connection that many people make at this moment, but a great university, like the best students, has to be flexible over time. Thirty years ago, no one would have imagined that someday Harvard might have a woman president, and yet here we are, in the midst of an unexpected but very exciting transition. Thirty years ago, no one would have imagined that a single comment from the former president, about women and their skills at math and science, would have erupted into such a public furor, pretty much demanding his eventual resignation. Harvard has come through a difficult moment in its history and been strengthened by it. The idea of this prestigious university as a home to avant-garde artists might seem as unlikely as a woman president—but by the time my great-grandson sends in his application, who's to say?

That's what excites me about being the fourth generation at Harvard. Whatever I end up wanting to do, I know I'll get the best possible education there. I might even surprise everyone and end up a lawyer, after all.

Ted poured himself a second glass of wine and flipped on his brand-new, fifty-inch flat-screen plasma TV, purchased right before school began with last year's accumulated Best Buy gift cards from grateful graduates' parents and a portion of the bonus check he had received from an equally indebted head of school. He and

Brad were going to have to have a talk, and fast, for whatever he was doing with these essays, he was not trying to get into Harvard. The first essay was too flaky, and the fact that Ted liked it was Ted's personal and rather unprofessional shortcoming; when he put his Harvard hat on, it felt light and more than a little goofy. The second essay definitely did not work, and on this one he had to agree with what he anticipated the neofeminist and the lumberjack would say. She would pull on the gold ankh charm she wore on a leather cord around her neck, he would pull on the untrimmed beard that always carried a remnant of his most recent meal, and they would mutter about subtext, about what Brad seemed to be saying underneath what Brad was saying—which was that he did not want to go to Harvard at all.

Ted reached for the binder where he recorded his notes about the essays, having abandoned margin notes a few years earlier after a run-in with a famously bestselling author dad who had taken issue with Ted's comments. The man had sent his daughter's essay to his equally famous editor, who was on the board of trustees of the very college the girl in question wanted to attend, and the editor had replied with a two-page, single-spaced critique of Ted's critique, which boiled down to the conclusion that Ted was an idiot. In truth, the editor found Ted's comments to be more than reasonable, but the editor had heard rumors of the dad's possible defection to another publishing house, so he did what was necessary to make his author feel beholden. In self-defense, Ted ordered a Levenger leather portfolio with a lock on it and never again shared written notes with a student.

He wrote Brad's name at the top of a page, printed WHAT'S THE AGENDA? right under it in big block letters, and turned his attention to CNN just long enough to read the tail end of a crawl about the possibility of an Ebola outbreak in some country whose name had already slid by. If it had been *E. coli* he would have waited for the item to lap and reappear, to make sure it had nothing to do with the burgers at In-N-Out, but Ebola was out of his zip code, a distraction unless it got on a plane and landed in a dorm in Boston or Palo Alto.

In the fall, television was little more than white noise. Ted had no time for anything but admissions. He got his hair cut shorter first semester than he did during the rest of the year, so that he could cancel his standing monthly appointment if a crisis arose without the head of school making nervous jokes about Ted's Afro. He rarely ventured past the prepared-foods counter at Whole Foods, except to buy precut and prewashed produce and bottled dressing, and he paid extra to have his dry cleaning and laundry delivered. He burned up his Netflix queue and barely remembered what he had seen. Every morning he donned a crisp pair of Ralph Lauren khakis and a starched, striped broadcloth dress shirt, unless one of the Ivies was visiting, in which case he hauled out one of the two equally dark gray Zegna suits that a grateful couple who owned a boutique had purchased for him on one of their buying trips to Florence.

During college application season, Ted was distilled to an efficient essence: He was not black, not male, not forty-five, not short, not slim, not a lapsed Baptist, not a Democrat, though all these things were true. Ted was his results.

❧

The big lesson of Ted's childhood boiled down to "Don't," a command uttered and obeyed long past the point of humiliation, though he never once complained. Ted Marshall grew up at the intersection of urban unrest and geographical misfortune; ten years or ten blocks in either direction and everything would have been different. He paraded in front of the television set, as proud as any baby who had figured out how to get the appendages to do something more than wriggle, while his parents and both sets of grandparents watched the Watts riots that kept them indoors for a week. He enjoyed a few seasons of dusk basketball after they fled to a tiny apartment in nearby Compton, only to be hustled indoors by his parents once the Bloods and the Crips designated his block as one worth fighting for. His father started walking Ted to and from middle school before and after his postal route, while his grandfathers split the responsibility of escorting his younger sisters. The girls loved the attention, but twelve-year-old Ted was ready to unfasten the latch that held him to his childhood, which mattered not at all to his terrified parents.

They moved again at the end of his sophomore year at Compton High, this time to the barely affordable fringe of Baldwin Hills, a middle-class black suburb where no one, as far as they could tell, cowered in fear. For the first time in his postponed life, Ted was allowed to walk to school alone. It was too late to matter. The students at his new school did not want to make friends with a boy who undoubtedly had a gang past, or at least knew gang members who might come looking for him some night; their parents told them to keep their distance, just as Ted's parents had instructed him to stay away from two previous neighborhoods' worth of trouble. His father might as well have continued to walk him to school and back for all the good his new autonomy did him. The only thing Ted could control was homework, which he went at with a vengeance. When he got a scholarship to UCLA, he took a perverse pride in knowing that some of the families that had snubbed him were probably having second thoughts.

His background gave him a certain cachet in college, as long as he was careful about discussing it. Ted could claim to have witnessed crucial moments in Los Angeles's black history only if he was among people who knew nothing about it, as his first-hand experience involved being marched away, quickly, from whatever was going to make the next day's headlines. He was smart enough to let people mistake his solemn silence for depth of feeling, though, and he managed to get more than one date with girls who assumed that there must be a great deal of emotion right underneath the surface. In fact, Ted had seen enough of what happened to people who got caught up in the thick of things—who found themselves the target of a cop or a rival gang, trouble either way—even if his vantage point was the sidelines. He wanted no part of it. He dreamed circumspect and solitary dreams, because any other instincts had long since atrophied.

He graduated with a BA in English and an agenda that involved a first novel and a first love, the former about to be written, the latter, he was sure, about to be met. A year later, he had ninety pages of unfinished manuscript, and a year after that, he had barely broken a hundred. Ted could no more step out of his head than his younger self could step off the curb without his father's permission, so he accepted his parents' offer to stake him to a teaching credential and got a job at a big public school, where he saw some of his students for the first time on the day he gave the midterm. Three years of that and he answered Crestview's ad for an English teacher. He told himself it was a temporary move, an advantage, really, in terms of raw material for his novel. Thanks to his parents' watchfulness, Ted had no serious misfortune to peddle. A detoured life as an English teacher might lack the exploitable depth of genuine bad luck, but it would have to do.

Inevitably, one of the seniors asked him to read a draft of her college application essay, and when she got into Stanford early, she and her parents let everyone know that Ted had made all the difference. He got so many requests for help that the head of school cut his teaching load in half and made him the junior member of what was then Crestview's two-person college counseling team.

He never wrote another page of his novel. The true love part of his fantasy eroded as well, when his most promising girlfriend broke up with him midway through his first early-decision season as department chair, as though her biological clock could not have kept ticking for a few more weeks, until he saw how the applicants shook out. He dared to suggest that she was not being reasonable, as his deadline was absolute and hers was not. She stomped out of his place, and he never heard from her again. His acceptance rate that year was 10 percent higher than his predecessor's had been.

He had a gift for other people's success, if not his own, so he let the job take up more and more of his time, until it eclipsed his old ideas of who he would turn out to be. Crestview parents generously assumed that he had secrets and occasionally speculated as to what they might be, but in fact he was a lower case enigma. Ted let them wonder, for whatever they imagined had to be more interesting than the truth.

Ted read Brad's flying essay one more time, wrote, "Nice writing, but let's get on course" in his notes, and moved it to the bottom of the stack, more irritated than made sense. He read an essay about solving the health crisis in Africa, "One of thousands," he wrote on his notepad, though when the boy came in Ted would make a flattering plea for something that better reflected the boy's dynamic range of interests. He read one about a personal epiphany inspired by the discovery, in the garage, of the applicant's parents' Pete Seeger albums. "Reed or Hampshire," wrote Ted, "and change epiphany." Lots of people rewrote their kids' essays, even if they swore their children had asked for input and all they had offered were copious notes, but subtlety was key, and "epiphany" was not a subtle word. He read a long essay by a girl who thought that buying only local produce, even if it meant forgoing apples in the middle of summer, qualified as profound self-sacrifice.

Katie's essay could not possibly be any worse than those. The last draft had been fine, and at this point he was reading only to buy her parents another week to persuade her to switch to Williams. He riffled through the rest of the stack and plucked hers out. It was always easy to spot Katie's drafts, because she had scrolled through the font list until she found a sans serif typestyle that she felt better reflected her straightforward personality than the standard Times Roman font.

I am the fortunate daughter of two people who have taught me so much about hard work, and good work. My father is an attorney-at-law and my mother is a physician, and I have learned from them the value of self-discipline and needing always to do my best.

Ted started to write "parallel construction" on his notepad, and then he stopped, certain that the teacher who gave Katie As in her AP class, despite syntax like this, would somehow manage to catch the error.

I have also learned that success is not enough in and of itself, but that I need to use my future success to make a contribution to making the world a better place. This is analogous to what I have already done in high school, where I have been very successful academically (NOTE TO MR. MARSHALL: How soon can I say I'm vale-dictorian? Grades come out after the early-decision dead-line, but I'm pretty sure) and also have made numerous contributions that have nothing to do with my personal life. In the summer before my junior year I went to Gua-temala for two weeks to help build houses. . . .

At a cost, thought Ted, that would have paid for an entire vil-lage of houses.

In the summer before my senior year I went to China to do the same. I will end my high school career with a skill-

set that makes me an excellent candidate for a rigorous
college program. In addition to my superior academic
profile, I have made myself something of a Renaissance
woman involved in many different kinds of activities.

He circled "Renaissance woman," which must have come
from Katie's mom.

My mother says that magazines used to talk about "jug
glers," because women had to try to figure out how to raise
a family and have a career, and be an attentive wife and
an interesting woman all at the same time. Somebody
should have asked her how to do it, because she really
has it all figured out, and I don't say that just because
she's my mom. I don't feel like I need more of her time
than I get. She has taught me to look at it a different way.
The time I'm alone is when I learn to be independent, to
get along by myself, which is going to help me in college
and after.

And my dad has taught me the benefits of what he
calls compartmentalizing, which means 100 percent attention to whatever you're doing at the moment, and then
you switch channels and give all your attention to the next
project. We joke about channel surfing and our invisible
remote controls, but his example has shown me that I can
do more because I'm more organized.

I'm honest enough to say that I'm not sure where the
next four years will take me—or maybe, like my dad says,
I'm self-confident enough not to need a major to tell me
who I am. I could be an attorney or a physician, although
my parents have set the bar high. I could combine my parents' interests and become both an attorney and a physician. In fact, I remind myself not to think just about working

for a law firm or a company that already exists. What's the next step from what my parents did? Perhaps I'll run my own company or succeed in a universe that won't exist until I create it. I might even run for public office.

Whatever I end up doing, I have to be all I can be.

The last line was new. Ted sang the jingle the Army had used for as long as he could remember—"Be. All that you can be. Da da duh duh, in the Army."—and wondered whether Katie had come up with the line without knowing its source, in which case she was a natural for a career in advertising, or, worse, if she knew where it came from, in which case she could be the first Crestview student to apply to West Point. For a wicked instant, he was tempted to let her use it, but he wrote on his pad, "Admissions officers probably won't get the last line." If she balked, he might call her dad, to make sure he was on record about his reservations. In Ted's experience, the more enthusiastic and effusive parents were at the beginning of the process, the angrier they got if things did not go as planned. He had to protect himself from accusations down the line.

The remaining essays were from early applicants Ted happened to like, even though he knew that their chances were not as good. The boy with too many Bs from the semester when his dad had the stroke, the girl with a B minus in physics because the teacher was too embarrassed to confess that he had misfiled her supposedly nonexistent homework assignments in another student's folder, the girl who pulled off straight As but only took APs in courses she actually liked, and the twins who between them were a perfect candidate, one with 2370 on his SATs and the other a basketball star. And Lauren, neither an angel nor an ambulance case, the kind of kid who in any other generation would have had her happy pick of schools. Lauren, who ought to get into Northwestern and probably would not. All these breeding, over-achieving baby boomers; wasn't anyone with bad SAT scores having children?

He pawed through the stack, skimming first lines, more African health care crises, more personal awakenings, a Habitat for Humanity from Fiji, and a note from Lauren:

Mr. Marshall, I hope you remember I'm going to look at some more schools with my folks. I promise I'll have a final draft the minute I get back (working on the plane both ways), and I'll still have plenty of time to make more fixes before the 1st. Thanks, Lauren.

When Ted first became a college counselor, his more experienced colleague had advised him to arrange the office furniture so that his back was to the door, to buy a moment to compose himself before he had to face a teary kid or an angry parent. Five seasons later, he no longer needed the hedge. Ted had calloused up. He could wrap a consoling arm around a devastated senior's shoulder while he debated privately whether to have the mozzarella and tomato on a baguette or the deli meats on a ciabatta roll for lunch. It was what made him a success. He had learned to fight for every senior who had a chance, and yet not to care where they ended up, or rather, not to care in terms of a teenager's broken heart. They mended, even if they did not know it yet.

All that mattered was the list of college acceptances that appeared in the annual report, the list that parents of prospective students compared to similar lists from competing schools when they were deciding where to send their seventh-graders to school. He reminded himself of that, sternly, when he looked up and saw Brad—saw Harvard—in the doorway. He beckoned the boy in and made great fuss of pulling his essays from the stack and turning to the proper page on his writing pad.

"So," he said, hoping that the delay might make Brad just uncomfortable enough to tell the truth, "Mr. Preston Bradley the Fourth, would you like to tell your hardworking college counselor what the agenda is here?"

"I'm sorry?"

"No, you're not. If you're sorry you would have given me a final draft of what I saw last time, like everybody else did."

Brad sighed. "Do you like either of them?"

"I like the first one fine," said Ted, "but not for a boy who's headed to Harvard. I only like the second one for a boy who's determined not to go to Harvard, which would not be you. So we need to straighten this out."

"Mr. Marshall, can I close the door?"

Back when Ted was Brad's age, he had used that very line on the day he told his father that he intended to major in English lit and become a writer. He had said, "Dad, can I close the door?" in the irrational hope that a sealed room would somehow contain his dad's disappointment, which it did not, as his father's definition of success for his son included regular hours, an office, and benefits. Bad news—the betrayal of a family plan—inevitably followed a request to close the door. For a wild moment, Ted wondered if he could prevent whatever was about to happen by insisting that the door remain open.

"Sure," he said, and nodded. After about a hundred years, Brad sat back down.

"Mr. Marshall, we have something like attorney-client privilege, right? I mean, I can tell you something and you won't tell my dad."

Ted felt himself smiling in terror.

"I don't want to go to Harvard," said Brad. "I mean, I really don't want to go to Harvard. You think if I send in one of these essays they'll turn me down? Or at least wait-list me? That would buy me some time to figure out what I want to do. Buy my dad some time to get over it."

"Isn't it a little late in the game to change your mind? Where would you go instead?" Ted had applicants lined up at all the other Ivies, and he did not want to be in the same county as Trey Bradley when he found out that his boy had been relegated to the Big Ten, or, even worse, the Pac Ten. Trey sneered at Columbia and Penn, as though there were two distinct tiers within the Ivy League, and he had lately let it be known that he was debating whether to endow Crestview's new science wing. There was much more at stake here than Brad's mysteriously revised notion of collegiate happiness. Ted waited while the boy scooped a handful of paper clips from a bowl on the desk, arranged them in the shape of a bird, and sat back to consider his creation.

"Brad."

He looked up, startled and abashed, and Ted saw in the boy's guilty expression a glimmer of opportunity.

"Brad. You understand how close you are to making this happen. You understand the advantage you have, I know you do, so you have to explain to me why you would turn away from this."

Brad dismantled the bird and dumped the paper clips back in the bowl. "I just think I'll be happier somewhere else. Maybe I ought to go to art school."

Ted saw the science wing vanish.

"I just don't want to be the fourth anything."

Ted pounced.

"Hey, that has nothing to do with where you should go to school," he said. "It's like the girl I had last year who was thinking about Barnard until somebody said the Columbia kids look down on the Barnard girls, and all of a sudden she's not going to apply. Not going to let anybody tell her she was second class. I asked her, if some nitwit said they looked down on the surfers from southern California, or they looked down on the Jewish kids, what would you do? And she said I'd write that person off, never speak to them again. Okay, if that's the case, then you have to ignore the person who looks down their nose at a Barnard girl. Not you, Brad, but her. But she got so caught up in what people were going to think that she didn't even apply, ended up at Wash U in St. Louis. That's not you. Your job is, anybody who treats you like the newest branch on the family tree, you ignore them. It's their narrowminded problem, not yours. You're not the fourth anything. You're the first you."

Ted only wished that he came across more kids who were named after their parents, because that business about being the first you was one of the best lines he had ever come up with on the fly. He would have loved the chance to use it again.

"Makes all the sense in the world, I guess," said Brad.

"Besides, you think they give you a sign to hang around your neck that says 'legacy'? For that matter, do the math: They don't take every legacy that applies. They don't have the room."

"Okay, but what if I'm right? What if I'd be better off someplace else? I don't think it's a good strategy to send in a great app and hope I'll be one of the legacies who doesn't get in, I mean, that's kind of leaving my future to chance, don't you think? And besides, if I want to be an architect . . ."

"I see," said Ted, "and somehow a school that spit out your guy, Gehry, and Philip Johnson, that's too old-school for you, okay, Thom Mayne, a school that has what's-his-name Koolhaas on the faculty, somehow this is not up to your standards?"

"How do you know all that?"

"It's my job to know all that." Ted moved in for the kill. "So tell me what could possibly be wrong with going to Harvard if architecture is your—"

"*You don't get it.*" The tone of Brad's voice rattled them both. "I'm sorry, Mr. Marshall. Really. But listen. I can't go to Harvard and be an architect, don't you see? If I go to Harvard I'm going to be a lawyer. Everybody in my family who goes to Harvard ends up a' lawyer. You have no idea, I'm sorry to say that, but you don't. I mean, I go there, my life is set for the rest of my life."

He took a deep breath.

"I am not going to be a lawyer," he said.

Ted reeled it in. "I believe you. Look, this is a stressful time. Let's get you in and then you can stand up for yourself, which I know you will. What do you think your father's going to do—show up in Cambridge to help you register? Pull the plug on tuition if you're not prelaw? Come on. Let's get some perspective here. Have you looked at their fine arts curriculum?"

Brad reached for a smaller handful of paper clips and lined them up left to right.

"Not really. No, not at all," he said, without taking his eyes off the paper clips. "Y'know, I'm not really working on the double helix so much anymore. Not so much. Not at all, really. There's not a whole lot of time for . . ."

"Clean up the first essay you showed me and send it in, okay?"

"Okay," Brad lied.

Ted came around the desk and clapped Brad on the shoulder. "I've got to tell you, Harvard's always seemed like the right match for you."

"You'd say if you didn't think so."

"I would," Ted lied, in return.

❧

Dan Dodson was one senior partner's retirement away from a corner office with a view of the Hollywood sign, but until the guy came to terms with reality, Dan had to settle for the standard Century City consolation prize, an office with an endless bank of windows that opened onto a vista of other endless banks of windows. He did not care about the view, because at his level there was no time for staring out the window. He did mind the positioning, and if he had a business lunch near Decorator's Row he occasionally stopped in at one of the showrooms to consider the latest styles in desks and credenzas, so that he would be ready when the inevitable happened.

He always planned ahead in that way, envisioning the future as he wanted it to be, in great and specific detail, as though a definitive dream would be likelier to materialize than a vague one. He did not even see these internal dramas as dreams, really, but as documentaries. Anticipatory documentaries. He occasionally rehearsed lines of dialogue to determine in advance how best to tell the story of his life.

"I have two kids at Williams."

"Both of our children are at Williams."

"My son and my daughter attend Williams."

He took stock twice a day—once right before he left his office, and again right before he went to sleep, even on Sundays, when he had to fight the soporific effects of what Joy called sex night. The office session enabled him to compartmentalize and make the transition from attorney to family man. The bedroom tally, which involved a nightstand notepad, ensured that he would wake up with his priorities intact.

When Ron had applied to college, all the Dodsons cared about was finding a school that appreciated an extraordinarily smart boy who on a good day aspired to nothing more than flatlined social skills. Anyone who accepted Ron was going to do so in spite of his personality, not because of it, so the Dodsons had endorsed Ted's strategy of focusing on small, prestigious schools outside but equivalent to the Ivy League—Williams, Swarthmore, Wesleyan, Amherst. Once Ron got in and Dan could relax, he embraced Williams with all the fervor of a man intent on building the family brand.

He defined success in terms of status and status in terms of money, a nicely quantifiable formula for happiness. Dan had grown up on the second floor of a Chicago three-flat near his father's liquor store, and when he was in junior high, old enough to stock the snack shelves, he got his first good look at people who had it better than he did. Every weekend a parade of snooty kids from Northwestern University and Evanston High, sentenced to spend their adolescence in a dry town, would drive down to Howard Street to make a buy. They pulled up in front of his dad's store and handed a ten-dollar bill to the nearest drunk, who reeled into the store for them and got a pint for himself with the change. Sometimes the kids waved at Dan and hollered that they were going to call the cops because he was too young to be inside a liquor store. He spent a lot of time inventing replies that he never had the nerve to deliver. He met Joy at the University of Illinois at Champaign-Urbana, and by the time they reached senior year, their combined ambition had jelled into a plan. He would go to law school, she would be a doctor, they would marry and pursue lucrative specialties, and together they would buy their way into exclusivity, one component at a time.

He used reverse volume as his leading criterion of value: the best things were those that the fewest people could acquire, which was why an AMG Mercedes was better than a standard model, a custom piece of jewelry was better than anything of which there was more than one, no matter how expensive it was, and a small school, preferably one that was hard to get to, was better than even the most prestigious university in a major airline's hub city. By his standards, Williams was collegiate paradise, a bucolic campus nestled at the base of the Berkshire mountains—Yale did not have mountains—with a cute little neighboring town—Yale did not have that, either—and intimate classes taught by the professors themselves. The life of the mind—the Fiske had used that very phrase—taught in an idyllic, East Coast setting.

He tried again.

"You can't do better than Williams. Unless you care more about brand names than education, right?"

Having both his children at Williams would be like having a wine locker full of bottles with nothing less than a Parker score of 92. It was knowing what lardo was—and knowing that no one else at his table would stoop to making jokes about eating pig fat. It was proof of his success, essential when what he considered failure, what he called the Howard Street era, was only years, not generations, in the past. After some debate, he decided not to argue relative merits with Katie, not unless she got headstrong about Yale. He had rehearsed his dinnertime presentation in the car on the way to work, as he was about to in the car on the way home. It was unassailably simple: on an objective level, Yale was no better than Williams, so he saw no compelling reason to endure the logistical inconvenience of having two children at two separate schools.

Tuesday and Thursday nights were the Dodsons' workweek family dinner nights, and Dan and Joy remained firm about that schedule, as well as a traditional Sunday night meal, despite ever more imaginative excuses from Katie. They had read articles that credited the family dinner with everything from improved SAT scores to higher lifetime income, they had read critics who with equal fervor debunked the claims, and they had decided to split the difference, just in case. Joy amused her friends by claiming that she and Dan did not have a kitchy-koo gene between them. They preferred an evidence-based approach.

Dan always started the conversation while Joy dished up one of a revolving set of takeout meals from the Italian restaurant in the lobby of her building. The latest management team had divined that authenticity mattered not as much as political correctness to their clientele, so tonight's entrée was what the menu called "chicken osso buco," even though chickens lacked shank bones, to say nothing of edible marrow. Real osso buco was veal, and veal was beef, adorable baby beef with its hooves nailed to the floor. A smart restaurateur responded creatively to customers averse both to the cholesterol level of veal and the torture of baby cows, but accepting of chickens bleeding out through the neck. Joy served the chicken with broccoli and a small scoop of generic pasta salad, chosen for color accent rather than flavor and measured out with a doctor's precision, grateful for the mindless task. She had spent her afternoon doing full-body skin cancer checks, and the dainty prodding of the skin behind people's ears, on their balding pates, at an obsolete bikini line, always left her worn out. Bad news could lurk on the skin between one's toes. Joy had to start referring these patients to someone else.

Dan started to speak as soon as she put down the serving spoon.

"So, Katie. You met with Ted today."

"Did you call him? You promised you wouldn't . . ."

Joy sat down and reached a conciliatory hand toward her daughter. "Katie, please. It's on the college calendar. Your father did not call anyone, and I think you owe him an apology."

"Sorry," Katie grunted.

"Accepted," said Dan, who in fact had confirmed the date and time of the meeting with Ted days before, when he dropped off the bottle of wine. "And he's happy with your essay."

"Sure." Katie shrugged. She would have replied in exactly the same way if Ted had fed her essay to his shredding machine. She had written him off when her parents pushed for Williams instead of Yale and he failed to push back hard enough. The absolutism that made her such a successful student, the belief that there were right answers in lit and history as well as in math and science, informed her attitudes about people as well, and once she assigned them a category she was unlikely to reconsider. Ted had proven himself her parents' ally when he was supposed to be hers. Every one of his suggestions about her essay was clearly suspect and stemmed somehow from his desire to see her at Williams.

Dan attempted a supportive smile. "So the only thing left is to resolve . . ."

"Katie, what your father's trying to say . . ."

"I'm saying what I'm trying to say, Joy. We need to resolve this Yale business once and for all and talk dispassionately about what approach is going to yield the best results."

"The best results?" Katie slammed down her fork and a globule of chicken osso buco sauce catapulted onto her T-shirt. Reflexively, Joy dipped her napkin in her water glass and reached over to wipe it off.

"Mom, stop it." Katie knocked her mother's hand away and started to push her chair back.

"Excuse me," said Dan. "People who storm out of rooms have a great deal of trouble figuring out how to walk back in, so we do not storm out in the first place, and you know that. We are going to talk this through."

"No, we're not," said Katie, inching her chair back into place. "Talking would mean I get to say what I want, which is not to go to Williams, but I can tell already I'm not going to get to say that. Or I can say it but neither one of you is going to listen to me. This isn't a conversation. Maybe my idea"—and here she mimicked her father's measured tone—"of *yielding the best results* is to figure out how to get me into Yale."

"Sarcasm does not help, Katie," said her mother.

Katie speared a chunk of broccoli so that she would have an excuse not to talk. She had always liked her parents better than anyone else's. Lauren's parents were nice enough, but they never seemed to know what to do, not like Katie's folks, who were always a good six months ahead of the curve. Chloe's parents were too busy fighting and Brad's parents were too smug to think about what was really best for their kids. Katie's parents had always told her she could do anything she set her mind to—and yet they refused to yield on Yale. They acted as though she could not possibly know what was best for her, having raised her to believe the opposite, which made her dig in simply for the sake of being obstinate.

There was no good reason for Katie to insist on Yale—surely she could navigate Williams without running into her brother, she knew that—but the more her parents insisted, the harder she pressed. It was exhausting, and she had begun secretly to wish that she could figure out how to give it up without hating herself.

She swallowed and looked at her plate. "I am just trying to say that I don't think you ever really considered whether Yale might be better for me. Never really considered changing your mind."

"Or you might give us the benefit of the doubt and consider that we've weighed everything very carefully," said Dan. "We have been extremely satisfied with your brother's experience, and we see no reason for you not to go to Williams. We see only benefits, in terms of the school being a proven commodity, in terms of not having to split our time between the two of you when we visit. In terms of what's best for you and for this family."

Dan took a sip of wine to see if Katie was going to object, but she was concentrating on arranging her remaining fusilli in the shape of the letter *K*, so he continued.

"And I have to say, Katie, that since your mother and I are the ones paying for this excellent education, we do expect you to take our opinions seriously, in the same way you expect us to take yours. So how about it?"

Joy chimed in. "Honey, can you just tell us what it is about Yale that makes you want to go there so much?"

Katie knew two things: whenever her mother began a sentence with "Honey," whatever followed was not a statement of genuine concern but the thing her mother knew she ought to say, and whenever her father mentioned money the conversation was effectively over. She had nothing to lose. She might as well try to make them feel as bad as she did.

"They had these reading rooms," she said, a tiny crack in her voice. "In every building. A quiet room where you could sit and read." In fact, Katie had not seen a single reading room, because her tour group lingered too long in the library to have time to visit the residence halls, but Lauren had gone crazy for the reading rooms and had sworn that if she had the grades for Yale she would have sat in one of those rooms for a quiet hour every single day before dinner. As Lauren did not have the grades, and Katie did, she felt free to borrow the story.

Dan allowed himself an affectionate chuckle. "I think we can assume that there are similar rooms at Williams."

The image of herself in a room she had never seen at Yale, sharing a pizza she would never eat with a handsome boy she would never meet, disappeared, just like that. Suddenly, Katie wanted only to be done talking about colleges.

"Never mind," she said. "I'll try Williams first. Done. Is there something for dessert?"

chapter 5

At six in the morning, an hour before his shift began, Steve was at the curb with three soft, clean rags, wiping down the Mercedes and wishing that he had covered parking, or at least a driveway where he could set up one of those aluminum-frame carports. The biggest of the three cottages on the lot got driveway and garage privileges, so the smaller two had to settle for being grateful for a space within a half block of home. It added twenty minutes to his morning routine, but he was not about to pull away from the curb with dew drying in dusty rivulets on every square inch of sheet metal. He wiped, folded the dirty side of a rag to the inside, wiped and folded again, and when he was done he rinsed the dirty rags with a garden hose and spread them on the fence to dry. He checked the cab's interior for discarded water bottles and crumpled-up protein-bar wrappers, placed a fresh six-ounce bottle of Evian in each of the rear-seat cup holders, and settled into the driver's seat with his thermos of black tea and a copy of *USA Today*, ready to catch the calls that came too early for his more shift-bound coworkers and too late for the night guys who were already on their way home. When the first call came, an airport run at an address less than a mile away, he told the dispatcher he had it, folded the newspaper and put it in the back pocket of his seat, for the customers, and took off down a side street that was much faster than the main street the other drivers used.

The door of the house was already open, and as Steve pulled up to the curb the man who stood in the doorway turned to yell

"Let's go" at someone still inside, turned again, and marched toward the cab. Steve was quicker. He had opened the trunk and the passenger doors and was on the sidewalk, arm outstretched to relieve the man of his suitcase, before his fare got the front gate open.

"Two more coming," Joel said.

Steve hoisted the bag into the open trunk. "Then you prefer to sit in front?" he asked. He had once had a neighbor who drove a town car for Music Express, until the night a couple of DEA agents altered his career path, and when Steve first got the cabbie job he had grilled the young man about the amenities that made a Music Express ride worth more than twice as much as the fare on Steve's meter, even though his cab was a Mercedes. The morning wipe and dust, the water bottles, the newspaper, the clean passenger seat in front so that a party of three would not have to crowd into the back, these were the extras Steve offered his fares, to distinguish himself from his coworkers and, with luck, to increase his tips.

Joel glanced at his watch and resisted the urge to make a guy's joke about how long it took his wife and daughter to get out the door. The distinction between him and them, which he thought about often, had nothing to do with gender: he stepped, and they leapt; he managed his time, and they burst through the door with a great antic eagerness. The difference was what he liked the most about them. When he proposed to Nora, he had offered her a deal. She would keep him from getting stodgy, and he would keep her from fretting herself to death.

Steve loaded the rest of the suitcases in the trunk, ran around to the driver's door, and settled in.

"LAX," said Nora.

"Delta," said Joel.

Steve smiled. He had driven his share of eager parents and silent teens to the airport early on a weekday morning. "College trip," he said. It was an assumption, not a question.

"That's right," said Nora.

With that, Steve rolled the Mercedes away from the curb. "My daughter too."

"On a college trip with your wife?" asked Nora.

"No. She goes to college next year like this girl. Like your daughter."

"Ah," said Nora. "But no trip. So she plans to stay in California."

Steve chuckled.

"No," he replied. "No need for trip. She want to go to Harvard and not to anywhere else." He glanced in the rearview mirror at Lauren. "You will visit Harvard?"

Nora tried to change the subject. "The fastest way is down Lincoln," she said.

"I get you there plenty of time," said Steve, who proceeded to shoot down a little street that curved over to Lincoln at a stoplight and spared them having to sit at the major intersection through six permutations of turn lights and one-way greens. Joel glanced at his wife and read the thought bubble hovering above her head: in what other ways was their obvious complacency getting them into trouble?

Steve was not done talking.

"My daughter at ten she say to me, 'Daddy, when I grow up I go to Harvard and you and Mom be so proud.' I say nothing. It is all up to her, there is no need to push. When she go to high school they call me and my wife to come in. Eleventh grade. We think it cannot be trouble, she get all As, why do they call us?"

He paused to recall and savor the delicious suspense.

"Why did they call you?" Lauren asked.

"It was to say, six AP classes, this is maybe too much even for Elizabeth—that is my daughter, Elizabeth. They worry because no one else in this school ever take so many in one year and what if she cannot do it? I say, 'Ask her can she do it, and if she say yes then that is what she must do.' The principal tell me I can tell her no, I am her father."

Steve laughed again. "And I say I will not tell her no. I will never tell her no when she wants to do her best."

They hurtled down Lincoln as Steve described the specifics of Elizabeth's best. Straight As in all of her AP classes, a 2400 on her most recent SAT, nothing below 780 on each of five SAT achievement tests, two more than required to show that she was well-rounded. Joel stared straight ahead, thinking that the saga of the perfect Elizabeth might end more quickly if he let the cabbie finish his spiel, rather than try to interrupt, and for his silence he got to hear about Elizabeth's prowess on the violin, her special science research tutorial, and her volunteer work on the pediatric cancer ward, every Sunday after church.

He wondered for an instant if Elizabeth had a sport, but he preferred to assume that she was a klutz, rather than ask and risk finding out that she was all-state champion in the fifteen-hundred-meter. The notion of a pinhole of human frailty, anywhere in her resumé, was a comfort to him—and from the deer-in-the-headlights expressions on Nora's and Lauren's faces, he assumed that they agreed.

When they pulled up in front of the Delta terminal, Steve pointed to a laminated wallet-size photo that was clipped to the cabbie registration next to the meter. "This is Elizabeth, my daughter. *Liz.* She prefers that." He smiled at Lauren. "Both of you graduates. It is a very exciting time. I wish you all good luck on your trip."

Lauren gave him a frozen smile, backed out of the cab, and stumbled directly into Nora, who had hopped out and rushed around behind the Mercedes to be at her daughter's side.

"I know her," Lauren whispered. "Well, I don't, but Chloe does. She's Chloe's math tutor. She goes to Ocean Heights. She's perfect."

"You're perfect in my book," said Nora, grateful that the cabbie's daughter had not set her sights on Northwestern.

Joel paid the cabbie and darted over to them, propelled by his own protective instincts. "Let's go find a latte," he said.

Steve waved, got into the cab, and headed back the way he had come until he got to the McDonald's–Taco Bell duplex that sat on a corner halfway to home. If the day started with an airport run, Steve treated himself to coffee on his return, working his way from one place to another, heading north up Lincoln Boulevard, a broad street that managed to snake through a great deal of prime residential real estate without ever giving up its predilection for cheap eats, lube and body shops, and massage parlors with smoked windows. He rode the wave of all the immigrants who had preceded him: he tried coffee and a bagel, a churro, a cannoli, a slice of strudel, a diamond chunk of baklava, a beignet, a pork bao, and, on the day he got the $50 tip for no reason at all, a mocha latte and a breakfast burrito from two adjacent shops in a mini-mall. One after another plump clerk shook his or her head at the small skinny man who remained a small skinny man no matter how many times he came back for a pastry, and he always smiled—the only part of him that seemed a little worn, for his black hair and his unlined face were as resistant to change as his waistline. Even the clerk who served him the latte, who would never be caught dead more than two pounds over ideal, commented enviously on Steve's physique. Steve gave each one of them the same answer.

"My daughter," he said, always relishing the opportunity to refer to her existence, "says I have the metabolism of a hummingbird." If he got any kind of a response at all, he pulled another copy of the cab photo out of his wallet.

Along the way, he developed a strong preference for McDonald's hot apple pie. After he ate his first one and bought a second, he pulled a worn copy of the *Thomas Guide* to Los Angeles County out of his bag, turned to a page with a folded corner, and began to

read. From west to east—he used the ocean as his starting point—
Romany Drive and West Romany Drive, Lucca Drive, D'Este Drive.
From north to south, Umeo Road, Amalfi Drive, Sorrento Drive,
Monaco Drive, San Remo Drive, down to Sunset Boulevard. Not
quite; the streets above Sunset wiggled and folded back on each
other, and he had to turn the map at an angle to get a sense of the
layout. He read each name aloud three times, and then he closed
the book and drew the grid from memory on the small notepad he
always carried in his pocket, labeling each street as he went. He
opened the book to make sure he had gotten all of them right, and,
satisfied, he closed the book, covered his drawing with a napkin,
and recited the names again in order. He lifted the napkin to check
his work. Only then did he eat his second apple pie.

Steve intended to work his way through the *Thomas Guide*,
week by week, to become a living map of every street between
downtown and the ocean, between Pacific Palisades and the airport. Other ambitious drivers used a computerized navigational
system and made fun of him for being so old-fashioned. His more
passive colleagues refused to learn either the street names or enough
English to facilitate a conversation about directions, and depended
for success on a wearying array of hand signals, shrugs, and excla-
mations from their passengers. To Steve, it seemed as though they
wanted to punish their American passengers for the fact that they
were no longer the engineers, lab technicians, or doctors they had
been at home. Steve harbored no such bitter feelings, nor any
nostalgic longing for his prior life as an engineer. He and Eun Hee
had invested their ambitions in Elizabeth before she was old
enough to vote on the matter, and driving a cab was better than
painting houses or being the night manager of a convenience
store. So he went to Thomas Brothers University, determined to
be the best possible cabbie, if that was his fate. No passenger was
ever going to lurch forward and poke a finger under Steve's nose,
yelling, "Left. Left, there, God, you missed it."

Anyone who lived with the chronic fear of rejection—which to Nora meant every parent of a high school senior, with the possible exception of the Dodsons, the Bradleys, and now the cabbie and his wife—remembered occasionally to entertain the opposite possibility, of stunning good fortune. It was the only way to keep from being too depressed to function. Nora made a mental note every time she heard a come-from-behind story: the unseeded player who trounced the reigning champ at Wimbledon, the dark-horse candidate who beat the incumbent, the dark horse, period, who passed the entire field to deprive the favorite of the Triple Crown. Tommy Lee Jones, for heaven's sake, who started out somewhere she had never heard of in Texas and ended up Al Gore's roommate at Harvard and an Oscar winner.

Of course, coming from a small town in Texas must have been an advantage for college admissions.

Nora forced herself to concentrate. What about her own life? A fired researcher one minute and a successful baker the next, without so much as a single week spent in Paris learning the proper wrist cock for cracking an egg one-handed. Tenacity, creativity, an indefinable spark: the unquantifiable parts of a personality had to matter as much as the numbers did, every now and then. No one trafficked in analogies anymore, now that the SAT had abandoned them, but surely it was possible to see:

Nora : Baker

AS

Lauren : _____

"Mom, this is the stop."

Nora obediently edged her way toward the door of the subway car. She had not even had time to create the multiple-choice options for Lauren's happy future. She would have felt better starting the tour if she had.

They climbed upstairs and found themselves right next to Columbia's massive iron gates, swept onto campus by a tide of people dressed like winter trees, as though someone had found a statistical link between primary colors and applicant rejections. Lauren turned toward the balloon clusters that were the universal symbol for prospective student events, and Nora scurried after her, distracted by a burnished leaf or two on the quadrangle maples, imagining how perfectly still the quad would be on the morning of the first snowfall. She hesitated outside the auditorium to take another look—and in that instant Nora was a freshman again, surrounded by memories. Not the boy who threw up on her new pea coat or the girl who stole her earrings but swore she owned an identical pair, not the day she started to sob because she had no idea what building her philosophy class was in, not the dizzy loneliness that occasionally sidled up behind her in the cafeteria line, or all of those things, but it no longer mattered. The point, really, was the skittish joy of knowing so much all of a sudden, without knowing anything at all in terms of how all this information was going to jell into a life. That great, bewildering excess, that experience, was what they wanted for Lauren.

"Now, this is a campus," she said. "I think I'm getting smarter just breathing."

"Mom, there is no way on earth I am going here."

"Did I say you were? I just said it's a campus, capital C."

"They take six percent of all applicants. Line up the whole Crestview senior class, pick the best six, maybe seven, and send everybody else home."

"It would be crazy to be in New York and not see it. No one is telling you to apply here. Besides, what if you just happen to be exactly what they're looking for? Could we stop acting like an A minus or even a B plus is the kiss of death?"

They could not. An hour later, on their way back through the gates, they reached an easy consensus: the tour had been a disaster. The number of applicants was up; the number of acceptances was down. The only constant was the qualifying numbers for the competitive candidate, the GPA and SATs and AP test scores, which were as stratospheric as ever. It did not take Nora long to figure out why the other parents in their tour group refused to make eye contact with her: they regarded her as the CEO of a competing company, whose product might knock theirs off the shelf.

"We should have left," said Lauren as they headed out the gate. "This is not what Ted meant when he said to look at other schools."

"You never know," said Nora, who no longer believed it.

"Oh yes I do," said Lauren.

"Look, Dad said to meet him for lunch, he's out of his meeting by now."

"You go," said Lauren, who wanted to avoid the instant replay. "Go have a nice lunch. I'll meet you back at the hotel."

"Are you sure? You have your cell phone, right? You okay?"

"Mom. I'm not brokenhearted. I really never figured . . ."

She trotted off before Nora could suggest that they at least ride the subway together.

❧

Ron's friends and enemies alike called him Flap: his friends because of the way he liked to bend his arms at the elbows and herd the oarsmen toward the boat before a race; his enemies because he flapped when he was on dry land as well. He gestured with both hands when he talked, and the more obscure the point he was trying to make, the more he waved his hands around, so that sometimes it looked as though his fingers were about to break off and fly into space. His lips were what the women who came into his mom's office for plumping injections were after. His hair bounced when he walked. His friends were not really friends, but math and science geeks who held him in awe. The kids who hated him—and they were legion, because he inadvertently made everyone feel as dumb as toast—liked to stand behind his back and mouth "flap flap flap flap flap" while he talked, safe in the knowledge that they could do so without him noticing. When Ron was deep into an idea, there was no such thing as distraction.

He said he loved quantum physics, and no one at Crestview had challenged him or inquired further, because he was the only one who understood what he was talking about, except for the UCLA professor who had worked with him twice a week once he outgrew the Crestview curriculum. Katie was mortified to be related to him and extremely relieved when he left home. She had confided to Lauren that her brother might very possibly have Asperger's syndrome, even though her parents had taken him to a specialist years before who confirmed that he did not. It was the cruelest rumor she had ever planted, far worse than the one about Brad, which had only enhanced his reputation, but Katie had to find some way to distance herself from her brother.

Lauren never repeated what Katie said, but as she walked down Broadway and saw Ron having a flapping conversation with a tall, thin girl, she wondered if there was any chance of getting into Gray's Papaya for a hot dog without him noticing her.

No. He had some sort of radar.

"Lauren," he hollered, lifting his arms higher and waving as she crossed the street.

"What're you doing in New York?" she asked.

"What're you doing in New York?" he replied.

"Looking at colleges," she said.

"Little late for that. You don't have the grades for Columbia, so is it Fordham? Hofstra? NYU? New School has some neat classes."

The exhausting thing about talking to Ron was that he was not malicious, so Lauren could hardly get mad at him for being hurtful.

Her dad said that Ron lacked an internal censor—his exact words were "That kid needs an in-house editor." The easiest thing was to ignore him. Lauren stuck her hand out in the girl's direction.

"I'm Lauren," she said. "I go to school with Ron's sister, Katie."

"The great-ee Miss Kate-ee, quite beleaguered Ivy Leaguer. I'm L'Anitra, glad to meet ya." She slapped Lauren a low five.

Ron wrapped his arm around the girl's waist.

"L'Anitra's a spoken-word poet," he said.

Lauren was dumbfounded. All she could think to say was, "L'Anitra. That's a very unusual name."

L'Anitra's smile made Lauren think of a Discovery Channel lion right before it tore a zebra into edible chunks.

An enraptured Ron continued to address Lauren as though L'Anitra did not comprehend English—which Lauren found entirely possible, at least as a first language, as the meter of her verse was a little bit forced. "How great is she?" he said. "She came to Williams for a performance poetry weekend and it was, it was, it was love at first adjective."

"Love at first electron, baby," said L'Anitra. *"Entanglement."*

She and Ron laughed as though that was about the funniest thing anyone had ever said, and Lauren wondered for a long moment what drug they had taken. But then Ron got flappy serious, all of his familiar energy in his fingertips, his eyes locked on Lauren, and she understood that he was merely high on acceptance. L'Anitra could stand to be with him for more than ten minutes, which was sufficient cause for elation on his part. He had no need of pharmaceuticals.

"Swear to me you won't say anything to Katie. Don't say anything to your parents. You didn't see me, okay?"

"Why? What's the big deal?" said Lauren.

Ron's eyes got wide. "Are you kidding me? I am standing on a street corner in Manhattan because L'Anitra goes to Barnard and she can't afford the train to Williams. . . ."

"Couldn't you pay for her ticket and take turns?"

"Lauren. Let me finish."

"Sorry."

"Where we are is beside the point . . ."

"Since we're always in the same place," said L'Anitra, and then she kissed Ron for long enough to allow Lauren to count out the exact change for the hot dog and papaya drink she regretted ever wanting.

"Say, Ron, I have to go meet my folks."

He broke away from L'Anitra slowly, his eyes darting furtively toward the subway, hoping her roommate would keep her promise to be out of the room by two.

"Anyhow, you can't tell them you saw us. You have to promise."

Lauren shrugged. "Fine. What do I care?"

"Great." Ron searched his mental list of appropriate behaviors until he found the one labeled "favor done/gratitude expressed." He fixed Lauren with as sincere a gaze as he could muster. "So, Columbia."

"Or Northwestern or Vassar or NYU or none of the above," said Lauren. "I'm just looking, Ron. Shopping. You don't say anything, either."

"No problem," said Ron.

And then L'Anitra did something Lauren had never seen before—she snaked her arm across Ron's skinny torso and tucked her fingers into the front of his waistband, eliciting a high giggle from Ron that Lauren hoped never to hear again. She was used to people lacing a finger into the back of someone's waistband as a way to assert proprietary rights, or to propel them toward the door, but L'Anitra had long fingers, and all four of them were tapping a secret code on the inside of Ron's zipper. Only her thumb remained in view, and it looked impatient. Lauren looked for another point of focus—the little mole above L'Anitra's left eyebrow, the purple butterfly tattooed in the well above her collarbone—but it was impossible not to watch the disappearing hand.

"Gotta go," said Lauren.

"Suh-weet," said L'Anitra, dismissively. Her slightly threatening tone made Lauren decide not to mention that no one used "sweet" as an adjective anymore, something a poet ought to know.

Lauren was halfway to the hotel, numb, when she remembered the hot dog she had forgotten to buy, so she settled for a handful of hard candy from a bowl in the lobby and went upstairs to collapse on the bed, trying to make sense of her distress. Lauren was not a prude; she simply had never found "everybody else is" a compelling reason to have sex, especially as she knew of too many girls who supposedly were but in fact were not. Lauren's last boyfriend had dumped her at the end of junior year in favor of a more compliant girl. Since then, Lauren had come to agree with Katie: any senior who still had a boyfriend was not spending enough time working on her college applications. They never once stopped to wonder if they were missing out on something. Fun in high school was as outmoded a concept as pajama parties, and a good time was likelier to be a 5 on the AP world history exam than a pep rally. This generation was all about purpose, at least until the fat envelopes arrived. Boys, like introduction to sociology or a survey course on Western intellectual thought, were something to look forward to freshman year.

She told herself that it was perfectly reasonable for two college sophomores to be indulging in foreplay on the way to the subway. The problem was that Ron was half of the happy couple, Ron, who failed to find a date to his senior prom despite the efforts of the crew captain, who had pimped Ron to his twin sister and her pals at the nearby girls school. Ron, who went to prom anyhow, got two girls to dance with him, once each, and spent the rest of the night hanging out with the photographer, pretending he was the guy's assistant. Lauren subscribed to the sustaining notion that freshman year was going to be full of all the happy experiences she was in the process of denying herself, but Ron's new life implied that the path was not necessarily a straight one. If he could turn into a sex object, there were no guarantees.

She turned on the television set, but her only options were a talk show about a husband and wife who each had had a sex-change operation ("Saves money on a new wardrobe," joked the husband-to-wife), a talk show about a couple suing their grown children for fraud ("They said the money was safe"), and three local news shows that featured breaking news on puppy mills, a raid on a store that sold knock-off Vuitton handbags, and a wedding photographer who collected his fee and never delivered the photos, respectively. Lauren curled up tight and put her hands over her ears. Sometimes it seemed to her that these particular stories ran in a continuous loop all over the country. She could have sworn that she had already heard them back home.

She turned off the set when Nora and Joel walked in.

"Boy, I would do a lot for a lemon cupcake right now," said Lauren.

"Oh, sweetie," said Nora, snuggling up next to her. "Feeling a little overwhelmed?"

Lauren hopped up off the bed and tromped toward the bathroom.

"I was feeling hungry. Could we not read something into every single thing I say? I'm going to take a shower and work on my essay."

⤜⤛

They went to NYU, which confirmed Lauren's preference for a rolling campus. They rented a car and drove to Brandeis, which made her feel insufficiently Jewish, and to Trinity, which had the opposite effect despite her father's joke about Curly, Moe, and Larry. They went to Bard, which made her feel like a Republican, and to Sarah Lawrence, which made her feel nothing at all, and then they headed north to Vassar, each of them careful neither to mention how many times they had doubled back, nor to raise the question of whose job it should have been to consult a map and create a more linear itinerary. Nora insisted that she loved the chance to see the same autumn leaves a few days apart and swore that she could see a difference in the colors, which was her way of putting her family on notice: she would not tolerate a single moment of strife over the curlicues they were driving.

Ted had suggested Vassar at the last moment because he felt that Vassar was in flux, eager to be considered competitive with the Ivies, not a consolation prize for their rejects, but not quite there yet. Better still, no one from Crestview was applying this year. Ted sold the gorgeous campus hard, and reminded Nora that the nearby Culinary Institute promised higher quality local restaurants than they would otherwise find in a rural setting.

Best of both worlds, he said, jotting that phrase next to Vassar on his personal crib sheet. He added the school to Lauren's list, in a vague open space that might be the bottom of the Stretches or the top of the Even Odds, depending on one's point of view and her first-semester grades.

So Lauren and her parents checked into the Crystal Lake bed-and-breakfast, whose brochure inflated the adjacent stream into a waterfront location and referred to the lobby as the living room, where the hospitality staff offered a full afternoon tea. Crystal Lake had started out as a flagship in the Nite-E-Nite economy motel chain, until outsourcing dried up the steady stream of satellite-office managers and sales reps who had been its dependable clientele. The bank manager who handled the foreclosure sale bought the place for a song and retrofitted it to serve the growing number of families who came to town for the college tour, as well as the lucky return visitors who came back straight through graduation. He replaced the monochromatic executive palette with the decorating equivalent of comfort food: floral prints and overstuffed chairs and his mother-in-law's scenic watercolors to give the walls some needed warmth. The only vestige of the previous regime was a slightly distorted flat-screen TV in every room.

Lauren and her parents arrived after dark, too late to appreciate the adjacent lake or the afternoon tea, and overslept the following morning because Joel had set the alarm on his cell phone but forgot that he had it on silent mode. Happily, hospitality was as endemic as chintz in Poughkeepsie. There was coffee and tea and fresh apple cider and what looked like homemade donuts in the cozy admissions office from which the tour embarked.

As the tour group set off for the freshman dormitories, a dad in full L.L. Bean autumn regalia strode up next to Joel, because having a son for whom Vassar was considered a safe school meant nothing without sharing. A woman who struck up a conversation with Nora made a pitying cluck when Nora said that Lauren had taken six AP classes.

"This year?" the woman asked, and Nora changed the subject to those marvelous donuts.

No one at all spoke to Lauren, because a hardened high school senior on tour knew that autonomy made a stronger impression than camaraderie.

At eleven, having visited several identical dormitory rooms and a bunch of empty classrooms, the two tour leaders herded their two dozen charges toward an auditorium in the oldest building on campus, which bore dignified witness to the amount of time that Vassar had been doing things right. A tall, slender, stern woman stepped to the podium and introduced herself. She was second-generation Vassar admissions, dressed in a first-generation uniform of silk blouse and sensible skirt; she wore pearls without irony and oversized bifocals, the ones with the earpiece attached to the bottom of the frame instead of the top, without shame. She smiled without sincerity.

"My mother liked to say that she would've rejected every single girl Mary McCarthy wrote about in *The Group*," she said, with a parched New England chuckle. "And I have inherited that high standard for Vassar's incoming class."

She proceeded to recite what she called the "recipe for success" at Vassar, which involved straight As, being in the top 5 to 10 percent of one's class, community service, extracurricular activities, an application essay about an absolutely unique topic, and incomparable test scores. She frequently mentioned her own version of the holy trinity, Harvard, Yale, and Vassar, as though Princeton, Columbia, and a half dozen other impossible schools no longer existed, as though these three schools bestowed the only diplomas worth having. Her job was to change the perception of the L.L. Bean dad, to make Vassar a destination college.

"If you don't have straight As," she said, "then perhaps you need to ask yourself if you should be in this room. Or will you be happier at a school that doesn't set the bar quite so high? As for the rest of you, the ones who've met every criterion I've laid out, I look forward to reading your applications in the coming months. And now, off you go to enjoy this beautiful fall day. Thanks so much for coming."

Lauren and her parents headed for the nearest exit and walked to the main gates without saying a word. Once they were safely on the street, out of view of the other tour families, Joel wrapped his arms around Nora and Lauren.

"You cannot tell me that every kid in that room had straight As," he said.

"That's for sure," said Lauren. "I don't."

Nora's voice was as bright as stainless steel. "They can't have you, is what I say. Let's go get free tea."

The full afternoon tea, as it turned out, involved two plastic domes, one covering striated multicolored cheese cubes and the other red grapes, alongside a carafe of coffee and another of hot water. There was a cereal bowl full of assorted tea bags, another of slightly dehydrated lemon wedges, individual plastic tublets of cream, sugar, and artificial sweetener, and a plate of bulbous muffins. A set of white plastic tongs hung from the lid of the cheese dome.

Joel went through the motions and took his plate over to the couch in front of the fireplace. Nora studied the contents of the cheese dome as though there were a difference between one cube and another, and Lauren drifted over to the picture window to stare at the Lilliputian puddle that imagined itself a lake. Five days, and all she had succeeded in doing was make Northwestern seem even more alluring. Evanston did not feel like a small town the way Poughkeepsie and some of the other towns did, and Chicago did not feel harsh the way New York sometimes did to her. Northwestern was the best of all possible worlds, which was exactly what she had come on this trip to stop thinking. She glanced over at her dad, who could not find a thing in the local newspaper worth turning the page for, and at her mother, who seemed to have decided that late-afternoon hunger was preferable to any of the muffins. Lauren rested her cheek against the glass.

"Are we close to anything at all?" she asked.

chapter 6

Alexandra Kirk Bradley understood from the day Trey slipped his great-grandmother's engagement ring onto her finger that her job description involved administering certain of the Bradley traditions. She considered herself a highly qualified candidate, third generation in everything that mattered, from the Pasadena Junior League to the mansioned hillsides of La Cañada to the dressage finals at the annual Flintridge charity horse show, where her father and grandfather had always purchased two ringside tables apiece to accommodate any last-minute guests. She knew a small sliver of life very, very well, and she was perfectly content to leave the rest to others who were as experienced in their specialties as she was in hers. Alexandra might not be a commanding physical presence—the first time Trey met her, he had the eerie sense that he could see right through her to the other side, she was that frail, that pale, that dainty—but she knew how to do what she knew how to do. Her oldest girlfriends, who had called her Birdy in high school, insisted now that she reminded them far more of a dove than a sparrow.

Privately, she felt more like a little chicken, a *poussin*, darting this way and that, trying to get her bearings. That was what Trey had called her on their Paris honeymoon, or had tried to, except that *petit poussin* came out *petit poisson*, and he had spent several days apologizing for calling her a little fish. It was the first and last time he behaved in a deferential manner. Trey was never

harsh, but he was definitive, on everything from her family's recipe for leg of lamb, which he summarily rejected, to the benefits
of living in Hancock Park rather than near her folks in Pasadena, to
the disposition of family names. Their first son, Roger, was named
after Trey's maternal grandfather, and their second son was Preston
Bradley IV, always to be called Preston and nothing shorter.

Alexandra dutifully insisted that the nanny call her younger
boy Preston, while other mothers and nannies, rendered inarticu-
late by love, referred to their toddlers as boo-boo or zee-zee, as
bunny-bun or m'hija. The Bradleys donated $25,000 to Best Step
Preschool, in return for which everyone on the staff was instructed
to avoid affectionate diminutives. The same order accompanied a
$50,000 donation to Ashland Elementary, but Alexandra had not
taken into account her six-year-old son's teary refusal to answer
to any name but Brad. He became the boy with three names—
Brad at school, Preston at home, and Four with and only with his
father, a small reminder from husband to wife of exactly whose
lineage was the dominant one.

She had fewer opportunities to call her son by any name,
lately, as Brad had long since stopped talking to her about anything of significance, and everyone's schedule was so full. October was the start of Alexandra's charity season, with an event every
weekend—a Junior League luncheon to gather supplies for home-
less families, whose members would enter the coming year wearing repurposed T-shirts commemorating everything from Fashion
Week to Lollapalooza; the Revlon Run/Walk for breast cancer
research; a church-sponsored 5K run for adult literacy, to which
she donated accumulated copies of *The New Yorker*; and a food
drive that involved the aggressive gifting of frozen turkeys and
boxed stuffing to families whose food heritage did not include
turkeys and stuffing.

Alexandra had inherited each of her target charities from her
mother, except for the breast cancer event, and she had decided

that this would be her last year for that cause unless the partici-
pants showed a bit more restraint. She wanted to raise money
without drawing attention, as her mother and grandmother had
done, and she was rattled by women, most of them newcomers to
the charity circuit, who wanted face time with their beneficiaries,
or whose passion was fueled by a personal saga they felt compelled
to recount. Trey's Jewish partner had once congratulated her for
aspiring to what his religion defined as the highest form of charity, giving anonymously to an anonymous recipient. While she
thought that was a bit excessive—one wanted to feel that those
who received help deserved it, and a little recognition was always
nice—she did like the part about never actually having a conversation with the people who benefited from her efforts.

This year, she had added to her roster a luncheon at the Pen-
insula Hotel, sponsored by the bank's private investment group
for families who gave away over a million dollars a year. Another
of Trey's partners handled the Bradleys' philanthropy, but Alexandra loved the idea that she was taking on new responsibilities, one
of the strategies suggested by the therapist who had come to
Crestview to talk to parents about the empty nest. The bank's
scheduled speaker was an expert on ethical wills, which enabled
the philanthropist to dictate from beyond the grave the good work
he expected his heirs to do on his behalf or risk disinheritance, a
topic of great interest to Trey and Alexandra, who were not about
to let mortality alter their long-range agenda. As one of the event
organizers, Alexandra had to show up early and stay late, but Trey
was not going at all, some double-talk about respecting his wife's
independence being a nice cover for wanting an afternoon to himself. Saturday was the one day of the week when Trey was neither
at the office nor on the golf course, and he was loath to give it up.

Brad was pacing circles in the entry hall when his mother
came downstairs wearing a navy blue suit that made her skin look
like skim milk.

"Hey, Mom, you look ready to take care of business."

She adjusted her jacket and checked the contents of her handbag.

"Well, that's a nice thing to hear from the young man of the house," she said, uncertain about what to do next. Alexandra stepped toward her son for a kiss just as he decided that he did not need a heavy sweatshirt, and she almost took an elbow to the forehead, which must have been the reason her eyes threatened to fill with tears. She looked away as though she were checking the way her stockings descended into her pumps, blinked fast, regained her inner balance, smiled too brightly, and was gone.

Brad stood at the door and waited until he heard the whir of the electronic gate. She was gone for at least three hours. With barely a week left before the Bradleys' self-imposed November 1 filing deadline for Harvard, Brad finally had the chance to approach his father without fear of interruption.

Trey was in his study, one of two twin rooms on either side of a back hallway that led to a large bricked patio, the only surface in all of southern California that a family in search of a New England gestalt could afford to finish in weathered brick; a patio might break up in an earthquake, but it had nowhere to fall. To the left, Trey's study, furnished in the high testosterone of the Ralph Lauren line, wallpapered in a deep red plaid, carpeted in the color of a mighty stag's blood after it was killed by a single perfect shot to the heart, lined with bookshelves stocked with leather-bound classics. Under the windows, an antique partner's desk that Alexandra's decorator had found in the little showroom with the British name that he favored for the extra 10 percent commission the owner padded into the price and split with him on top of his normal cut. In front of the bookshelves, the big black leather and cherry wood Eames lounge chair and ottoman that Trey's father had bought for him when he passed the bar exam.

To the right of the hallway was an equally large room done up to look as though it had survived decades of salt air and Atlantic chill. Bleached wood couches covered in chemically aged cotton stood on bleached wood floors against bleached linen walls. On a long wooden table the color of driftwood, Alexandra kept a set of fabric-covered boxes, a sewing machine she never used, and a large wicker basket filled with yarn that was suspiciously color-coordinated to its surroundings. Occasionally Brad would notice a pair of knitting needles sticking out of one of the balls—today there was a globe of marigold yarn anchored by two big natural wood needles—but he never saw a finished project, never got so much as a homemade scarf at Christmas, and he had come to realize that the yarn and needles were part of the set dressing, like his dad's books or the bottle of single-malt scotch whose level had not wavered in years.

Along the full length of the long back wall of his mother's room, arrayed on a single shelf, were souvenirs of the one aspect of her former life that mystified Brad—a row of framed photographs of Alexandra on horseback, posed always on the same white horse, a ribbon dangling from its bridle, her parents and sometimes the trainer standing next to her holding a silver cup or a silver platter and some flowers. His mother had been brave enough to ride a horse and good enough to win some blue ribbons. It made no sense to him at all.

He had asked her about it once, and she had waved him away with an airy, "Oh, it was just something you did," as though getting a horse to do her bidding were as easy as riding a bicycle. For all Brad knew, it was. Trey had done his best to make dismissiveness sound affectionate.

"Let's remember," he said, giving his wife's elbow a playful squeeze, "it's not like they ever moved very fast or left the ground. Dressage. Horse dancing, isn't that what you called it?"

"Yes," Alexandra had said. "Horse dancing."

Brad stood in the hallway and forced himself to focus. When he had successfully excised the image of a dancing horse from his brain, he took what he hoped was a decisive step into the doorway of Trey's office.

Trey was watching the Stanford-Cal football game while he cleaned his golf clubs. Two simultaneous tasks was the closest he ever got to doing nothing.

"Dad."

Trey looked up, reached for the remote control, and hit MUTE, but he did not turn off the set.

"Yes."

"Can I talk to you?"

Trey gestured at the Eames with his putter. Brad hated the chair, which made him feel at a disadvantage, splayed out like a bug on a mounting board for his father's inspection, but it was either there or the desk chair, which would make this seem too much like a meeting.

He settled in, looked at his dad, and wondered how old he would be when he woke up one morning and looked like that—like a bad watercolor of his former self, a thin, diluted, smudged version of who he used to be. In old photos, in the annual family reunion shots, in white tie on his wedding day, Trey looked unnervingly like Brad. In newer photos, he looked like he had vinegar in his veins. The handsome that got in Brad's way burned out quickly, it seemed—the bright eyes faded, the hair lost its heavy sheen, and slender became gaunt. Or perhaps Trey's life made him look like a ghostly version of his former self. Brad wanted to believe that being an estate lawyer took its toll on the living, even if the estates belonged to famous people with wacky codicils and questionable witnesses, because if that was true, if that was the defining variable of Trey's life, then Brad had a chance of not growing up to be like his dad. Over the summer, he had made a derisive joke about how his dad saw dead people, an opening salvo in his campaign to liberate himself from the Bradley legacy. In response, Trey had drawn up a list of his current clients, annotated with their Oscar and Emmy and Tony nominations, if they were any good, or their box office triumphs, if they were not.

They had stopped just short of an argument. They always did, thanks to an unspoken agreement struck six years earlier, when Brad started at Crestview and his older brother dropped out of Harvard, three weeks into the fall term, to join a dance commune in Portland. None of them had heard a word from Roger since the day he appeared on the doorstep to announce his decision, sending Trey into an impotent rage that lasted the subsequent night and half the next day and involved a bottle of Glenfiddich, a putter, and a wall clock. His only reference to his older son, once he had awakened from a sodden nap and taken a long, hot shower, was that he was glad he had not squandered the name Preston on such a loser.

Trey was ashamed that twelve-year-old Brad, now the single repository of his ambition, had seen him like that, and Brad was frankly terrified that he had. No one mentioned it again, just as no one mentioned Brad's crying jag about his name, but from that day forward Brad had tried not to give his dad a hard time. Until now, that is.

"Application ready to go." Trey presented it as a statement, not a question.

"Yes, sir. I thought I'd send it tomorrow. Like the good old days. Early."

Like the good old days? Brad winced at how dumb he sounded.

Trey shook his head. "End of an era. And nobody I've talked to there can give me a satisfactory explanation as to why they had to

let early decision go. Because financial aid kids need to know all
their options? Great. In the meantime, don't we lose some of the
best kids?"

Brad wondered how many nobodies his dad had called, and
who the "we" were who lost the best kids.

"Dad, I don't want to go."

Brad had to look down when he said that, so he did not notice
his father's eyes flit to the screen for the Stanford touchdown. He
worried, instead, that his father had not heard him, that the knot
in his throat had muffled his voice. He coughed to clear the way
and repeated himself.

"I don't want to go to Harvard, Dad."

Trey considered the head of the putter, which was cleaner
than it had been on the day he bought it, store dust being what it
was. He slid the putter back into the bag, put the leather cover
over the head of the club, and only then looked at his son.

"Don't you think it's a little late in the game to make that announcement? No, that's not the correct first question. Are you
saying you don't want to go to protect yourself in case they turn
you down, which is patent nonsense? If not—if you believe you
can make a substantial case for another school—then I have to
question your sense of timing. So. Is this nerves, or have you convinced yourself that there is a better school than Harvard, which
will be news to Harvard?"

"Boy, good thing you didn't become a prosecutor," said Brad
with a shift, his discomfort registered by the upholstery, which responded with a resentful squawk. He stood up. He had no chance
of winning as long as he was thrashing around on that chair.

"I am not confusing nerves with lack of desire, though there
is no such thing as a sure bet," he began. Trey started to protest,
but Brad held up a hand and his father, surprisingly, went back to
his clubs. "There is no such thing as a sure bet, but I'm probably
the valedictorian and everybody acts like I'm Crestview's best

chance at Harvard, so sure, if anybody's going to get in it'll probably be me, especially with the legacy thing, unless . . ."

"Thank you for including the family in your list of assets," said Trey, dryly, cutting him off before he could raise the specter of Roger's behavior.

"*Dad.* I just don't think I'll be happy there."

His father polished his three wood and waited, wondering what chromosomal ding on Alexandra's side produced boys who perceived an imaginary link between rebellion and happiness. He cautioned himself to remain calm at all costs. His first, unguarded response to Roger's news, a loud "You've got to be kidding me," had not put the boy in the mood for reasoned deliberation. Self-control was essential to a positive outcome.

"I just don't think I'll be happy there," Brad said again, stuffing his hands into his jeans pockets and starting to pace. "I just don't see myself being a lawyer. I don't know, maybe I should be a sculptor, or maybe an architect if that sounds more responsible. . . ."

"Brad, please." The imperative in Trey's voice worked as it always had. Silently, Brad watched as his father walked over to the floor-to-ceiling bookcase behind his desk, knowing exactly what was coming next. Trey retrieved a small, slightly battered rectangular black case, placed it on the desk between them as though it contained an heirloom jewel, and flipped the two metal clasps that held it shut. Brad smelled the musty smell that he associated with every unpleasant lecture he had ever sat through and waited to see how the clarinet pertained this time.

Over the years, Trey had used his childhood clarinet to illustrate a variety of life lessons. When Brad was a toddler, his father showed him the clarinet but did not let him touch it, because we respect other people's possessions unless they give us permission to use them. At nine, bored and frustrated by soccer, Brad found out that his father had practiced the clarinet diligently, even though he disliked the daily hour's drill, because you get out of life what you put into it, and nobody has anything coming to them without hard work. In middle school, the clarinet represented dedication—and if that lecture backfired when Brad started paying what Trey considered to be too much attention to woodworking, a reprise came in handy a few years later, when it was time to decide how many APs to take. For a time, Brad had lived in terror of the day when he would find out how the clarinet fit into his father's lecture about responsible sex, but happily, Trey seemed perfectly willing to leave that conversation to his wife, who never broached the subject but told her husband that she had.

Brad watched with a new horror as his father lifted the segments out of their worn velvet nest and started to fit them together. Until today, his father had settled for using the clarinet as a visual aid, but now it looked as though he might actually play it. Brad could not decide what would be worse, a show of surprising talent or a pathetic musical misfire. He felt a tiny thrum of panic. He would have preferred a know-it-all little sister to the damned clarinet.

"Hey, the famous clarinet," he said, with a weak smile.

Trey held up the clarinet and peered down its shaft as though he were a marksman sighting his prey. He had no intention of playing a note, but he needed something to do with his hands.

"My prep school orchestra needed a clarinet, so I began lessons in third grade. In high school I played with both the orchestra and the marching band. When it was time to apply to college I considered applying to Oberlin to major in music."

Brad squirmed and waited. The bit about Oberlin was new information, but he could tell that this was a pause for effect, not an invitation to respond. His father sat up a bit straighter and locked his gaze on his son.

"And then my father asked me a very simple question: what would happen if I did?"

"Were you good enough?"

Trey waved away the question. "There are things we have to set aside as we grow up," he said. "The question of whether I was any good is beside the point, and my father helped me to realize that. Imagine what our life would be like if I had pursued music. How would I support your mother and you? How would I provide not just financial support but the kind of emotional support, the constancy, the stability that a family needs?"

"But Grandpa was rich. You could have done anything and we wouldn't have been broke." And you would have been a musician, Brad thought, so Roger might have hung around. With almost ten years and a wing of the house between them, Brad barely knew his departed older brother, so there was not much to miss. Still, he had to wonder how things might have turned out if Trey had done what he wanted to do.

"And my father's wealth buys me what? What kind of a son would I be if I exploited his wealth so that I could sit around and play the clarinet? A parasite. An opportunist."

Trey left the clarinet on his desk and walked back over to his golf bag, where he began to polish his three wood for the second time. "Children always think that they're the first generation to want to do something interesting," he said, glancing up as the silent Cal quarterback got knocked to the ground by a silent Stanford linebacker. "They think their parents were born this boring. This limited. That's how they see adult responsibility. My father thought it about my grandfather, I thought it about my father, and now you think it about me. But here is the truth: Every dull parent was once an interesting person with ideas his parents did not want to hear. No, not every dull parent. Some of them were dull from the moment they were born. But not your father or your grandfather or your great-grandfather. We were adolescents"—and here his pacing slowed, as though each word were a complete thought—"and then we came to understand the obligations and challenges of adulthood. You have that same great opportunity.

To continue a tradition of excellence and accomplishment. That is not dull."

There it was. In this season's lecture, his dad's clarinet symbolized a discarded and irresponsible passion, the musical equivalent of an adolescent fling, or Brad's interest in architecture, or anything else on the list of things the Bradley men did not do once they became men. Trey considered even a fleeting infatuation with the arts to be a condition one grew out of.

Trey raised his arm in a sweeping gesture, encompassing not just the study but everything it stood for.

"Someday you'll own this house, and your mother and I will be out in Palm Springs playing golf. This is a good room for a hobby. Tear out the bookshelves. I'll take the desk with me. Make it a wood shop. Make it the place you go to catch your breath and build things." He put the three wood back in the bag and looked at his son.

"So. Are we all set?"

"Yes, sir," said Brad.

"Good," said his father. He hit the MUTE button to bring the sound back up, and the room filled with the Stanford marching band's rendition of "California Dreamin'."

Brad slogged upstairs, opened his laptop, and cut and pasted the Brewster McCloud essay into the last vacant space in Harvard's online application. Without hesitating, he clicked SUBMIT. There. He had done his dad a big favor and not used the legacy essay.

He fell back onto his bed. This was what four generations of ambition had bought him, five if he counted those anonymous Welsh ancestors who decided that Tregaron was not the place to start an empire. Brad was heir to enough money to make his grandchildren rich, even if Trey reconsidered and wrote Roger back into the will. The day after he graduated from law school, he could start work at his father's firm, incurring the resentment of every employee who was not the boss's son. He could have this house or a bigger one, a weekend place and a philanthropic presence. That was what his mom liked to call it, a philanthropic presence.

He could inhabit his father's life. Brad groaned, rolled over, and buried his face in the pillow. The future that Preston Bradley III had in mind for Preston Bradley IV was essentially a maintenance job.

Maintenance.

That was Brad's presumptive fate. Somebody had to manage the family empire, and Brad was the obvious, in fact the only, candidate. Roger was not even in the running. Roger got to dance and Brad got to be responsible. Some reward system: the prize for not driving his parents nuts, it seemed, was the opportunity to continue to do what they thought he ought to do. Brad's life was to be the epilogue to generations of cumulative success. He was the family's fiscal tree trimmer. He was the fiduciary pool guy.

◦✦◦

Liz awoke to a silent house on Saturdays. If her room had been darker, or the neighbor's Chihuahua quieter, she might have slept until noon. But her bedroom curtains were no match for the eastern sun, and the nervous little dog felt a compelling need to chronicle the slightest motion outside the apartment building on the corner, so Liz never got the chance to feel guilty about sleeping through half of her parents' workday. The greatest indulgence of her weekend morning was to lie in bed, stare at the ceiling, and imagine what might happen next.

She had to be a little careful when she talked to her parents about the future. They might say they wanted nothing more than for her to go to Harvard, but there had to be a bit of envy tucked into the folds of that dream. How could there not be? Her father had been an engineer who worked on roadway overpasses and hoped someday to build a bridge over water instead of over pavement, and now he drove a cab six days a week. Her mother had all but run a children's clinic for three doctors, and now she squandered her compassion on patients whose biggest challenge was to look the age they lied about being, and spent her Saturday mornings driving the mother of one of those patients to the beauty salon, because the woman was embarrassed to be seen in Beverly Hills in the van from the assisted-living center. If their lives had unfurled in a logical and just fashion, with the kind of fantastic momentum Los Angeles advertised, they would have had more today than when they started. It did not work that way when passports and job recertification were involved. Liz's parents had traded personal accomplishment for Liz's future, which made their ambitions for her complicated. She had to go to Harvard to pay them back, but if she did, the gap between them would be enormous.

At eight o'clock on an unfettered morning, she wanted nothing more than to fulfill their expectations, not because she wanted to be away from them but because she wanted an education that made her immune to circumstance. She wanted to prepare herself for a career so safe, so essential, that fate would never show up at her door to inform her that her native land had hit the skids and starting tomorrow she would be a cocktail waitress or a dog groomer in a booming oil-rich nation in the Middle East. She wanted always to be in demand, doing something substantial enough to compensate for what had happened to her folks. With a cool pragmatism, she had begun to clip articles about autism, Parkinson's, Alzheimer's. Nobody was going to figure those out in her lifetime.

For that matter, she wanted to be at a school where everyone was as smart as or smarter than she was. She wanted never again to walk by a sniggling gaggle of girls who called out to her, "Hey, Ivy, you know, like in League?" Liz had pretty much given up on finding friends at Ocean Heights. She settled instead for working nonstop and told herself it was an investment in a happier future.

Valedictorian heaven. That was where she would be in the fall.

She got out of bed, smoothed the sheets and blanket and plumped her pillow, and put on the hoodie and sweatpants Yoonie had brought home on Friday, the store tags still on them, one of the occasional bequests from Dr. Joy, who sometimes bought the wrong color for Katie, or a sweater she did not need. Dr. Joy insisted that it was easier to give the clothes to Yoonie than to take the time to drive back to the Grove or the Promenade to return them, so in a way Liz was doing her a favor by accepting them. Dr. Joy was glad that the girls were the same size, and that was that. She refused to listen to a single word of protest from her nurse.

Liz was particularly pleased with this latest inheritance, which was incredibly soft, and much more to her liking than the last offering, a wraparound cardigan whose long tails flopped like octopus tentacles unless she bound herself once, twice, three times and tucked up the ends. Liz did not really have taste, which would have required wasting time paying attention to clothes, but she had severe criteria, and she rejected most of what passed for fashion because it was nonsense. There was no structural reason for those ridiculous tails, but the sweats were soft, and loose without being baggy, and a comforting shade that the tag identified as sea foam. She was happy to have them.

Liz was taller than either of her parents, slender like both of them, and the planes of her face could look harsh when she was tired. The sweats smoothed the edges a bit, and the color made her think of the ocean, which as far as she was concerned was the best thing about Los Angeles. In these clothes, on a solitary morning, Liz almost felt at ease.

The final copy of her Harvard application was stacked on the kitchen table next to a wax-paper-wrapped bagel with cream cheese and a room temperature chai latte, clearly an early-morning purchase by her father, who equated excessive amounts of dairy products with prosperity. Next to the plate, a coffee cup filled with the pink alyssum that overran everything else Yoonie tried to plant on the parkway. Liz carried the bagel over to the sink, squeezed both halves together until she reached what she considered the proper proportion of bagel to filling, and scraped the extruded cheese into the garbage. She poured the latte into a little saucepan, skimmed off half the foam, and reheated it. Satisfied with breakfast on her own terms, she sat down at the table.

There were two little adhesive notes attached to the application. The first one, in her mother's handwriting, reminded her that she had volunteered at the public library the summer after tenth grade, a comparatively insignificant achievement but worth including. The second one, from her father, requested that she count the words in her essay one last time, to make sure that the added phrase they had discussed the night before did not take it over the five-hundred-word limit. They had heard that some schools simply lopped off the overage and then penalized the applicant for a sentence fragment.

Liz was sure but never smug, so she reached for a pencil and counted one more time, tapping each word in turn as she whispered, "one, two, three . . . thirty-eight, thirty-nine . . . four ninety-four, ninety-five, ninety-six." Four hundred and ninety-six words. She reread the essay to make sure she did not have a four-word thought she wanted to insert—and then, as though the counting had made the room too warm, she hopped off the chair and strode into her room, turned on her laptop, added the business about the public library, checked her name and email address, and clicked SUBMIT, all in one single, heady rush. She jumped up again, spun around, ran back down the hall, and flung open the kitchen door. If she had been one of the heroines in any of the movies she had watched during her American musicals phase, she would have burst into song, or at least lip-synched to someone who could carry a tune.

Gone.

Liz closed her eyes and saw herself arriving at Harvard for the start of her freshman year. It was a well-worn image, one that had been her secret companion since ninth grade. She was standing on the sidewalk in front of a beautiful, redbrick dormitory, flanked not by her parents but by two effusive, welcoming Harvard undergrads, one boy, one girl, each reaching to help her with a suitcase. There was a light, clean, refreshing breeze, nothing at all like the bully Santa Anas that set the southern California hills on fire every fall. It was, as she envisioned the scene, a Saturday. She had traveled all this way on her own. Her mother had quit Dr. Joy and started working in the emergency room at St. John's. Her father, who now drove a town car for a private firm, had with great fanfare made her his first fare of the day, before he started shuttling celebrities back and forth to a charity carnival in a park in Beverly Hills.

That was as far as she ever got. Liz's imagination had only a supporting role in the private drama known as getting into Harvard; aside from being activated to complete the occasional creative-writing assignment in English class, it was a marginal presence, not quite up to the task of daydreaming on such a grand scale. Harvard's catalog and website provided Liz with a detailed sense of the physical setting, enough information to create an opening scene—but she had little idea of what she would do once she got there, beyond continuing to excel in class.

She wandered back into her room and opened the application again, to the screen that contained her essay.

I traveled across the world to a new home, a new language, a new life, when I was three. I learned English in my kindergarten class, but no one ever had to teach me to be determined, to aspire to a larger life than my immigrant parents could have managed. They decided to change their lives for my benefit. There is no need for me to feel guilty—I did not ask them to do so—but I have a great desire to extend myself out of recognition for what they did. During my high school career, teachers or administrators occasionally asked me to consider taking one less AP, or to cut back on an extracurricular activity, out of concern, they said, that I was taking on too much.

I know myself better than that—and, as my record attests, I was able to meet the challenge. My parents traded their potential for mine, and I am aware, always, that I must show them how much I appreciate my opportunities.

She closed the file without reading the rest, suddenly disgusted by how stuffy—how dull, how trite—she sounded.

"Could you be any more predictable?" she muttered to herself, hoping that Harvard had some kind of remedial class for the children of driven immigrants, one that might help her to develop a sense of humor.

A west side teen with any self-respect stayed away from the beach in the summer, rather than be mistaken for a tourist and have to endure the indignity of an Iowan leaning across the sand with presumed familiarity to ask, "Where you girls from?" A west side teen knew that the best time to go to the beach was between Halloween and Thanksgiving, when the ambient noise was a self-satisfied purr, not the liberated squeals of normally landlocked visitors, when the beach had everything going for it but too many people. Los Angeles rewarded its full-time residents with an exclusive treat: late fall at the beach felt like late summer in all the places where less fortunate people lived.

Lauren and Chloe arrived at the beach at eleven o'clock sharp, knowing full well that Katie would be late because she liked to make an entrance, even when the only onlookers were a formation of seagulls watching the tide. Everyone had a girlfriend like Katie, whose biggest crime in elementary school had been the need always to be first in line, first to speak, teacher's pet, in the front row at the assemblies. She took her pals with her, in those days, to form a flying wedge of energy, and year after year they melted the hearts of adults who got pushiness and independence confused, particularly when it came to girls. Parents approved of their daughters playing with Katie, back then, because Katie was a girl who never let anyone stand in her way.

It took middle school and puberty to expose the ruthless edge to Katie's selection process, as girls who had always been at her side suddenly found themselves replaced by girls with prettier hair, any breasts at all, and money to spend on makeup and clothes, as long as none of those assets were competitive with Katie's. She ditched friends who did not measure up and acquired new ones who did. Her single saving grace was that she did not engage in the kind of high-profile, mean-girl shenanigans that marked a girl for eventual vengeance, or at least she had not so far, though the business about her pretend sex life with Brad had made Lauren wary, in case it signaled a downward spiral. Katie cut and culled her girlfriends using more of a CEO model, refining and improving her associates' group profile without ever making the rejects feel rejected or the new hires feel temporary.

Chloe made the cut because she was a goofy mess, and Katie's notion of alpha-girl perfection required that she have one sidekick who was living proof of her compassionate nature. Lauren survived because she was fun and smart and pretty enough, but not a direct threat in any way. They hung around with Katie, in return, because they always had, and because at this point there was no reason to change. College would take care of that.

Chloe caught Lauren looking at her cell phone for the third time.

"Well, c'mon, her time is so much more important than ours," said Chloe. "Except really she hates herself, that's what they say about people who are late, you know, she's so insecure she has to be late, to prove to herself that she matters."

"Where did you read that?"

"My mom did. Someplace."

"Or maybe she just said it so you'd be on time."

"Nice. There she is. Hey, Katie. Katie."

Katie ambled across the sand slowly enough for the cute boy in the wetsuit to have second thoughts about leaving the beach so soon. She stopped to pretend to check her cell phone, but when he failed to pursue her, she dismissed him as gay and sped up.

"You don't have to yell. Sorry I'm late."

Chloe pulled a copy of *Nylon* out of her bag and turned to the feature on boot heights, hoping for advice on how best to make short legs look longer, certain that the answer would require her to buy something new. Lauren flopped on her back and closed her eyes.

"Don't you want to know why I was late?"

Lauren and Chloe glanced at each other. Katie clearly was not going to sit down unless one of them asked.

"You had to stop for Tampax?"

Katie ignored Chloe and turned to face Lauren.

"I filed." Without waiting for a reply, she plopped down between her two friends. "So I'm actually not going to stay long. I have to get a dress."

Chloe sat up and wriggled her shoulders in a way that made every part of her body shimmy. "Well. We're special."

Katie shrugged. "I need a dress. My folks are taking me out to celebrate."

"Celebrate what?" asked Lauren

"I just said. I filed."

"Everybody files," said Chloe. "Don't most people celebrate when they get in? What if Williams doesn't take you?"

"Right," said Katie. "Or, fine. If they don't, we won't go out to dinner then, but for now we are, so I have to get a dress." She lowered herself carefully onto the blanket, glanced up at the sun, and adjusted her position three times, which required Lauren and Chloe to adjust theirs as well. She untied the straps of her bikini top, wriggled out of her shorts, and tucked all the edges of her bikini bottom around each other, to make it an inch smaller in every direction. She lifted her head and set it down again, once, twice, to make sure that her hair was piled properly beneath it, and then she wiggled one last time, ever so slightly, and let out a tiny resting breath.

"Is there more?" asked Chloe.

"So I'm going to the Co-op if anyone wants to come and help me try things on," said Katie, who knew how to shut Chloe up. Some people wanted to see the Sistine Chapel; if Chloe in fact wanted to see it, and the subject had never come up, she dreamed first of buying her travel wardrobe at Barneys Co-op. The one time Katie had dragged her along, Chloe had come this close to embarrassing them both, swooning over T-shirts indistinguishable from all the other T-shirts in the world except for their three-figure price tags. Katie understood that the whole point of the Co-op was to shop with passion and without emotion, to build a wardrobe and disdain the impulse buy, but Chloe was by nature a Forever 21 girl, happiest in a store where she could buy three sweaters she did not need and still come in well under $100. Still, Katie invited her along, as though Katie were a colonial empire and Chloe a small underdeveloped nation—because it was good for her, because she might learn something. She invited Lauren because she trusted her taste, and because it was nice to have a friend to retrieve another size and bring it back to the fitting room if the salesperson was not around.

"I don't think so," said Chloe, who was dying to go. "I try to limit myself to being jealous maybe once or twice a week."

Normally, Lauren would have preferred the beach to being Katie's handmaiden, but October of senior year was a tough time to kick back on the sand. Not having anything to do, usually a welcome state at some point on the weekend, inevitably devolved into having too much to think about—like the fact that Ted had added UC Irvine to her list of Best Chances when she returned from the college trip without a better solution. People drove to Irvine for an afternoon of antiquing, and Lauren thought that college ought to be more of an adventure than looking for a vintage lamp, but Ted had insisted, and her parents, the traitors, had chimed in about what a great writing program Irvine had. She did not want to sit on a beach towel and think. Busy was better, even if it meant listening to Katie agonize over which expensive dress to buy or whether she would get any long-term use out of the adorable little clutch purse the salesgirl had suggested to go with one of them.

"Fine. We'll go," said Lauren, wondering if at this time next year she might be sitting at the edge of Lake Michigan, talking to girls she did not yet know. "We can get sushi after."

"Sushi at the Farmers Market?" asked Katie. "I can't believe you eat at that place. How fresh do you think it can be?"

"I love that place," said Chloe. "I'll go."

"It has a really good Zagat rating," said Lauren, defensively. "My mom loves them too."

"Well, fuck me," said Katie. "Fine. The Co-op and then sushi, and if I have to leave early to get ready, you can both make fun of me behind my back for being a food snob."

"I don't need to wait until you're not here," said Chloe.

"Oh, I'm sure of that," said Katie, fighting a sudden urge to get up and stomp away. "Honestly, Chloe, you know, I invite you so we can all do things together and you are such . . ."

"Oh my God," said Chloe, nudging Katie with her foot, on purpose, to make her move over a half inch.

"You're kicking me," said Katie, her voice starting to tighten.

"I am not kicking you," Chloe replied. "Maybe you could take up less than most of the blankets."

"Maybe you could move closer to the edge and we wouldn't all feel so crowded."

"I don't hear Lauren complaining about me. Lauren, am I shoving the two of you off the blankets?"

Lauren got up and grabbed her tote bag. "Will the two of you stop it? You sound like . . . like . . ."

"My parents?" said Chloe.

Lauren started to laugh. "Exactly."

"Thank you," said Katie. "Because that's how I want to think of myself, as . . ."

"Stop," said Chloe. "Only I get to bad-mouth my parents. C'mon. Let's go watch you spend money."

"Already?" said Katie. "Okay, fine. Whatever you say."

They gathered their belongings and headed across the sand toward the parking lot. Katie drew up close to Lauren.

"Haven't you filed?"

"It's not like they start reading before the first," Lauren snapped, surprised at the exasperation in her voice. "I've got a week yet. I want the essay to be right. I mean, you don't get points for being there early."

Katie was offended at Lauren's response—she had filed already because she was efficient, not because she was looking for an edge, which implied self-doubt—but she worked hard to maintain a tone of sincere concern.

"Maybe not," she said. "And I can imagine, I mean, it's got to be hard, them not deferring. I mean, you're out, you're out. That's tough. Well, see you guys there." She turned away and headed for her car.

Chloe grabbed Lauren's arm and propelled her in the opposite direction. "When she doesn't get in and you do," she said, "promise me you'll make her life hell."

chapter 7

Nora should have questioned the order when it first came in. The talent agency that was one of her biggest regular customers wanted its usual Halloween party order, three dozen each of the pumpkin mini-cupcakes, the white chocolate ghost cupcakes, the gravestones made from iced slabs of sheet cake, the chocolate skulls with edible pearls where their eyes used to be, the gingerbread bats—and eight dozen of the mini-coffins made out of chocolate wedges robed in powdered nuts.

No, they wanted three dozen of everything, as always, which the delivery boy discovered when a new agency assistant, who had spent her first workweek enduring all manner of verbal and psychological abuse, started her second week by unloading on him in the agency's towering two-story lobby. The eight was obviously a three. The delivery boy could turn around with those extra boxes and take them right back where they came from, and the screeching assistant was going to watch for the bill to make sure nobody tried to pull a fast one on her.

So the delivery boy came back to the bakery, dumped the extra boxes of chocolate coffins on one of the prep tables, repeated exactly what the assistant had said to him, punctuated by the frequent repetition of the epithet "that little bitch," and stormed out without another word to take the rest of the afternoon off. Nora gave a dozen coffins to each of her two bakers and a dozen to the woman who had taken the order, because everyone made mistakes and it was just as likely that the agency kid was being obnoxious to cover her own error. She took the last two dozen home with her, hoping that they would give Lauren a laugh, and that a laughing Lauren would take the overstock to school.

On any other night, Nora would have regaled her family with the story at dinner, complete with an impression of the delivery kid doing an impression of the assistant, but ten o'clock that night was midnight in Chicago, the last minute of the November 1 deadline for early-decision applications, and for some reason Lauren had yet to send off her application. Nora intended to keep as low a profile as humanly possible, to get her family fed, fast and early, so that Lauren could get back to work.

She was in hiding in her bedroom when Nora got home; still in hiding when Joel breezed in the front door an hour later. He tossed his briefcase on the couch, pulled a sheet of paper from it, and came toward his wife with one of his big, lifesaving smiles.

"You have to take a look at this," he said, "because it's going to keep us from going nuts. Somebody at the office printed these up." He yelled, "Lauren!" and turned back to Nora. "Where is she?"

"Upstairs. The better question is what she's doing, and . . ." She broke off when Lauren appeared in the doorway.

"Dinner ready?"

Joel held up the sheet of paper, puffed out his chest, and began to read.

"The *Jeopardy!* list of famous college dropouts. Listen to this. Tolstoy. Rush Limbaugh, okay, nobody wants you to grow up to be Rush Limbaugh, but how about Carl Bernstein. Yes, indeed. No degree after his name. Or Bill Gates."

"Joel . . ."

"Dad . . ."

"Okay, I have more, which do you want? Stupid people who went to great schools or great people who went to stupid schools?"

Lauren covered her face with her hands.

"Dad, what are you doing?"

"It doesn't matter," said Joel, triumphant. "You go to a great school, you start a war over oil. You go to a crappy school, you start spending money on women's health."

Lauren grabbed the piece of paper out of her father's hand, crumpled it up, and threw it into the kitchen sink. "Okay, I get it. Great school, bad person, not great school, better person—wait, if I don't go to college at all I can be the best me ever."

"Lauren, honey, I don't think your father . . ."

Lauren glared at them. "I'd be worried if I were you two. If I get into Northwestern who knows what might happen? I might turn into . . ."

She hesitated, and her parents waited, silent, rapt.

"A spoken-word poet. And I could have a geeky boyfriend and you'd never know it."

Joel and Nora waited to see if additional threats were coming, but Lauren had run out of steam. She moaned, "Really, I can't believe you did that," and then she slumped onto a kitchen chair.

Joel sighed helplessly. "I thought it would give you a laugh," he said. "Take the edge off. Clearly, I miscalculated."

Nora was stuck several steps back. "Why a poet?" she said.

"Why not?" said Lauren. "You don't really think you get to pick out my entire future, do you? Call me when dinner's ready."

❧

The house was locked down before nine, the dinner cleared, the dishwasher loaded, the daughter, despite her parents' attempts to find out how she was doing, once again sequestered in her room. There was nothing left for Nora and Joel to do, so they retreated to their room and pretended to read sections of the *New York Times*, which could just as well have been upside down for all the information they retained.

Since the start of Lauren's senior year, Nora had set aside time each night to read the international and national news, with the same grim diligence with which she approached the stationary bicycle. Before Lauren was born, Nora had had an opinion about everything, but once Lauren arrived she settled for asking other people questions and switched her attention to whatever Lauren happened to be reading in school. It was a conscious and happy choice. She could have done a better job of keeping up with the news, but she preferred to be ready in case her daughter ever felt like chatting about fate and free will, or social caste and destiny, or *Jane Eyre* or Daisy Buchanan or anything at all.

But in a year she would be back at the adult table, so she had to get into mental shape. She relied on mnemonics to help her remember who, exactly, was trying to topple whom. If there was a story in the paper about Iraq, she chanted, "Shi-*I*-tes say, *I* am in power, while *Suuu*nnis say, Our day is coming *soon*." She had more trouble when there was a triumvirate, because the dynamic lacked logic. For weeks she had worked hard to process the relationship between the Sudanese government and the insurgents and the Janjaweed, only to learn that the current strife was an overlay on an older civil war: same region, completely different set of combatants. How did anyone know whom to shoot at when they went to battle every morning? Did they wear colored jerseys, like sports teams? She yearned for the era when nighttime reading meant *Charlotte's Web*, for a world where moral intervention made a difference and death had at least a glancing acquaintance with nature, but she doubted she would be invited back to anyone's house for dinner next year if all she could talk about was the larger meaning of Wilbur's spared life.

At nine thirty, Lauren wandered into her parents' room to say good night, praying that they would not say anything about anything, not her dad's list, not her reaction, not her application, not her nerves, not anything.

"So," said Nora, cautiously. "Early night. You're all set."

"You bet," said Lauren. She dove in for two quick kisses. "Night, Mom. Night, Dad."

"Night, honey," said Joel, who had started channel-surfing.

"I guess we officially have an early-decision candidate in the family," said Nora as Lauren got to the doorway. "How does it feel?" She regretted having asked the moment the words were out of her mouth, but old habits died hard. Did you go potty? Did you finish the broccoli? Did you brush your teeth, floss your teeth, put in your retainer? In the early days, the last question of the night had been code for undying affection, one final maternal inquiry to bridge the time to a wakeup kiss. Lately, it felt tacked on. Nora vowed for the umpteenth time to try harder not to finish the day with a knee-jerk question, even as she waited nervously for the answer.

Lauren turned and shrugged.

"Night," she said again.

Joel waited until he heard Lauren's door click shut, and then he hit MUTE.

"You asked the wrong question," he said. "What you wanted to know was, did she file yet. Not how does it feel. You're always going to get a shrug with how does it feel."

"Well, I couldn't ask did she file yet."

"Why not?"

"Because it would sound like nagging."

Joel rolled toward her and kissed her cheek.

"And you wouldn't be nagging, no, not you."

"So how do we know she filed?" asked Nora.

"The deadline's midnight, Chicago. Twenty-seven minutes. Of course she filed."

"But how do you know that?" She turned toward him. "You like that question better? Don't play hotshot journalist with me, bub. Maybe I got fired, but it wasn't because I didn't know what I was doing."

Joel sat up, disoriented. He had no idea how to behave in this situation, and yet it was clear that he ought to do something.

"I'm going to have coffins and milk," he said. "Want some?"

"No. Honey?"

"Yeah?"

"See if she wants some. I mean, she's being a jerk, but it's a big day."

The big difference between Katharine Hepburn and my mother is that Katharine Hepburn kept her job in the research department even after the computer moved in. In *Desk Set*, one of my favorite movies, technology comes to a publisher in the form of a huge computer that's supposed to be smarter than the research department staff. But it's a romantic comedy, so of course the star gets to keep her job, and she gets the guy as well, in the form of Spencer Tracy, the consultant who's brought in to improve efficiency.

Real life is something else again. My mother used to run the research department at *Events*, the news magazine where she met my father, but three years ago that department disappeared in a wave of cutbacks. She likes to say she was replaced by a search engine. Whatever you call it, she lost a job she loved, along with four other people, and now research involves an IT employee who fields requests from the few writers who don't know how to do searches themselves. My dad, who's still an editor at *Events*, says that those reporters will likely be the next ones to go.

But this isn't an essay about getting fired. It's about

what comes after you get fired. In my mom's case, she turned her life around because she was not about to let circumstance do her in. She says she spent a good month feeling entirely lost, and then she made a list entitled Other Things I Do Well. Now she runs a local bakery. She has successfully reinvented herself.

I was frightened when she got fired, because it was the first time I'd seen someone's life change from the outside in. It would have been different if she had decided to switch careers. With the decision made for her, she had to get past a lot of negative feelings pretty fast, and she had to think for the first time in a long time about what she wanted to do. I think she was really brave not to run out and look for another research job right away. I think probably the hardest part of what she did was to try something new just because she thought it would be a satisfying way to earn a living. And my dad was great to support her in her decision.

What I learned from what happened was that I need to have faith in myself, even if the world hands me a major disappointment. It will, at some point, because nobody's life is smooth forever—and whatever it is, whenever it happens, I have to believe that I can get past it, and that I can create a solution. A lot of my friends think that deciding right now on what they want to do is the best way to move ahead, but for me college means the chance to explore my interests further and then to decide where my focus is. If I get fired a quarter of a century from now, I'll have other skills to fall back on!

It was still fifteen words too long. Lauren grabbed a pencil and scratched out "big," "one of my favorite movies," and "of course," and then she counted the number of words in the sentence about the reporters who would get fired next, scratched it out, and put the other words back in.

She turned out her bedroom light and crawled into bed with her laptop and her cell phone. She had twenty-five minutes before the filing deadline, twenty-five minutes to wrestle one last time with Northwestern's no-deferral policy. Other schools gave their marginal early-decision candidates a slim thread of hope, a deferral that dumped them into the regular applicant pool and gave them four more months to send letters reaffirming the spurned applicant's devotion to her first-choice school. Not Northwestern: the moment she sent off the application, she made herself vulnerable to a flat rejection in mid-December, just in time to be upbeat enough to complete the rest of her applications and ace her first-semester finals.

She texted Chloe.

"What are you doing?"

"You done?"

"Almost."

"Just do it. The moms are going to the financial aid meeting together."

"Fun."

"Need me to call?"

"No."

She texted Brad.

"You are so lucky not to have early decision."

"Filed anyhow to shut my dad up. What are you waiting for?"

"Who said I am?"

"Did you file?"

"Sure."

"Cool."

She thought about texting Katie and flipped the phone closed, as Katie would only make Lauren feel crazier than she already did.

9:46. She guided the mouse up and to the left until the blinking cursor sat right on top of SUBMIT, and her finger sat right on top of the mouse, like the guy with his finger poised over the red KILL button in *Syriana*, right before he blew up George Clooney and the emir and his family. He had looked like he was enjoying himself, like he was playing a video game with great resolution, concentrating hard and yet somehow unconcerned. The image on his monitor looked so very real, but there was no sense of consequence. Lauren was choking on consequence.

9:52.

What if Chloe was right and Lauren had a whole different set of priorities next spring? What if the reader thought an old movie was a silly reference?

9:55.

A knock, followed by a thin shaft of light and her father's waggling fingers. His voice came from the other side of the door, the era of barging in having ended the day he walked in before she had properly adjusted the first bikini she ever owned.

"I thought I saw a light," came his disembodied voice. "Want a coffin and milk?"

She slid the laptop under the covers and dove for her pillow.

"Already brushed my teeth. Thanks anyhow."

He opened the door wide enough to poke his head in.

"How about an abject apology before you fall asleep."

It would be quicker than an argument, she thought.

"I'm really tired, Daddy."

He stepped in, and when she did not snap at him he came over to sit next to her.

"I meant well, I really did," he said, brushing a nonexistent lock of hair off Lauren's forehead.

"It's okay, really it is," said Lauren. "G'night, Dad."

"Mom and I only want—"

"Daddy, *please*. I have a calc test tomorrow and I want to study some more before breakfast."

"Okay. I just needed to say I was sorry, and I hope you accept the apology."

"I do." She sat up quickly and kissed him on the cheek. "I have to go to sleep."

"Right." He smiled again and she tried very hard not to scream at him to get out. "Okay. I'm going to go have my dessert. There are only maybe twenty of them left for you."

She closed her eyes and turned toward the buried laptop. "Night."

"Night."

She listened to make sure he was headed downstairs, and then she dove under the covers, flipped open the laptop, repositioned the cursor, and clicked SUBMIT.

An eerie stillness sank in at Crestview on the following morning. The inland heat sucked a blanket of moist ocean fog over most of the west side, and the thick, dull gray dampness made more than one Crestview senior decide that getting out of bed was too much of an effort. Ted saw more of it every year. "Bird flu," he called it, as in early birds, which was what his predecessor had called the early-decision applicants, since shortened to Birds and used by everyone who had to deal with them. There was always a slump associated with the filing of a single, high-profile application. For twelve years—fourteen for the kids who were on Mommy and Me waiting lists before their mothers went into labor—Crestview seniors had been told that they were the masters of their fates. And then, with a single keystroke, they handed their futures over to a bunch of overworked strangers who might or might not fully appreciate how special the candidate was. For the first time in their lives, they ceded control. Sometimes the effort wore them out, and they spent a day in bed.

Regular-decision applicants like Brad came to school because they had no reason not to, but the Birds who came to school had something to prove. Katie showed up to remind everyone that she had nothing to worry about. Lauren, who might have stayed home if her parents had not worked so hard to act as though it were just another morning, took advantage of the fact that seniors did not have to show up for free periods that fell at the beginning or end of the day and skipped the early-morning anxiety stampede. She slipped in at ten, fully intending to sit out the morning break as well, and headed up to the computer lab to send her mother an email.

The fastest way to make a mom happy, all the girls agreed, was to talk to her when there was not an issue on the line. Moms figured you had to talk to them, or at least pretend to listen, when the topic was drinks in open containers or the four thousand excuses boys would use, not any time soon, of course, but someday, to avoid having to wear a condom. Random communications were something special. A daughter who instigated even the most mindless chat was a daughter who had not yet gone over to the dark side—and the comfiest refuge Lauren could think of, at the moment, was to email her mom to find out what she was going to make for dinner.

chapter 8

When Dave moved out, Deena donated the old queen-size bed to the Salvation Army and splurged on a Tempur-Pedic California king, a bed big enough to accommodate a suitor the size of a basketball star, an outsized and life-embracing bed that had yet to welcome any guest but Chloe when she had cramps. At the moment, the side where Deena did not sleep was covered in clothing. When Deena rummaged around in the closet, it was a genuine hunt for identity. She was what she wore—or rather, she wanted to be what she wore, which was why finding something that fit was such a challenge. She blithely bought clothes that ignored the passage of time, childbirth, and anything resembling propriety. She was quite possibly the most disgruntled size 4 on her block, and surely the only one over forty who owned a pair of burgundy velour sweatpants with the words "Class Act" appliquéd across the seat.

Getting dressed had gotten even harder since Dave moved out, because he took with him the two sure ways to stop Deena: one was to say that whatever she had on made him want to rip her clothes right off, and one was to thrust his wristwatch in her face and say he was leaving without her. Either way, she had to walk out the door or risk missing the very event she was dressing for.

Chloe had not yet devised an equally effective tactic, but she had set a time limit of fifteen minutes for these episodes, ten if she heard profanity, after which she staged an intervention. She perched on the edge of the bed, next to a pair of jeans that Deena had not worn since Chloe was in middle school, even though they were almost always part of the selection process. They seemed to exist only so that her mother could try them on and reject them.

"Mom."

Deena wrestled herself free of a black V-neck sweater without ever letting it come to rest on her hips. "Hand me the red top. No. Next to it, over, over, that one. Quick. I'm going to be late."

"I forget where you're going."

"Financial aid meeting."

"Wow. I didn't know we had a financial aid person."

Deena pulled the turtleneck over her head, faced the three-way mirror, and turned this way and that, smoothing the sweater over imaginary bulges. She yanked it down and sucked in her stomach, clasped her hands where a belt would be, sighed, and ruched it up for a softer profile. It was too long, and that was the irremediable sadness of Deena's life. At five feet tall when she stood up straight, she would never be willowy. She was cute, tiny, even—heaven forbid—petite. She was officially small, despite a mane of highlighted and low-lighted blond hair and a closet full of four-inch heels, and she worried about not having much of a presence.

"Mom. I'm talking to you."

When Deena turned around there were tears in her eyes and little dots of mascara on her cheeks.

"It's at Crestview," she said, in a tone of voice more appropriate to the discovery of a large red wine stain on a favorite blouse. "Thanks to your father, who just so happens to have a prior engagement tonight, ha ha, and we know what her name is, I get to go back to Crestview to humiliate myself by reminding everyone that, also thanks to your father, we don't quite see how to come up with the money we should have to send you wherever you want to go. I'm going to sweat to death in this."

Chloe reached for a blue silk top, which she handed to her mother as the red sweater landed on the floor.

"But, Mom," she said. "Rich people won't be there. How can you be humiliated if everybody else is in the same position you are?"

"Because I'm not supposed to be in that position," said Deena. "And I don't need Katie's parents looking down their noses at me to feel humiliated, thank you. I can manage that all by myself."

"Efficient," said Chloe.

"Brad's father organizes it, so he'll be there," said Deena, as though he put out a newsletter identifying everyone who attended. "Hand me the black shirt."

Chloe picked it up. "Is this new? Wow, Miu Miu? Where'd you get this? I've never seen it."

Deena snatched it away, put it on, and started to feel better before she got to the third button. "Seventy percent off, thank you. I would never pay full price for something like this," even though she had, the day she found out that Dave's girlfriend's age was a full 30 percent discount off of her own.

"I didn't ask you if you did. And you say *I'm* defensive." Chloe considered the black top, which looked nicer than anything that had preceded it. "Of course if the speaker knows anything about fashion, he's going to throw you out. Or tell you to stop shopping."

She hopped up, cried "Homework" a bit too gaily, and left Deena to finish getting dressed. She was back to inflating her extracurricular activities when Deena appeared in the doorway, a triumphant look on her face.

"Looks nice," said Chloe, who felt vaguely guilty for baiting her mother about the price tag.

"And just for the record, I know what you think. You sit there watching me, and you think, God, my mom is the biggest walking cliché on the planet. My mom is a shopaholic. How totally dumb is that?"

"I do not," said Chloe, who did, absolutely.

"Well, think about this," said Deena. "Think about how a cli-

ché doesn't exist unless there are lots and lots of people who behave that way, because otherwise no one would have thought it up
in the first place. A cliché is just lots of reality. Volume reality." She
giggled. "I am the Costco of truth. No. I'm better than that, and
you know why?"

Chloe shook her head.

"Because I know I act like a cliché, which just maybe means
I'm smarter than other people who act like me."

Deena stood up a bit taller, not easy in four-inch heels, and felt
her knees compress and complain. "I might be one of those women
caught in a web of circumstance. By a society that didn't prepare
me for life as a single parent."

Chloe smiled. Deena had been watching too many daytime
talk shows.

"You could go back to school," said Chloe, in her best supportive voice.

"Honestly, I'm late," said Deena. "You have any tests tomorrow?"

"G'night, Mom."

"G'night, Miss Smarty."

There were not enough Crestview families to fill the school library
for a financial aid workshop—or rather, there were not enough
Crestview families willing to admit publicly that they could use a
little help coming up with the over $200,000 price tag for an under-
graduate degree at a private school, not even with their retirement
accounts shrunk to pre-offspring levels and pundits predicting a
flat year, or two, or decade. So Trey, who provided the expert and
the refreshments, insisted that Crestview open its annual program
to the overtly less privileged public school parents from Ocean
Heights, whose Odyssey mini-vans and Chevys the security guard
discreetly directed to Visitor Parking, a section of the lot a safe

distance away from the Crestview parents' pristine BMWs and Mercedes.

Even with the open invitation, fewer than thirty people showed up. Ocean Heights families worried about their image as well. The ones with money or home equity stayed away to show that their public school altruism was not merely a cover for being broke. The ones who lived paycheck to paycheck and would no more pay private school tuition than they would purchase a Sub-Zero refrigerator—cold was cold, after all—had been socking money away since the kids were born. They defined the college universe as the UC system, and they wondered what was sillier: paying more than twice what the UCs cost for a private university or a tiny private college in the middle of nowhere, or wasting an evening learning how to fill out forms.

Every year, Trey drafted Brad to help set out the Pepperidge Farm cookies and powdered lemonade, and every year, Brad arranged Milanos on plastic platters, ran the wheeled trolley back and forth to the school cafeteria to refill the pitchers with lemonade, and invented a new excuse to leave early. As people began to file into the faculty dining room, he took his place behind the refreshment table, next to his dad, and leaned over to explain that he could not stay until the end.

"I'm cutting out at the break," he whispered. "Calc test."

His dad nodded. Like all of his friends, Brad used "calc test" as a generic excuse for getting out of other obligations, whether there was a test or not. Parents never asked a follow-up question about calc tests, the way they might about an in-class essay on *Hamlet* or a multiple-choice exam on World War II. Nobody remembered enough to be able to drill a kid on calculus. It was the world's safest excuse.

Ben Miller, who ran the workshop, was in charge of retirement planning at Trey's firm, earning four times his previous salary as director of financial aid for the Claremont Colleges. The financial aid workshop was his way of thanking Trey for a lucrative midlife career change; once everyone was seated, he cleared his throat and smiled his most practiced and benevolent smile.

"How many of you have been to the doctor in the last six months? Almost everybody. Great. Then pay attention. Paying for college is like going to the doctor. I had a colonoscopy recently, I'm fine, thanks, it's something we all should do, but I got a bill from the facility for over $5,000, and from the doctor for over $2,000, and from the anesthesiologist for $800, which is a pretty good hourly rate when you consider I was out for twenty minutes, tops."

He had been using the colonoscopy anecdote for so long that it was almost time to make an appointment for another. "So I called the doctor's office and you know what they said to me? 'Ben, you're not supposed to pay those amounts. That's what we bill your insurance company for, because we know they're only going to pay a tiny percentage of the total. So the more we charge, the more we stand to get back. You'll get an adjusted bill, and that's the real bill. We don't expect you to pay the first amount.'

"College is exactly like having a colonoscopy, and I'll leave it to you to make the bad jokes after I'm done up here," Ben continued. "Nobody expects you to pay the first amount. Go home and look at the websites for the big guys, for Columbia, Harvard, Yale, NYU, Northwestern, you name it. Nobody pays sticker price. Nobody! Upwards of seventy percent of the kids at these schools get some kind of help. So take out your pens and pads, and let's get to work.

"The question is not, 'Will I get financial aid,'" he intoned, with a gravity that made everyone write down what he was saying. "The question is, 'What kind of deal will I get?' Trust me. If your credit is good, if you pay your bills on time, if you beat everyone else to the punch, you, too, can go further into debt."

With that, Ben launched into the alphabet soup of financial aid—the government FAFSA forms, which overlapped but did not duplicate the College Board's CSS Profile, the Business/Farm supplement for the self-employed, which required even an urban baker to confirm that she did not own any livestock, the letter of special circumstance to explain how a family that looked fat on paper could be really strapped, somehow.

"Which leads me to another family issue that impacts your aid," said Ben. "I don't want to embarrass anyone, but how many of you are divorced, a show of hands, please?"

Deena listened for the rustling of clothes in the rows behind her before she put up her hand, and even then she raised it no higher than her shoulder, where the gesture might be mistaken for a hair flip or a neckline adjustment.

"Okay, about half of you. How many of your children live most of the time with Mom? Almost everybody. Great. Next question: How many of those moms work? Almost nobody. Anybody remember that book by what's-her-name, Betty Freedman?"

"Friedan," said Nora. "*The Feminine Mystique.*"

"There's the A student," said Ben, pointing at Nora. "Anyhow, the good news is that you're better off not reading it, and your child is better off living with Mom if Mom doesn't work." He paused for a moment, savoring the suspense. "Here is why: the government does not consider Dad's earnings if the child lives with Mom. All you have to do is have a form signed by Dad stating that the child lives with Mom. If your school only asks for the FAFSA, you move to the front of the line as far as financial aid goes."

Deena clasped and unclasped her purse in happy, nervous disbelief. Here was her life's silver lining: Chloe would qualify for a lot of money because she spent most of her time living with Deena, who had been so smart to barter time for Pilates instead of asking to be paid. Finally, they had an advantage over their married friends. She hoped that Chloe would have the sense of humor to see it that way.

After the first hour, Ben called a ten-minute break and the members of the audience descended on the cookies, their usual restraint replaced by the need for sugar and fat and chocolate and the endorphins they promised to release. Money was still out there—that was the good news. To get it, though, parents would have to tell strangers about the yawning chasm between their lifestyle and the house of cards that supported it, or simply to confess that they had fallen short despite eighteen years of economic good intentions.

For a generation that had made sexual liberation a social movement, finance was the last frontier of intimacy, and yet schools demanded to see the fiscal equivalent of their genitalia, the most private details of the financial corpus. Worse, they wanted the information online, which meant that it would fly over the same Internet that regularly belched up the sour details of people's personal lives because they had forgotten the first rule of cyberspace: Never put anything in an email that you would not want to see on a billboard. More than one parent wondered about the odds that someday their sons or daughters would fall in love with a slightly older classmate who had seen the family's file while holding down a work-study job in the financial aid office.

Brad poured lemonade and smiled at everyone who approached. He smiled even harder at the girl who had come in late and sat in the far back corner, as though he could will her to look up at him. She had long, liquid black hair that fell in a single, heavy sheet from a precise center part. It swung when she made the slightest move, and he wondered if someday he would design a roof that flowed like that, or if Gehry had cornered the market on liquid architecture, and he would have to do pleats, or maybe organ-pipe tubing, like those chocolate pipes Lauren's mom used to build a wall around a cake.

C'mon, he thought. You really need some lemonade or you're going to be way too thirsty by the end of the next part. C'mon. You need to come over and get a glass of lemonade. Please.

She did. He wrapped a napkin around a cup to make sure his fingers did not slip on the condensation as he handed it to her.

"How come you're here?" he asked.

"My dad's working," the girl replied. "My mom's at—Katie's in your class, my mom's at her house. Dr. Dodson has a party tonight." The girl flashed a wicked, slicing smile. "For the turkey packers."

"Sorry?"

"Every year she packs turkeys for poor people, and to thank the volunteers she has them over for a party before the packing day. That way they feel too guilty not to show up for the actual work."

"Your mom's a turkey packer?"

The girl considered the cookie tray and carefully selected a Milano that seemed to her more delectable than its companions, evaluated the amount of chocolate showing at each end, turned it around, and took a small bite. When she looked up her smile was not quite as wide.

"My mom is Dr. Dodson's nurse," she said, as though that explained everything. "Dr. Dodson thinks it's important for my mom to take part in the effort because that's the American way, you know. But not really take part. She passes trays of little sandwiches to the turkey packers—"

"I didn't mean to—"

"Little sandwiches made of cheeses from a friend of Katie's mom who used to be a lawyer until she gave it up to raise sheep and goats." The girl's mouth tightened in a little smirk of disapproval. "I know because she gives the leftovers to my mom every year and I have them for lunch. So does my mom. And my dad. He drives a cab. The bread's really nice, some kind of whole grain with dried cranberries and walnuts."

She cocked her head and waited to see what he would say, but before he could get a word out, two moms descended on the table, and the girl stepped aside to make room. Brad just had time to blurt out, "What's your name?" before one of the women reached over to give him a hug.

"Liz," the girl said. "You?"

"Brad," he replied.

"For heaven's sake," said Deena, who had embraced him, "don't you think I know what your name is? Or have you already forgotten me and Chloe, and you figure we forgot you, too?"

Brad turned reluctantly to Deena and Nora. "Grand, I said grand, Mrs. Haber."

Deena winced; she could not decide if she wanted Chloe's friends to call her Deena, which seemed to diminish her even further, or Mrs. Haber, which might no longer be true but implied that she had honored her commitment and Dave was the jerk, or by her maiden name, Warner, which made too much of her unfortunate change in marital status but asserted her autonomy.

"Nobody says 'grand' anymore," said Nora, reaching over for her hug, in turn. "You're spending too much time in English lit, I think. Polishing those As for Harvard."

Brad wondered where Liz was going to college. Had Nora spoken loudly enough for Liz to overhear, and would she be impressed or dismiss him as a stuck-up rich boy?

Nora hung on to Brad's hand for a moment when he gave her a lemonade.

"Oh, now, I shouldn't have said that about Harvard. I'm sorry. You kids are under so much pressure. I didn't mean to say anything. You must be counting the days. I know Lauren is. But it's not like you have anything to worry about."

"It's okay, Mrs. Chaiken. Really. I figure what's going to happen happens, y'know?"

Deena slung a brave arm around Nora's shoulders. "It's us Brad should be careful around, not us around him, for heaven's sake, how many generations at Harvard, three or four?"

"I would be fourth," he said, in the smallest voice imaginable, wishing that Liz would go back to her seat.

"Four then," said Deena. "I sometimes think they tell people like you early, on the sly, I mean, you don't have to tell, I'm just saying. Our poor girls, four more months and no idea what's going to happen. That's who needs sympathy."

She stopped, as though she had suddenly remembered something, and turned to Nora. "I told Chloe she's crazy. Why would Lauren change her mind? But . . . Wait. There's Ted. Maybe he'd answer a question for me for old time's sake."

An electrical current of hot prickles shot from Nora's shoulder blades to the crown of her head. Lauren changed her mind? About applying early? Why else would Deena say the girls had four months? But if Lauren had changed her mind, then Lauren, beloved Lauren, their only child—being a distracted parent was no excuse, how could Nora have missed this?—had lied, over and over again. Everything she had said about college since midnight on November 1, even the slightest offhand exchange, had been a deception.

Suddenly, Nora could not remember Lauren saying anything about college since November 1.

Lauren changed her mind. It was not possible, it was not feasible on any level. Then why did Deena say the girls had four months?

The prickles exploded in Nora's brain like firework stars, and she began to sweat. She drained her glass and held it out to Brad for a refill, drained it again and waited for her thermostat to drop, to no avail. She could have sucked on ice cubes without making a dent. This was flop sweat, not heatstroke, and the only thing that would make it go away would be for Deena to apologize for getting Lauren confused with someone else.

Instead, Deena came back over to the table, gave her friend a scrutinizing look, and leaned over to whisper in her ear.

"Are you having a hot flash?" she inquired.

❧

The second half of Ben's presentation was an utter blur to Nora. She spent most of her energy figuring out how to get to Ted first when the event ended, in much the same way that she charted the fastest path to the nearest exit door whenever she got on a plane. She evaluated the obstacles, identified the competitive sprinters, and defined the quickest route, which might not be the shortest. She had a strategy in place, only to watch Ted slip out of the room as the conversation about need-blind aid got heated. She had to clamp her hands to the folding chair to keep from running after him.

She listened to the rest of Ben's presentation in a daze, preoccupied by the new question of what she would say when she got home.

"... highly emotional, very stressful time ..."

"... big checking account balance—will they think we're too rich?"

"... small checking account balance—will they think we're too poor?"

"... sixty-five years old? Great. The government thinks you're retired."

When Nora got to the point where she thought she might burst into tears, she nudged Deena, mimed getting a text message, and whispered that she had to leave.

❧

This was the first year that Liz had not been home doing homework on the night when Yoonie passed sandwiches to the turkey packers, and as she drove up Carmelina Street, looking for the

Dodsons' house, she wondered if she might catch a glimpse of her fashion benefactor when she picked up her mom. If Katie seemed pleasant enough, Liz might attempt a careful, mutual compliment, something about sharing National Merit and probably valedictorian, as well as sweats. There was a good basis for potential friendship here, she thought, surely a likelier connection than with too many of the girls at Ocean Heights.

Liz pulled up in front of the Dodsons', hurried to the door, and rapped the heavy bronze lion's head against it twice. Her first thought, when Katie opened the door, was that they were not the same size at all. Katie was a good four inches taller, bigger-boned, with the shoulders of a girl whose parents had put in a pool and hired a private instructor when she was a toddler. The business about Dr. Joy giving Katie's fashion mistakes to Yoonie to give to Liz was a hoax. Liz stared at Katie and wondered if she and her mother were co-conspirators. When they went shopping, did Dr. Joy steer Katie toward the sale rack to see if there was anything the anonymous Liz might like? The inherited clothes had always made Liz feel ever so slightly superior—her mom's boss might be rich, but she did not even know how to dress her daughter—but now she saw the discards for what they really were, charity disguised as fashion errors to hide the element of pity. For an instant she wondered if her own mother had known about the charade, if Katie had dropped by her mother's office one afternoon, or come out of her room during an earlier turkey packer meeting, confronting Yoonie with the two-size gap between her boss's daughter and her own. Liz would not be able to bring herself to ask, because she thought it entirely possible that Yoonie would have endorsed the deception, would have pretended not to notice, in the name of providing for her only child. It was all she could do not to bolt and leave her mother stranded.

"I'm here to pick up my mom," she said.

"Right," came the uninterested reply. Katie turned to head back down the hall, yelling, "Yoonie, your daughter's here," as she did so. She pointed to the left—"In there"—and peeled off to the right, leaving Liz to wonder what would happen if she left off the "Doctor" in "Doctor Joy" some day. At that moment both mothers appeared in the doorway, and Dr. Joy held out a Victoria's Secret bag to Liz.

"Tomorrow's lunch," she said.

"Thank you," said Liz.

She and her mother drove home in silence. Yoonie was tired enough to accept without question Liz's suggestion that they save the financial aid report for dinner the next day because it was so late and Steve would already be asleep. Liz sat on her bed in her clothes until the sound of her mother's footsteps stopped, and then she sat for fifteen minutes more, to give her mother time to fall asleep. She tiptoed to the end of the hall, where her father had wedged a tiny stacking washer and dryer and a set of shelves into what had been a closet, and pawed through the folded clean clothes until she found the hoodie and sweats she had worn on the day she filed her Harvard application. She would miss their softness, but she congratulated herself on what she was about to do. She stuffed them into her backpack behind the textbooks, so that she could deposit them in the lost-and-found when she got to school the following morning.

Nora dropped Deena off at home, pulled into the parking lot of the first mini-mall she saw, and called Joel.

"Where's Lauren?"

"Upstairs, want me to get—"

"No. Listen to me. She lied to us."

"About what?"

"She didn't apply to Northwestern."

A loud computerized voice filled the ensuing silence, bleating, "Cross Ocean Park Now, Cross Ocean Park Now" into the empty crosswalk. The city of Santa Monica, the institutional equivalent of a helicopter parent, watched out for all of its citizens in all aspects of their daily lives, including the unsighted pedestrian who might appreciate a sound cue to avoid being run down by a silent hybrid. Nora watched the traffic light's signal count down the seconds of her husband's surprise, 15, 14, 13, as the mechanical voice continued to bleat into the void.

At 3, Joel finally cleared his throat. "Honey, sure she did. I saw her."

"You saw her."

2, 1, flashing orange hand, solid orange hand, and then the little white man who always crossed from left to right. Nora wondered: Didn't he ever want to cross back the other way, to go home?

"I went in, it was almost midnight, in Chicago, I mean, it was almost ten. I was seeing if she wanted dessert, remember, you said to. I'm sure she was done."

"But you didn't see her."

"No."

"She wasn't sitting in front of the laptop?"

"Stop. Let me think this through." Joel had been raised by a father who thought he was a prince and a mother who thought he was a god, but all their loud talk of his perfection had had an unintended effect. While he might be smarter than almost all of the occupants of any given room, on any given day, he was quicker to doubt himself because no one could possibly live up to his parents' expectations. Even Marv and Sheila seemed to know that. Having deified their son at an early age, they spent the rest of their lives questioning their faith, enumerating the ways in which Joel's day-to-day execution fell short of the perfect abstraction

GETTING IN

they worshipped. They had a list of the superlative things Joel could have been or done if he had not married so young, if he had gone on to graduate school, if he had picked law or medicine, if his wife had not lost her job, if Joel and Nora had not spent all that money on a private school, to say nothing of real estate in California, when Pittsburgh had such beautiful homes for less than half the price.

He had moved as far away as he could without having to flee the country, but his image hung over him at moments like this. When confronted with his own fallibility, his response was always the same: denial, defensiveness, attack.

"Who the hell says she didn't file?"

"Deena."

"There's a reliable source. And she would get this from Chloe, right, the James Frey of her generation. Just come home and we'll ask her what's up."

"You get to go first," said Nora, slapping her phone shut, knowing that he wouldn't. Optimists had it easy. All they had to do was delude themselves a bit longer, and the impatient realists of the universe would step in to figure out what was really going on.

❦

Lauren was in her room when Nora got home, so she and Joel set the stage for civility: a pitcher of milk, a bowl of apple slices, the maple walnut cakes they had already had three times this week, while Nora struggled to make them not look so unrelentingly tan.

"Honey," Nora called upstairs, "take a break. Have dessert with us." She turned to Joel with a black look. "There. Your turn."

"Jesus, Nora, what does it matter . . ."

"What does what matter?"

Nora looked up as Lauren came down the stairs, knowing that they were less than a minute from trouble, and her brain, displeased with the evening's programming, sought refuge in reruns of earlier episodes. Lauren the eighteen-year-old took a step and became Lauren the birdy twelve-year-old, all eyes and braces and bony angles; took another step and became Lauren the stern eight-year-old, who knew more than anybody about anything, including how much she would hate her mother into all eternity for endorsing a more practical short haircut; became Lauren the five-year-old dirigible, a floaty little pillow with limbs; became Lauren the barely two-year-old, who yelled "I go myself" before she launched herself down those stairs in an extended somersault that required three stitches under her left eye.

What does what matter, indeed, thought Nora. For an instant, she considered letting Lauren play out the charade, because in the next scene, there would be no Lauren on the stairway at all, which was the part of the college plan that nobody talked about much. Right now, at this exact moment, they were together and she was a happy kid—a liar, but a happy liar, and maybe a happy liar was better than an honest but miserable child. That made no sense, of course, unless Lauren had lied because her parents put too much pressure on her and it was the only way she could keep from collapsing under the strain. If lying was self-defense, then Nora and Joel were the guilty ones for not realizing how tense Lauren was. That made no sense, either: what was the point of working so hard at Crestview if not to get to the next step? And what would they do on December 15 if they said nothing—pretend not to notice that there was no letter, fat or thin, from Northwestern?

"Y'know, I don't care if you never get these things to look right as long as you keep making samples," said Lauren, sliding into the booth and grabbing a little cake. Brad had texted Lauren to warn her about what Chloe's mom had said, but he could not say for sure if Lauren's mom had actually gotten it—so there was no point in confessing right off the bat, not until she had a better sense of how much her parents knew. The smart move was to act as though everything was fine, and to hope that too many college-era rock concerts had blown out her mother's high-range hearing, about as realistic a hope as imagining that Ted would engineer a last-minute save, which was what had kept her from confessing so far. If only a miracle had happened, and Northwestern had rolled back the hands of time for her, she would have retired the truth for ten or fifteen years, by which point it would have aged into funny. That had been her plan until she got Brad's text. Now she had to wait for her parents to make the first move.

They did not, which was a bad sign.

"Aren't the two of you sitting down?"

Nora and Joel slid in on either side of Lauren, and for a long moment there was no sound except for appreciative chewing and swallowing.

"Honey, you're all set at Northwestern, right?" Joel asked the question without raising his eyes from his plate.

The room had been quiet before Joel said anything, but now it was tomb silent, soundless for miles and miles and miles down toward the center of the earth.

"What do you mean?" asked Lauren. When confronted with the accusation of fraud, no matter what the circumstance, the accused always asked first for clarification, in case the interrogator knew so little that evasion was still a possibility.

Joel sighed. "Deena said to your mom that you were applying regular like Chloe, and I said she must be mistaken . . ."

Nora put down her fork with unnecessary force. "Which makes me the only one who thinks Lauren lied to us? Great, Joel."

"That's not what I meant and you know it. We have to consider the source, is all."

"Of course, but can't we ask a simple question and get—"

"Excuse me. If the two of you are going to argue I can go back upstairs."

"Never mind," said Nora, determined to get a straight answer. "Did you file? You said you filed."

"No," said Lauren, dividing her remaining cake into microscopic wedges. "Yes, I did, but I missed the deadline. And I didn't actually say I filed. I sort of didn't say anything."

"How could you miss the deadline?" asked Nora. "You were done when you came in to say good night. All you had to do was submit it."

"I know that. I finished but I didn't send it, and then I missed the deadline."

"Dad said he came in to say good night . . ."

"And why did he walk into my room without knocking?"

"I did knock," said Joel. "It was five to ten. You still hadn't filed?"

"Does Ted know?" asked Nora.

Lauren rolled her eyes. "I went in to see him the next day. I went as soon as I got the email saying thanks and we'll let you know in April. I've been to see him three or four times. He said if I have great first-semester grades it could end up being a good thing, which just means he wouldn't call them."

"He's known all this time?" asked Joel.

Lauren ignored him. "The very next morning, I said please can't you call them, say we had a power surge, say the clocks were wrong, *say my parents thought dessert mattered more than college.* But I'm not Katie. Why should he bother with somebody who took regular science?"

"You can't expect him to ask them to take a late application," said Nora, who had no idea why she was defending a man who had not bothered to call her or Joel. Why should he call them? He probably assumed their daughter shared this kind of news with her parents. "I mean, if they did it for you they would have to do

it for everyone. A deadline's a deadline. I really don't understand
how—"

Lauren cut her off.

"I know why Dad came in. Because he figured I was going to
screw it up." Lauren's eyes got huge as she realized where her
bobsled logic was taking her. She recoiled from Nora as though
her mother were wearing a sandwich board that read, "I have an
antibiotic-resistant staph infection."

"You told him to come in, didn't you?" Lauren said. "You
said, 'Honey, I bet she fell asleep or she's not watching the clock,
go be a good dad and pretend you just wanted to say good night.'
That worked really well, didn't it? Maybe if the two of you acted
for once like I wasn't going to blow it, then maybe I wouldn't
have blown it. Except now that I have, you get to say I told
you so."

Her parents were too stupefied to reply.

"I'm going to go finish my homework now." She glared at Nora.
"I need you to move," she said, and Nora, not knowing what else
to do, dutifully got up and let Lauren out. Without another word,
Lauren shuffled toward the staircase, slogged up the stairs, and
quietly closed her bedroom door.

"Well, that's that," Nora spat. "I give up." She, too, headed for
the staircase, though she did not bother to be quite as careful about
how she shut the bedroom door.

Joel rubbed his scalp with the fervor of a Boy Scout trying to
pass the kindling test, hoping to spark an inspiration, and when
none came, he trudged up the stairs, still rubbing, still hoping. He
stood outside his daughter's room and listened to the kind of
abandoned sobbing that guaranteed this episode a slot on her psy-
chotherapy top ten, and then he knocked.

"Go away."

He headed for the other end of the hall, leaned against the
bedroom door, and listened to his wife's remorseful weeping, an

infrequent but bottomless sorrow specific, as far as he could tell, to women who thought too much. During the fall and winter holiday season, an exhausted Nora joked about wanting to be Deena in her next life, not working and not caring, so that she could spend her days shopping and exercising and beautifying and trying new recipes, without ever feeling that she was wasting time. During the slow months, she spoke admiringly of Joy's initiative and made up seasonal promotions to keep from having too little to do. Occasionally, she preferred to be herself, but never without self-doubt. Sometimes it seemed to Joel that baking was what Nora did to occupy herself while she questioned her life—but now he wondered if a bit more introspection on his part might have given him a clue about how to behave at this exact moment in time. He was of no use to either of the crying women in his life; he knew better than to knock on his and Nora's bedroom door, be-cause behind it was the kind of second guessing that defied inter-vention.

"Well, I'll be downstairs," he announced in a loud voice, "if anyone feels like talking." He retreated down the stairs, wrapped up the remaining cakes, and washed all the dishes. No one was moving upstairs, so he collapsed on the couch and turned on CNN, in the hope that one international disaster or another would help him put all of this in an appropriate context. A few hours later, he awoke to the latest on the first high-profile heterosexual male prostitute to surface inside the Beltway, surely a blow for gender equity. He took a few notes for the following day's edito-rial meeting, turned off the lights, and headed upstairs, to find Nora awake in the dark.

They confessed to wondering the same thing: Was North-western—was any school—worth all this arguing? Whether Lauren had lied to them was beside the point. All that mattered, finally, was whether she would talk to them in the morning—or had they unwittingly stepped over a line that only became visible as the parental foot landed on the far side?

"There's a happy thought," whispered Nora, reaching for a matted tissue. "Our daughter? Oh, yes. We're very proud. She got into her first choice, Northwestern. We haven't heard from her since."

chapter 9

Nora surveyed the backyard and automatically started running a tally in her head. Not a canopy but a drop-sided tent, a tuxedoed three-piece combo, a portable dance floor to protect the lawn, bistro tables on the patio and around the pool, a full bar and two bartenders, glassware not plastic, flatware not plastic, china not plastic, cloth napkins and tablecloths, not paper. She was at $4,000, and still adding, when a moonlighting aspiring actor appeared in front of her with a tray.

"Pigs in blankets," said the server, who had just been told by a pretty female guest that he looked like the young coroner on one of the cop shows. "Actually not, since it's Niman Ranch organic beef and pigs in blankets are pork, aren't they? Anyhow, it's artisanal garlic mustard, and besides, how weird would it sound to say cows in blankets? Big old cows. Not a tasty image." Nora took three just to make him go away and handed two of them to Joel. Lauren, who had been at her side a moment ago, had already taken off in Chloe's direction.

"You have to admire the chutzpah," said Nora.

Joel raised an eyebrow.

"What if Katie hadn't gotten into Williams?" asked Nora. "I mean, you have to have a pretty positive outlook on life to schedule a party the weekend after the early kids find out."

"I don't think they spend a lot of time on what-if," said Joel. He peeled off toward the bar.

Joy and Dan threw their annual holiday party on the first Sunday of winter break, before any of their close friends left for Vail or Napa or Santa Fe. Their other dinner parties involved no more than twelve people, seating charts, and multiple catered and served courses, and the most highly prized invitation among those choreographed events was the spring dinner, which always involved an unusual theme and the hosts in appropriate costume. The holiday party was a clearinghouse event: the Dodsons got to reciprocate for every invitation they had received during the past year, catch up on what everyone else was doing, and remind the guests that their life was hard to beat.

Nora wandered over to the dessert table, as she did every year, to see who had won the job. Fugusweet. Of course. Little desserts designed to look like sushi rolls, with Rice Krispies and flavored marshmallow paste replacing the rice, and chocolate, fruit, flavored cream, or all three in place of the fish. Standing in for the nori wrapper, a thin, brittle band of chocolate that melted almost immediately, which was why they were served with miniature chopsticks and plated on a tray inside a tray, surrounded by a moat of ice that had to be refreshed on the half hour. Nora hated high-maintenance food, but Fugusweet had a publicist and three celebrity investors, women who never ate an entrée, let alone a dessert, but who hosted the launch party and provided quotes to the food magazines. They had been featured in *InStyle*. She should have guessed.

Joy came up next to her and adjusted one of the platters a half inch to the left. "I know. I know. I order the desserts and then at some point at three in the morning I always wonder why I didn't call you. We have this conversation every year, don't we?"

"We do, and then you say, 'Because I think of you as Lauren's mom who happens to bake, not as a baker who happens to be Lauren's mom.' It's okay. Really."

"Oh God, do I say exactly the same thing every year?"

"Pretty much," said Nora. "But seriously, if I did the food I wouldn't have a good time, which is what I say every year."

Joy smiled, adjusted the tray back to its original position, fixed her gaze on a row of mango and papaya rolls with green-tea marshmallow filling, and waited for Nora to say what she was supposed to say.

"Oh, listen, forget dessert, congratulations on Katie and Williams. It's great, really great. Sort of makes this a big celebration for all of you."

"Well, we're thrilled for her, I must say. You holding up okay?"

"I'm sorry?"

"Well, Lauren not filing at the last minute like that. It must've made you crazy. Having to wait now with everybody else must . . ."

"We talked it over." Nora was amazed at how easily the lie slid out of her mouth, how nimbly she and Joel and Lauren had transformed a foolish error into a consensus strategy. "She wanted more time. I understand that. We're fine. She'll have a nice choice in April."

"I'm sure she will. I just don't have the stamina, I have to tell you." Joy reached over to grab a chunk of white-chocolate roll and pointed her laden chopsticks in Nora's direction. "Want to give me your professional opinion?"

Nora shook her head. "No, no. Too many good appetizers before I get to dessert. Where is Katie? I should congratulate her in person."

Joy waved in the general direction of the house. "Do I know? Changing her dress or something. Making an entrance. Where's Lauren? I'm going to tell her to hang in there."

Nora made an equally vague gesture toward the tables by the swimming pool, betting that the demands of being the perfect host would keep Joy from following through. There was no such thing as privacy midway through senior year, and she might as well stop trying to act as though there were. She could be more productive saving Joel, who was being bored silly by the tax attorney who lived next door to Dan and Joy. They saw him every year at the party, and every year he assumed that they had forgotten him.

"It's easy, really," he always said. "I'm the only guy from my class at Yale who didn't join the CIA," and they would laugh and talk about spook movies until an empty plate or an empty glass gave them an excuse to move on.

Katie was ready to go as soon as the little dashes of blood dried. She had almost made it out the door, but she lingered a moment too long in front of the mirror, and it hit her, as it did on an almost hourly basis, that she was the envy of pretty much everyone but herself. She was in early at Williams, she was the other seniors' dream come true, except that she would always wonder if she would have been happier at Yale. No. She would always wonder if she would have been happier with a choice she had made herself.

She sat on her desk chair, the skirt of her dress hiked up and wrapped around her waist and her underwear down around her ankles, and considered her fingernails, which was where the trouble had started. A week before the beginning of junior year, Katie had decided that shredded cuticles and battered nails were no way for a college applicant to present herself to the world. Her stubby nails barely made it to the end of the nail beds, and ellipses of dried blood marked the places where she had tugged too hard on a hangnail. An Ivy League admissions officer was not going to want to shake hands with those mangled paws, so Katie had announced to her parents that the bad habit ended that day. She never did it again.

While her mother marveled at her self-discipline and her father praised the quality of her handshake, Katie cast about for a replacement activity to soothe her nerves. She found it by accident one day, when her brand-new Tweezerman slipped past her left eyebrow and nicked her left hand, which was pulling the eyebrow taut for easier tweezing. A single drop of blood bloomed in the space between her thumb and forefinger. It hurt, enough to notice but not to last, enough to be exactly the kind of wicked little thrill she was looking for.

It felt good and bad all at once, and the only question was how she might do it again without drawing attention. Because she spent a lot of time in public in a tank suit, she had few options—and because she had far more self-respect than the real cutters she heard about, the ones who went at themselves with no regard for the possibility of permanent scarring, she was not going to slash hash marks on the insides of her thighs, even if she could. This was not that. This was her own private joke until she left home. She settled on the line between her pubic hair and her belly, which she punctured with the point of the tweezers, not often, but every now and then, never more than two cuts at a time, none of them longer than a quarter inch. She waved her hand back and forth over the two little marks and pressed a finger against them to make sure they were dry. Almost.

She ought to be happy. She knew she ought to be happy, which made everything worse. She got no pleasure from being better off than friends who had to wait until April to find out where they were going. She took no solace from Ted's sermonette about the seniors who went to "Whew U," which was whatever school accepted them, because the fate of kids who were lucky to go to college at all had nothing to do with her. That was like saying she should be grateful for soggy French fries because people somewhere were starving—not that Williams was the equivalent of soggy fries, obviously not, but the point remained. If the world as her family defined it was the Ivy League universities plus Williams, and if her personal rankings put Yale ahead of Williams, then in a way, she had failed.

Katie stopped herself. She would feel better, she knew she would, as soon as she got out of this house and away from Crestview and the circle of friends that was beginning to smother her. She had no idea that it was possible to be seventeen and happy, because she mistook her chronic dissatisfaction for ambition and assumed that true happiness was by definition farther down the road, after she had reached some of her goals. Anyone who seemed to be enjoying herself now—Chloe, or even Lauren—was not working hard enough on her future.

She rubbed her hand more vigorously across her belly and turned her palm up for inspection.

Done. Good. She pulled up her new ivory lace bikinis and smoothed her dress. Time to get downstairs and accept congratulations. Some of the guests probably were not aware that Williams was number one on the *U.S. News & World Report* list of liberal arts colleges.

⚜

This year's party was a particular minefield, because so many of the guests had children at Crestview. The seniors took refuge at the far end of the pool; whenever Nora looked over she saw Lauren, Brad, and Chloe huddled at a table, joined occasionally by Katie and her posse of early-decision friends, Mike at Williams, Jim at Wesleyan, Jeanie at Penn, the latter allowed into the inner circle because she posed no threat to Katie in terms of the boys, not until she got her complexion under control. If a parent veered in their direction they scattered like nervous prey animals, pretending to need more food or drink, settling back in their seats only after the threat had faded. And it was all too easy to distinguish parents of earlies from the rest: they mingled aggressively, trolling for adults who had not yet heard the good news, while the parents of deferrals and regular applicants gravitated toward the dance floor or tried to engage a server in small talk.

"I'm thirsty," said Nora, to the strains of "White Christmas" with a salsa beat. "How's the bar look?"

Joel peered over her shoulder at the bar. "Trey's just ordering a drink, Deena's up next, and the guy who always says his son is on the Harvard track is drinking something blue."

"This is crazy. We have nothing to be worried about. Do we?"

"I like the way you phrase that. 'We're fine. Aren't we?'"

"I just hate it when Joy noses around."

"Oh, please. What's the second-best thing about your kid getting in early, other than your kid getting in early?"

Nora drew back to look at him.

"I'll bite. What's the second-best thing about your kid getting in early?"

"Somebody else's kid's not. People don't put decals on their cars because they need to be reminded where their kids go to school. They put them on to impress the person behind them at the traffic light. Joy's happy about Katie going to Williams, but she's happier"—and he pushed the *er* for emphasis—"because Lauren doesn't know what she's doing yet."

❧

Trey did not believe in luck, but he did appreciate coincidence, and he was pleased to see Alexandra walking toward him with a plate of desserts as he started talking to Lauren's parents. Now he had a reason to stay put for a while, and they had an obligation to sit with him, because Alexandra could be counted on to flit right off again and it would be rude to leave him there to eat alone. Ten minutes earlier and he would have been stuck talking about financial aid with that daft woman whose kid had left Crestview before junior year. Ten minutes later would have put him who knows where. He was grateful for his wife's timing, if a little sad that it in no way illustrated a special sensitivity on her part.

He had hated parties since the days when he and his brothers sat halfway up the curving stairway of his parents' house, each of them in powder blue pajamas with navy piping that were just like their father's, while below them the adults washed down the workweek with martinis made by a white-jacketed bartender. He could never make sense of it—the random noise, the milling people, the unexpected outburst from a friend's mom best known, during daylight hours, for her generous dexterity with a waffle iron. Parties seemed to him an unpredictable and inefficient waste of time, and large ones, like the Dodsons', were the worst, because the odds of getting caught talking to an idiot increased with the size of the crowd.

He gestured to one of the little bistro tables and settled in with Nora and Joel.

"So," he said, debating whether to use the pair of chopsticks as intended or a single one as a spear, "you decided to wait it out. Interesting choice. May work to Lauren's advantage in the end."

Joel felt Nora reach for his hand under the table.

"You think so?" Nora asked. She had no idea how failing to file could possibly be a good move, but she had been a researcher for too long to lead with her own ignorance. The trick was to inquire as though you already knew the answer and were merely being polite enough to seem interested. That was how you found out things you wanted to know and kept yourself from giving anything away.

"Sure I do," said Trey. He picked up a single chopstick, impaled the slice of sushi roll that looked to contain the most chocolate, and popped it in his mouth whole. He swallowed without much chewing. Nora shuddered slightly. Trey would have been the first member of the Donner party to take out his collapsible picnic ware, she was sure of it.

"Think about it," he went on. "The early apps are all valedictorians, all ranked athletes, all legacies, you're swimming with sharks. Sharks. How do you distinguish yourself in that rarefied environment?"

"But Ted says they fill a quarter of the class early," she replied, feebly, "maybe more."

"Let them have the first slots," said Trey. "They would have gotten them anyhow. Those spaces were never really in play, I don't care what Ted says. Never."

Nora felt Joel lean forward slightly. "But if she waits for regular admissions she's at the top of the heap for the rest of the class," he said.

"Exactly," said Trey. "Now she stands out. Now she's one of the ones they really want. Long shot for the early spaces or standout for the rest. What makes sense to you?"

"Then why would Ted push so—"

"Yield," said Trey. "The colleges aren't the only ones who want their numbers to look good. The more kids Ted gets locked in early at the top schools, the better his year looks. What does he care if Lauren's a long shot? Maybe she gets lucky, and if she doesn't, he hasn't lost a thing. Besides, once he has the earlies socked away, he knows where he can lobby. If Northwestern doesn't take an early, it's a clear field."

"They took two kids," said Nora, mournfully. Whiplash, this was all whiplash, no better than the studies that said do not take hormones, except whatever you do, take hormones. Trey was making an utterly logical argument that contradicted everything Ted had ever said.

"Two? Who?"

"The boy who's in all the musicals . . ."

"No competition. Different department. The other one?"

"Boy," said Joel. "The kid who wins the Latin prize every year, what's his name?"

"Irrelevant," said Trey. "Minority candidate. And no girls. This is a great opportunity. Did she interview?"

"When we visited last spring." Nora's head was spinning.

"Doesn't matter. Get her an alumni interview out here. Here's the thing," said Trey. "You can agonize over what was the right thing, or you can make this the right thing. Take advantage of all the time you have before April 15. Mount a campaign for Lauren."

He speared another piece of sushi, but the combination of dried fruit and rice was too sticky, and he mutely waggled a finger in the direction of Nora's iced tea, which she pushed toward him. Trey took a drink, swallowed hard, and waited a moment to see if he could breathe—which gave Nora enough time to locate what was left of her sanity.

"Sometimes," she said, "sometimes I'm just not sure about doing that. I mean, sometimes I think why break her heart investing so much in a single school. We're not even sure who else is applying there. I mean, we hear rumors but she can't go up to some kid she barely talks to and ask what her GPA is and whether Northwestern's her first choice."

Trey let out a short, impatient breath. "She's a great girl. Don't assume she's going to get her heart broken. Stand up for her."

"It's not that," said Nora. "I wish she didn't have a first choice, to tell you the truth. Everybody gets so caught up in having a first choice. I mean, it's different for Brad."

Trey allowed himself a dry little smile and tried not to think about his older son. "Yes, I think for us the challenge was simply to make sure he didn't do anything so bizarre as to draw attention," he said. "The boy was born on the on-ramp, I guess you could say. He would have to work awfully hard to lose his place in line."

He mistook Nora's wide-eyed expression for admiration until he felt a hand on either shoulder.

"Wow," said Brad, who had come up behind his father with Lauren and Chloe in tow. "I thought I was born on the donor floor at Cedars. Who knew?"

Trey flinched and berated himself for talking about Brad without looking around first to see where his son was. Ever since the clarinet conversation, he had been careful to provide at least the illusion of taking Brad's concerns to heart—an admiring comment about a professor at another school who had won an architecture prize, or, better still, days in a row when he made no reference to Harvard at all. Now he had let down his guard for a moment and betrayed his real feelings, which boiled down to a collegiate version of manifest destiny.

He was scrambling for a clever response when Nora came to his rescue.

"Everyone should have such a problem," she said. "On-ramp to Harvard. Must be on the freeway past the bakery, because I haven't seen it."

"I can't believe you guys are sitting here figuring out our futures for us," said Lauren. "Can you give Chloe's mom a ride home so we can take her car? We're ready to leave."

✦

They were gone, and Trey was trying to change the topic to football. Nora excused herself to collect Deena, who was standing in front of the desserts but not taking any.

"Please," said Nora, with surprising exasperation. "Just eat the damn things."

"Easy for you to say," said Deena. "Joy said I looked great, considering. What the hell does that mean?"

"Look at it this way," said Nora. "You probably burned a couple hundred calories just torturing yourself, so you're even. Eat the dessert. We want to go home."

"Nice," said Deena, wolfing two pieces before her taste buds had time to process the flavors. "Let's go."

Joel was silent all the way to Deena's, grateful to have her around, for once, because she, like Chloe, talked more when she was nervous. They sat in front of her house for five minutes while she finished a tirade about Dave and the financial aid forms, but happily she ran out of breath as Joel was about to run out of patience. He waited until she had closed her front door, and then he took off down the street, ignored a yield sign, and roared through a yellow light that turned red before he was halfway across the intersection.

"Joel."

"Sorry." He jerked the wheel toward the curb, pulled up at a bus stop, and pounded the steering wheel a couple of times. Joel rarely lost his temper, so when he did get angry he tended to overdo it; no point in settling for being slightly miffed if it only happened a couple of times a year.

"Feel better?"

"How many legacies you think there are at Penn by now?" he asked, not expecting an answer. "Or Wisconsin, if you want to be helpful here. Hundreds of thousands? Millions?"

"She doesn't want to go to either of those."

He hit the steering wheel again, and Nora jumped. "I know that. I'm just saying, we are not exactly a huge help. I knew a guy at Northwestern's journalism school. Maybe I should have called him, but no, wait. I forgot. He got fired for thinking new technology meant an electric typewriter."

"You're exaggerating."

"Maybe."

A shadow, a knock: a large, uniformed gut blocked the afternoon sun, and a black-gloved hand rapped on the car window and made a rolling gesture to get Joel to lower it.

"Good afternoon, sir. Is everything okay?"

"Good afternoon, officer," said Joel. "Everything's fine. Did I do something wrong?"

The officer rested one hand on the roof of the car to steady himself as he leaned over.

"Well, sir, the yellow light was a judgment call, but you hauled over to the curb pretty hard, you're occupying a marked city bus zone, and I notice you've been hammering that steering wheel." He leaned forward, so that his eyebrows and mustache were inside the car. "Are you okay, ma'am?"

"Oh, for God's sake, she's—"

"Excuse me, sir. Are you okay, ma'am?"

"I'm fine," said Nora, who was desperately afraid she was going to start laughing. The last time a cop asked her if she was okay was two nights before they got married, when they were inspired to consider sex on a darkened side street as the best antidote to an influx of relatives. Happily, that cop had shone his light in the car before they got around to anything for which they could be hauled in, but Nora was thinking about it, and she knew Joel was, too, and she prayed that this cop would give up before one or the other of them fell apart. The officer did not strike her as someone who would enjoy the joke.

"Officer, really, I'm to blame," she said. "My contact lens slipped, it's so painful if you've never had that happen, and my husband didn't know what was wrong, just that I was sort of shrieking." She smiled. "And then of course once he found out it was only a lens, well, that's the pounding on the steering wheel part. Because it scared him, you know, the shriek, never a good thing when someone's driving. I'm so sorry."

Joel almost choked. Nora had conned the previous cop into believing that her disheveled appearance was the result of wild grief, something to do with a nonexistent but credible and ailing maiden aunt. Where did she get this stuff?

"Even so," said the cop, "driving your feelings. Very bad thing."

"You're right, officer. I should be more careful."

"Okay, then, folks. You have a good day, and drive safely."

He got back on his motorcycle and roared off. Joel pulled into the first mini-mall he saw, parked the car, and rested his forehead on the steering wheel.

"I liked the first bust better, somehow. Poor Aunt Bertie."

"I knew you were thinking that," said Nora.

"Maybe we should have pushed her harder," said Joel. "You're supposed to push girls, up to a point, aren't you?"

"Stop," said Nora. "We did what we did. It's my job to second-guess, not yours."

"But if we didn't make a mistake, then the schmuck's right," said Joel. "We have to figure out what else we can do."

Chloe chased dusk north past Topanga, past the Malibu Colony, out to Zuma Beach. She was not one for the big, smog-tinted summer sunsets that drew people to the beach like so many pilgrims to Mecca; she preferred the way a winter sky deepened to indigo, and when she had the car she liked to drive the coast to watch it happen.

The problem was that eventually the sun set, the sky stopped changing color, and three goal-oriented seniors found themselves driving aimlessly, not something that a senior was supposed to do, not even on winter break.

"Hey, turn around and we'll go to La Salsa," said Brad.

"How can you be hungry?" asked Chloe.

"Because, I don't know, I am." He rolled down the passenger window and stuck his head out like a dog collecting scents. "Pull over and we can turn around. And then you can drop me at the on-ramp to Harvard."

Lauren leaned forward from the backseat. "I should go home," she said. She had seen the concern in her father's eyes as they approached the table. She was used to that look from her mom, but her dad was a master of the poker face, an occupational hazard, he said, born of too many years of trying not to look rattled when publishers in $2,500 suits announced more budget cuts. If her dad was worried, then life was not so good, a notion that folded right into her doubts about getting to the first week of April in one piece. When Lauren got upset she deflated like yesterday's birthday party balloon, at which point she needed to be off by herself.

"It's winter break," said Chloe. "What's this 'should go home'?"

"I have apps," said Lauren.

"And you have weeks still," said Chloe, "so stop it."

They doubled back and drove to La Salsa, and the girls waited in the car while Brad ordered. He emerged moments later with a cardboard drink caddy and a bag too big for a single meal, handed each of them an order of chips and guacamole and a Diet Coke, and went to work on his chicken taquitos. He adjusted the passenger seat backward, reclined, and sighed with satisfaction. Chloe lowered her seat as well, Lauren lay across the backseat, and they ate in silence, staring out the windshield at the huge plaster gaucho who towered over the little restaurant, perched on a T bar as high as the roof, holding out a plaster tray of plaster food visible only to the gulls flying overhead.

"Y'know," said Brad, his diction compromised by sour cream and guacamole, "that beam he's on isn't flat like a balance beam. It's round. Not easy for him to hold steady like that."

Chloe snorted. "Not easy for him to be two or three times normal size."

Lauren chimed in. "Really not easy for him to be not a real person."

"Harvard's definitely going to take you," said Chloe. "You're very perceptive."

Brad bit off another chunk of taquito. "Yes, they are," he said.

When they ran out of food and purpose, Brad wordlessly collected and discarded the garbage and Chloe started up the car. The ride back was always a sobering one, like waking from a happy dream; they were at the curve where the Pacific Coast highway turned its back on the ocean and dissolved into the Santa Monica freeway, where the romance of a beachside cruise yielded to unmitigated traffic, when Chloe's cell phone started to buzz.

"Want me to?" asked Brad, reaching for the phone.

"Sure."

He flipped open the phone and read the text message aloud. "Liz wants to know are you coming. You're twenty minutes late."

"Shit," said Chloe, hauling right across two lanes onto an off-ramp. "Can you guys wait ten minutes and then I'll take you home? I forgot. I was supposed to go by today to pick up a calc thing I did that she graded."

"Sure," said Brad. "Let's go get it." He read Liz's cell phone number twice more, until he was sure he had it memorized, and then he put Chloe's phone in the cup holder, took out his own as though it had vibrated, muttered, "Who the hell is this," and input Liz's number as he pretended to respond to a nonexistent text message. He had not done anything about contacting her since the financial aid meeting, but that did not mean he lacked interest, only that he temporarily lacked initiative.

"Let's go, as in sure, before I take you home? You hoping for a glimpse of your future fellow classmate? I could be very helpful here."

A giggle floated up from the backseat.

"You told Chloe you met Liz?" Lauren poked the passenger seat with her foot.

"He did *not*," said Chloe, who slapped at him with her right hand. "I was just thinking Harvard and Harvard. You *met* her? How could you not tell me and you told Lauren?"

"Self-defense," said Brad. "Fuck you both. I'll stay in the car."

Chloe smiled. "Like I care if the two of you have genius babies someday."

When they arrived, Liz's father opened the door and pointed Chloe down the hall with an efficient, "She's waiting for you." Lauren trailed after her, but Brad stood where he was until Steve sat down at the kitchen table and gestured at an empty chair.

"Sit down, if you would like," he said. "Liz's mother is at the grocery, and I am almost done here."

"Thanks," said Brad. He sat, silent, watching as Steve traced his index finger along a page of the *Thomas Guide* as though he were reading Braille, top left to bottom right. He was about to speak when Steve closed his eyes, which implied a process that was not to be interrupted; he was about to speak, again, when Steve opened his eyes and began scribbling furiously into a spiral-bound notebook. Brad watched, transfixed, inexplicably concerned whenever Steve paused, irrationally relieved whenever the writing began again, hoping, without knowing why, that the girls would stay in Liz's room until this exercise had ended.

Finally, Steve put down his pencil and closed both the map book and the spiral notebook, and Brad stared at him, waiting, until his curiosity won out.

"May I ask," he began, "I mean, what are you doing?"

Steve opened the map book again and waved his hand over the open page. "I memorized the area around the Hollywood Bowl," he said. "I drive a cab, and I set myself the goal of memorizing much of the *Thomas Guide*. Certainly the areas where cabs are in demand. Many people think it is no longer worth the effort to park for a Hollywood Bowl concert."

"You know it by heart?"

"I do."

Brad had no idea how to respond. "Gee, that's cool" would sound condescending. "Wow, I wish I could do that" was a lie, and

"Don't you have GPS in your cab?" seemed rude. Maybe Liz's dad had some kind of brain injury and this was rehab.

Steve smiled at his bewilderment. "I was an engineer in Korea," he said. "I like puzzles, patterns, grids."

Brad smiled back and looked around, hoping that a change of subject would present itself. He pointed at a three-panel bamboo screen, the kind Pier 1 had been selling since long before bamboo became the darling of eco-decor, that blocked off what Brad imagined to be a dining area. Whatever was behind it was the reason for the card table wedged into the kitchen, which, according to Brad's tape-measure brain, made it impossible to open the refrigerator and the oven simultaneously.

"What's back there? If you don't mind me asking, that is."

Steve stood, folded the screen, and leaned it against the refrigerator. He gestured at the contents of the alcove with the pride of a game-show host showing off a new car to eager contestants. A big whiteboard labeled "Summer/Fall," with a list of deadlines, Harvard's in red and the rest in black, sat on a small dining-room table that was pushed against the wall; next to it, a smaller whiteboard labeled "Financial Aid" with a similar set of color-coded deadlines; next to the table, a set of plastic file boxes, one red and the rest black, stacked alongside a two-drawer steel file cabinet. On a small sideboard, an orderly display of all the office supplies Liz could possibly need to complete her applications: stamps, letter-size and manila envelopes, erasers, tape, a coffee mug filled with sharpened pencils, another filled with pens and highlighters, and a saucer stacked with multicolored tabs of the sort that Brad's father used to indicate signature lines.

Brad whistled. "That's some operation," he said. "Liz files everything hard copy?"

Steve, who had not traveled this far to be pitied by a kid for whom geography was not destiny but an amusement park, took a moment to collect himself. He monitored his irritations carefully and never allowed himself to speak until they had subsided.

"She has a PowerBook to file," he said. "But she makes these copies for her mother and me to read. You do not show your applications to your parents?"

"Sometimes," said Brad, who never did. He stepped forward to read the entries on the bigger whiteboard: Harvard, Yale, Princeton, Columbia, Penn, Swarthmore, Cornell, Chicago, Stanford, Berkeley.

"Wait," said Brad. "What's her safe school, Berkeley?"

"Yes," said Steve.

"I was joking. They turn down California valedictorians. It was in the paper."

"They will not turn down Elizabeth," said Steve. "Of course, all the California campuses can review her application and accept her, so I suppose we have a network of very safe schools she has no interest in attending. But in terms of real options, Berkeley would be her fallback."

All of a sudden, Brad wanted Liz's father to like him, or at least to respect him.

"Her first choice is Harvard, though," said Brad. "I applied to Harvard."

"Applied," came Chloe's drawling voice behind him. "Oh, please. I thought your dad just called up to let them know when to have your room ready."

Brad spun around and willed her dead, to no avail.

Chloe smiled, emboldened by Steve's sudden look of interest, because usually he ignored her. "Brad's fourth generation to go to Harvard in his family," she said, turning to Liz. "You guys've met, I hear."

"You know Chloe's friend?" Steve asked his daughter.

"He was at the financial aid meeting," said Liz.

Steve pondered for an instant. "Why would a boy fourth generation need money?"

Chloe's laugh was too big for the house. "Exactly, Mr. Chang," she said. "His dad runs the meeting. Please. Preston Bradley the Third could pay for everyone in this room to go to college and still keep his golf membership."

"Chloe exaggerates," said Lauren, who caught the pinched look on Brad's face. "Or she doesn't, but she makes it sound worse than it is."

Brad instructed his facial muscles to smile, squeezed Chloe's elbow too hard, and guided Lauren and her toward the door.

"Nice to meet you, Mr. Chang. Sorry we have to rush, but my parents have dinner waiting." He had no idea if his parents were home, with or without food, but this sounded to Brad like the sort of thing a boy worthy of Mr. Chang's respect might say.

Steve nodded his approval. "And perhaps next year you and Liz will see each other on campus."

"Well," said Brad, "who knows. I mean, it would be nice. I'm not, I'm thinking, it might be . . ."

"C'mon," said Chloe, "subject, verb, object, you can do it."

Brad blurted his confession. "I haven't decided that's where I want to go," he said.

Steve shook his head and put the screen back in place.

*   *   *

The best and worst thing about Chloe was that, like her mother, she made no distinction between monologue and dialogue. Once she got going, it was hard to chime in, but remarkably easy to hold up the other end of what she considered to be a conversation. An occasional monosyllabic response was all she needed to feel that an intimate exchange had taken place.

She had learned far more than math during her weekly tutoring sessions, all of which she was eager to share in her new role as matchmaker.

Money: "Liz buys her shoes at Payless, and not because it's a fashion statement, I promise you."

Outside interests: "She's got a whole shelf of what's-her-name, the one who wrote, we saw the movie, Italy, the girl almost marries the wrong guy but she's in love with someone else. Edith Wharton."

"No," said Lauren, "that's E. M. Forster. Edith Wharton's the guy who does marry the wrong girl but he's in love with someone else. Or the girl who doesn't marry the right guy or the wrong guy and she ruins her life, that's the other one."

"Right," said Chloe. "I mean, why read that stuff if you don't have to?" She continued with her list.

Home life: "Lauren saw it, but Brad, her room I swear is the size of the pantry in your kitchen, and her dad's got a drawer in her desk because he pays the bills there. How glad is she going to be to be in a dorm and have a little privacy?"

Parents: "My mom may be a total ditz, but at least she's fun sometimes, and my dad's about a month away from being really bored with his girlfriend. I'd go crazy if they were on my case all the time like Liz's parents."

By the time she had critiqued the snacks Liz offered during their tutoring sessions, they were in front of Brad's house.

"Thanks for the ride," said Brad, fingering the cell phone in his pocket.

"Hey, you could fall in love and take her away from everything." Chloe laughed, such an easy, liquid laugh. Brad envied her that.

"Leave him alone." Lauren reached forward to pat him on the shoulder. "Remind me why we like her."

"Oh, please," said Chloe. "Can you see Brad's parents having dinner with the in-laws? I'm only saying what you're both thinking."

Brad laughed and got out of the car. He took a deep breath at the front door to steady himself, but he need not have bothered. The house was empty, and there was the usual bag from his mother's favorite cheese shop on the counter. Brad poured himself a half glass of orange juice, carried it and the bag into his bedroom, and set out his meal as he always did: he spread a towel on the bed as though it were a place mat, to avoid getting Brie or cranberry relish—it was always Brie and cranberry relish on a whole-wheat baguette, a bag of Sun Chips, and an apple—on the bedspread. He retrieved a mini-bottle of Stoli from his sock drawer, emptied it into the orange juice, screwed the top back on tight, and stashed the empty bottle in the bag where he carried his laptop charger and Ethernet cord so that he could throw it out on the way to school in the morning.

It was that easy to stay under the radar. All he had to do was buy those little airplane-service bottles from the display at the gourmet market and remember to throw away the itemized receipt before he got in the car. His parents assumed that a $15.95 charge meant San Daniele prosciutto and sottocenere cheese on an olive roll and a bottle of imported mineral water, but in fact it paid for a generic hero sandwich with extra peppers and three mini-bottles, rung up by a clerk who was far more interested in Brad's smile than in asking him for a picture ID. He kept the bottles buried in his sock drawer in mute collaboration with the housekeeper, who occasionally took a mini-tequila for herself and never turned him in.

Since the beginning of senior year, he had allowed himself one bottle before turning out the light each night, never two, not even on the night after the clarinet lecture. Brad had a built-in sensor that kept him from ever going too far, developed at a tenth-grade party when he lost count of his refills and suddenly felt the room torque, ever so slightly.

"Whoa," he had yelled, to cover the possibility that he was wobbling enough for people to notice. "Was that an earthquake?" His equally woozy friends had muddled to their feet to stand in the doorway, or was it anyplace but the doorway, away from the windows, under a desk or never under anything, outside but watch the power lines and the palm trees, who could remember? Brad had slunk into the bathroom and hid there with a cold, wet guest towel over his face while he waited for the moment to pass. He never again forgot to keep track.

He sighed and took a bite of the sandwich. He figured he ought to be grateful for the cheese, at least. Alexandra Bradley went for the healthy alternative whenever possible, but she made nice exceptions for any imported cheese or cured meat that cost over $20 per pound, as though expensive fats and nitrates posed less of a threat than cheap ones.

Brad took a long drink, inhaled the rest of the sandwich, took out his cell phone, and started a text message to Liz.

"Great to see you," he wrote. "Want to have coffee tomorrow? I can meet you at four at the Coffee Bean near school."

"Near your school."

"Near Ocean Heights."

"Your Coffee Bean."

He stared at the message.

"Nice, fuckhead," he said. "Don't bother to tell her who it is or anything."

He hit CANCEL. Too enthusiastic or too bullshit, depending on how she interpreted it. Where was the balance of desire and indifference he was looking for?

He tried again. "Hi, it's Brad. Coffee tomorrow. Four at your Coffee Bean?" He hit CANCEL a second time. He left the phone on his bed while he rinsed his plate and glass and loaded them in the dishwasher, and then he banished the phone to the bathroom to be recharged, to show that he did not care. Not that he needed proof.

Brad was finding it increasingly difficult to do much of anything, especially anything new. He got into bed, turned on the flat-screen, an early Christmas gift from his parents, and surfed the directory for a movie, any movie, that was being broadcast in HD.

When Alexandra got home, she found him asleep in his clothes with the Discovery Channel playing on mute. She had to look away and point the remote control over her shoulder to turn off the set. Insects were so frightening in HD; Alexandra could not understand how anyone could look at them right before they went to sleep, and she hoped that her brief glimpse of a spider the size of a seat cushion would not haunt her dreams. For a moment, she debated whether to wake Brad up to get him to brush and floss, but surely his teeth would survive a single night of neglect, and she would be spared the possibility that he would snap at her for being a nag. Nothing made her feel older than being called a nag, except perhaps the puppet lines starting to bracket the row of vertical hash marks above her upper lip, which she fought with every emollient and procedure this side of anesthesia.

chapter 10

Brad finally sent Liz a text message two weeks into sec-ond semester, on the day he saw Katie coming down the hall at lunchtime wearing a brand-new Williams sweatshirt. He had no expectation of love, and certainly not of sex, not with a girl who presided over an entire room devoted to college applications, not in his own bleached state of mind. He had almost talked himself out of bothering at all, but the sight of Katie in that sweatshirt made him send the text. Suddenly it seemed very important to Brad to have a conversation with someone who knew next to nothing about him, including the fact that his father had purchased a Harvard sweatshirt a year earlier and put it in his bottom desk drawer, where Brad discovered it one afternoon when he was looking for a ream of printer paper.

He ducked into the bathroom and texted, "Hi, it's Brad, Chloe's friend. Can you meet me at the Ocean Heights Coffee Bean today at four?"

A moment later, she texted back, "Sure."

He felt like an idiot for not having asked sooner. As soon as class got out he hurried toward the parking lot—or rather, toward Katie, who stepped out from behind an Escalade as he turned the corner, requiring him either to stop or to knock her over.

"I'm really in a hurry," he said.

She ignored him. "Did you get all As first semester?"

"Yeah."

"So did I."

"Okay," said Brad, computing the odds of still being able to get to the Coffee Bean ten minutes early if he spent five minutes listening to Katie, or of Katie trailing him in a rage if he didn't hang around long enough to wrap this up, whatever this was. "Congrats. Makes you valedictorian, right?"

"I'm not sure. I had that A minus in honors geometry. Sophomore year," Katie confessed in a tone of voice more appropriate to a disclosure of chlamydia or herpes.

"I had an A minus in AP chem," said Brad, trying to be helpful.

"Exactly," said Katie. "Which is worth more than my A minus because mine was only honors. And I took ceramics. What other A minuses did you get?"

"Katie, I'm late for a doctor's appointment," said Brad.

"I don't think so, but never mind."

She waited. Did he really think he could tell Lauren where he was going after school without Lauren calling Chloe from the bathroom? To be fair, Lauren had been more discreet than that. She had texted Chloe from the bathroom. It was Chloe who called back instead of texting, to press for details. Lauren's only mistake was failing to look for feet in the stalls before she replied.

"Whatever," said Brad. "What do you want?"

Katie gave a furtive glance left and right. "I want to be valedictorian," she said. "If I'm going to be stuck at Williams—"

"That's hardly stuck."

"If I don't get to go to Yale, then I want something that I want, not something my parents want for me. I want to be valedictorian. I mean, my parents want me to be, too, but I do and that's all that matters. If you get an A minus in anything this semester, then I will be."

"Assuming you get all As."

"We're both going to get all As. It's our reward for working so hard."

"Says who?"

"My brother. Never mind. No teacher wants to be the one who keeps a kid from being valedictorian, trust me. We're going to get all As unless we do something really bad. Something they can't ignore."

"You want me to what, tank a test on purpose?"

"It's better than writing a bad paper. Somebody could pretend not to notice a dumb paper, but, you know, you can forget part of a bio lab or leave something blank on a calc test. You don't have to blow it entirely. Just enough."

When he hesitated, Katie leaned in close. "You've got everything you want. You can always fight with your dad in April when you get in everywhere. I have no choice. So you should let me be valedictorian. What do you care?"

Brad was surprised, and slightly dismayed, but he did care. He felt a little knot of resistance in his throat, a prideful lump that made him worry about his resolve for the first time. A guy who really wanted to turn his back on Harvard would not care about being valedictorian. In fact, he would welcome Katie's suggestion. Crestview submitted third-quarter grades, and the Ivies took them seriously. Get a B on a test—get a C, do it right—and he might lose his place in line at Harvard. Blowing a single math test was a minor revolt compared to what Roger had done. Why was he so reluctant?

Because he could not quell the fear that a single test grade might actually be enough to tip the odds against him. As long as he believed that his Harvard acceptance was at stake, there were only two possible explanations for his hesitancy: either he lacked the resolve to walk away from his legacy, despite all his big talk about wanting to do exactly that, or he had let a prospective coffee date alter his world view and make Harvard seem appealing. He was either a coward or a romantic idiot, and whichever it was, it was not good.

What if his dad had ignored his protests, all these months, because he knew that eventually Brad would cave in?

Like anyone confronted by the limits of his own bravery, Brad got belligerent.

"And if I do step aside? What do I get in return?"

Katie smiled flirtatiously.

"I won't tell the doctor you're meeting at four, right, that you've slept with half the senior class, you slut."

Brad spun away from her so fast that he rammed his thigh into the fins of the basketball coach's 1969 Caddie, and screamed "Shit!" loud enough to draw the attention of the uniformed security guard, who emerged from his kiosk to make sure that the source of the expressed torment was psychological, not physical. He saw a boy crumpled on the ground next to his backpack, but the girl with him had a big smile on her face, so clearly there was no need to intervene. A moment later the boy straightened up, rubbed his leg, slung the backpack over one shoulder, and hobbled away, and the girl hustled off in the opposite direction.

The security guard returned to the kiosk and the unfinished spoils of the Crestview trustees' luncheon, a chicken quesadilla made with breast meat only, which he knew because the mother who brought it to him insisted on lifting up the corner of the whole-wheat flour tortilla so that he could have a peek at the ingredients, washed down with one of Mexico's true contributions to fine dining, a bottled Coca-Cola made with real sugar instead of corn syrup, which he bought every morning on his way in, at the little taqueria near his house. He glanced toward the parking lot once more to make sure that the girl and the boy were headed for their cars, but he did not expect a problem. His brother, who worked at Ocean Heights, had a diagonal scar four inches long on his forearm, the souvenir of a knife fight he had broken up the first week of school, but Crestview students lived in their heads. Most of the torture was self-inflicted—kids seemed determined to suffer one way or another, so if they had no worries they looked for ways to make them up—which left him with not a lot to do.

The next intrusion on his day, he figured, would be in about ten minutes, when the mom returned with whatever the trustees had had for dessert. She always brought dessert separately, and she always made the same little joke about whether she could clear his plate, and was he ready for the next course.

❧

Ted made a pilgrimage to Starbucks every afternoon for an Americano and a fifteen-minute breather, and he was headed for the driveway when he noticed Brad's mother carrying what looked like a chocolate hockey puck, to his left, and Brad buckled on the ground next to Katie, to his right. Instinctively, he stepped in front of Alexandra Bradley, to give her son the chance to make a getaway. He had no reason to assume trouble, but Ted thought it was risky, on principle, to let parents roam the campus unattended.

"Alexandra," he said, gesturing at the plate. "Where are you going? My office is back there. I'm ready for dessert."

She had a laugh like a chittering mouse.

"Take this one," she said.

"I'm joking," said Ted, who cared only about delaying her. "Somebody must be waiting for that one. I'll survive without."

She looked genuinely hurt. "Don't you think it looks good? I think Lauren's mother made them, I'm not sure, but I think so."

"In that case, I'm not joking," said Ted. "I can go get it myself, though. You needn't bother."

"It's no bother," she replied. "Surely you have more important things to do."

"Not so much," said Ted, figuring he needed to stretch the chat for another minute or two. "Early's over, and regular-admissions people aren't ready to hear from me. Call them the end of January and they think I've got something to be anxious about. So I wait."

"The calm before the storm," said Alexandra.

"Not in your house," he said. "Your only disappointment is that they stopped doing early decision."

"Indeed," she lied. The first time she got pregnant, Alexandra had hoped for a girl, despite the fact that the Bradley line was relentlessly male. When the baby turned out to be Roger instead of Priscilla, her body rebelled and refused to conceive again. Secondary infertility, the specialist explained, an allergic reaction to Trey's sperm that made a second pregnancy almost impossible. In the name of being a good sport—that was what Trey had called it, being a good sport—she had tried two courses of Pergonal and pretended to try two courses more, while she read all the literature about side effects. She pretended to experience enough of them to scare her husband, who reluctantly agreed to abandon his plan for two boys. Ten years later, the allergy wore off, and Alexandra spent nine months hoping again for Priscilla, until Preston IV was born.

She loved her younger son. She loved her older son, for that matter, though it was easier now that they never spoke, easier to cope with him in theory than it had been in practice. Alexandra had yearned for a girl because a girl would have been a full-time job, while a boy had all those cousins and uncles, who admitted him into their fraternity as soon as he could walk. She did well enough when Brad was in elementary school, when her primary responsibilities involved scheduling, driving, nutritional supervision, and the modulated expression and receipt of affection. Middle school and puberty had tipped the balance toward Trey and his tribe, who had rather absolute notions of what it meant to be a Bradley man, and toward Brad's new sense of self, which seemed to depend for its health on never being in a car with his mom if there was another way to get from here to there. Alexandra was irrelevant without ever having felt essential, but she felt it would be ungrateful to confess her disappointment, so she kept it to herself.

Something in the parking lot caught her eye.

"Look, there's Brad," she said. She waved at his departing car even though there was no way her son could see her. "I could've said hi."

"My bad," said Ted. "I got in your way."

"My bad," she mimicked, with an admiring smile. "How hard it must be to keep up on all the slang."

Ted shrugged. His job successfully completed, he stepped aside to let Brad's mom deliver her dessert.

When he got back to his office, Rita handed him a phone message from Fred Ottinger, the father of the best student in the junior class, who turned out to have a simple question: would Ted be interested in doing some outside consulting, for a fee, of course, to help the boy get into Columbia?

Ted's surprised silence worked to his advantage, because Fred read it as reluctance and decided on the spot to make his first offer $10,000 instead of $5,000. When Ted took another moment to collect himself, Fred apologized.

"Look, better yet, let's start now instead of next fall and make it a flat twenty thousand for eighteen months, now until Joe graduates. I hadn't thought about the summer months when I said ten thousand." Fred felt slightly nauseated. He spent his workday rearranging people's intestines, but his surgeon's detachment failed him when it came to the eldest of his three children. "Let me buy you lunch Saturday and we'll work out the details. Have you been to Bocca?"

"I haven't," said Ted, as dumbstruck as a boy in the presence of a naked girl for the first time. Bocca probably held the record for consecutive months when the only available reservation seemed to be at four o'clock, whether for a late lunch or an early dinner.

But his initial hesitation, about both consulting and what would surely be a three-figure lunch, had nothing to do with ethics, for what he did on his own time was his own business, and anyone who got the kinds of gifts Ted regularly got had long since made a convenient peace with being bought off. In fact, he found Fred's offer refreshingly frank. He wanted help with Joe, beyond what he felt he could reasonably expect as just another Crestview parent, and he was prepared to pay for it.

No, what confounded Ted was his own shortsightedness: why had he not thought of this himself? Private consultants charged anywhere from $5,000 to $25,000, depending on the difficulty of the placement, and he had better contacts than they did. As long as this did not encroach on his day job—his day job, now that was funny—he could become a very rich man in a very short time.

And why limit himself to Crestview families, when there were ten private schools on this side of town? If he averaged $15,000 per student, twenty students without breaking a sweat, he made $300,000 in his first year.

It was enough to make Ted forget that Fred was still waiting for a reply.

"Then are we set?"

"Oh, sure. Great. I was just checking my calendar."

"I bet you were. I told my wife, Ted's got to be in demand, but he knows Joe. He'll find the time for us."

Ted chuckled. "He's a great kid," he said.

"One o'clock then, Saturday, Bocca," said Fred.

"Done," said Ted.

In a trance, he picked up the portfolio where he kept his college essay notes, and labeled a back page "Consulting." He multiplied $15,000 by 20, by 40, by 100—he could hire assistants—and subtracted imaginary income tax. It was still very serious money. He quadrupled the amount he contributed annually to his retirement fund and imagined himself, a much younger man than in previous escape fantasies, traveling through Europe, perhaps renting a villa, settling into a vibrant new life, eventually presiding over an empire via teleconference from wherever he preferred to be.

He started sketching little mock-ups of business cards, as his enduring but unformed and underpaid daydream of being a novelist evaporated, replaced by a firm offer of $20,000 for helping a single kid. Fred Ottinger had shown Ted the way out: he could have a client list of two hundred students and a suite of offices with rooms for private consultations. He might even have the architect design a private entrance and exit, like a psychiatrist's office, so that families could get help while perpetuating the illusion that they did not need any.

He heard Alexandra's voice in the reception area, heard a timid single knock on his door, and a whispered "Dessert, Ted." He held his breath, knowing that she would not open his office door unless he answered, not caring if she left the plate with Rita or took it back to the kitchen, unwilling to return to earth quite so soon.

Brad felt like a buffoon. In a giddy, disoriented moment he had ordered a Black Forest Ice Blended, in which coffee was merely the vehicle for lots of chocolate espresso beans and maraschino cherries, all of it blanketed by a pyramid of whipped cream. Liz was sitting across from him with her chaste chai latte, and he had ordered a clown drink. He poked at it, took a small sip, and grimaced, in the hope that she would find the drink dumb, and not him. So much for the scion of the Bradley family and his inherited social graces.

"I have no clue how to eat this thing," he said.

She smiled.

He could not recall the last time he had had a conversation with a new person, let alone someone who did not go to Crestview. His friends might talk about joining Doctors Without Borders or

studying at the London School of Economics, but they were isola-
tionists when it came to friendship and romance. They rarely ventured outside the Crestview family, and their conversations were
studded with incestuous references to what went on at school. Brad
was out of his element and wanting to impress, a deadly combination, a minefield. There were probably a dozen things he could say
to Liz that would put her off irrevocably, and another dozen that
would endear him to her, but he had no idea which was which
because he did not really know anything about her, except that he
did not know anything about her, which was the allure. It might be
safe to talk about celebrities and rehab, or the health-care crisis, or
the Middle East, or how about those Lakers, those Dodgers, those
eco-terrorists, but there was no way to tell until he opened his
mouth and put his foot in it. If this was a preview of life as a college
freshman, he might never leave his dorm room.

"So. Can you believe graduation is so close?" Dumb, pale,
vague. He sounded like his grandfather, who began every long-
distance phone call with "How's the weather?" because he could
not think of anything else to say.

Liz took a sip of her latte and waited, and it hit Brad that she
was waiting because she assumed, charitably, that he had more
to say.

"You wouldn't believe the Crestview graduation. Very formal. White caps and gowns, jackets and ties, dresses. No denim.
They have a rule, no denim."

"Nice," said Liz, with the little smirk he remembered from
the financial aid meeting.

Brad abandoned the straw and concentrated on folding the
whipped cream into the body of the drink with a spoon, which
turned it the color of mud. "It's no big deal," he said.

"Right," she replied. Liz was prepared to like Brad, primarily
because he seemed to lack Katie's snobbishness, but she had her
guard up. She expected private school kids to be spoiled unless

they convinced her otherwise—and if he turned out to be one of those entitled kids, then at some point he would be condescending about her life and that would be the end of it. Liz was quick to judge and harsh in her assessments; there was too much at stake to waste time. She had to make a concerted effort to be merely curious.

"Where do you have your graduation?" she asked.

"Soccer field," he said. "They cover it, set out chairs, the seniors sit on bleachers. In a tent, so nobody sweats too much. You guys?"

"Track-and-field field," she said, "same deal without the tent, and if it rains we go to SaMo Airport, to the hangar where they have the Barneys sale. It's packed. Kind of like the cows in *Hud*. Maybe less dust."

He smiled, lost and not sure if he minded.

"*Hud*," she said. "Paul Newman's the rotten son, the cows all have hoof-and-mouth disease, he wants to sell them before anybody finds out, but his father lets the government guy round them up in a big hole in the ground and shoot them. Crowded. Like that."

"Haven't seen it," said Brad, feeling the need to pretend that he did not care.

Liz sat up straighter. "My father got me Netflix for my sweet sixteen," she said. "First I watched the AFI hundred best films, most of them, not the war ones so much, and then I got more movies with anybody I really liked, and musicals."

Brad concentrated on flattening his straw wrapper and making a knife crease down its side with his thumbnail. Liz and her movie list, her dad and his map book. He did not know many people who built up extra tasks for themselves like that. In his world, success was defined as the handing off of tasks, not the accumulation of them—the less you did for yourself, the better off you were. He was hardly going to romanticize ironing, for heaven's sake, but he liked the idea of inventing interesting projects, and for a moment he wished he had built the balsa wood double helix after all.

He folded the straw wrapper into accordion pleats. "I have this idea for your house," he said, even though he had none.

"I'm sorry?"

"Your house," he said, fishing in his backpack for a pad and pen. He drew a rectangle and started filling in walls and doors, and to his surprise, he did have an idea, one he must have been working out since the day he had come by the house with Chloe. His conscious brain might be in an extended coma, anesthetized by uncertainty, but his subconscious was striking out for new territories. He sketched in little boxes to stand for pieces of furniture, and in Liz's room he drew a shelf and laid in a row of hash marks.

"Know what those are?"

"No."

"Your DVDs," he said, triumphant.

She reached over for his pen and drew little lines to connect the tops and bottoms of adjacent hash marks, turning them into rectangles.

"Except we rent four at a time," she said, "so you left too much space. Now they're my books." She put down the pen and studied the drawing. "I like it," she said, choosing not to point out that her parents rented the place and had to get written permission to install the washer and dryer. "I could live here."

With a flourish, Brad drew a side view with an exploded roof that wafted two feet above the building.

"There," he said. "You can do that. Makes the whole place feel bigger, and you can set in a skylight, get sunlight during the day and install shades to make it dark at night."

He kept his eyes on the drawing.

"Look, you want to go to prom with me?"

A small breath escaped Liz's lips, a *heh* that could turn out to be surprise or the dry first syllable of rejection. Brad could not tell.

"Prom?"

"Well, yeah."

"Isn't it in, I don't know, May?"

"Yeah. Couple of weeks before graduation."

"It's January. Why aren't you taking a Crestview girl?"

"Look, you can say no."

"I didn't say no. It's fine, I mean, sure, but . . ."

"So you'll go. 'It's fine, I mean, sure' is your way of saying yes."

"Right," she said. She tapped the drawing with her index finger. "Can I have this?"

"Sure."

She folded it carefully, put it in her purse, and stood up.

"I have to meet Chloe at five," she said. "Thanks for the latte."

"We're on then," said Brad. "For prom. I mean, I'll see you in between, we could—"

Liz cut him off. "Yes," she said. "I said yes. But I have to go. See you." She was out the door before Brad had gathered up his things.

❧

Yoonie's humming began one afternoon after lunch, a thin little scrap of what must have been considered melody in Korea, though to Joy it sounded more like aluminum cans cascading into a recycling truck. She found herself listening too hard, waiting for the notes to resolve themselves in a way that felt familiar to her Western ear, which they obstinately refused to do. Instead, the line of notes embedded itself in her brain, so that at any given moment she was hard pressed to say whether the music was coming from Yoonie or from inside her own head. It got on her nerves.

Jim Arden had held the last slot on the first Tuesday of the month ever since Joy could remember, testimony to his vanity, his hypochondria, and a misplaced belief that diligent examination prevented, rather than exposed, disease. His collected MRIs, viewed in a single sitting, would require popcorn and a large Coke, but a retinue of specialists was happy to indulge him because he never mentioned insurance and always paid at the end of his visit. He was one of Joy's easiest patients—Botox across his forehead four times a year, a reassuring look at the same mole she had examined a month earlier, and he went home happy.

As Yoonie held out the first of six syringes filled with Botox, the humming seemed to get louder, not enough for Jim to notice, but enough for Dr. Joy to glance over at her nurse, who hesitated, the needle in midair.

"I am so sorry," Yoonie said, although she had no idea what she was apologizing for. "I thought you were ready for the first injection."

She reached forward just as Dr. Joy did, their hands collided, and the needle fell to the ground.

"Hey, butterfingers," said Jim. "Should I let you anywhere near my forehead with shakes like that?"

"It was entirely my fault, and I am very sorry," said Yoonie, who dove in one continuous arc to retrieve and discard the needle and reach for a replacement, which she handed to Dr. Joy with her other hand. Joy took it with exaggerated caution and held it up, immobile, six inches in front of her patient's face.

"If you have any concern, Jim, I'll refer you to Dr. Josephs and he can handle your treatments."

"No, butterfingers, I meant the nurse. Not you."

Yoonie took longer than usual cleaning up after Jim left, but when she came out of the examination room Dr. Joy was waiting in the hallway.

"You're humming," said Joy.

"Oh," said Yoonie. "I disturbed you, again, I am sorry, I will not do it again."

"Yoonie."

"Yes, Dr. Joy."

"Come in my office for a moment."

Yoonie followed her but did not sit down.

"You never hum."

"No."

"But now you hum. Why is that?"

Yoonie mistook irritation for interest.

"Liz is going to the prom and I am very happy for her, so today after school and after work there is a dress she found that she wants me to see."

"Prom? Well, someone must be crazy about her to invite her so early, perhaps you'll want to keep an eye on this. Prom. When is the Ocean Heights prom? And where? In the gym?"

"I do not know. Liz has been invited to the Crestview prom. To your prom. In fact you must know, do most of the girls wear long dresses or short? The one to see today I think is short, but I say she ought to look at long ones. What will Katie wear?"

Joy was instantly disgruntled, doubly so, at Yoonie for having a reason to be happy that Joy did not yet have, and at herself for caring that Yoonie had a reason.

"Katie hasn't decided who she's going with yet," said Joy. "And of course once she sees what group she's going with, she and the other girls will probably decide what they're wearing. I expect she'll want a long gown, but some of the girls do wear short."

"Ah, groups," said Yoonie. "I do not know if the boy who asked Liz mentioned a group."

"How did she meet him? What's his name? I bet I know him."

"His name is Brad. Like Liz he hopes to go to Harvard."

"Good grief, he's one of Katie's best friends," said Joy. "He's a very popular boy. Plenty of girls at the prom are going to hate your daughter, let me tell you."

"She cannot help it if they are jealous. He asked her. He did not ask them." Yoonie had no patience for, no understanding of, the envy that drove some girls into a cruel frenzy. To her, worrying about beating another girl at anything—better grades, a more popular boyfriend, being the first to acquire whatever the magazines said a girl had to acquire this season—seemed a tremendous waste of energy. She and Steve always told Liz to challenge herself and to ignore everyone else, because the victory was excellence, not comparative excellence. She was surprised at Dr. Joy, who in turn was a bit surprised at the flinty tone in Yoonie's voice.

"True enough, he did not ask them," said Joy, sitting up a bit straighter and pretending to consult a patient's file. When she spoke again, she did not look up. "I'll be ready for Joan in a minute." Yoonie was dismissed.

$11,565.

Steve wrote the number at the top of a blank sheet of paper and let it sit. He had driven to work as usual but circled back an hour later, once Yoonie was at work and Liz was at school, to finish the single aspect of the college application process that he refused to share with his wife and daughter—the financial aid forms, which he had completed a month before the government deadline, because he wanted plenty of time to prepare for whatever the computer said to him. He reviewed the online application one last time, clicked on SUBMIT, and within seconds the computer spit back the Changs' Expected Family Contribution. Steve needed to find a minimum of $11,565 toward Liz's $49,000 freshman year, and Harvard was supposed to provide the rest: $37,435. He would not allow himself to think about what he would do if Harvard gave her any less.

He had seen the headlines about Ivy League schools starting to offer even more financial aid, but he worried that it was aimed at more comfortable families than his, at people who had cars and a mortgage and still could not absorb the cost of a college education. He worried about shrinking school endowments and the dwindling supply of loans. He had pored over the list of websites that Liz brought home from school, including one that promised to search for appropriate private scholarships if the applicant filled out a basic questionnaire. Steve completed it without telling her, but the results were meager. Liz was not related to Emily Dickinson or the Plains Indians, nor was she of Slavic descent and a serious bowler. She did not have the time to write a three-thousand-word essay on freedom for the chance to compete with ten thousand other students for $1,500. The members of her immediate family did not work at a Coca-Cola bottling plant or belong to the Elks. She had just found out that she was a finalist for a National Merit scholarship, but to Steve's dismay, not all of the finalists got money, the ones who did received only $2,500, and there was nothing Liz could do to affect her chances. It was up to Steve to find $11,565, and more to bring her home on the holidays and buy her books and give her spending money.

He divided the sheet of paper into columns labeled Income and Expenses and filled them speedily, because he knew his family's finances as well as he knew his ever-expanding inventory of addresses and alternate routes. The government might look at his finances and determine that he had almost $12,000 available to spend on a single year of college, but Steve worked and reworked the numbers in both columns and came up with less than $7,000.

Beyond that, he was left with the kinds of strategies that appeared in advice columns aimed at recent college graduates, for whom forty years without gourmet coffee might actually amount to something. He could never again stop at a fast-food restaurant, Yoonie could eliminate Liz's latte allowance, they could spend more on gas to get over to the big-box store to buy bulk paper goods that they had no room to store. He could cancel Netflix, although he hated to do so before Liz left for Boston. They could sell the car and he could drive Yoonie back and forth to work in his cab, but what was a 2001 Sentra worth?

Everything that might be considered an extra, in his family's circumscribed life, and not enough trade-in value to close the gap for one year, let alone four. Steve tore his worksheet into vertical strips and tore the strips into bite-sized pieces, which he wrapped in a paper napkin and buried under a layer of carrot peelings in the kitchen garbage can.

A merit scholarship was the key, one of those tantalizing stipends dangled in front of the most deserving applicants to lure them to School A instead of School B, thousands of dollars that never had to be repaid, a tool used more and more frequently to snare the best kids. A gift. There was no way to apply for a merit scholarship, though, so Steve could not depend on it. He decided that he would borrow the limit on his two credit cards if need be, as distasteful a high-interest solution as that was. This was a puzzle. Not figuring it out was not an option.

Dan wandered down the hall toward the kitchen, drawn by habit more than anything else. Sunday night was Joy's version of his childhood chicken dinner, the same roasted trinity of chicken, potatoes, and carrots, the components acquired at a little French bistro every Sunday morning on her way home from the gym and extracted from the refrigerator an hour before dinner. She called it *cucina al fresco* to make disregard feel like preference.

Not that he had loved having dinner with his parents, but he had enjoyed the anticipatory smells.

He instinctively stepped to the left at the sound of Katie barreling down the stairs.

"It's dinnertime. Where are you off to?"

Katie waggled her towel in his face.

"I don't know, Dad," she said. "What's your guess?"

She turned away without waiting for an answer, left the sliding glass door open behind her, and switched on the pool lights. A moment later he heard the very specific sound of Katie entering the water—not a splash, not a plop, but a more precise sound that reminded him of a piece of stationery being torn in two.

He headed to the back of the house to close the door. Dan did not enjoy swimming. His parents could have lived downstate, landlocked, for all their interest in Lake Michigan; they only visited the lake in street clothes for the occasional picnic, and by the time they thought to sign twelve-year-old Dan up for summer swim camp he had outgrown a little boy's oblivious courage. He knew the camp counselor was lying when he said that everyone floats, because his arms and legs started to sink every time he tried.

He quit camp after a week. "They call it *dead-man's float*, don't they?" he told his dad. "Don't you think there's a reason for that?"

When he met Joy, who swam with a baffling and offhanded ease, he bartered coherent poli sci essays for swim lessons from his roommate, and by the end of the semester Dan could impersonate a recreational swimmer. Now he did weekly laps with his wife in the pool that had made buying the tear-down on the adjacent lot such a smart move. No one would have guessed that his internal metronome beat to the four-four rhythm of "do not drown now, do not drown now."

He stood in the doorway and watched Katie, although there was little of her to see. She moved through the water like a torpedo, silent and unwavering, and when she came out of the water for the breaststroke or the butterfly she did so with little of the fuss that hobbled the slower swimmers. Freestyle, she sat right below the water, the only signs of life a bouquet of exhaled bubbles on

every fourth stroke and her bent elbow surfacing and disappearing along the length of the pool.

Like a baby shark's fin, he too often thought, both delighted
and mildly disturbed by her discipline in the water. He closed the
door behind him and went into the dining room to set the table,
vowing to start a list of things he and Joy could do once both kids
were at Williams. He had considered and dismissed learning Spanish and taking a wine appreciation class, and was debating whether
they could retain a private yoga instructor without feeling like fools,
when Katie appeared at his side and leaned over to correct the
alignment of a water glass.

"I am going to miss that pool," said Katie, who in fact had
decided not to swim for the team second semester simply because
she no longer had anything to prove. "What a waste, I mean, you
guys almost never use it. Hey. You could pave it over, put in a tennis court." She giggled. "Ooh, no. A putting green."

"You're dripping," he said.

She stood there for an extra count of five to irritate him before
she turned for the stairs. Dan took it all in: the squishy wet foot-
prints on the dining-room rug, the trail of water along the hardwood
floor in the hall, the threadbare tank suit Katie so proudly wore at
home. Her drag suit, she called it, and the first time she did he had
Googled the phrase rather than confess his ignorance. Her drag suit:
the old, worn suit she wore to practice because it created more resistance in the water than a sleek, skintight new competition suit
would. If she was fast in the old suit, she would be faster in a new
one without making any additional effort.

He understood the rationale, but he hated the drag suit. It was
like the clothes the kids wore when they drove down to his dad's
liquor store, the beat-up khakis and the battered loafers, the dress
shirts with frayed collars and cuffs, the clothes that said, I'm so
rich I don't have to bother to impress anyone. Dan and Joy had
managed to spawn an Evanstonian, a second-generation snob, and

he had to work hard not to take his daughter and her little jokes as seriously as he had the boys who had tormented him. As though he would ever install a putting green, as though his lessons with the club pro had not made him proficient enough to survive the requisite rounds with clients.

chapter 11

Lauren was sprawled on the couch with the television on when Nora got home, a flagrant infraction of the rule about no television until your homework is done, which could not possibly be true at six o'clock at night. Nora swallowed the sanctimonious comment forming at the back of her throat. Lauren was not the kind to flaunt. If she was breaking the rule, there had to be a reason.

Or perhaps Lauren had snapped altogether. She was watching *Threesome*, a nighttime soap that she had never bothered to watch before.

"Honey," Nora began, tentatively, "what're you doing?"

"Ssshhh," said Lauren. She hit the PAUSE button and shot her mother a long-suffering look. "That's Madison Ames. Chloe had last season on DVD."

There was a trio of women on the screen, a blonde, a redhead, and a brunette, each one in her forties and desperate to prove otherwise. Three face-lifts, three bust lifts, three sets of false eyelashes, three shiny, low-cut, strapless dresses held in place by a combination of corset boning, double-sided tape, and sheer will.

"Which one?"

"The redhead," said Lauren. "Can we be quiet please so I can watch this?"

"But . . ." Nora was drawing a blank.

"The Northwestern interview. Madison Ames. She's the one I'm talking to."

Nora peered at the screen. "She went to Northwestern?"

"What's that supposed to mean?"

Nora sat down on the couch next to her daughter. "Nothing. Can I watch her with you?"

Lauren shrugged and hit PLAY, and Madison Ames's character continued her conversation with the other two women about whether her second husband was abusing alcohol, cocaine, the new single neighbor, or, in a trifecta of prime-time cliffhanger narrative, all three. The blonde's housekeeper was threatening to destroy her candidacy for mayor by disclosing that she had never taken out withholding taxes or paid Social Security, and the brunette's son had run away from home with an ATM card, a jar of peanut butter, a loaf of bread, and his father's gun, but Madison Ames was the most famous of the three stars, so her fidelity and substance abuse issues took priority. She launched into a long speech about the dreams her character had dreamt, back when she was waitressing to support her first husband, a medical student who had died in a terrible accident but still appeared from time to time in a flashback sequence. Lauren and Nora sat, transfixed, waiting to hear what she was going to do about her current spouse.

"This is really awful," said Lauren.

"Ssshhh," said Nora. "Aren't we supposed to be listening?"

Lauren started to squirm. She turned to her mother, tossed her hair back the way Madison Ames did, and batted her eyelashes.

"But, Mother," she said, in a breathy voice. "I haven't yet told you, Mother, about, oh, can I say it? About what Jonathan said to me. Yesterday. When we were strolling through the garden, and . . ." She flung herself on Nora, racked by phony sobs. "Mother, I didn't want to tell you, I shouldn't tell you, but how can I keep from saying it? Mother, I'm pregnant. With triplets. It was the drugs, he said the injections were vitamins, how could I know? Or wait! Do you think, is it possible"—and she broke into a beaming smile—"maybe I'm not pregnant. Maybe it was all that cake, you know I love your chocolate cake, Mother. Could the test be wrong? Could I just be, heavens, could I just be bloated? Oh, I'm so relieved—but wait. What's that terrible pain in my head?"

Nora wrapped her in a hug and they sat there laughing until they ran out of breath, at which point they watched a minute more and dissolved again, back and forth until the segment ended, Nora wondering to herself how long it had been since they had had anything that resembled fun.

❧

Madison Ames—renamed for her mother's and her father's midwestern hometowns, respectively, as Susan Miller did not sound like stardom—sprawled across the billboard at the entrance to the Fox studios in all her forty-foot-long, bathing-suited, airbrushed glory. She caught Lauren's eye as Lauren edged into the left-turn lane, which caused her to overshoot the double yellow line and forced the driver of the oncoming Santa Monica city bus, who only a week earlier had taken off the open door of an old Volvo, to swerve into the next lane. The driver of the adjacent UPS truck slammed on his brakes, sending his Seven-11 Big Gulp all over the inside of his windshield. From behind a liquid curtain of Mountain Dew, he glared at Lauren and made her grateful that she could not read lips.

Lauren corrected her trajectory and sat through a full cycle of traffic lights, waiting for her knees to stop trembling, oblivious of the honking horns behind her. If she could have pulled out of the turn lane and driven a calming loop around Century City, she would have, but she had five minutes to get to Stage Nine, so she clamped her hands at ten and two, stared straight ahead, and made a left into the driveway that led to the security guard's little hut.

"Name?" he asked, without taking his eyes from the computer screen.

"Lauren Chaiken," she replied.

He ran his finger down the list on the monitor.

"And you're here to see?"

She cleared her throat and tried to sound authoritative. "I have a two o'clock appointment with Madison Ames. On Stage Nine."

"Well, Lauren who has a two o'clock appointment with Ms. Ames on Stage Nine, I do not have you on my list, so I cannot let you in." Not a week went by without a kid pretending to have an appointment, in the hope of seeing someone famous once he got onto the lot. The guard had made his one mistake a year ago, with a USC freshman whose fraternity hazing required him to get a spec script for *The Simpsons* into Matt Groening's hands. The people who worked on the show still gave him grief about it.

Lauren leaned out the window for emphasis. "But I have to be there. In four minutes. I can't be late."

The guard was already waving at the car behind her. He pointed toward the curb. "Pull over there for me, please," he said.

Madison Ames continued to pout rather than respond to the first knock on the door. She was tired of these kids and their attitude, and crankier still because she knew she would have to answer the second knock, and three more like it this week. A whole season of Northwestern alumni interviews, when all she had done was walk over to the twenty-four-hour Gelson's at two in the morning, in her pajamas, to buy a steak. Everything would have been fine—women walked around in tank tops and penguin-patterned flannel pants in broad daylight in the Palisades and nobody blinked—if Gelson's had not run out of New York strip steaks, bone in. If she had not crumpled to the floor and started to sob, if the night-shift butcher had not owned a cell phone with a video camera, if the middle-aged cashier with a motherly streak had not called 911.

The next morning, Madison was on YouTube, YouTube was all over the entertainment news, and the show runner was in her trailer talking about damage control.

It was true, what people said: if you took Ambien longer than the label said to and washed it down with a glass or two of chardonnay, you could end up wanting a steak at three in the morning, even if the next day you failed to remember either the craving or the empty refrigerator that had gotten you into so much trouble.

There were people at the cable network who considered "forty-two-year-old sex object" to be an oxymoron, so she did everything the show runner asked her to do to repair her image. Madison appeared on *Showbiz Tonight* to discuss the physical and psychological pressures of being a forty-two-year-old high-definition sex object, while her lawyer quietly investigated the possibility of an age discrimination lawsuit if she got written off the show, and she was tentatively scheduled to testify at a congressional hearing about strengthening federal warnings on prescription sleep aids, depending on whether anyone but C-SPAN intended to be there. The head of production was one of those rabid alums with Northwestern license plate holders, so she signed up to conduct alumni interviews, figuring that a couple of quick chats with some eager seniors would be a small price to pay for getting back in his good graces. She never imagined that there would be so many, and that they would expect her to pay attention.

The second knock. "Come in," she called.

Lauren stepped into the trailer. Madison Ames was sitting at her makeup table dressed as a member of the Red Guard, probably the only member in the history of the Chinese Revolution to show quite so much cleavage, lining up a row of lipstick tubes in front of the mirror. She did not get up.

"I'm so sorry I'm late," said Lauren, trying not to stare. "The guard didn't have my name on the list and I had to . . ."

Madison held up her hand for silence and gestured toward a chair piled high with bikinis. "Sit down," she said. "He's an idiot. Dump them anywhere." She caught Lauren's gaze and tugged irritably at her jacket. "It's a dream sequence. I'm adopting a Chinese kid."

"Right," said Lauren. She put her shoulder bag on the floor, scooped up the bikinis with both hands, and looked around for a break in the clutter. She lengthened her arms and pointed with one index finger at the top of a little cabinet. "Is that okay?"

"The floor is okay," said Madison. "I'm joking," she said, as Lauren started to lower her arms. "Put them right where you said."

Madison consulted the list of questions she used for every interview.

"So, tell me a bit about yourself," she said, much more concerned with finding a lipstick that stood up to the bilious khaki of her costume than with any answer Lauren might give. She held up an open tube of MAC Viva Glam next to the Red Guard jacket. "What are you interested in?"

"Journalism," said Lauren. It was not true, but it was not exactly a lie, it might be true someday, and in the meantime she knew enough about it to sound convincing. Lauren sensed that being undecided was not a viable response.

"Journalism," said Madison. She set aside the Viva Glam and reached for Chanel Red No. 5. "You're not going to be one of those reporters who camps outside my house, are you?"

Lauren had forgotten about the business with the steak.

"Oh, no," she said, "of course not, I think what those people do is despicable, and . . ."

"Let's not get carried away," said Madison, with a tight laugh. "If they don't write something, then maybe people forget me."

"Oh, no," said Lauren, "but not that kind of journalism. My father's an editor. I can imagine myself being an editor."

"Really. Where?"

"*Events.*"

Madison wrote this down next to Lauren's name on her inter-view list. "So you're thinking about the family business. Did you apply to, what's its name?"

"The Medill School. Of journalism."

"Right. Did you?"

This was the real reason not to lie, Lauren realized. Tell one and inevitably you had to tell another.

"Well," said Lauren, trying to remember why her parents made fun of the one guy on the magazine with a degree in journal-ism, "I can get a summer internship to give me on-the-job experi-ence in whatever aspect of journalism I decide to pursue. I think it's important to major in something else, or even have a double major, so that when I graduate I'm knowledgeable in my field. Otherwise you end up knowing how to say things but you don't have anything to say."

She smiled. Good save.

"And I can always take journalism classes," she added.

"Yes, you can," said Madison. She looked at her list of ques-tions, which one of the publicity kids had drawn up for her back in the fall.

"But Northwestern's not your first choice," she said, con-fused. "You didn't apply early. Why is that?" She remembered the time she had pretended to be on vacation in Fiji so that she could avoid committing to a part while she waited to hear about a big-ger one. "Was your first choice someplace you didn't get into?"

Lauren bit her lower lip. Ted had circulated a list of the twenty things alumni were likeliest to ask, and this was not on it, because not applying early usually had to do with trolling for the best money package, and that was nobody's business outside of the financial aid office.

"Not at all, no," said Lauren, flailing about for the answer to the question she knew was coming next. "Northwestern's my first choice."

"Then why didn't you apply early?"

Having credited her parents for her choice of major, Lauren decided to blame them for her timing. In the algebra of falsehood, perhaps two lies canceled each other out.

"My parents feel," she said, and then she stopped, dismayed at the good-girl tone in her voice. If she was going to make things up, at least she ought to have a sense of humor about it. "You know, parents. They have this notion that senior year's a big year. My mom says I shouldn't limit myself in the fall when I'll be a different person by May. And, well, I mean, parents. They think I'm going to get in wherever I want. They're so proud of me. My dad says I should let schools fight over me. I mean, I'm not conceited, I know how hard it is, but he has a point—if you have confidence in yourself then why would you limit your options?"

She stopped short. She could not let it sound like she agreed with her parents.

"But I'm going to Northwestern if I get in," Lauren announced, even though it was clear that Madison had stopped listening back at the business about being a different person in May. A moment later, a production assistant walked in without knocking, on cue; it was her job to interrupt every one of these interviews after ten minutes. Madison Ames stood up and flashed her most apologetic smile.

"Great to talk to you," she said, "and I'm sorry I'm out of time. I will tell the Northwestern people what a lovely conversation we had. Thank you for coming by."

"You're welcome," said Lauren, edging her way to the trailer door. She turned back before she took the first step. "And thank you. For taking so much interest in my application."

"No problem," said Madison.

Nora listened to every grotesque detail, even as she should have been filling four custom Valentine's Day orders, one of which involved hiding an engagement ring in one of six tiny velvet boxes, each of the remaining five containing a chocolate truffle. It was painstaking work, so she handed it over to one of the bakers whose hands were not as likely to shake with rage and retreated to a quiet corner of the bakery to debrief her daughter. Lauren barely got as far as the bikinis before Nora decided to assassinate Madison Ames.

She had been having very primitive and definitive fantasies of late, any time she perceived the slightest threat to Lauren's happiness—and at this point in the process, it was all too easy to confuse a small bad moment with the apocalypse. Her targets, at various times, had included Ted at his most officious, Joy at her most patronizing, even the Northwestern alumni rep, whose only crime was that he took two days to return Lauren's email about setting up an interview—and now Madison Ames, for the crime of narcissistic inattention. Anyone who did not treat Lauren with the proper respect got a miniature pecan pie spiked with a single drop of cyanide—where would Nora find it?—or a quick jab between the ribs with Nora's favorite paring knife, even though it was too short to do any lasting damage and she could never remember whether real killers used an underhand or overhand thrust. Faced with a choice between depression and fantasy, Nora chose fantasy, which at least entertained her while she worked.

She wrapped her arms around Lauren, who burst into frustrated tears, leaving the two women who were packing gift boxes to wonder how a mother and daughter lucky enough to live in the same city, no, in the same country, could be so very sad. Nora hung on until Lauren wriggled free, and did not protest when her daughter blew her nose into the nearest prep towel. She simply guided Lauren toward an empty work table with one hand, tossed the snot towel into the laundry bin with the others, and set out bags of lemons, eggs, and sugar, two cutting boards, and two knives.

"Lemon curd, what do you say?" she asked. "For all those nice people who don't happen to be in love today."

For an hour they stood side by side, Lauren cutting and juicing, Nora measuring sugar and separating eggs, Lauren stirring at the double boiler, Nora filling jars, talking about nothing more pressing than whether the lemons were juicier this year than last. The crazier college applications got, the more the bakery hummed. In the comforting and finite world of dessert, a teaspoon was always a teaspoon, never a teaspoon and a half. Melting chocolate seized up if it got wet, cream biscuits were lighter mixed by hand, a pastry crust that spent an hour in the freezer baked up flakier than one that had not been chilled. Baking was reassuringly rule-bound. It was solace for baker and customer alike.

Second semester was an eternity. There were no deadlines, no goals, and homework only mattered if a student had applied to an Ivy or an Ivy-equivalent or stopped turning it in altogether. The seniors wondered how they would fill the empty months that spread in front of them like whatever the name of that African desert was on their tenth-grade geography exam. The teachers, exhausted after a semester of writing recommendation letters and fending off prying parents on top of everything else they had to do, were perfectly happy to spend a week's worth of class periods watching any DVD that had a tangential relation to their subject. Ted could stroll the English lit corridor and hear dialogue from film adaptations of *King Lear*, *Beloved*, or *The Crucible*, chosen, he imagined, to remind seniors of the larger world and put college apps into context. It never helped. The kids in the bottom half of the class had already perfected an I-don't-care façade, but the top students felt as though they were living one variant or another of that awful anxiety dream, the one about waking up late for a test, or being inexplicably naked in public, or the popular Crestview hybrid that involved showing up late and nude for the SATs.

Alliances shifted. Lauren stopped telling Katie anything, because Katie had such a gift for making her feel worse than she already did. Reluctantly, she stopped confiding in Chloe as well, because for Chloe the difference between a closely guarded secret and public information was five minutes, tops. Instead, Lauren said that she needed the *Threesome* DVD for a paper discussing the effects of a stifling status marriage in popular culture and in *The Great Gatsby*, and Chloe believed her. But Lauren needed a confidant, so she told Brad she was going to see Madison Ames, and he promised to say she was at the dentist's, if anyone should ask.

In return, Brad told Lauren about the parking-lot ambush and Katie's ultimatum, and she made him swear not to miss so much as a minus sign on Katie's behalf. He had promised, in the hope that taking a vow would enable him to stop debating. Weeks later it had not, though he chose not to tell Lauren about that part. He told her instead that he liked the coincidence of her interview being at the same time as his calc test, which he was sure was a good sign for both of them.

Brad always took math tests the same way: he read a test from start to finish to make sure that he understood each problem, and then he went back to the first page and worked straight through to the end. He rarely found a problem that stymied him, but if he did, he worked it first, out of sequence, to get it out of the way. There were no surprises on this calculus test. Brad finished the first five pages before class was half over, so he took a break before he tackled the final page, and scribbled some notes on his scratch paper.

Under the heading Tank, he wrote:

No legacy?
No valedictorian
No Katie trouble
No Liz

Under Ace he wrote:

Legacy
Valedictorian
Katie trouble
No Liz

He could blow the test and risk never seeing Liz again because she would be at Harvard and he might not make the cut, in which case buying Katie's silence hardly mattered, because there would be no relationship to protect. Or he could ace the test and see Liz every day next year, maybe even be in the same dorm, except that she would refuse to talk to him because Katie had filled her head with lies about his nonexistent promiscuous past, out of concern for Liz's happiness, of course. He wanted to think that she would see right through Katie, but this was his worst-case scenario, so he scratched out "No Liz" on both lists. He liked the idea of Liz better than Liz at this point, anyhow, as he barely knew her. It would be crazy to make a decision about his future based on a relationship they did not yet have.

No, the lasting impact, in either case, would come not from Liz but from his dad's reaction—either his rage and disappointment, if Brad missed the cut at Harvard, or his belief that Brad finally had come to his senses, if Brad got in. He worked the last page of problems on the scratch paper, got all the answers, and turned in the test at the bell with the sixth page completely blank, which had to be good enough for a C, possibly even for a written progress report that would have to become part of his official record. As he walked down the hall toward his locker to grab his other books and head home, he felt a hazy little thrill, a disoriented sense that only someone who had been a good boy for eighteen years, with minor infractions, could appreciate.

By the time Brad got to the parking lot, his calculus teacher was standing by the security guard's kiosk, brandishing a sheaf of papers that had to be the calc test. Katie said that all they had to do to get straight As was stay awake and turn in the work, but she had underestimated the school's commitment to its stars. From the look on Mr. Winter's face, a candidate for valedictorian could stay awake, turn in the work, leave an entire page of problems blank, and get away with it.

"Brad, Brad, I'm so glad I found you before you went home," said Mr. Winter, his face pasty with fear. He was a first-year teacher whose sole ambition was to be a lifer at Crestview, and he was not about to draw attention to himself by costing Preston Bradley IV his near-perfect GPA. He had just opened escrow on a pillbox condo an ungentrified mile from the wine bars of Culver City, and in forty-five days he and his PhD were finally moving out of the garage apartment behind his parents' bungalow. There was too much at stake to be done in by a careless boy. He put his hand on Brad's elbow to make sure he did not get away.

"I don't know how this happened, but your test, your copy of the test, look at this, a page missing, everyone else had six pages and you, you, look at this, page six is missing. I am very sorry. I don't know how this happened, but we're going to set it right, right now if you have fifteen minutes. Ten. C'mon."

Brad took the test and noticed two tiny punctures below and to the left of the current staple. In his haste to remove the original staple and the blank sixth page, Mr. Winter had failed to align the new staple over the old staple's holes, not that Brad could call him on it. Mr. Winter was trying to save Brad. He could hardly accuse his teacher of lying and confess that he had intended to leave the whole page blank.

That, he realized, was his mistake. If he had left one problem blank on each page, Mr. Winter would have had no choice but to deduct those points from his total score. The whole page gave his teacher a way out—and Brad had never stopped to consider that Mr. Winter's determination to save Brad from himself was as strong as Brad's desire to cut himself loose. Stronger. He sighed and patted the man on the shoulder.

"Y'know, Mr. Winter, I wondered how I got it done so fast. I mean, I get the material . . ."

"Which is why I came looking for you."

The teacher herded Brad back toward the math wing, relieved at how willingly the boy went along with the charade, pleased that he had found a way for Brad to redeem himself.

"Here we are," he said, opening the door to his classroom and putting a blank sixth page on the nearest desk. "I'm going to sit here and give you ten minutes, which is what I budgeted for this page when I made up the test, so you finish up, it won't take you that long, and that way no one will come down on my head for failing to give the valedictorian his whole test."

"Oh, Mr. Winter, nobody was going to come down on you. I can survive a C. Teach me some humility."

"No, no, not on my watch, I don't think so. Let's save the life lessons for after you graduate."

Brad rooted around in his backpack for his pencil case, his eyes squeezed shut. The boardroom in his brain was getting crowded—not just the Bradley men but Ted and Katie and Liz and Lauren and, now, his math teacher. He blinked hard, sat up, and held a pencil aloft to show that he was ready. Mr. Winter looked at his watch, pointed at Brad, and said, "Now." Five minutes later, Brad handed him a complete and completely accurate page of answers, guaranteeing both his GPA and his math teacher's ability to keep his new job and pay his new mortgage.

Brad got in his car and turned right out of the school driveway instead of left, meandered in the shadow of the 405 until he got to Olympic Boulevard, and headed west toward the ocean, knowing that every block guaranteed him another deadlocked rush-hour block going east, toward home. He did not care. He drove all the way down to the beach, looped around past Liz's street, and pulled into the parking lot of a little art supply store, where he bought some single-ply cardboard, a tube of Zap-a-Gap and an Olfa knife, and a set of fine felt-tipped pens. Satisfied, he headed over to Olympic, turned his back on the setting sun, and took his place in the five-mile-an-hour slog toward the center of the city.

Deena got up from the built-in desk in the kitchen and wandered the house with increasing frequency—what started as half-hour breaks, when she first sat down after lunch, had increased by dusk to a lap every ten minutes. It was hard enough collecting all the bank statements that Dave had asked her for, but every time she went online to find a missing page, the website chastised her for printing what she needed. All around the world, trees were falling over dead because she was trying to get her daughter some financial aid. This should have been Dave's job; this was Dave's forest toppling to the ground. But getting him to do it would have required letting him back into the house, so she printed, and fumed, and took another break.

She walked toward Chloe's deserted room and told herself she was looking for enough dirty T-shirts on the floor to fill up a load of laundry. Deena had no agenda beyond the vague curiosity of a derailed mom who thought she ought to know more than she did, and when she found a black elastic-bound notebook she had not seen before, wedged behind a boot box behind Chloe's laundry hamper, she took it out, vindicated, certain that it contained information she needed to know to be a better parent. She would take a quick glance and put it right back.

To her disappointment, it was not a journal but a sketchbook, page after page of pencil drawings of clothes, not on stick-figure mannequins but on shorter, rounder, more Chloe-like figures. She closed it quickly and put it back behind the boot box, far less pleased than a mother might have been at the discovery of an only child's unexpected talent. Deena was not focused on the possibility that Chloe had a skill she could use to get a job someday. Deena was stuck on the news that her daughter had a secret life. Most parents who snooped feared discovering evidence of drink or drugs, random sex or Facebook shenanigans. Chloe's big news was that she could draw.

Deena corrected herself: the news was that Chloe continued to draw. For a long time, the house had been a minefield of color: fat, greasy crayons, finger paints, watercolors, chalk, until Dave sat down in the wrong chair and stood up to find a peach-colored line across the seat of his good khakis, pastels but only in the kitchen after that, cunning metal trays with six Caran d'Ache wet-or-dry colored pencils, with twelve, with forty, drawing pens with tips so fine they made a dry scratching sound against the paper. But by sophomore year, Chloe's output had dwindled to the occasional napkin doodle, and her parents assumed that she had lost interest.

It seemed instead that she had gone underground. She had shut her mother out. Forget Dave, whose definition of fashion involved a clean T-shirt, pressed jeans, and athletic shoes that had never seen a sport. Deena knew something about style, and yet Chloe had never once confided in her about so much as a stand-up collar. She backed out of the room, climbed into her own bed, wrapped herself in Nana Ree's sunburst-pattern crocheted afghan, and started to cry. No cloudburst, no drama, just the thin leak of reflexive tears that usually came only during a sad movie or that commercial about the two sisters whose dad had Alzheimer's.

"Bullshit," she muttered to herself. She stormed into the kitchen, filled a bowl with ice, carried it into the bathroom, filled the sink with cold water and dumped in the ice, and plunged her face into it until she felt little pinpricks on her skin. Nana Ree had done this every Saturday night before she went out because she had read that Paul Newman did it to keep his skin taut. Lacking a social life, at least for the moment, Deena did it to cover any puffy traces of self-pity. It was not every day that a mom found out she had no idea who her daughter was. Deena was used to the familiar, dysfunctional Chloe, the one who seemed barely able to string together a set of college applications, let alone set off on a new life. A girl with a book full of sketches might do heaven knew what, might sign up for junior year abroad in Paris or Milan or London or anyplace else that was far away and fashion-forward, never to be heard from again unless she remembered to send her mom a plane ticket and an invitation to the fall runway show.

She lay in the growing dark until the last possible moment, and then she grabbed the papers she had printed, stuffed them in her bag, and headed for the Valley. Deena had told Dave that she liked the Sisley's in the Valley because it was halfway between the house and his apartment, but in fact she chose it because no one she knew would see her there, and because a public venue reduced at least the decibel level, if not the likelihood, of an argument. When she got there he was already in a corner booth tucked away from the early crowd, not a good sign, for under normal circumstances Dave loved to be at the center of things.

"Hi. You been here long?"

"No. How you doing?"

"Well, I don't know." She slid into the booth. There was one stack of papers in front of Dave and another on her place mat. "You tell me. What was I printing if you already had a plan?"

Dave ignored the question. He had long since looked at all the statements online, but he had hoped that if Deena printed them out she might actually read them, might show up in a more coop- erative frame of mind. He forced himself not to snap back at her.

"It's no big deal, Deenie. We're going to go through it. How about we order first."

"Sure," she said. Dave beckoned to the waiter and ordered a chicken Caesar for Deena and the cacciatore plate for himself, iced tea for her, a Diet Coke for him, and made a gesture like a whisk broom to dismiss the kid. It was one of the few peremptory things Dave did that once had made Deena feel special. She used to think he was so attuned to her every desire that he could antici- pate what she wanted to have for dinner. Now she found the same behavior insulting—was she so predictable?—and she would have said so, except that she really did like the Caesar here.

She opened the folder and tried to look mesmerized by the numbers Dave had written on the top sheet of paper. "Fourteen thousand dollars—does that mean she's going to get $14,000 if a school accepts her? That's pretty good, isn't it? I mean, $14,000. How'd we get so much?"

Dave adjusted and readjusted his place mat. "Deenie, you got to do the math here before we jump ahead. The number that matters is what they say we can afford to pay." He tapped the sheet of paper with an instructive forefinger. "That's this here, the Ex- pected Family Contribution: $33,000."

She waited.

"So listen," said Dave, gathering speed. "I'm saying a school costs maybe $47,000, and that doesn't include money for travel, she comes home for vacation, we go visit her for some parent thing and it's two hotel rooms, she gets homesick, who knows what, and then you got supplies and books. Spending money. So figure a year, it's really $50,000. Four years, we're talking $200,000."

"Minus $14,000 every year times four years. So."

"So $200,000 minus $56,000."

"That's a good deal."

Dave smiled. His ex-wife espoused a cockeyed fiscal philosophy that made very expensive sense. She never focused on how much she spent, preferring to revel in how much she saved.

"It is a good deal. But it's still almost $150,000 out of pocket. It's kind of like if you found a leather coat that was $3,000, but now it's a third off, so $2,000, a really good deal except you have to have the $2,000. I mean, a deal's only good if you can afford it. The chunk you save is kind of invisible."

"I know that."

"And we know she's not getting a scholarship, so it's loans. We have to pay them back. With interest. It ends up being even more."

"I was at the meeting," she said, drily.

"If she went to a UC it would be under $100,000 even if we paid for the whole thing," said Dave. "Much less."

"So we'll see where she gets in and then we'll know how much it's going to cost."

Dave folded and unfolded the corner of his place mat. There was no good way to do this except fast.

"Deenz, we can't afford a private school. Even a UC's going to be tight."

"But she applied to all these places. What am I going to say to her, that she can't go?"

"C'mon, she applied like you shop—a joke, it's a joke, don't go all pissy on me. She applied to lots of places, I mean, she saw lots of things she thought she'd like, but how many do you really think are going to take her?"

"I don't know. What if it's just one but it's the one she likes the best?"

The food arrived, and Dave, grateful for the interruption, took his sweet time considering the waiter's stock query about whether he could get them anything else. After considering and rejecting offers of white wine, red wine, grated Parmesan, and fresh-ground pepper, he dismissed the kid and turned back to the work at hand.

"One thing we can maybe do," he said, "is talk up the UCs a little, point her in the right direction."

"Because you feel like we have a lot of influence with her at this point, is that it? If I say UC you know what she's going to do? Decide she has to go anyplace but."

Deena had a point. Dave speared a chunk of chicken.

"OK, look," he said, "if it's so important there's one way maybe we can pull it off, but you're not going to like it."

"How do you know?"

Dave smiled. "Because the one way is we sell the house and find you an apartment until we have to buy something else because of taxes, but we get two years to figure that out and then we look for a condo for you, maybe Mar Vista. That way we can send her wherever she wants, except I have to check how that screws up financial aid. Equity in the house they don't care about, remember, but if one year we've got profits from selling it then I'm not sure. But if it's so important to you, I'll find out. She won't know from all the schools for a month. We can figure it out by then. Should I do that?"

Deena moved her fork around the salad bowl as though it were a ouija board and the spirits were going to tell her what to do. What would Nana Ree say? She had lived the way she wanted to live, sent the bills to her ex-husband, and told Deena it was time to practice her phone-answering and message-taking skills if she did not feel like having Saul yell at her. Nana Ree had refinanced the house to send Deena to UCLA, sold it and rented a lovely condo for years with the profits, and had the good sense to expire before she ran out of assets.

Short of dropping dead, Deena had no idea how to respond to Dave's suggestion. Zip codes were destiny in Los Angeles. It was bad enough living in upper Sunset Park, where the only single guys were divorced or gay or both. Mar Vista had not caught up with the news that half of all marriages ended in divorce and Birkenstocks were on their way out for the second time, so there was no potential for a new life in that neighborhood. As for Palms, that was merely the name someone had slapped on the blocks and blocks of dingbat apartments that sat on real estate's Death Row, waiting for the day that developers tore them all down and invented a new beachside community, beachside meaning any thing on the sunset side of the San Diego Freeway. These were the only west side neighborhoods left that were cheaper than where she lived, and Deena was not prepared to consider any of them.

"I am not moving out of the house," she began.

"Well, look, I know it's a tough thing but think about it. When Chloe's gone you got three bedrooms, three baths, I mean, c'mon, how many showers can one woman take?"

"It's not funny."

"Nobody's saying you should move into some hole some-place . . ."

"And I should be grateful for that, right?"

"Hey, let's take it down a notch."

"No, I mean, I don't see why I'm supposed to move out of my house. Maybe the solution is, you make more money and then we do everything we're supposed to do."

"I make plenty of money."

"You're a successful guy," said Deena, cautiously. "So be a little more successful and then we don't have to have this conver-sation."

"What do you think, I can go to Jay and say hey, Jay, I need a big raise this year? Have you maybe seen the headlines about the economy? Nobody's buying air time, so the price goes down, so I make less, so how am I supposed to do this?"

"Well, maybe if they advertised more they'd sell more stuff."

"Great, I'll call somebody right now," he said, brandishing his cell phone, "and tell them my ex-wife says they ought to spend more of the profits they don't have on thirty-second spots."

Deena stared at her plate. "When we got married you never said we can only do this much and no more."

"When we got married I didn't figure to support two households."

"More like two and a half households. Do we get to talk about how much you spend on Linda, or is that not open to discussion?"

The busboy had been lingering nearby with a water pitcher, waiting until it seemed safe to approach the corner booth, and when the silence lasted for ten seconds—he counted to himself—he made his move. He filled both glasses and was about to make his getaway when the woman picked up her plate and held it out to him.

"Can I get this packed up right away, with some extra dressing, and are there any more breadsticks?"

He nodded and backed away.

"What are you doing?" asked Dave.

"I am taking my dinner home where I can eat in peace and quiet. I think I should stay in the house and Chloe should go to school where she wants and you should figure it out. No, you know what? You talk to Chloe. You break her heart and tell her she has to go to a UC."

"Deena, what the hell is wrong with a UC? You went there. I went there. How is that going to break her heart when she never said there's someplace she's dying to go?"

Deena retrieved the statements from her bag and shoved them across the table at Dave. "Maybe she's just afraid to say she likes a school because she thinks you'll let her down," she said. She slid out of the booth and headed for the door without waiting for her

leftover salad. Dave watched her retreating back, ordered a tira-
misu to go despite the vow he had made that very morning to lose
twenty pounds and get into better shape, and left with it and the
bagged Caesar and his notes and the statements. He waited until
he was at a red light, on a busy section of Ventura Boulevard, and
then he opened his window and hurled the container of salad with
enough force to startle both himself and the Labradoodle that was
starting to pee on a bicycle chained to a parking meter. The dog
skittered sideways, stepped in its own urine and stepped on its
owner's foot, leaving a paw-shaped spot on a brand-new suede
boot just three hours out of the box. The woman stared at her foot
and at the scattered salad, and when she looked up to see where
the missile had come from, Dave gave her a jaunty little salute.
She held her fist aloft and ceremoniously raised her middle finger,
one of the legions of people who used sexual references—middle
fingers, cocksucker, fucker—when they were angry.

Deena always wondered why men who loved blow jobs acted
like "cocksucker" was an insult. She thought they might be worried about their own sexuality, about whether they'd be happier
gay, getting blow jobs all the time. Or maybe men used "cocksucker" as a putdown—she had come up with this theory after one
of her own displays of prowess—to keep women from thinking
that they ruled the world for any longer than it took to perform
the act.

She said things like that every so often, out of the blue—not
often enough for anyone to mistake her for an original thinker, but
it was the very unpredictability of her pronouncements that Dave
enjoyed. He corrected himself: that he had enjoyed, back when
conversations had lasted long enough for her to have the opportunity to surprise him.

The driver behind him sat on the horn. Dave roused himself
to yell "Fuck you" at the dog owner, but she was already huffing
down the block, her traumatized pup in tow, stopping every few

steps to hold up her left toe and evaluate the drying stain. Dave looked long and slow in his rearview mirror, held up his middle finger, and edged into the intersection at a crawl to let the other driver know that he was moving forward because he wanted to, and not because he felt anything like remorse.

chapter 12

Ted had a tell, like any gambler: he drummed exactly as many fingers on his desk as there were seniors likely to be admitted to the school whose admissions director was on the phone. College admissions people never answered their phones in March, using voice mail as a filter to control the timing and rhythm of their disclosures, so anyone Ted called would have to decide to call him back. If they did, it usually meant a measure of good news, although everything was relative these days. Good news might mean a single probable acceptance among five applicants. More and more, admissions people modified whatever they said with the word "probable."

Ted never picked up his phone during the month of March either, but to provide the illusion of eager accessibility he relied on the college counseling receptionist to field his calls, rather than use voice mail. Every morning he gave Rita a prioritized list of the calls he was waiting for, and if the first school on his list called while he was talking to the eighth school on his list, she scribbled the name of the first school on a Post-it, walked silently into his office, and placed the note on his desk. She never stood there long enough to hear how he finessed hanging up on the eighth school, but he was always ready for the more important call by the time she got back to her desk, after which he somehow managed to get back on the phone with number eight without playing a new round of phone tag.

The first year on the job, Rita concentrated on working the list quickly and efficiently, and at the end of the season Ted handed her a Nordstrom's gift card that turned out to be worth $300. The second year, she merely let a particularly pushy set of parents know that Ted had heard from Bowdoin, in return for which she received a gift certificate for six sessions with a personal trainer. Soon after, discreet notes and small gifts from other parents began to appear on her desk ("Why wait until graduation to thank you for all your help?" "Dear eagle eyes, if Donny ends up at Brown we'll have you to thank for watching out for him."), until she had enough high-end skin-care products to stock a small boutique. All that they wanted in return was a quiet heads-up when Ted took a call from their children's first-choice schools, so that they could coincidentally call to check in later the same day.

It was easy enough to accommodate them, as she was not being asked to divulge content. Rita was an ambitious girl who had lost her development job at Paramount because she believed an article about office romances posing less of a risk than they used to. Now she dreamed of being made a full-fledged counselor just in time to derail the college aspirations of the current ninth-grader whose father had cost her the studio job. While she bided her time, she looked for ways to be even more indispensable than she already was.

She always knew which school was on the phone. The next step was to watch Ted as he talked, to look for clues—and once she noticed the tapping, to look for a pattern. At the end of her second year at Crestview, she had drawn up a list of presumed acceptances, which she compared to the official list the school published every June. Based on Ted's tapping, Rita had been right on twelve of the fifteen calls she had tracked. This year, her third, she was sure enough of her technique to share information with a very select group of parents.

Ted was on a call with Skidmore when the phone rang.

"He has the head of school in his office," she lied. "But he did ask me to let him know when you called. Just a moment, please." She did not take the time to write. She got to the doorway of Ted's office, held up one finger, and he nodded and got off the phone.

It did not take long. Ted talked, Ted listened, Ted drummed on the desk, Ted hung up and smiled. Rita took a small Moleskine notebook out of her purse, pulled the elastic strap out of the way, and wrote down, "Harvard—2. 1/1?" She had a hunch that gender played a role in Ted's tapping, that he tapped one-handed if it was all girls or all boys, and two-handed, like a typist, the phone cradled against his shoulder, if both girls and boys had gotten in. She had yet to figure out if he always used the same hand for the same sex, but there was no rush. Parents were satisfied to know that he had made contact. The rest of her sleuthing, the attention to gender-specific tapping patterns, was a puzzle for Rita's personal entertainment. The more sophisticated her code-breaking skills, the greater the risk she would be found out.

She pulled up the final application list on her computer screen and found the five students who had applied to Harvard. One set of parents always called her Rhonda, so they would not be getting a call. The remaining four had been attentive to her in varying degrees, but two of their children were long shots, so only two sets of parents would hear from her.

At this time of year, her calls always went through.

"Hi. How goes it?"

"He just got off the phone with Harvard," she said, "and he was smiling. There may be two yeses. I'm sorry I don't know more about who it is."

"That's fine," said Trey. "Thank you."

"No problem."

She hung up, put the notebook back in her purse, and glanced up just in time to see Ted riffing with two fingers on each hand as he chatted with the rep from Skidmore. When he finished the call, he dialed another number and swiveled his chair so that he was facing the back wall, and Rita assumed that he was making his own call to Trey.

❧

The University of California schools dumped notification emails throughout the month of March, as though being first gave them any meaningful advantage over the East Coast schools. Crestview parents who had grown up in Los Angeles wanted to send their kids east to prove that they were cosmopolitan, that they appreciated the existence of a larger world, where men shaved every day and women of a certain status and zip code dressed as though they were on their way to either a funeral or a foxhunt. Parents who had fled the East Coast and migrated to the promised land, on the other hand, had to prove that they had not gotten lazy, that they still appreciated the character-building aspects of frostbite and vertical architecture, and they dreamed of sending their children back to the very cities they had fled. For most Crestview families, a UC application was little more than a sunlit insurance policy against the unthinkable on April 1.

The single exception was UC Berkeley—Cal to the people lucky enough to go there. Cal, a vestige of the time when it was the one and only UC, the first, the sufficient, the definitive, the model·for the satellites that followed. Berkeley was as difficult to get into as a private school, the site of an ongoing and escalating battle between white and Asian students, each of whom thought their acceptance rate was too low and the competition's too high. A Crestview senior might bide his time in March by bragging about a Cal acceptance, but most of them tallied their UC acceptances with the same nonchalance that enabled them to fill up their cars with their parents' credit cards and never once look at the price.

There were no surprises for Lauren, as she had checked off only three UC campuses. Three emails popped up on a single evening, a rejection from Berkeley and acceptances from UC Santa Barbara and UC Irvine. She reported the news to her parents without disappointment or relief. As far as Lauren was concerned, there was little difference between a no from a great school like Berkeley and a yes from a school she had picked because Ted said she needed three Best Chances.

"But it's your first yes," said Nora. "Yeses, excuse me. We could stop for a second and think about that." She tried to put her arms around Lauren. "You're going to college."

"Not in Santa Barbara or Irvine I'm not," said Lauren, backing off.

Joel stopped loading the dishwasher. "You would have preferred getting turned down?"

"Stop it. Don't pretend to be happy about something we're not happy about. I mean, what do you think I should major in, surfing? Antiques? I'm going back to work. We don't want Northwestern to accept me and then take it back because I flunked out."

She disappeared, leaving Nora and Joel to finish cleaning up the kitchen. Joel waited until he heard Lauren's door close before he leaned over to whisper to his wife.

"What are we, living with Groucho Marx? 'I don't want to go to any school that would accept me as an undergraduate'?"

"Something like that."

Disdain, ingratitude, tempests of self-hatred and rage and sarcasm, and the occasional ultimatum that equated UCLA with prison, UC Santa Cruz with summer camp, and UC Davis with the boonies: as April 1 got closer and closer, Crestview seniors began to fall apart. With Ted's fingers poised in midair more often than they made happy drumming contact with his desk, there was precious little good news, or even good rumor, to go around. Worse, everyone assumed that the acceptances and rejections were by now loaded into every school's outbound email bins, waiting for a bureaucrat to launch them at the end of business on March 31, or at a minute after midnight on April 1—cruel inconsistency—so that heartbroken families would have to wait overnight to call to appeal. Like cows being herded into the slaughterhouse chute, like dead men walking, seniors lived the last days of March with a cold inevitability, knowing that there was not a single thing they could do to alter their fate. Bad news was coming to someone, but no one knew how much or to whom.

The tunnel vision got worse every day, even among families that had in the past acknowledged the existence of more substantial threats to their happiness than a college rejection: rogue nuclear nations, a global food shortage, phenomena that people with stacked degrees from illustrious colleges and universities were having a great deal of trouble solving. The mood was only slightly more festive at Ocean Heights, where the demographics included families for whom a UC acceptance was heaven on earth, proof that they were about to send a first generation to college, or that they would spend fewer years in debt than they had feared. But the best Ocean Heights students were as crazed as their Crestview counterparts, hopeful that they would show to advantage in the public school population, terrified that an Ivy would discount a public school A because the curriculum lacked rigor. Liz's Berkeley acceptance registered as little more than confirmation of her competitive status for Harvard.

On April 1, Steve dropped off his last fare at 2:15, complained to the dispatcher of a terrible stomachache, possibly food poisoning, and headed for home, as did Yoonie, who at 2:15 feigned an identical stomachache and left Dr. Joy in the lurch for the first time in her life. They met in the parking lot of the Coffee Bean so that they could arrive at home simultaneously, and when they pulled up, Liz was already standing on the sidewalk in front of the house, staring at a pile of mail stacked on the stoop. She could have checked her email before she left school, and for a moment she regretted not having done so, but her parents had always talked about what the three of them would do when Liz got her good news, not what Liz would do by herself. The unspoken assumption was that they would find out together. It would have felt like cheating to look at her email.

Steve and Yoonie came up next to her, silently, tallying the number of big manila envelopes. Six. They had a mail slot in their front door, so there was no way to tell if there was a thin envelope without going inside, but for a long moment they did not move.

Six large envelopes.

"We should go inside," said Liz.

"You said you did not want us to open the mail," said Yoonie. "We are waiting for you."

"Right. Okay. I'll go first and pick up the stuff on the stoop but I'm not going to look at the return addresses. I'm going to open the door and take in the mail and not look either. I'm going into my room. I'll come out and tell you what happened once I look at everything."

She could not make good on the business about not looking at the return addresses, but she picked up the outside stack and opened the door to collect the inside stack without giving anything away, and then she disappeared down the hallway into her room, leaving the front door open behind her. Yoonie waited for Steve to move, and Steve waited for Yoonie to move, and neither of them did until a sound behind them made them jump. They turned, as one, and the mailman smiled and saluted as he locked the back doors of his truck and came around to the curbside driver's door.

"Lotta mail for you folks," he said, with a knowing smile. For ten years he had been delivering school news to the families on his route, from preschool acceptances on up to college, and he knew what a pile of fat envelopes meant.

"I can see there's going to be some celebrating here tonight," he said as he got into the truck.

Steve and Yoonie waved, mimicked his neighborly smile, and went inside. Yoonie put on water for a pot of tea, but Liz was still in her room when the water boiled, still in her room when the tea had steeped. The optimistic flush that Steve and Yoonie had felt at the mailman's reference to a celebration began to fade, replaced by the awful sense that the delay had nothing to do with Liz being overcome by joy.

When she did emerge, holding a single sheet of stationery in her hand, there was none of the drama that her parents had anticipated. She simply placed the letter on the table between them and said, "I didn't get in." She went to the cabinet, got a mug from the company that made Dr. Joy's favorite retinol preparation, poured herself some tea, and sat down, so that they could all stare at the letter together.

"Would you like something with your tea?" asked Yoonie, who needed to be busy. Dr. Joy often bought cupcakes for the staff, even though she refused to go near refined sugar and the two younger nurses were on a lifelong diet that only included cupcakes if no one was watching. Yoonie always brought three of them home.

"Sure," said Liz.

Yoonie cut a double-chocolate cupcake into thirds and put the pieces on a small plate. Steve picked up the letter and studied it, as though he might find a clue to his daughter's fate in the watermark, or the typeface, or even the cushioned wording of the bad news. A friendly rejection letter had a familiar and disingenuous sting, like the fare who complained about the cab's air-conditioning, left a chunk of almond bark to melt into the creases of the backseat, and departed the cab with a cheery, "Have a nice day."

Yoonie studied the cupcake segments and took the smallest one, and when Steve put down the letter she pretended to read it with great interest.

"Mom," said Liz, taking it from her mother's hand and folding it in careful thirds. "There's no point to reading it." She stood up, cupcake wedge in one hand, mug of tea in the other. "I'm sorry I let you guys down," she said.

She was halfway down the hall before her father came to his senses.

"Elizabeth," he called. "All the big envelopes. What were they?"

She answered without turning or stopping. "Yale, Swarthmore, Princeton, Columbia, Penn, Chicago." She shut her bedroom door behind her, and her parents, as depressed as though they had received nothing but bad news, finished their tea and wondered what they would do with the rest of the afternoon.

Liz stacked the acceptance packets on the floor by her desk and picked up her cell phone. She sent a text message to Brad.

"No from Harvard. You?" but he did not reply.

✤

Brad wandered over to Starbucks after school and wasted an hour pretending to read his biology homework, and when Liz's text arrived he went back to school and slipped into the empty computer lab to find out his own fate before he answered her. He started to open his email once, twice, and closed it both times without reading the contents of the in-box, waiting for the excited tightening in his chest, the flutter of anticipation, that he imagined a senior was supposed to feel. All he got was a tight little tug in his right shoulder blade, which he knew was from hiking his shoulder when he used the mouse, but which felt like a knot of his father's gathered expectations.

Enough.

He called up his email and there they were, eight emails lined up like little soldiers at attention, awaiting his inspection. He clicked. He was in at Brown, as though his father would ever let him go to a school with no set curriculum. Click, click, click, in at Penn, at Williams, at Cornell. At Wesleyan and Princeton. With Berkeley, he was batting a thousand, and the momentum of all this good news carried him, click, into the Harvard notification without hesitation, because for a single, sheer, clear moment he felt confident enough not to care what happened.

Brad read the message, read it a second time, forgot completely about Liz, and called his dad on the inside office line. Trey picked up on the first ring.

"Son, I called the house and no one is home. Where are you?"

"I'm on the wait list, Dad. I got the email. I got accepted everyplace else, but Harvard wants to put me on the wait list. Go figure."

"That's not possible."

"Want me to forward the email?"

"I don't understand."

"They send out emails. Besides the letters, so I opened mine. They didn't take me, so what do you think? Penn might be good." Brad heard the clacking of a keyboard and panicked. "Hey, who are you emailing? Don't do anything. Please wait until we get home."

The clacking stopped.

"Who got in?"

"I'm sorry?"

"Well, we're all sorry, but we'll get this straightened out. Who got in?"

"How would I know? I'm in the computer lab. Who cares who else got in?"

"I care," said Trey, who went back to the email he was drafting to the head of the alumni association. "I'd like to know who there has a more attractive record than a fourth-generation legacy who's going to be valedictorian."

"A maybe valedictorian," said Brad, feeling a sudden, small urge to give his father a hard time. "What if it's Katie instead?"

"Please. Let us not get distracted. Go ask Ted who they took."

"I will not."

"Brad, I need you to go ask Ted who they took."

"You need me . . . I don't want to know, okay? Talk to you later. Thanks for all your sympathy." He hung up and forwarded the email to his father, who called back a moment later. Brad thought about not answering. His friends ignored their parents' calls, or pled bad reception or a low battery, but Brad always assumed that his father would see right through that kind of fakery.

"Dad, I really don't want to talk about it," he said.

"Son, is there anyone else in the lab?"

"No."

"Listen to me. It may be that Roger's behavior has cast a pall here. He certainly did not do the family any favor by making such a noisy exit."

"Dad. Maybe they just didn't take me."

"They did not reject you. They offered you the wait list, and we're going to clear this up. In the meantime, talk to Ted, but if you should see one of your friends I see no reason to make a lot of noise about not knowing yet."

"If somebody asks me I have to say."

"No, you don't." Brad had never heard his father sound so brusque. "You say you're in. I don't want to hear any more about this. Talk to Ted and call me back."

"You want me to lie and say I got in?"

"I want you to appreciate that this is an error we are going to resolve."

"Right. See you at home."

"Call me after you see Ted."

"I *will*. I said I would."

"Actually, you didn't, but now you have. Don't worry. We're going to straighten this out."

This time Trey hung up first, before Brad had a chance to say that he was not worried, that there was nothing to straighten out, that he would appreciate the opportunity to enjoy all the other good news. Instead, he reread the acceptances, tried to feel elated, felt only confused, and shuffled downstairs to find Ted waiting in the counseling lobby, wearing the determined expression of a man who had already been briefed. Brad followed him into his office and fell into a chair.

"My dad already called you," he said.

Ted nodded.

"I'm supposed to ask you who got in."

Ted shrugged. In fact, Harvard had offered a spot to a female basketball star who had already been promised a full ride at Stanford and was conveniently on the road to Palo Alto for a visit at that very moment. Ted's first job in the morning would be to convince his Harvard contact to swap her out for a legacy boy, Caucasian, of no athletic prowess whatsoever but possessed of a dad with profoundly deep pockets, without waiting for the formal wait-list process to begin on May 1. He was already working on the script in his head. It would be tinged, ever so slightly, with righteous indignation—because the officer had implied that Crestview was getting two acceptances and because the disappeared second space obviously should have gone to Brad.

"And he wants me to say I got in because he thinks he's going to figure out a way to do that."

Ted squirmed. "I'm not telling you to lie, but your dad has a point. Not that you should say you got in, which is pretty bald-faced. But tell people you have way too much choice, which by the way is true. Or say you don't have a clue what you're going to choose, also true. Not really, I mean, you're getting into Harvard, but at the moment you can say you don't know, while I get this error resolved. That's my job now . . ."

"That's what my dad said. An error we're going to resolve. How big a check you think that's going to take?"

"Uh-uh, stop it. This is where I earn the big bucks, I get on the phone before dawn tomorrow and get this straightened out . . ."

"That's the other thing he said."

"Look," said Ted. "Your dad loves you, Harvard's a big deal in your family, you've got to let us play this out and then you make your choice. I mean, you can tell people whatever you want, but do you really want to spend the last six weeks of your senior year answering the question, 'How's the wait list going?' "

"Not so much."

"So finesse it. I mean, after all, it's nobody else's business. You have to look out for yourself."

Brad shrugged. "Like somebody's really going to decide not to go to Harvard and I get the empty slot. You guys do what you do. Maybe I'll go to Princeton, what do you think? Or Brown. Design your own curriculum. That'd drive my dad nuts, don't you think?"

"If that's your first criterion," said Ted, more harshly than he had intended to.

"Right," said Brad, who heard the accusation in Ted's tone.

"Go home," said Ted, retreating into empathy mode. "Play sick tomorrow. Give yourself a day to think it over."

"I can't."

"Why not?"

Brad laughed a strangled laugh as he got up to leave. "C'mon, Mr. Marshall. The only people who stay home on April 2 are the people who got shot down. If I'm going to bullshit everybody I have to be here."

Ted sighed. "Stay away from crowds, what can I say?"

He held his breath while Brad said good-bye to Rita and opened and closed the outer office door. He counted to five, got up to close his door, sat down in one of the club chairs and leaned over, his hands clasped at the back of his neck, stretching, pulling down hard, turning his head to one side and then the other, to make sure that his anger did not clot in his carotid arteries and kill him on the spot.

Preston Bradley IV was supposed to be the closest thing Crestview had to a sure thing, a gimme, and Ted had failed to get him into Harvard, had failed to sell those *asshole tight-ass jackass fucking asshole* members of the admissions committee on a candidate who should not have needed selling. He bit his lip to keep from saying out loud what he was thinking to himself. What was that sly smile from the admissions guy back at the NACAC conference—bullshit? Was he, Ted, such a negligible presence? He felt his father standing next to him in his mailman duds, the polyester shirt with its awful slimy sheen, the stupid wide Bermuda shorts that made his knobby legs look like a couple of walking sticks, a cautionary hand on Ted's shoulder, as though he worried that his son would paint a target on his chest and go looking for a drive-by. Ted was furious at himself for ever thinking that good luck—even informed, researched, strategic good luck mixed with hard work—was the same thing as power.

Ted did not run the show, and he had been a fool to think that he did. He straightened up in the chair and walked over to slam the desk drawer shut. In the morning he was going to sell this kid and his dad and their blank check until he seduced the admissions committee into changing its mind. He was going to deposit the

$5,000 he had in his wallet, Fred's down payment on his son's future, and more checks like it. Rita had commented that very morning on the increase in calls from junior parents, and he was not about to let Brad's angst get in the way of what those calls promised.

chapter 13

No, no, no, not, not, not, the slamming of doors along an endless hallway, despite an array of linguistic devices designed to soften the blow: rejection letters never referred to an applicant's limitations, preferring to follow the bad news with an inevitable and empty phrase about the terribly competitive landscape. They often sounded far too much like acceptance letters, except for the presence of the word "not" and the absence of "Congratulations!" Worse, thanks to overzealous spam filters and postal workers capable of confusing Chaiken on Forest Street with MacDougall on Third, the agony of notification dragged on for almost two weeks. A large school mailed its letters in stages, leaving parents to speculate about whether they were sorted alphabetically or by zip code or type of news. A small school's new email notification system failed to work. Parents in limbo checked the digital readout before they picked up the phone, rather than talk to someone whose child had already received good news. Seniors who had not yet heard studiously avoided seniors who looked happy, and seniors who got bad news avoided everyone. One boy Brad barely knew accosted him in the cafeteria line to ask if he had been accepted at Brown, and when Brad said that he had, the boy yelled, "Well, fuck you," and stormed off.

Lauren stopped going to the cafeteria altogether on the day she saw Katie gleefully bouncing up and down with one of the other Northwestern applicants; she could not bring herself to ask if the girl was happy about Northwestern or about someplace else. Every day or so she received an email or a thin envelope containing a rejection from a Stretch, which caused her father to say something empty and philosophical, or an Even Odds, which caused her mother to bake. A wait-list form arrived from Skidmore, which put the entire family into a cold sweat. Chloe had gotten into Skidmore.

They broke discipline and called Ted, who insisted that Joel put him on speaker phone so that Nora and Lauren could hear what he had to say first-hand.

Ted said exactly what he had already said to four other families and would repeat to five more before the end of the day, that a single rejection was in no way indicative of a trend, that even multiple rejections were a set of unrelated coincidences, that Best Chances were putting highly qualified applicants on wait lists to protect their yield, because a highly qualified kid might prefer to go somewhere else. Ted said there would be what amounted to a second acceptance season in June, when schools tallied their commitment letters and saw how many empty spaces they had to fill, as though the opportunity to wait for two more months was good news.

At this point in the process, Ted's life was defined by the crisis card he kept in his wallet, a short list, updated nightly, of the things he absolutely had to fix. Right now, Brad and Harvard held the top slot, and the trustee's daughter with the lowest score any Crestview student had ever received on the math SAT rounded out the list at number seven. Anyone who was not on that index card got the appropriate canned speech—particularly someone like Lauren, who had yet to hear from her first-choice school. Ted was a counselor, not a magician, and if he was going to be effective he had to establish priorities and keep to them.

He was distracted and he knew it, so he relied on a proven second-tier strategy. He offered to make Skidmore happen, banking on the Chaikens' common sense to keep him from having to try when he had more pressing problems to solve. They came through: there was no need to spend his energy pushing for a school Lauren did not care about, merely for the sake of having an acceptance. They would wait to hear from Northwestern. In gratitude, he reminded them again that nothing had anything to do with anything else, as far as envelopes were concerned.

"Northwestern knows it's your first choice by far," he said. "The other schools didn't hear that from you, so maybe they don't want to take the chance you're going to turn down their offer."

"See?" said Joel, after they had hung up. "He's saying all of this could be good news. They know they're not your first choice, they know you're good enough to get into your first choice, so they cut their losses and take someone who isn't as strong. Skidmore knew you weren't going to settle."

"Then how come Brad got in everywhere?" Nora whispered, as soon as Lauren had left the room. She held up her hand to keep Joel from answering. "Never mind," she said. "What's going to happen is going to happen. I just wish it was over."

❧

Nora had been driving home at lunchtime for a week without telling anyone, wolfing yogurt at red lights from a container wedged into the cup holder, so that she could be around when the mail arrived. She had known about every single thin envelope before Lauren got home, which meant that she always knew first, for Lauren was not about to risk exposure by checking her email during school hours. The day after the conversation with Ted, Nora was in place when the mailman delivered yet another sheaf of letter-sized envelopes along with the standard batch of Realtor and insurance solicitations. She riffled through them, and there, second to last, was an envelope from Northwestern—but not quite a skinny one. Not bulging, but definitely not skinny, definitely full of something more than the single sheet required for a Dear Reject or a Dear Wait List letter.

She went inside, dumped the rest of the mail on the kitchen table, and held the Northwestern letter up to the light, in case the afternoon sun happened to illuminate the word "please" or "welcome," or the infinitive "to accept," although that was a less dependable clue, since it could conceivably follow the phrase, "We are sorry to say that we have decided not." All she could make out was the university logo and "Dear Lauren." The rest was a slaw of all the letters on several folded pages. Try as she might—and she turned the envelope from front to back and upside down—she could not tease out the opening line.

In a giddy instant, she knew what this was. Clearly, Northwestern was concerned about the environmental waste involved in sending a four-color glossy brochure to every accepted candidate, as some of them would choose another school. Clearly, Northwestern took its carbon footprint seriously—really, what a great choice for Lauren—and chose to send out the good news in a couple of pages. After May 1, the members of the freshman class would get everything else, the pamphlets, the campus map, the move-in checklist, the calendar of welcome week events.

She called Joel.

"Northwestern's more than one sheet."

"You're home?"

"I was near the house—"

"So you stopped by to weigh the mail."

"Joel, it's more than one page."

"Wasn't Skidmore more than one?"

"No. One page, sign at the bottom and we'll put you on the waiting list. You don't think that's what this is, do you? It has to be three or four pages. I think it's a yes, and all the paperwork comes after she says yes to them."

Joel was silent.

"You don't think I'm right."

"I don't think you're wrong. Is it more than two pages? Can you tell?"

Nora sighed. The man she depended on to evaluate the universe was no longer moored to the steadying dock of reason.

"Oh, it's four easy," she said.

"Good," Joel replied, trying to reclaim his role as final arbiter. "I think that's good."

"Good," said Nora. "Try to get out of there early."

She jammed the mail back into the mailbox in case Lauren got home before she did, drove back to work, and spent the rest of the afternoon making buttercream frosting because she could do it in her sleep, mindlessly separating eggs and unwrapping bricks of butter, slitting vanilla beans and scraping out the tiny seeds. She left work early, but so did Joel, which meant that they had far too much time to waste waiting for Lauren to get home from the graduation choir rehearsal they had forgotten about, until she called at her break to remind them. They retrieved the envelope from the mailbox and held it against the reading light in the living room, the illuminated magnifying mirror in the bathroom, the light on the ventilator hood above the cooktop. They discussed briefly the ethics of steaming, as opposed to merely looking, and tucked the letter back into the middle of the stack in the mailbox for Lauren to find.

At the sound of the front door opening, they got busy looking busy, Joel pouring ice water, Nora arranging and rearranging three chicken breasts on a small platter. Lauren walked into the kitchen and dropped her purse and backpack so that she could sort through the mail. When she got to the Northwestern envelope Nora turned away, as though a meal designed to survive neglect might require further attention. She knew, in the moment before she really knew anything, that she had misinterpreted every sign, that the zeal with which they had pursued the perfect school had made them crazy enough to believe that such a place existed, and worse, crazy enough to ignore every cautionary comment, to hurtle toward this single moment propelled by the belief that Lauren was going to get what she wanted purely because she was beloved. Nora heard the swish of paper being pulled from the envelope and unfolded, and it was all she could do not to grab the pages from Lauren's hand and feed them to the garbage disposal before anyone could read a word. They were wrong to care so much; she and Joel had made a complete botch of this even though they had tried always to do what seemed right and reasonable. They had gotten caught up, and in a millisecond they were going to pay for it.

She thought all of this in the time it took Lauren to open the envelope and read the first sentence of the first paragraph on the first page of four.

"Wait list," said Lauren, tossing the pages onto the kitchen counter, "and then there are some more pages to explain the wait list and a sign-up form. I don't have the energy for this."

"Honey . . ."

Lauren stalked out of the room. Nora reached for a sponge and wiped down all the kitchen counters, and Joel decided not to point out that she had done so only ten minutes earlier. He picked up the pages.

"Formal notice, two-page explanation of the waiting-list process, a little bit of don't give up cheerleading but no promises, and the do-you-want-to-be-on-the-wait-list form. Due May 1."

"The hell with them."

"Look, that's how you feel right now, but it's three questions on a form, I mean, maybe it can't hurt. In for a dime, in for a dollar."

"They can't have her," said Nora. "Her heart's broken, can't you see that? Where is she going to go to school?"

"She got into Santa Barbara and Irvine."

"But that's not what she wants. Where is she going to go to school that she's happy about?"

"I don't think we know that less than a minute after the big letdown. Or maybe not a letdown in the long run, but we have to talk to Ted, don't we? And then maybe we have to figure out a way to be happy with what she's got, which, let's face it, is not the end of the world. I don't know. Let's eat and let it sink in."

"I'm not hungry," said Nora. She leaned against the kitchen island and pulled shreds of chicken from one of the breasts.

Joel filled up his dinner plate and sat at the empty table, immobile, until he realized that he had lost his appetite, too. He wanted nothing more than to spend the evening with his family—but as the point person for emotional restraint in that trio, he knew that he dare not confess to such a need. It would only make Nora and Lauren feel worse.

Before he could figure out what to say, Lauren appeared at the bottom of the stairs and announced that she was going to sleep over at Chloe's.

"You know, maybe she'll loan me an acceptance someplace."

"*Lauren.*" Nora's tone was so sharp that they both stopped what they were doing and stared at her. "Please, honey."

"Sorry. I'm sorry," Lauren said. "This is just all so creepy. Please, can I go to Chloe's and we can talk about it more tomorrow?"

"Sure," said Nora.

Just like that, the house was silent, but in an unstable, aggressive way, and belligerently empty. Joel took to the couch with the *New York Times*, and Nora sat down next to him because she had no idea what else to do.

"What're you reading?"

"Obits," he said. "Looking for a correlation between where people went to school and how happy they were. Not finding one."

He held up the page and jutted his chin toward a death notice that ran almost an entire column in length. "This guy? Everybody loved him. Renaissance man, philanthropist, took up skiing at seventy, died in his sleep at ninety-four. Went to Covered Wagon U before Iowa was a state."

Nora stood up with the kind of sigh that a less-distracted Joel would have recognized for the storm cloud it was, and walked into the little extra bedroom where they kept the desktop computer.

When Lauren was in first grade she had taken Joel's visiting college roommate and his wife on a tour of the house, and had explained to them, with a great seriousness of purpose, that PC stood for Parents' Computer. Those were the days, thought Nora, when the simple ability to link a letter to a sound to a word was accomplishment enough. The memory only made her feel worse. Living in nostalgia's swamp was not going to be easy. They might have to get a dog.

A moment later, she called out, "Hey, come see what I found."

Joel folded the newspaper slowly, hoping that whatever it was had nothing to do with college, knowing as he walked down the hall that it did. She edged over so that he could pull up a chair, and she started to read aloud.

"Well, somebody sure as F made a big fat mistake they're going to regret forever when they rejected me. After I go to Harvard Law, after I clerk for a Supreme Court Justice, when I'm weighing offers, like maybe what public office should I run for first, who do you think is going to get credit for sending me on the path to greatness? When I'm on the road to the White House! Not Northwestern. Colgate is going to see that application spike because other people are going to want their kids to do what I did. I have a 2290 on my SATs and who cares about Bs in science if

I'm going into politics? You took a kid I know with only three APs, and if I cared at all I'd challenge the rejection because I bet you made a mistake. Your loss, bozos."

Joel looked up from the screen, praying that they were going to play this for comedy. "Where did you find this?"

"I Googled 'Northwestern University undergraduate acceptance,' and I found a blog of nothing but kids who applied there, all the way back to last fall. He posted this on the school's own website. Can you believe it?"

"What I'm having trouble believing is that you Googled 'Northwestern University undergraduate acceptance,'" Joel replied. "What did you expect to find?"

Nora shrugged, embarrassed but defiant. "And if I scroll down, he posted the same thing every hour. It shows up every five or six posts, so no matter when you look, you're going to see it. That's how angry he is."

"How do you know it's a boy? Could be a psycho girl."

"Named Bob."

"If you were that nuts, would you use your real name?" Joel scrolled further down the screen.

"Maybe we should have—"

Joel cut her off with a curt "No!"

"How do you know whether we should have or shouldn't have when you don't even know what I'm going to say?"

"That's not what I meant," he said. "I meant no, there's no point to second-guessing. For all we know, she was the next kid up at every single school she applied to."

"Then she'd be on the wait list at all of them. So we know she wasn't. Next kid up, that is."

"Don't be so literal. You know what I mean."

"Actually, I don't know what you mean."

Joel's voice got tight. "You heard what Ted said. Any other year and she'd be a gimme at these schools, but this is not any other year. Last year wasn't any other year, next year won't be any other year, these kids are trapped because too many of their parents had too many kids at the same time. And because we get *U.S. News & World Report* confused with the ten commandments. And because everybody has to apply to two dozen schools."

"But we didn't figure it out for her," said Nora, her voice strangled by coming tears. "Maybe we should have—don't you dare stop me—maybe we should have had her apply easier places, and who knows if Ted really fought for her. But like you say, it's beside the point."

She sputtered and looked around the room. "Why is there never Kleenex in here?" Joel waited while she stomped into the bathroom, blew her nose once, twice, splashed water on her face, and came back in.

"If you want a big mistake to agonize over," he said, closing the blog, "we should've waited longer to have a kid. The boomlet crests in maybe two years, three, five at the most."

"That's ridiculous."

"Of course it is."

"I don't mean ridiculous to wait. Ridiculous to think it's going to end. Not for kids who think there are only ten schools worth going to and their parents will do anything to send them there. All the Crestviews, all over the country, still have the same number of kids applying to the same number of schools, and that's before you even think about Ocean Heights. Maybe it gets a little easier getting into preschool, but after that? It's only going to get easier at the schools Crestview kids don't want to go to. Like the ones Lauren gets to pick from.

"And how sad is it," she went on, "that I feel a little bit better knowing we're not going to suffer alone?"

"There's a hole in your logic somewhere," said Joel, "but fine. You're right. It's never going to end. I don't have the energy to figure it out. She's going to be fine."

Joel wrapped his arms around Nora in what he hoped was a suggestive embrace and pointed out that sex required neither debate nor research.

She slumped against him. "Oh, honey, I don't have any energy. We could get up early tomorrow. She still won't be here." She kissed him, but not in an encouraging way, and slipped upstairs.

The sirens of middle age, the couch, the newspaper crossword puzzle, and the television set, lured him back from disappointment, but not for long. The guy in the erectile dysfunction commercial looked no older than Joel was, and he seemed to have no trouble coaxing his energetic wife away from responsibility and into a bathtub, a hammock, a sunlit bedroom. Joel's success rate in terms of even creating the opportunity for dysfunction was as bad, lately, as was his daughter's college acceptance percentage. He might be suffering from chronic ED without even knowing it, brought on by the prolonged stress of making sure that Lauren could go to a school she seemed to hate. He wished he could assign a story on the toll college applications took on parents without his colleagues questioning—or, worse, making assumptions about—his motivation.

The notorious exception to all the misery was Chloe, who found herself in the midst of what Nana Ree would have called a laugh riot—or rather, a laff riot, for she rewrote English at will to convey the uniqueness of a particular feeling or event. A laff riot was better than a joke, better than a funny movie or a sitcom, because it was unexpected. For Chloe's grandma, a laff riot was finding a size six in exactly the dress she wanted, hanging by mistake among the size tens she passed on the way to the ladies' room, after having been told definitively that all the small sizes were gone. But

GETTING IN

each generation defined the phenomenon for herself; it was the
antithesis of tradition.

Chloe had not previously experienced anything that qualified
as a true laff riot, though she lived her life in anticipation of one. It
got her by happy ambush: In a single week she got packets and
emails inviting her to attend Bard, Skidmore, Sarah Lawrence,
Goucher, Hampshire, George Mason, the New School, Hunter,
and the universities of Arizona, Colorado, and Florida, though she
honestly did not recall filing the Florida application. She could go
to UC Santa Cruz or UC Irvine. She got thin letters from the top-
ranked schools she had put on her list only because her old friends
at Crestview were applying, and she threw those envelopes out
without bothering to open them. Chloe had volume. She had the
academic equivalent of a closet full of new clothes, and she had
the new respect of classmates who might have heard that still wa-
ters run deep, but had no idea that there was anything of substance beneath Chloe's effervescence.

Lauren padded down the carpeted hallway behind Chloe, past
Deena's closed door. No muffled television, no music, no nothing.
The loudest sound in the house, at the moment, was the refrigera-
tor motor.

"Is your mom asleep already?"

"Yeah, she read that the hours you sleep before midnight are
better sleep than the hours after," said Chloe. "She believes those
kinds of things."

Lauren hesitated. "It's a little weird."

"Hey, things have changed since the big breakup, you know
that. Trust me, if you didn't need to get away from your parents
we'd be sitting down to one of your mom's desserts right now."
Chloe took two bowls out of a cabinet and two spoons out of a
drawer. "I like your house better."

265

She pulled open the freezer door of the side-by-side, and Lauren let out a surprised little breath. The shelves were full of pints of ice cream, row after row, arranged by brand.

"Häagen-Dazs chocolate chip, chocolate, and coffee, Häagen-Dazs Light that's never been opened, Ciao Bella sorbet for when Mom buys jeans too small, Ben & Jerry's for when Mom's depressed that she bought jeans too small." Chloe grinned, hard. "All of it's supposed to be if friends drop by unexpectedly. What do you want?"

"I don't want to take her favorite."

"She doesn't have a favorite. This is our medicine chest. Two tablespoons before bedtime to improve your mood. The only time I ever saw her actually eat ice cream like a normal person was the night my dad moved out."

"I don't care."

Chloe grabbed one pint from each shelf, except for the low-fat, and filled the bowls with a scoop from each pint. Lauren looked over Chloe's shoulder as she did, and sure enough, there were no scoop-sized indentations in any of the containers. Nothing but shallow little craters of the sort that a tentative, abashed tablespoon might make. All of a sudden Lauren hated herself for being a brat, which was what she had been, as far as she could tell, ever since the night she missed the early-decision deadline. Chloe's parents were kind of useless, when they weren't downright embarrassing. The worst she could say about her own parents was that they took everything so seriously. They wanted to do a good job, which they defined as something more than what they were doing at any given moment in time.

"You waiting for it to melt? C'mon."

"Sorry." She followed Chloe in a minor but familiar daze. When she was five her parents had let her sleep over at Chloe's house for the first time in her life, and it was in this hallway, in front of Deena and Dave's closed door, in the middle of the night, that she had demanded to go home right that minute because she was scared. Deena had called her parents to say that Dave would drive her home, but Joel and Nora had insisted on driving over in their pajamas—discussing, they told her when she was older, the damage they must be doing by not encouraging her independence.

She thought about driving home, but she did not yet know what she wanted to say to them. Stuck in self-pity as thick as coastal fog, she could not see her way clear to anything as simple as I'm sorry, or I love you guys. Not yet.

Instead, she and Chloe sat on the floor and listened to Chloe's Life Sucks playlist, songs about suicide and tragic accidents and love affairs gone wrong.

"My mother hates these songs," said Lauren.

"Mothers are supposed to hate these songs. Her mother hated her songs."

"No, I mean specifically," said Lauren. She did her best to imitate Nora's deadpan. " 'Whiny white boys,' " she intoned, " 'fed up to here with getting rich and touring the world. What do they think, you wake up the day after you're dead, still conscious? Heaven is clubs and girlfriends and attitude?' That's what she says."

Lauren turned her attention to her ice cream.

"Look, can I ask you something disgusting and you don't have to answer?"

Chloe grinned. "Go ahead."

"Look, I know you're smarter than you let on and all, you know that, but, I mean, you're the only one I told . . . and you've got . . ."

"All these acceptances and you want to know why the fuck I got in every place when you didn't."

"See, you're mad, I shouldn't have . . ."

Chloe held up her hand to silence her friend. "Here's how I got in, so listen. Partly I got lucky because Ocean Heights doesn't weight grades or report minus and plus, so my B minus is as good as a B plus. I picked schools on purpose that nobody else was applying to. And I told them what they wanted to hear."

She reached up, retrieved her laptop from on top of her desk, opened a Word document, and turned the computer around so that Lauren could see the screen.

"See if you like it."

I could start out with a joke about how people in Los Angeles discriminate against anyone who isn't a size two, because humor is pretty much the only defense against that kind of stupidity. And I guess I just have, but being a size six is a superficial issue. In fact, sometimes I'm glad that genetics have made me what I am, because it gives me something to laugh about while I figure out how to handle the other challenges I face.

My parents say I've always been a pretty trusting person, which I guess is why I proudly told my third-grade class that I was part Sioux when we did our family tree project. I thought it made me a little bit more interesting. I never would have thought that other kids found it weird. I still remember the day a boy I liked came up to me on the playground, on my birthday, to give me a present he made himself, a war bonnet he made of feathers glued to construction paper. When I ran to the teacher, crying, she told me I shouldn't be so sensitive, and what a lot of effort he must have put into that gift.

Maybe a more cautious person would have learned a lesson—or maybe my commitment to personal honesty made me brave—but in high school, in the world religions unit, I decided to make famous agnostics the subject of my oral presentation. A list of well-known agnostics includes Matt Groening, who created *The Simpsons*, Zac Efron, of the movie *High School Musical*, and rock star Dave Matthews. As a curious and questioning person, I embraced agnostic beliefs. I wasn't sure that God existed, but I wasn't prepared to say He didn't. I was proud of the fact that I was willing to be uncertain.

This time some people got angry, and the others made fun of me again. They said I had commitment issues, like I was a boy who only wanted sex and didn't call again if he didn't get it. They said I was indecisive. One girl said if I was smarter I would at least say I was an atheist, because being an agnostic only meant not knowing what to do.

My parents were as supportive as they could be, but when I was in tenth grade they went through an acrimonious separation and divorce. I spend half my time with my mother and half my time with my father, and they try to pay attention, but they each only have half-time, so many issues fall through the cracks.

The unexpected benefit of this is that I have become an even more independent person, I think, and self-sufficient because I have to be. I am still amazed at how intolerant some people can be. I think it's because they are so insecure in their own beliefs that they need everyone to agree with them so they don't have doubts. As for me, I don't back down.

Lauren handed back the laptop. "You never told me any of this," she said.

Chloe smiled. "My English teacher said she cried when she read it. She actually offered to do a recommendation, I didn't even have to ask her."

"I tell you everything, Chloe."

"I'll just wait until you catch up here, genius."

Lauren read again until she got to "part Sioux."

"Oh my God," said Lauren. "You made it up. You're not part anything, except maybe liar."

"I prefer to think of it as a sales document," said Chloe, paying great attention to the slick of melted ice cream at the bottom of her bowl. "I didn't exactly say I was part Sioux. I said I *said* I was part Sioux. I can't help it if people believed me."

Lauren stared at her friend.

"Look," said Chloe, "if somebody like you can't get in places, what the hell chance do I have? I go to a school where college counseling is a joke. I'm white. I'm not rich and connected like Brad. Any way you look at it, I'm average, which is the kiss of death. So I did what I had to do to make myself not average."

Lauren looked at the screen again.

"'Acrimonious separation and divorce.'"

"That's the truth," said Chloe.

"It doesn't sound like you."

"You mean 'acrimonious.' This is why God invented the thesaurus. Or didn't. Us agnostics just aren't sure."

"What about the *Simpsons* guy?"

"Wikipedia."

"What're you going to do if they find out?"

"Pay attention," said Chloe. "I only picked things they won't ask me about. It's not like I said I have a limp and they'll see me running across campus. Nobody's going to stop me on move-in day and ask me to prove that my great-grandmother was an Indian. A Native American, sorry."

Lauren giggled. "So I should have said I was, I don't know . . ."

"A Pacific Islander," said Chloe.

"Wow."

"With an alcoholic dad you had to help take care of."

"I couldn't do that to my father."

"An alcoholic neighbor. Out of the goodness of your heart. Who you helped when you weren't lobbying people in front of the supermarket to stop using individual plastic bottles. And collecting neighbors' old clothes for a shelter for women returning to the workplace."

"A part–Pacific Islander who took care of a drunk when I wasn't saving the environment and helping women turn their lives around."

"Have we left anything out?" asked Chloe. "I don't think attention deficit's worth it at this point, too many people say they have it. Look. You did exactly what you were supposed to do, and I love you, you know I'm not insulting you, but it got you pretty much nowhere. Which is crazy, because those schools should be happy to have you."

"Please don't say that. My parents say it all the time."

"But they're right."

"But you lied."

"Sort of. Yes. Why should I play by the rules if the rules fuck over people like you? It's a crappy system, so I say do what you need to do to beat it."

Lauren rubbed the carpet nap this way and that, until the palm of her hand started to tingle. "Too late for that."

"Maybe you'll get off the wait list. They have to take somebody."

Lauren shrugged. "No, they don't. Can we change the subject?"

"Sure," said Chloe, who had been waiting for the opportunity. "Paul asked me to prom."

Lauren lay back on the carpet and stared at the ceiling. This was the last straw. Her college choices were the equivalent of a bad date; no, that was unkind, the equivalent of a date she did not care about. She had no date for prom and no plan to get one, as she had always imagined she would follow in the tradition of the Crestview girls who ended up going stag and proud of it, girls who loudly proclaimed that they could celebrate just fine without a date, which they had been too busy to bother looking for, by the way. She had intended to buy a ticket and bring Chloe along for comic relief, and now Chloe and her zillion college acceptances had a date with a boy who was going to Princeton. A handsome, fairly funny date who Lauren had occasionally imagined was looking over at her in a meaningful way from the baritone section of the choir. Clearly not—or, if he was, it was because she was a friend of Chloe's.

"Did you hear me? Paul asked me to prom."

"I'm going to be the only one there without a date. I'm not going. That's it." Lauren got up. "I have to go home."

"Don't go home. You've got weeks yet. Find somebody. Want me to ask Paul?"

Lauren groaned, because on some hideous level she wanted exactly that and would never say so. Until this moment, she had not even been aware of how much prom mattered, and now it was probably too late to find an acceptable date, let alone a great one.

"I am not getting fixed up for prom."

"Then you have to get asked or ask someone. You can't not go."

"Right."

"You think I was terrible to make stuff up. You're going to go home and never be my best friend again, aren't you? I would give you one of my acceptances if I could, I would, and we have to go to prom together because otherwise we will wish we did for the rest of our lives."

"I hope not," said Lauren, grabbing her bag and planting a kiss on the top of Chloe's head. "I really hope that none of this matters in about an hour, but I think that's not happening. Talk to you later."

❧

Mr. Nelson, the Crestview student newspaper's faculty sponsor, had dyed his prematurely gray hair brown over winter break, but bad brown, the kind that oxidized and turned brassy in the relentless southern California sunshine. Nora said he looked like Lucille Ball. Joel said he looked like an idiot, as though anyone needed further proof. Lauren appreciated her parents' attempts to ridicule the man who had denied her the editor's job, but her problem with the dye job had nothing to do with the quality of the workmanship. She hated the new look because it made Mr. Nelson and Don, the editor, look even more disturbingly alike than they already did.

They were waiting for her in Mr. Nelson's office after school on Friday with their usual mutually perturbed air, as though it was her fault that she had a class instead of a free period at the end of the day. Two wan, round, expressionless faces, two small and tidy bodies in Brooks Brothers and J.Crew, respectively, their lollipop physiques topped off by their matching carrot tops, one fake and the other genuine. They had pale eyes and eyelashes the color and texture of bee pollen. If life were a science-fiction movie, Lauren thought, they would turn out to be insects who assumed human characteristics in the hope of infiltrating and then conquering the world.

Stop it, she told herself. She needed to stop finding reasons to dislike her life.

"End-of-year issue coming up," said Mr. Nelson as soon as Lauren sat down.

"End-of-year issue," said Don, as though Lauren had not understood.

"End-of-year issue," said Lauren, pulling a spiral notebook out of her bag and pretending to consult a nonexistent list of topics. "College roundup, sports roundup, graduation ceremony instructions, grad night rules, dress codes, prom photo spread, farewell editorial." The final issue of the school paper was meant for parents, not students, a keepsake to be packed away along with the diploma and the mortarboard and the graduation program.

Don did his best to look down his insufficient nose at her. "That's all you've got?"

"That's what the last issue always is," said Lauren. Seeking the truth had lost its appeal since Chloe's disclosure about how she got into so many colleges. Between her friend's engineered victories and her own seemingly limited destiny, Lauren was not in the mood for vigorous inquiry.

"Don has a couple of good ideas that aren't what the last issue always is," said Mr. Nelson.

"Okay," said Lauren, holding her pen poised above her notebook.

Don leaned forward. "Let's find somebody who didn't get in anywhere good and get them to write a first-person thing."

"With their name on it?"

"Lauren, I'm surprised at you," said Mr. Nelson. "Since when do we use anonymous sources?"

"I don't mean anonymous sources," she said. "I mean why would you ask someone to confess to the whole school that things didn't exactly go so well?" Lauren assumed that she was not the only Crestview senior keeping a secret, and that the others were as determined as she was not to divulge the truth. Don only liked the idea because he had gotten in early at USC and had no idea what trouble was; he was the high school equivalent of someone who watched *Storm Chasers* on television, not for the science but for the vicarious thrill.

"Because it's a great story," he replied. "I mean, c'mon, I heard about one school that had a wall of shame, people posted their rejection letters on a big board in the cafeteria and they had a vote, which school wrote the coldest rejection. Where's your sense of humor?"

"I don't know, maybe someplace where you laugh at funny things instead of laughing at people who are less lucky than you are, what do you think?" She shoved her notebook back into her bag and stood up suddenly. "You have no idea what you're talking about. Like you'd step up and confess in public if ten places turned you down. I don't think so, which makes you what? Kind of a hypocrite."

She sat down again and waited for a reply.

Mr. Nelson wondered why it was that the girls on the staff—even a girl like Lauren, who had journalism in her genes—eventually let their emotions get in the way. He made a mental note to mention this incident to the head of school, who was pressuring him to name a girl to the editor's job for the coming year and did not seem to appreciate that Mr. Nelson evaluated candidates based on ability, not gender.

Don wished he had presented the idea as an assignment for Lauren, which might have made it harder for her to turn down. Now he was going to get stuck looking for a subject himself.

"Is anybody going to say anything?" Lauren asked.

"I think Crestview seniors know how to say no if they don't want to participate," said Mr. Nelson, "but if the idea upsets you, Lauren, I'm sure Don can handle it."

"I'll get on it," said Don, intending to draft one of the juniors to do the leg work. If that did not work, he would complain bitterly about having to make room for all the traditional articles, and then he would kill his nonexistent story for space.

"There you are," said Lauren. She got up and left before either of them could respond. After a long moment, Mr. Nelson walked over to his desk and imitated a man checking his email.

"You see, this is where you get into trouble," said Mr. Nelson, who had never actually worked for a newspaper but had written his master's thesis about the limitations of advocacy journalism and had trouble distinguishing between passion and bias. "You let your feelings cloud your judgment and you miss out on a good story."

Don stared at the empty doorway, wishing he had ever had the nerve to ask Lauren out. The best thing about working on the school paper was the guarantee of seeing her at least once a week, even if she always seemed to be looking just past him, and over the course of the school year his interest in her had become inflamed to something more like worship. His disdain was merely camouflage. He never once thought to wonder why she had reacted so negatively to his suggestion. If anyone had asked Don how Lauren had done with her college applications, he would have speculated that she had gotten in everywhere.

chapter 14

Brad had envisioned an escalating series of encounters with Liz in the months between asking her to prom and prom itself, but he had failed to take her work ethic into account. Extreme diligence was not a situational personality trait: Liz treated second semester of senior year as though it were first semester of junior year, so there was no letup in her workload, no hope of more than an occasional after-school coffee in a week without deadlines or exams. She finally agreed to spend a Sunday morning with Brad instead of at her desk—but then the notifications came, and it took three days to reply to her text about Harvard, so she put him off for one more week while she sorted out how she felt about him being both rude and luckier than she was. Brad had planned to take Liz to the Getty, but by the time he pulled up in front of her house he had decided instead to take her to the Venice boardwalk, in the hope that it would feel more like a date and less like an art history field trip. The drive down to the beach felt like nothing at all.

Brad loved Venice because it was goofy. No matter how many art collectors bought adjacent shacks, tore them down, and built a single showplace home in their stead, no matter how many movie directors installed security systems, Venice refused to tidy up completely. He and Liz walked past a farmers' market set up in a parking lot, a sausage cart, a skateboarding Sikh with a flute. They stopped to watch the bodybuilders at Muscle Beach, men and women the color of rotisserie chickens, who failed to see the irony of bodies built to last covered by skin about to kill them. They turned around and headed north, past a row of old Russian Jews on new woven folding chairs, past a knot of gnarled, argumentative men kibitzing over a speed-chess tournament, without once talking about college. They studied the guys who swung along the rings like happy apes, swapping one arm to the next, ring to ring, until they flew off at the far end and landed facing the ocean. Brad put his arm around Liz's shoulder and thought he saw her smile, at least a little bit. She was not one for large expressions.

"I don't see how they do it," said Liz. "I mean, I see how they do it, I see how they pull down on the back swing to get the momentum going forward. I think I would crash right into the upright." She leaned against him for a moment, thought better of it, and straightened up. "See, that's why I didn't get into Harvard. Idiot me. I should've said I was an ace on the rings. I bet nobody said that."

I didn't get in either.

That was his first line of dialogue. All he had to do to make her feel better was open his mouth and say it.

Instead, he said, "I think Yale's great. Katie would kill to be you."

"I haven't decided for sure" was all she would say. Brad decided not to push. He could hardly ask Liz who had offered her the most money, and it would be cruel to talk about Yale if Yale was not the answer to the question he could not ask. They got as far as the Santa Monica pier, where a bunch of kids clutching presents streaked across their path on their way to a birthday party at the carousel, and then they turned around and headed back toward the car, grateful for the ambient noise that covered the sudden silence. Even on the far side of acceptance letters, college could kill a conversation more quickly than the unexpected appearance of a nosy parent or a gossiping friend.

By midday, the boardwalk started to fill up with locals trying to forget who they were during the workweek and sidewalk entrepreneurs getting ready to open for business. Vendors carrying collapsible canopies and boxes of merchandise piled out of pickup trucks and vans, and five minutes later they were selling T-shirts and sunglasses and straw hats, saris and lucky-hand charms and henna tattoos. The sausage cart was flanked by carts selling Mexican ices, popcorn, and cotton candy. The skateboarding Sikh with the flute had competition from guitars and steel drums, from congas and a violin and a guy singing along to instrumentals blaring from a boom box.

Liz stopped in front of the violinist and cocked her head to one side, as though changing the angle at which sound waves struck her ears might improve the quality of the sound. A moment later, she straightened up and turned away.

"I don't think more practice is going to help," she said, with a small shake of her head. "Maybe he ought to try another line of work."

Brad tagged after her, trying to ignore the fact that she sounded, in that moment, exactly like his father. Silently he calculated who all these musicians would have turned out to be if Trey was right about discipline and the responsibilities of adulthood. The Sikh undoubtedly would have negotiated a lasting peace between India and Pakistan, and the black guy with the boom box had surely taken his eye off the ball and missed out on a seat on the Supreme Court. The three steel drummers? A medical research team, consigned to the boardwalk because no one had cared enough to wrest those instruments out of their hands and insist that they finish their chemistry homework.

Brad knew he was being unfair, which made him feel a twitch of sympathy for his father, a fleeting shudder that came and went in a heartbeat. He understood what it was, just as he understood the cold, vacant feeling that followed it. What if Preston Bradley III knew something that Preston Bradley IV did not? What if his devotion to the goal of a Harvard legacy for his younger son was actually a positive spin on a negative truth, which was that the Bradley men were very good at being Harvard lawyers and not so good at anything that required a little creativity. Brad did not even bother putting a question mark on that second what-if, because it came into his head accompanied by an old memory of Roger, who really was not much of a dancer as far as Brad could recall.

It was entirely possible that Brad's father was the smartest guy around, not the dullest. He might be trying to spare his son the heartbreak of whatever Brad's clarinet turned out to be; might be trying to protect him from the hard lesson Trey had long since learned about accepting one's own limitations. Getting Brad into Harvard could be his father's version of a great kindness. If that was true, then Brad was expending an awful lot of energy guaranteeing his own unhappiness down the line.

Liz was going on about the dismal level of teaching in the English department at Ocean Heights, and Brad made what he assumed were the proper encouraging noises in response, because she kept talking. He waited in vain for his father to get out of his head. If only Trey had a more mundane obsession than the family legacy, one that he kept to himself instead of using it as the foundation of his parenting philosophy. If only Trey were having an affair, like other people's dads, Brad's life would have been much easier.

But it was clear to Liz that Brad was not listening; her two questions about Crestview's English faculty got the same noncommittal responses as her comments about her own teachers. What was his problem? She continued talking only because she felt that he might as well be required to feign interest if he was suddenly going to be moody about nothing at all. Brad's unpredictable silences were as frustrating as Chloe's dependably endless talk; Liz had begun to wonder if it was possible to be both well-off and well-tuned, to be rich and consistent. Based on her admittedly small sampling, the most pervasive side effect of having money, even the supposedly paltry amount Chloe always griped about, was the loss of conversational equilibrium.

Liz decided that she would look back on this part of her life, once she was successful and comfortable, and be oddly grateful that she had been able to afford so little latitude when she was young. She was glad that some instinct had kept her from blurting out the news about the offer of a full ride from Yale, which effectively had eliminated the need for her to make a choice. She would text Brad during the week, when distance and a 160-character limit imposed a protective restraint on the exchange.

chapter 15

Katie was tired of being old news. The worst thing about getting in early was that everyone ignored you in April and expected you to be as happy for them as you had expected them to be happy for you back in December. She looked forward to prom as a chance to reclaim her place center stage, and she was not pleased to find out that Ron intended to ruin everything. She picked a little green bit out of the penne and glared at her parents across the dinner table.

"I do not understand why Ron has to come home the weekend of prom," she said. "And I don't know what you mean, a girlfriend. Lauren saw him with somebody last fall, but her name wasn't Carol."

Joy and Dan exchanged a brief reproachful glance. If there had already been a girlfriend acquired and lost without their knowing about it, one of them was not doing a good enough job of asking leading questions.

"Perhaps Lauren misunderstood and she was just a classmate of his."

"Yeah. Right. In New York and he goes to school in Massachusetts. Whatever. Can't they come another weekend instead of ruining the most important day of senior year?"

"The girl has an interview for an internship."

"Well, she's not staying in my room."

"She'll stay in the guest room," said Joy, "and I doubt that ruining prom is high on their agenda. Ron remembers how important prom was."

Katie sighed. "Ron only wishes his prom mattered."

"I think she wants to be a writer," said Joy. "Won't you be embarrassed if she turns out to be terrific."

"Yeah, embarrassed." Katie pushed her plate away. "I'm done."

As soon as she got upstairs she closed her bedroom door and called Lauren.

"You're sure her name is Carol?" Lauren asked.

"Yeah."

"That's a shame. The one I met had a weird name. L'Anitra. That's it." Lauren mimicked the girl's rhythm. "'I'm L'A*neee*tra, glad ta *meee*tcha.' Your mom would have died, I'm not kidding."

"Well, this one better stay out of my way. Listen. You come over on Friday and we'll do prom stuff."

"I wasn't planning on getting dressed until Saturday."

"Funny. I am not going to spend ditch day watching Ron and his girlfriend do whatever they . . . I'm not kidding, you have to come over."

"Okay. We should ask Chloe, too."

"She's coming?"

"Paul asked her."

"Well, he's been in love with her since sixth grade. I assume she's just using him to get to a decent prom."

"Nice, Katie."

"Thank you," said Katie, preening. "Do we have to invite what's-her-name who's going with Brad? Liz. Do we have to invite Liz? In the name of absolute democracy?"

"Not a chance," said Lauren, laughing. "I wouldn't be that mean to her."

Ron's flight arrived at around one on Friday, so Katie invented an entire day of activities and laid in a stock of magazines, in case the girls needed the latest information on trends in nail polish or a tutorial in the application of liquid eyeliner. The only difference between their day before prom and their mothers' was the politically correct ambivalence they expressed as they debated the relative merits of toenails that ran the color scale from infant pink to ebony. Girls who had been raised to believe that they could do anything sometimes had trouble figuring out if anything properly included a fleeting obsession with gel blush and strapless bras.

They were finishing up an extra-large pizza and a liter of Diet Coke when the front door opened and Ron called out, "Anybody home?"

Katie yelled, "Coming," and turned to Lauren and Chloe. "Do I have pizza in my teeth?"

"Yep," said Chloe.

"Where?"

"Fooling," said Chloe, reaching for another slice.

"Why did you bring her?" Katie asked Lauren. She stood up, straightened her shoulders, and headed downstairs with Lauren and Chloe trailing behind.

Ron and the girl were standing in the front hallway, and when they looked up, Lauren wished that he had stuck with L'Anitra, at least for Katie's sake. The new girl had the same basic build—tall and slim—but everything else was different. L'Anitra's hair had fuchsia stripes and no sense of direction; Carol's hair was shiny and deep brown, and it rippled in beautiful, thick waves. L'Anitra had raccoon eyes and a dead mouth; Carol had liquid eyeliner nailed, and she wore one of those pale lipsticks that managed not to look fake. L'Anitra had the kind of jerky, nervous energy that made Lauren wonder about drugs, but Carol was so at ease. Katie's mom was going to love her.

And then Lauren noticed two more things: a tiny mole at the crest of the girl's waxed left eyebrow and a dot of purple that peeked out of her boatneck T-shirt when she reached to shake hands with Katie. L'Anitra had a mole above her eyebrow and a purple butterfly tattoo in exactly that spot. Lauren stared at the girl, and the mole, and the purple dot, until Carol reached out again to shake hands with Chloe, this time exposing an entire butterfly wing.

Carol was L'Anitra in disguise, or the other way around. Lauren had no idea which, or why, but this definitely was the same girl.

"Katie, let's go upstairs, c'mon, we have so much to do," said Lauren.

"I thought you were the one who said we had nothing to do today." Katie was giving Carol a severe once-over, looking for the single flaw that would enable her to feel superior, and not finding it.

"No, really . . ." Lauren gave Ron and Carol her best smile. "You don't mind if we abandon you, do you?"

Carol smiled exactly the same smile she had smiled when she—when L'Anitra—had hooked her hand into Ron's waistband. Lauren hustled her friends upstairs and shut the door as soon as Katie and Chloe were inside.

"That's her," she whispered. "That's L'Anitra."

"I don't think so," said Katie, who was not in the mood for intrigue.

"Who's L'Anitra?" asked Chloe.

"Ron's wacko sex fiend poet girlfriend."

"I don't think so, either," said Chloe. "That girl's Katie's mom, give or take a generation."

"Shut up," said Katie.

"Look at her shoulder. By her collarbone on the left side. Purple butterfly tattoo. And that little mole over her eyebrow.

I'm telling you, it's her. I don't understand why she looks so different."

"Because she's not the same girl," said Katie. "Besides, this is prom weekend. Are we going to try the dresses on or what?"

"I'm going first," said Chloe, who over the last two years had become all too adept at drawing fire from a quarreling duet. She took her dress down from where it hung on Katie's closet door, untied the plastic bag at the bottom, and pulled the bag up over the hanger with a flourish. It took the girls a moment to respond, which was exactly what Chloe had hoped for. No one else was going to show up at prom in a sleeveless white dress decorated with bubble grids.

"Where on earth did you get that?" asked Katie, vowing silently not to stand next to Chloe in any of the group photographs.

Lauren stepped behind Chloe to look at the back of the dress. "I don't get it. It's all real stuff filled in, your name, your address, Ocean Heights."

Chloe yanked her T-shirt over her head, pulled down her jeans, pulled the dress over her head, and stood on tiptoe to approximate her mother's four-inch heels.

"Ta-da," she said, taking a slow turn. "It's a Chloe Haber design, thank you very much. A kid at the Art Center did the lettering for me with a Sharpie, and he has a friend who sewed it, I mean it's nothing, two seams and a couple of darts, but c'mon. Nobody is going to have as cool a dress as this." She struck a pose. "I was their senior project. They got an A."

It was the only Chloe Haber design ever to have been produced, and it was nothing like the drawings Deena had found in the hidden sketchbook. Chloe usually drew to prove to herself—and with luck, to an employer someday—that she was dependable, consistent, capable, all the things she doubted herself to be. But this dress was meant to make the opposite point, to remind every single member of the Crestview senior class that Chloe was special, a renegade, not a reject.

"I think it's great," said Lauren.

"Lauren next," said Katie, dismissively.

Lauren's dress had a plain ivory top, a slim gray skirt, and a thin rose-colored velvet ribbon uniting the two. When she put it on she looked happier than she had in a while.

"Where'd you get it?" asked Katie, who had not seen anything like it at the stores she had gone to.

Lauren smiled.

"It's my mom's prom dress," she said. "I kind of like it."

Chloe walked a slow circle around Lauren, reaching out to adjust the skirt slightly, and then she stood back for another look.

"You look beautiful," she said. "I don't think I'd wear a thing of my mom's except shoes."

Lauren twirled. "Nobody's going to show up in the same dress, that's for sure."

"That's for sure," said Katie, with a slightly different intonation. "Well. Ready for mine?"

She stepped past Lauren, stepped into the closet, and, for maximum impact, turned her back on the others as she took the dress out of the bag, so that they could not get a good look until she spun around. It was strapless and fitted and the color of a cloud, made of layers of silk so fine it made chiffon feel like mayonnaise. A cascading column of pleated plumes ran down the front, held against the dress by a single stitch here and there. It was a dress designed to destroy the self-image of any girl within a five-mile radius.

"Does it come with its own spotlight?" asked Chloe.

"Are you going to try it on?" asked Lauren.

With barely a gesture, Katie slipped out of everything but a silvery thong, slipped into the dress, and stepped into a pair of silk high-heeled sandals. She turned toward her friends and struck the sidelong pose that celebrities used to make two hips look like one and a half.

"So what'd you do?" asked Chloe, unscrewing the top on a bottle of nail polish. "Buy the thong to match the dress or the dress to match the thong?"

"It's gorgeous," said Lauren, in just the awed tone of voice Katie had wanted to hear.

She lifted the dress over her head, settled it carefully on its velvet hanger, and climbed back into her jeans and T-shirt, lost in imagining the look on Mike's face—for that matter, the look on Brad's face—when he saw her in that dress. She had almost succeeded in forgetting about Ron and Carol, or Ron and L'Anitra, until a slamming door, followed by loud laughter and a boyish whoop, reminded her.

"Nice," said Chloe. "Hope you're not planning to get a lot of sleep tonight."

Katie got very busy piling paper plates and dirty napkins in the empty pizza box. "Anybody want a latte? Help me throw this out and let's go get one."

Despite Katie's entreaties, Lauren and Chloe went home an hour later, having run out of enthusiasm halfway through ten great ways to incorporate a braid into an up-do. Katie was alone with her beautiful dress, her hateful brother, the duplicitous girl, her imagination, and hours to kill before her parents got home. She called her mother and happened to mention that Ron and his girlfriend had arrived at around two and had been in the guest room ever since, but her mother missed the implication of impropriety. So Katie sat in her room, stewing, logging every groan or sigh that wafted down the hall, convinced that Lauren was right. This was the same girl. Anyone who could stand to spend a whole afternoon in a closed room with Ron was, by definition, crazy.

Katie felt compelled to tell her mother. It would break Joy's heart to think that she had known and chosen not to tell. Katie had a moral obligation to out the girl, whatever her name was, and to do it quickly, before her mother fell under the spell of Carol's pageboy.

The logistics were tricky, because her parents were coming home only long enough to change clothes and head out to dinner with friends. Katie bided her time through the requisite introductions and small talk and her parents' wardrobe change, hovering near her mother the entire time. As soon as her father left to get the car out of the garage, and Ron and Carol pretended to retreat to separate rooms to pretend to get ready for a movie, Katie pounced on Joy.

"Mom, I have to talk to you about Carol. It'll just take a second."

"Ron seems very happy, don't you think? It's nice to see him—"

"Mom, she's not who you think. Lauren saw her in New York, she's crazy, I mean it, she thinks she's a poet, she does these crazy performance things, and she has a tattoo and that's not how her hair really is. You have to talk to him."

"Honestly, Katie, I'm a bit surprised at you."

"You and Daddy can't let yourselves be taken in . . ."

"Katie, that's enough. I frankly don't understand why you feel the need to make up such a story about Carol. She's quite a lovely girl. You should be happy for your brother."

"Her name isn't Carol. It's L'Anitra. Lauren thought she was a nut case when she met her. You have to make him stop seeing her."

Her father sat on the horn, once, twice, three times, and Joy turned to check her appearance in the hall mirror.

"I have to go. I think it's time for you to focus on the big day tomorrow and let your brother—who is not as comfortable socially as you are—enjoy this little relationship." Her lips almost made contact with Katie's cheek, and she was gone.

"Great." Katie spun and ran upstairs just in time to see her brother cross the hall from his room to the guest room with a bottle in his hand. She retreated to her own room and methodically rubbed cuticle cream around each toenail, twice. Finally, she heard a door open.

She marched into the hall as Carol reached the head of the stairs, clad in nothing but an old Wilco T-shirt that one of the rowers had given Ron for his birthday, as though Ron had any idea who Wilco was, as though Ron had any idea, period.

"Hey," Carol said.

"Hey, Carol," said Katie. "Or maybe L'Anitra. Would you rather I called you that?"

Carol smiled. "That friend of yours, she's the one we saw in New York, isn't she?"

"She is. I told my mother."

"Really? Did she believe you?"

"No."

"There you are, then. Want anything from the fridge?"

That was it. Katie could not stand the idea that this interloper, this phony, thought she could take whatever she wanted out of the refrigerator without addressing Katie's accusation.

"I think you have bigger worries than the fridge right now."

Carol's smile curdled into a smirk. "Oh, now I'm scared. Look, here's the deal. This is me, Carol. Greenwich, Connecticut, Miss Porter's before Barnard, old money, I mean really old, like my parents would think of your parents as working class. Okay? If I'm somebody more fun than this when I'm at school, what business is it of yours? You think I'd be stupid enough to show up here looking the way I do at school?"

"Your parents don't know?"

"Oh, come on."

"So you lie about all this stuff."

Carol rolled her eyes. "Right. And you've always told your parents absolutely everything you've ever done, haven't you."

"That's different."

"No, it's not. You're just more limited in what you can get away with because you're still at home. My parents know what I tell them, and what I don't tell them they don't know, and as long as I go to class and keep my grades up, they honestly don't care, no matter how much they pretend they do." She regarded Katie with a new interest. "So if you get tired of being Miss Perfection, you can give it up the day you get to Williams. You can dye your hair and get a tattoo and sleep with the TA in your French class and be any old thing at all you want."

With that, she trotted down the stairs, and Katie, who was trying very hard not to cry, backed into her own room, shut the door, and leaned against it, gnawing on her thumbnail until she realized what she was doing and dove for an emery board to repair the damage. She put her dress back in its bag and the bag back in the closet, she stuffed her sandals with tissue and tucked each one into a felt bag, and she folded up all the magazines that Lauren and Chloe really could have helped to stack before they left. She lay down on the bed and put a pillow over her head, which was not enough to muffle the sound of Carol's footsteps coming back up the stairs and the door to the guest room opening and closing.

Who was happy? Ron and his schizo girlfriend, her parents who were out to dinner with their boring friends, Lauren and Chloe and Brad and even Liz, who probably got her prom dress on sale at Ross Dress for Less or Loehmann's, even though none of them had as much reason as Katie to be pleased with life. Who was unhappy? Katie, which made no sense at all. Without moving the pillow, she reached over and felt her way along her night table: hair elastic, nail file, lip balm, pad and pen, Tweezerman, scented candle, cell phone, back to the Tweezerman. She picked it up and spun it around like a miniature cheerleader's baton, poked her head out from under the pillow, and held it still, poised, pointing at the zipper of her jeans.

"Hah," she said, and put the tweezers back on the night table. She was not unhappy, she was exasperated, which was different. Exasperated was a good thing because it meant she was impatient with her high school life and ready for a new one. She glared at the tweezers. She was as done with puncture wounds as she was with biting her nails.

It was always a struggle to find an acceptable venue for the Crestview senior prom. This year's class had already attended bar mitzvahs on movie soundstages, sweet sixteens at private clubs taken over for the occasion, and a quinceanera at the biggest country club in town. They had eaten lobster tacos and white-truffle mini-pizzas; with the swipe of a handmade rosemary cracker, they had decapitated molded swans made of duck pâté, salmon mousse, or goat cheese, each one with a black-truffle beak, all the while pretending that what they really wanted was quesadilla, which was their way of saying that luxury was commonplace in their lives. They had danced to up-and-coming disc jockeys and famous bands on the decline, and they disdained the look-at-me Hummer stretch limos that the kids at Ocean Heights rented for their prom, preferring a discreet town car and a driver or a six-seater, tops.

This year, prom was at the Marbella, a doubly oppressed downtown art deco hotel that had been abandoned for the first time in the beach hejira of the 1950s, and ignored again in the recent redevelopment craze whose epicenter was a deserted half mile from the property. The Marbella had been a signed offer away from becoming a parking structure and a big-box store when it caught the eye of a New York hotelier who had made his fortune on what he called vintage real estate. Two years and an Italian interior designer later, the Marbella was back, dignified by a press agent who used phrases like "recycling panache," made accessible to the rest of the new downtown by a fleet of shuttle buses designed to look like the city's long-dead Red Car trolley fleet. The entire block behind the hotel—a Spanish-language movie theater, a Laundromat, a single-room-occupancy hotel, and a taco stand—was demolished to make way for an authentic reproduction of the type of gardens that had never existed downtown in the first place.

The Crestview faculty chaperones gathered at the entrance to the ballroom to form a corridor of flattery for the celebrating seniors, and Ted positioned himself discreetly toward the back of the group in the hope that students would drift the other way before they got to him. By prom night, most of them were perfectly happy to avoid him. The seniors who had gotten into their first-choice schools were dismissive, satisfied with a smug smile and a little wave, because of course they had gotten in on their own merit, with no outside help. The kids who had been disappointed steered clear of Ted because they blamed him. The ones who were still in play on a wait list somewhere avoided him like the plague, in case he had heard something earlier in the day that would wreck their evening. Short of graduation, this was as safe as Ted felt all year.

What he liked best were the groups of kids who flew by as one, their attitude toward him always defined by the pack's luckiest member, because no one was about to betray anxiety in front of friends. As Brad and his friends rolled past, Ted ran a private tally and decided that this might be the most successful constellation at prom: Brad at Harvard, where an admissions officer faced with a $350,000 donation quickly found the vacant slot that of course should have gone to Brad all along, what an unfortunate oversight, and his date at Yale, a bit of information Ted had picked up in a congratulatory call to Trey; Katie and her date, Mike, both at Williams; Paul at Princeton and Chloe, the volume winner according to Lauren, going to Santa Cruz, which was fine for an Ocean Heights kid.

As for Lauren, she had managed so far to use disappointment to her advantage. When people asked her where she was going, she replied that it would take her every single minute until May 1 to decide. She did not say that it would take that long because she had no good options, so the other seniors assumed that she must be facing a deliciously tortured choice, Northwestern or Columbia, Northwestern or NYU, Northwestern or whatever school had just turned the listener down. Ted had no idea whether she was going to pick Santa Barbara or Irvine, because her parents had stopped calling and Lauren had stopped dropping by. Ted figured they were in the purgatory known only to families who were figuring out how to put a good spin on bad news.

Lauren had less than a week until the truth narrowed down to the truth, and she had to send a commitment letter and a check to one school or the other, but for tonight she looked like she belonged at the best table, her status enhanced by her last-minute escort, Jim, whose longtime girlfriend had been sidelined by a herpes sore that made a public appearance unthinkable. Jim and the girlfriend, now there was a happy ending, both of them safely enrolled at Wesleyan despite the remarkable similarity in their end-of-semester papers on *King Lear*. Ted preferred to dwell on the victories instead of the failures, not that Lauren was a failure, but she certainly was not on the list he had drawn up to show his private clients, currently five of them confirmed, with another five sure to sign up by week's end. The welcome letter that he intended to send out, as soon as he had his official chat with the head of school, talked about Brad and Katie and Jim and his girl-friend, about Paul and the girl who ditched Harvard for Stanford. Lauren was the cautionary example on his list, anonymous, of course, the girl who had it all, except that other candidates had a bit more.

He watched her search for her table with the others, the girls' long dresses floating behind them, lapping at the boys' tuxedo pants. That is the way prom is supposed to look, Ted thought, gowns and tuxedos and upswept hairdos that won't last the night. When he started out as a college counselor, everyone dressed that way, but in the last couple of years a style chasm had begun to develop between the top kids—who were either going to their first-choice schools or adept at faking that a second-choice school was really their favorite—and the rest of the seniors, who had never dreamt upper case dreams in the first place. The chosen few stayed formal, the boys in tuxedos or in Grandpa's vintage white dinner jacket and the girls favoring the Greek goddess look, usually in no stronger a color than gray. As for the rest, the boys wore suits and ditched their ties before dessert. The girls wore short, shiny dresses that showed lots of leg and lots of cleavage, made of satin or taffeta tortured into pleats and ruffles and ruches, all of it in neon pastels—not buttercup but egg yolk, not peach but salmon, not sky blue but turquoise, and never pink if that little strapless number with the corset top came in coral. Their caterpillar eye-lashes were heavy with mascara, and their lips were so thick with gloss—Ted tried and failed to censor himself in time—that a boy's boxers would likely stick to his penis after the blow job.

He took a deep breath to try to empty his mind. He vowed next year to fake a bad cold and stay home, and then he reminded himself that by next year, with luck—no, with continued effort—his attendance at the Crestview senior prom might no longer be required. Thanks to the speed with which Harvard had reversed itself on Brad, Ted had regained his balance. He planned to submit his resignation letter about a week before graduation—early enough to promote the illusion that he cared about letting Dr. Mullin start the job search before everyone scattered for the summer, late enough to avoid an endless stream of anxious calls from the parents of juniors.

❧

Katie's family had stopped drinking tap water about five years earlier, when her father returned from a golf weekend to find a forgotten glass of water on his desk, a half-inch of the liquid equivalent of smog settled out at the bottom. He walked into the kitchen holding the glass at arm's length between thumb and forefinger, as though it were a dead rodent, and announced to his wife and children that he was going to order a water purification system for the entire house so that even the bathwater would run clear.

Away from home, the Dodson family drank only bottled water. The recent pro-tap backlash was for people who worried about the larger environmental consequences of all those plastic bottles. Dan Dodson's priority was his family's personal eco-system, which was why Katie carried a larger purse to prom than the other girls did. She polished off one bottle of Evian before the entrée arrived, handed the empty to the waiter who placed her salmon fillet in front of her, and leaned down to fish a second bottle out of her bag, which sat on the floor at her feet.

Chloe reached over for Katie's untouched water glass and took a long swill. "Am I glowing yet?" she said.

"Pick your poison," said Katie.

"So's your dad going to pop for a filtration system at the dining hall?" Chloe asked.

Katie smiled at the extent of Chloe's ignorance. "Somehow I'm thinking they have bottled water at Williams," she replied. "There's no need to make fun."

Liz broke in, determined to find common ground. "At Yale the residential colleges each have their own dining facility," she said, "although I imagine that college food is college food."

It did not matter that Katie was done with Yale and done with Brad, that in her assiduously rewritten life story neither her ex-first-choice school nor her ex-boyfriend had measured up. Liz seemed completely satisfied with both of them—and that, combined with a room that was suddenly too warm, salmon that was too rich, and a band that was too loud, made Katie feel the need to reestablish her personal equilibrium. She had worked hard to forget that she had ever preferred Yale, and she needed to make Liz just a bit less thrilled with her choice.

"All the boys at Yale are gay," said Katie. She glanced at Brad. The last time she had asked, he swore that he was going to tank a math test for her, but what if he was lying to get her to leave him alone? She should have asked to see it, as proof that he had kept up his end of the bargain. Perhaps she ought to let him know—a little coded comment, nothing obvious—that she had not forgotten their deal. "So the dozen guys who are straight have to be sleeping with everybody. That's going to be weird. Who would you rather go out with? A slut or a gay guy?"

Brad stretched his arm protectively across the back of Liz's chair, and Lauren nudged her foot under the table to poke at Katie, but Katie smiled and took a nice, long moment unscrewing the cap on her water bottle.

"At least you know they're gay," said Chloe, desperately hoping to prevent trouble. "At some places there's a saying, Gay by May, like these boys show up having no idea what they are and just about the time you figure out which one you're interested in, it turns out he'll never be interested in you. But I never heard that about Yale. I don't know about Santa Cruz. I figure I'll save myself the agony and just wait for sophomore year to fall in love with someone."

"Check it out," said Brad. "Maybe I'll transfer. Improve my odds."

"Yeah, like you'd go to Santa Cruz," said Katie.

"Hey, don't bash my someday alma mater," said Chloe. Katie ignored her. Katie was staring at Liz, who was staring at her plate, and in that moment Chloe recalled all the times Katie had condescended to her, whether the issue was Chloe's grades or her figure or her prom dress. The only difference was that Liz was too polite or too surprised to give back as good as she got, and Chloe was not.

She addressed Katie with an eager venom, slowly, so that no one missed her point. "But, Katie," she said, "I thought you were dying to go to Yale. Lauren, didn't you say Katie was so mad at her parents for . . ."

Katie took a long sip of water, long enough to glare at Chloe and then turn and glare at Lauren through the bottom of the bottle.

"I considered it last fall," she said. "It may be right for some people. Not me."

"I don't get it," said Mike, who had been idly figuring the odds of getting Katie to himself, and beyond that, of determining exactly where that dress undid. He knew that his chances of getting past the dress improved with the appearance of interest in something other than sex, so he made the occasional comment to preclude being dismissed as a boy who had but one thing on his mind. "I don't get it" was not one of his best, but it implied at least that he was listening, while he figured out whether that little gray knot on the side of the dress was decorative or functional.

"I mean," he continued, leaning toward his date to get a closer look, "once you're talking Williams and Yale, how can there be a wrong school?"

Katie rustled herself into a more authoritative posture. "Reputations change. Policies change. Schools make decisions that don't work out in the long run and maybe that school ends up not the great place it was in its heyday."

"Heyday," said Lauren. "There's a word you don't hear much."

Katie turned her laser gaze on Lauren. "My father uses it," she said, "and I think it's appropriate. Look at Yale, if we're going to play this out."

"Oh," said Brad, in a low, warning voice, "let's not."

"Look at Yale," said Katie, ignoring him. "One of the top three schools in the country forever, and like everyone else they're facing an upheaval . . ."

"Hey, upheaval, watch out," said Chloe, clutching at Paul as though to steady herself.

"Facing an upheaval in terms of numbers of applicants and quality of applicants and diversity . . ."

"Somebody stop her," said Lauren. Brad reached under the table and patted Katie's knee as quietly as he could, but he might as well have set the tablecloth on fire.

"You know," Katie went on, ignoring all of them and picking up speed, "I'm sure everyone wants to do the right thing, but you cannot turn around, having evaluated applicants purely on the basis of quality forever, and suddenly you decide that what you need is a . . . a . . . a *buffet* of students. As though variety matters more than excellence."

"There's nobody at this table who isn't quality," said Chloe, "except maybe me, who is not who you're talking about."

Katie grabbed a roll from the basket, swiped a point off the star-shaped butter pat, slathered the butter on the roll, and took a ferociously big bite. The others waited while she chewed, all of them but Chloe hoping that the carbohydrates would slow her down, Chloe spoiling for the next outburst. No one spoke. Katie finished the roll and attacked the wild salmon in champagne sauce, and slowly, the others picked up their forks and began to eat, one eye on their plates, one eye on the dormant volcano that was Katie. They talked about summer plans, about jobs and internships and family trips. When it was Liz's turn, she said that she had a job at the Gap for the summer, but she was quitting a few weeks early because her father had decided to drive across the country to Yale.

"So that will be our summer vacation, the three of us," she said. "Because my father loves to drive, and there is so much we have never seen. He found a service, we drive someone's car across the country for them and then he and my mother can fly back, because they can't take that much time off work, of course."

"Right," Katie muttered into the rim of her water bottle, "because every cab driver counts."

"Shut the fuck up, Katie," said Brad.

"You shut the fuck up," she said. "But, see, this is what's happening. A school like, say, like Yale, can take a freshman class from the top kids in the country. But no. They want one of everything. Suddenly how much does it matter that you've got perfect scores and perfect grades and all these activities and a great essay and terrific recommendations. Because if you're me, say, if you're this rich white girl, and it's harder for girls . . ." She took another sip. "Anyhow, so you're this rich white girl and all of a sudden that's a disadvantage, and normally Yale would have begged me to come, but all of a sudden what if they need to diversify, you know, and I am in the position of being discriminated against for being not a minority. What kind of solution is that, what kind of affirmative action is that, if all it does is somebody new gets left out for no reason except for who they are."

"That's usually the reason someone gets left out," said Chloe. "Guess it's your turn."

"Says who?" said Katie. "Says you?"

"Katie, you would've gotten into Yale, so what's the big deal?" Lauren hoped to flatter her friend into submission. "You chose Williams early, but you still would've gotten into Yale."

Katie was not about to admit that she had caved in to pressure from her parents. She slid into fiction as easily as she had slipped into her prom dress, not a snag, not a hitch, a seamless internal rewrite that transformed a months-long power struggle into an informed consensus.

"I did a lot of research, and I chose Williams early because it seemed that anyone—*anyone*—might get turned down at Yale this year for no good reason. No good reason. Except that there might be a less qualified candidate who made a school feel, you know, like it was doing the right thing."

"I am not a less qualified candidate."

They all looked at Liz.

"I am the valedictorian at Ocean Heights," she said. "I am as qualified as anyone at this table."

"More," said Chloe, trying to be helpful.

"And what you've said is very sad," Liz went on, "because I am not to blame for what has happened to you, and because you seem unable to be happy about going to Williams, which would make a lot of people very happy. You're embarrassing yourself. We ought to change the subject, I think."

Brad considered blurting out the truth about his Harvard acceptance, to make himself the focus instead of Liz, but a confession, he realized, would play right into Katie's hands. If Preston Bradley IV could not sustain the family line at Harvard without help, then clearly Harvard was using faulty criteria, which was exactly her point. The best he could do was to get Liz away from Katie before the next, inevitable outburst. He put down his fork, folded his napkin, and wished the band would start up again so that he could ask his date to dance.

Lauren stared at her hands. None of this sounded very funny when Katie said it, not half as funny as quoting from Chloe's phony essay over ice cream, imagining a profile built out of fake roadblocks that were only amusing to people who had never faced any. She glanced over at Jim, who had yet to say a word, but he was busy taking cell-phone pictures of the room to send to his girlfriend. Everyone else seemed suddenly obsessed with the pattern of their woven dinner napkins, mortified into silence by Katie's behavior. Lauren was seized by the desire to speak up, to say something that would make senior prom a watershed event in their lives. To make a statement about profound advantage and the equally profound shortsightedness that seemed to accompany it.

Wow, she thought. How pompous is that?

She wanted to challenge her friends to consider their obligation to a world that had always been awfully kind to them.

No better.

What doesn't kill you makes you stronger.

Trite. Each of her parents had said that within the last two weeks and had apologized almost immediately for sounding so dumb.

If only she could think of something to say that did not sound like the topic sentence of a bad five-paragraph essay. She was still working on the best way to share her feelings when Katie lurched halfway out of her seat and sat down again with a thud.

"Lauren," she said, in a forcibly gay tone. "Come with me to the bathroom."

Something in Katie's voice said that this was not the traditional retreat, in which girls headed to the bathroom to criticize other girls' dresses and calculate the likely trajectory of the hours after the dance was over. Lauren caught Chloe's eye, and together the three girls peeled off like drill team members working a formation. A moment later, Liz got up and followed them down the hallway. Brad, who had no interest in listening to Mike's post-prom agenda, caught up with Liz and propelled her toward the others.

The girls were at the door with the silhouette of a bathing

beauty on it, when Lauren turned and beckoned to Brad and to Liz to hurry.

"C'mon," she said.

"Inside?" Brad asked.

"You stand outside. Liz can come in. Don't let anybody else."

Lauren and Chloe stood on either side of Katie while Liz pushed open the door. Once they were safely inside, Katie sagged against Lauren, who tried to prop her up at arm's length, motivated by a reflexive desire to save her dress from whatever was rumbling so loudly in Katie's stomach. She inched around behind Katie without ever letting go of her entirely, and motioned to Chloe to do the same. Together they nudged Katie toward the row of sinks, arriving just in time for her to open her mouth and spew a stream of salmon in champagne sauce, buttered sourdough roll, and stomach acid into the nearest bowl.

"Bull's-eye," said Chloe, turning on the faucet full blast and wrinkling her nose. "Nice."

"Think she's done?" asked Lauren.

"How would I know?" Chloe replied. "Better question. What are we going to do with her?"

"She needs to go home," said a low voice behind them. Liz took her cell phone out of her purse and laid it at the far end of the counter, out of Katie's range.

"Please don't tell anyone," begged Lauren, who would not have blamed Liz if she had.

"I was only going to call my father," said Liz. "I can ask him to . . ."

Katie waved a vague arm in Liz's direction and looked as though she wanted to say something, but all that blood rushing to her vocal cords left her leg muscles without the will to go on. She did not quite faint. She crumpled in slow motion until she was flat on her back on the floor, her dress splayed around her and one high-heeled sandal caught in her hem. She writhed back and forth to free herself until Chloe caught sight of the trapped shoe and eased it loose, and then Katie lay there, motionless—the only thing in her world, at that exact moment, that was not moving.

Chloe moistened a paper towel and held it out to Katie.

"Here," she said. "Wipe your mouth."

Listlessly, Katie placed the wet towel across her face and left it there.

"That's effective," said Chloe.

The three girls stood, frozen, silent, waiting to see what Katie would do next. After she had managed to hold still for an entire minute, Liz picked up her phone and hit her dad's number on speed-dial.

As Liz began to talk, Katie propped herself up on her elbows and the damp towel slid to the floor. Her eyeliner and mascara had melted into two black crescents across her cheekbones, and her lipstick was a soggy half-inch wider than her mouth in all directions. Her hairline looked as though she had just finished a half-hour workout.

She moaned.

"My head," she said, batting at Lauren's hem with one vague arm.

"What is it?" Lauren knelt down next to Katie.

"My brain," Katie said, with rising urgency. She tried to sit up and point at Liz, but she needed both hands on the floor to keep her balance, so she lay back down. Her voice rose in a wail. "I don't understand what she's saying! Nothing makes any sense. Oh my God. What's wrong with me?" Her breath got fast and shallow, and then she burped, loudly. Instinctively, Lauren hiked her dress up and checked the floor.

"Katie. Listen. I don't understand her either."

"You don't? Ask Chloe if she does. What's wrong with us?"

"Katie, stop," said Lauren. "You just understood me. None of us can understand her. She's talking to her dad. In Korean. There's nothing wrong with your brain."

"Except that it's pickled," said Chloe, who was flicking little shreds of mascara off her cheeks and wishing that she had used her mother's good stuff instead.

"You think?" Lauren asked.

"Or we're all about to have salmonella," Chloe replied. "Personally, I'm hoping for drunk."

Katie sighed and turned her head so that her cheek rested against the cool tile. Her fingers scrabbled uselessly against the floor, as though she was trying to take hold of it.

"Floor's moving," she mumbled.

"Remember Brad?" Chloe asked, happily. "When he got drunk that one time? 'Whoa, is that an earthquake?'" She leaned over Katie. "Floor's not moving."

"I remember," Katie chirped. "I do. Where's Brad? Want to go get Brad?"

"Outside. Sssh," said Lauren, wishing that she could gauge the intonation in Liz's voice. It was remarkable enough that Liz's generosity had survived Katie's monologue about who deserved what. It might not last through a round of Katie's inflated reminiscences about her nonexistent romance with Brad. Lauren turned to Chloe.

"Let's get her standing up."

"I don't think so, not until we have someplace for her to go." Chloe peered at Katie. "Very pale, pretty sweaty. Leave her there."

"I'm fine," said Katie, who sat up too fast and vomited down the front of her dress.

Liz slapped her phone shut and turned to the other girls. "If you each hold her under one arm you can get her over to the sink," she said. "We need to clean her up before it dries. But hold up her hem or it will get on the floor."

They did as they were told. Lauren stood at Katie's left side, Chloe at her right, and they escorted her over to the counter, where Liz somehow separated the folds of Katie's dress and got the soiled ones into the sink. She ran hot water straight through them, one leaf of fabric at a time, and after a few minutes the water in the sink ran clean.

"Chloe," said Liz, still holding the fabric over the sink, "can you get Katie's water bottle so she can rinse her mouth."

Chloe tipped Katie toward Lauren and reached out with her foot to nudge Katie's bag closer. She bent down without letting go, and with her free arm rooted around in the purse until she found a water bottle. Rather than hand it to Liz, she propped up her side of Katie with her hip, unscrewed the bottle top, and took a tiny sip.

"Not salmonella," she said, with a delighted grin.

"What do you mean?" asked Liz, gently squeezing the sodden pieces of Katie's dress.

"I mean vodka is what I mean." Chloe poured the contents of the bottle into an adjacent sink, rinsed it twice with hot water, filled it with cold, and handed it to Liz, who held the bottle to Katie's mouth but did not let go.

"Take a little sip. Little. Swish it around in your mouth and spit."

Katie had come around just enough to remember the usual order of things, and she started to back away from Liz, only to have Lauren and Chloe tighten their grips. So she swished, and she spit, and she awaited further instructions.

Liz washed her hands, stepped over to the hot-air dryer, and gestured for the girls to follow. She held the wet segments of the dress under the blower, chiffon leaf by chiffon leaf, until it was almost dry. When she was done, she washed her hands again and walked over to the door.

"My father will be in the parking lot by now," she said. "Probably best to take her home." Without another word, she pushed open the bathroom door.

⚘

Ted was assigned to the serpentine hallway that led to the ladies' room, but every half hour he took a break and slipped out the back to pop an Altoid and disengage. He was deep into his fantasy of wealth and autonomy, amusing himself with the philosophical question of which was more appealing, money or not having to answer to anyone but his clients, when a cab pulled into the small service lot by the garden exit and the driver got out, the engine still running, to open the back passenger door. The limos were all parked in the Marbella's valet lot, and the kids were supposed to come and go only from the front entrance, given the opportunity for all sorts of misbehavior in the dimly lit gardens behind the hotel. Ted's inner institutional voice told him that he was about to witness an escape attempt, and, while he was not in the mood for anything that required intervention, he was curious. Who would be dumb enough to get into trouble only weeks before graduation? He stepped into the shadow of the building, hoping to get a look at the senior who had interrupted his reverie without the senior seeing him.

He was a second too slow. Lauren caught sight of Mr. Marshall the moment she and Liz and Chloe and Katie stepped outside, having left Brad behind with instructions to head toward the ballroom and divert anyone who threatened to wander by. She maneuvered Katie into the cab, tucked the trailing, damp ends of her dress into the backseat, and sat down next to her as close as caution would allow.

"We'll leave in just a second, Katie. I'm going to go talk to Mr. Marshall and then I'll be right back, okay? He saw us come out. If

KAREN STABINER

I don't go over there he's going to come over here, and you don't want him to see you like this."

As she backed away, Katie called after her, "What's the big deal? It's not like I ran over a dog or anything."

Two years earlier, on prom night, a boy had lost his spot at Princeton when he ran a four-way stop and hit a Boston terrier on its nightly stroll with a public school teacher who cared for foster dogs until the rescue agency found them a new home. The boy's beverage of choice was a bottled margarita, four of which were empty in the backseat, two of which were open in his and his date's cup holders. The last thing the teacher had drunk before she told her story to the police was a bracing cup of sencha tea.

Standing in the deserted intersection, their conversation illuminated by the headlights of a squad car and an animal control truck and punctuated by the sobs of both the dog walker and the rookie nightshift animal control officer, Ted and the boy's father had agreed that getting drunk at prom was as much a part of the ritual as a white dinner jacket, a corsage, and a boutonnière. The issue was not partying but getting caught—in this case, by a horrified and sober witness whose story was now part of an official record that might require Crestview to make good on its impressively stern drugs-and-alcohol policy. The challenge, with Princeton at stake, was for Ted and the dad to construct a credible counter-narrative. Together, they paced the death route and agreed that the untrimmed ficus definitely obscured the stop sign. They suggested to the cop that a $2,000 donation to the ASPCA, along with the purchase of the teacher's purebred puppy of choice, might reduce this to an unfortunate life lesson of no lasting consequence or blame. The cop, mindful of his own drunken prom, decided to let the boy off with a stern warning, and gently suggested to the teacher that she wear brighter colors or a fluorescent armband when she walked her soon-to-be-acquired bichon frisé late at night.

The animal control officer was not so malleable. She called

Crestview first thing the following Monday morning, and the head of school made the mistake of mentioning the fine young man's future at Princeton. The road to vengeance, for a young officer who had had to bag her first corpse, was now clearly marked. Ted's only hope was to get there first, which turned out to be no hope at all.

The admissions director at Princeton listened to Ted's carefully rehearsed defense of the candidate, which included a brief social history of ritualized and unpunished prom night drinking, sympathized, and pronounced sentence.

"That was then," he said, wearily, "and this, I'm afraid, is now."

In a buyer's market, schools revoked slots in the freshman class for infractions that had never before been enforced, and college counselors found themselves trapped. If Ted defended the boy too strenuously, he lost credibility with Princeton, which might have an impact on future applicants. If Ted sacrificed the boy and allied himself with Princeton, he risked a significant ding in Crestview's reputation, one that could have repercussions with other schools. The only safe exit was a fabricated one. By mutual agreement—Ted must have been on the phone with the admissions guy for a solid hour—Princeton dumped the boy but allowed him to weave a gap-year fiction that would enable him to apply somewhere else, unsullied, the following year.

Faced with a senior's actionable stupidity, Ted far preferred secrecy to diplomacy. As long as the cab got Katie home without further incident, Ted would be spared having to beg on her behalf, and she would join the endless ranks of drunken seniors who managed to avoid detection and proceeded, unimpeded, into the glorious future that awaited them. He would have loved to turn her in, but he would settle instead for a smaller pleasure, for making sure she knew that he could have ratted her out and had chosen not to.

Before he saved her, though, he intended to enjoy himself a bit. He smiled as Lauren approached.

"Seems to be a prison break going on here," he said. "No one is supposed to leave until eleven, and never by the back door. Want to tell me what's going on?"

"It's ten minutes of, Mr. Marshall," she said, glancing over her shoulder. "It's almost eleven. Please."

"I can't grant 'please' unless I know what I'm agreeing to, Lauren. Why exactly are we bundling Katie into a cab?"

"Mr. Marshall, I will tell you the truth but you have to promise me, promise me, that you won't do anything that'll get her into trouble."

He raised an eyebrow.

"Okay, I know you won't, right, because it's bad for her, for Crestview, for Williams, and it was the kind of mistake anyone could make," Lauren said. "Somehow, somehow, maybe her brother played a trick on her, but there was something in her water bottles, I think she got drunk without knowing it, I mean, vodka doesn't smell, that's what my parents say, I don't drink, I don't think Katie drinks either. Let's just say somehow she ended up drunk and we got her into the bathroom and she got sick and now we need to get her home. And you're the only one who saw her, so if you just let her go now, I know she's really sorry and she's learned a good lesson, except, really, I bet it was Ron playing such a mean trick, Mr. Marshall. Please. Can I just take her home?"

"Yes, yes. Of course you can."

"Oh, Mr. Marshall, I'm so glad it was you who saw us and not somebody else."

"I need a promise back."

"Anything, you name it."

"Figure out how to keep Chloe from telling everyone."

"Oh, sure. It was the salmon. That's what we'll say, okay? Can she go now?"

"Sure." He waved in the direction of the cab, in the malicious hope that Katie had her eyes open, and went back inside.

Lauren hurried back to the cab.

"My dad wants to know is someone coming with her," said Liz, "in case she doesn't feel well on the way home."

"I figured Chloe and I would—"

Chloe broke in, having learned moments before Katie's collapse that her date had the keys to his family's weekend cottage in Santa Barbara. "Yeah, but if two of us disappear to take her home it kind of screams crisis, don't you think? I mean, I'll come with you if you want, but if you're good alone, well, you're so good at this kind of stuff. Me alone, I'd . . ."

"It's okay," said Lauren, deflated. "It's fine. I'll take her. Somebody tell Jim for me."

Chloe hugged her and disappeared inside before Lauren could change her mind, so Lauren opened the cab door and settled in next to Katie, while Liz checked out the backseat like a claims adjustor, making sure that Katie had not drooled or in any other way defaced Steve's upholstery.

Lauren reached out her hand and squeezed Liz's arm.

"Look, it was so nice of you to fix up Katie's dress like that," Lauren whispered. "Can you imagine her mom if she came home—"

Liz cut her off. "I didn't want her smelling up my dad's cab." She said something to her father in Korean that made him laugh, and walked away.

As he pulled out of the parking lot, Steve glanced over his shoulder and asked, "What is the address where I am taking you?"

"That's a good question," said Lauren. "I guess we should go to my house." She gave him her street address and launched into directions, but he held up his right hand for her to stop.

"I know," said Steve. "How is the girl?"

Lauren looked over at Katie, who was clutching her purse in one hand and the door handle in the other, her forehead and cheek plastered against the cool window, her eyes closed.

"Well, she seems to be done throwing up, which I guess is what matters most at the moment."

Liz's father chuckled. "Yes, my cab and your dress are then safe, a good thing."

Lauren desperately wanted to talk about anything else.

"By the way, that's so great about Liz and Yale," she began. "You must be so proud."

"I am, and my wife is too," said Steve, whose lingering affection for Harvard had been diminished if not erased by Yale's offer of a full ride. "And your parents. You have made them proud."

Lauren pretended to be ministering to Katie, who was in fact asleep. She still had not told anyone where she was going to school, hoping to hide behind an enigmatic smile all the way to graduation, and for now the Mona Lisa act had led to a nice new theory, that her parents had put down double deposits at two schools to buy her the summer to make up her mind. Come August, she intended to slip quietly up the coast to Santa Barbara, and anyone who still cared could gossip behind her back. She had come to regret that she had sent in the Northwestern wait-list form. She did not need to be turned down again.

She stared dully at the back of Liz's father's head, wondering why everyone she met felt that they had the right to inquire about her future.

"I say," he repeated, thinking that she had not heard him, "you have made your parents proud."

Lauren leaned back against the seat. There was no question mark in that sentence. Liz's dad seemed to believe that there were two categories of children—those who let their parents down by swilling something that was not water and ruining an expensive dress, and those who behaved well and made their parents proud—and with very little evidence, without even asking where she was going to school, he had placed Lauren in the second category, alongside Liz. For the first time since she had missed the early-decision deadline, Lauren considered the possibility that her parents were proud of her, had always been proud of her, and that perhaps pride was not conditional on acceptance letters from fancy schools. What she had read as their disappointment in her could have been their disappointment in it, in the process that had made her sad, or even their disappointment in themselves, for not being able to protect her.

"I did my best," she said.

"Then you are like Liz," he said. At the stoplight he turned to look at her. "I tell her, this is Harvard's loss not to take you. It is their mistake, not anything you did wrong. At first I say it to her to make her feel better and do not quite believe it myself, but the more I think the more I am convinced. The more I think about it, this has nothing to do with her."

"Of course you're right," said Lauren, although she had gotten angry when her father made an almost identical speech about Northwestern. Katie let loose a reedy snore. "It's crazy this year. My parents say the same thing you do. It has nothing at all to do with us. Or at least not very much."

The light turned green, and Steve banked the car into the curve of the freeway entrance ramp. Lauren sat back and stared out the window, and when they got to the exit near her house she cracked open the window an inch, so that she could smell the ocean.

They pulled up in front of her house and she nudged Katie, hard.

"Listen, wake up," said Lauren.

"Where are we?"

"My house," said Lauren. "Open your door, take a couple of big breaths, and then right up to my room. My mom always wakes up the minute I open the door, but do not talk to her, do not do anything but walk straight into my room and flop on the bed."

"Is there a reason you're being such a bitch?"

"If you don't do what I say I'm going to have Liz's dad drive you home and you can explain to your mom why the front of your dress looks like old salad."

Katie stared down at her lap.

Steve's voice came from the front seat.

"Do you need me to help you get her to the door?"

"No," said Lauren, as though she could will it to be true. "I'm sure we're fine. Aren't we, Katie. Can you stand up?"

"I am fine, thank you," she said, swinging open the door of the cab and wobbling to her feet. She clung to the open door while Lauren got out.

Lauren turned to Steve. "Thank you so much for taking us home," she said, and then she stopped, flustered, and reached into her purse for her wallet, not knowing whether a twenty would be enough or an insult.

"No," Steve said. "You are Liz's friend."

"Well, barely," said Lauren.

"You should get her upstairs."

Lauren pried Katie from the door and put an arm around her waist in what she hoped looked more like friendship than aid, in case anyone was at the window. Steve waited until they were standing under the light at the front door before he drove away. Once he was gone, Lauren took a deep breath and grabbed Katie's elbow.

"Okay. We had a great time and we took a cab home because we weren't interested in driving all over town to after-parties. Got it?"

"You said I shouldn't say anything to your mom."

"You shouldn't. But don't say anything if I say anything, either. Ready? One, two, three, and we hit the bedroom."

"God, you'd think I was incapable of knowing how to behave."

Lauren turned so that her face was inches away from Katie's.

"I think you're an incredible bitch and you don't deserve any of the nice things people do for you, but here we are." She opened the door, they sailed straight to the stairs, and by the time Nora had thrown on a robe and moved to intersect them, Lauren was at the door to her bedroom with a ready story, and Katie, who had flopped onto Lauren's bed, managed a wave and a gleeful "Hi, Mrs. Chaiken. What a night!" before Lauren gently closed the door in her mother's face.

chapter 16

An idea lodged itself in Ted's brain like a parasite cling-
ing to a host: he had to get Lauren into Northwestern.
He fought it all day on Sunday, to no avail. Every time he let down
his guard, he heard her pleading for a friend who did not deserve
it and, even worse, expecting him to behave in a compassionate
manner. The degree of her decency was irrelevant to his mood;
there was no such thing as spiritual valedictorian. What mattered was that he had short-changed a good kid without even realizing that he had done so. He had given her less than his full
attention and convinced himself that he had done enough, while
a star from an important family, like Brad, or a perfect specimen
with pushy parents, like Katie, drew him right into their drama
and got more.

It was his behavior, not Lauren's, that nibbled at him. At
$20,000 per outcome, every one of his new clients was going to
be a first-tier customer who expected Ted to give his all. By six
o'clock, collapsed in front of the Travel Channel, he had come to
the terrible conclusion that he had to intervene with Northwestern, had to get results to prove to himself that he could. He had
an inviolate rule about never going into his home office after the
first week in April—any loose ends after that could be handled
during regular weekday working hours, and if he did not draw
boundaries the job would consume him—but the day after prom,
for the first time since he ascended to the top job in the counseling department, he turned on his computer to take a look at

Lauren's application. All of his seniors submitted copies of their final applications to him; privacy was for kids who were arrogant enough to think they could get in without help, and he had swapped them out to a junior counselor the previous September.

He reread the application, looking for proof that she never really had a chance. Regular sections in science were reason enough to excise a candidate, these days. B pluses could be the kiss of death, especially in those unweighted regular science classes. Very high test scores, but no 800 to draw the eye away from the B plus in physics. The same was true of her extracurricular activities—impressive, and yet not enough to tip the balance. Choir, which relied on the God-given ability to carry a tune, carried less weight than an activity that required ambition and mastery, like debate or student government. Lauren should have been editor in chief instead of news editor, but even that might not have been enough, as every decent high school had a newspaper and every newspaper had an editor who deluded himself into thinking that any school with a great journalism department— like Northwestern—was a lock. Lauren had not even applied to the journalism program, which made the newspaper matter even less.

His left calf began to seize up, so he walked around the house to loosen it. If he felt like selling, if he was really on his game, he could recast all of these elements in a better light. Lauren had taken real lab sciences instead of going for an easy A in the various punt sciences Crestview sprinkled through its curriculum for grade-grubbers. Any SAT score over 720 might as well be an 800, and could have been, with a handful of different vocab questions. She ran the alto section of the choir, or so said the choir director, whose offer of a recommendation Ted had turned down, as singing was irrelevant to the task at hand. Without her the editor of the paper would have had no story ideas to claim as his own. In truth, the worst thing Ted could say about Lauren was that she tried things and rejected them—introduction to ceramics never became AP studio art, freshman volleyball never became a starting position on the varsity team. She spent high school being curious, and he berated himself for not seeing the thread sooner; curiosity, journalism, curiosity, life, it would have made a good essay, one that exalted her record, that made it sound more strategic than it was. Unadorned general interests might be admirable in any other generation, but they were death for a candidate who had the bad luck to grow up in the middle of a population boom and had a counselor too busy to conceptualize on her behalf.

Ted was bleeding altruism out of every orifice, which scared him. He composed an email to his Northwestern admissions contact and did not send it, called the guy's private line to leave a voice mail but hung up before he got connected, and drove over to Whole Foods to keep from doing anything rash. A half hour later, he stood in the express line with a grilled boneless and skinless chicken breast, a container of brown rice pilaf, a container of steamed spinach, a little tub of rice pudding in case his courage soured into despair at the whole wretched mess, and an overpriced bottle of garage wine for later on, no matter how he ended up feeling.

He drove home a bit too fast, strode straight into his office, dumped the grocery bag on the floor, got his draft email up on the screen, and hit SEND without bothering to sit down:

"Bob, do me a favor, dig out Lauren Chaiken's app. It's Sunday. I'll call you Monday. Ted."

Ted burst out of his office first thing on Monday morning, dropped a Post-it on Rita's desk, and disappeared down the central corridor. He fell into step next to Katie when she came out of AP French and cut her off from the rest of the herd with nothing more than a tense "Come with me" and a no-nonsense glance. As they passed Rita's desk, Ted raised an eyebrow and Rita mouthed the words "Got him." He nodded and ushered Katie into his of-fice. He did not reward Rita's success by leaving the door open.

"How're you feeling, Katie?" he asked, not because he cared but because he wanted to give her the opportunity to tell the truth before he lowered the boom. It would not make any differ-ence to the verdict, but he was curious to see what she would do.

"Fine," she said, looking right at him. "What's up?"

Not a hint of remorse. He supposed he ought to be grateful. It made his job easier.

"So, Katie, I doubt this is going to come as a surprise, but under the circumstances we're not going to be able to ask you to deliver the valedictory address this year."

"What do you mean? Who's going to get it?"

"Which would you rather I answered first?"

"What do you mean? My GPA's the highest, isn't it?"

"Katie, let's not pretend here. I doubt you registered that I was in the parking lot when you left prom. Still, I am aware of the drinking and your being sick and leaving in a cab. You could be suspended for that. Actually, you could be expelled."

Katie had waited all day Saturday to see if her parents no-ticed that Ron had swiped a bottle of scotch the night before, but they never said a word. They only kept hard liquor in the house for parties, ever since a famous local chef had come out of the kitchen to chastise Dan for ordering a martini, which dulled the taste buds, before the foie. Her dad had surveyed the inventory midday without comment—he often did that on Saturdays, as though they knew anyone who ever dropped by unexpectedly for any-thing, let alone a drink. He checked only to see if he needed to restock, not because he thought anyone in his household was drinking on the sly. The kinds of excessive behaviors other people worried about were not an issue with his children.

After he went to the club for his weekly tennis lesson, and her mom went upstairs for her weekly massage, Katie had crept into the study, emptied two water bottles into the ice bucket, filled them both just past halfway from an open bottle of vodka, and topped them off with some of the water. She dumped the rest of it into the bar sink, dried the ice bucket, screwed the caps on the water bottles extra-tight, and stashed them in her purse for the evening. Brad liked vodka. He once said that a sip at bedtime took the edge off, which was exactly what she had in mind. She would sip like he did, and cope, and no one would be the wiser.

She could not have anticipated the combined effects of the vodka and a stomach denied anything but a plain piece of break-fast toast, thanks to a wildfire rumor among the girls that a more substantial meal, eaten within twenty-four hours of an event, would result in visible bloating. She got only as far as the ballroom entrance before the few sips she had drunk in the limo took hold of her brain and misinformed her about the temperature in the room, the stability of the decorative palms, and the exact location of the seat of her chair at the dinner table.

The simple logic of the first-time drinker told her to eat to correct the imbalance, as though food would absorb the alcohol and nullify its effect, but dinner rolls and butter and rare salmon only made things worse. Katie had no memory of the cab ride, and only a vague sense of charming her way past both Lauren's parents and then her own on Sunday morning. A few blithe words about what a great evening it had been and she was safe in her own bedroom, where it was hours before she felt anything like herself.

Like any amateur drunk, she thought she had deceived everyone—except Lauren, of course, and she would keep the truth a secret because she was too nice not to. As for Ted, he might know or he might be bluffing. He had not said that she was suspended or expelled, only that she could be, which to Katie signaled that this was a negotiation, not a sentencing.

She did not flinch. "If what you say about me drinking is true, then maybe you're doing something to find out who spiked my water bottle. You could expel them instead."

Ted had to smile. Someday this girl would be the press secretary for an administration that needed to rationalize an unjust war, or run a government regulatory agency involved with hazardous materials or covert operations; she was that good at turning disaster to her own advantage. Katie had an instinct for the feasible lie—not the whopper that betrayed her, but the completely plausible story that he would have fallen for if he had not seen her. She was even savvy enough to risk the spiked water bottle story instead of salmonella, which sounded good but would not hold up because no one else had got sick.

"Perhaps you have an inkling of who might have done such a thing to you?" he replied, happy to play along because he knew he would not have to for very long. He placed a cool, composed hand on the telephone. "Look, if we're going to mount an investigation we better do it fast, so let's get your dad and mom in here to help us figure out what to do."

He held her gaze and counted silently toward ten. If she called his bluff he was going to have to place the call, which he did not want to do.

At nine she held up her hand.

"Y'know, Mr. Marshall, I'm sorry to say this, I mean, I love Crestview and all that, but I am, I am, so, I don't know, so over it."

"You are?"

"I'm so over it." As soon as Ted mentioned her parents, Katie began to craft a story for them about why she had decided not to give the valedictory address, one that dovetailed neatly with her explanation of why her prom dress looked as though she had gone swimming in it. Katie was more than up to the challenge of a credible narrative, and the one about prom involved Chloe getting drunk and sick and Katie coming to her aid, a gesture of sisterhood followed by a pact not to tell Chloe's mom because she was under enough stress as it was. In Katie's version, the girls were in the hotel bathroom after dinner, checking their hairdos and makeup, when Chloe took what turned out to be her fourth Vodka Cruiser out of her purse. When Katie gently tried to take it away, Chloe spilled it down the front of Katie's dress and insisted that she had to help rinse out the dress in the sink. Leaning over must have made her head spin, because Chloe vomited as they were finishing up, and Katie had to start over and rinse out the dress a second time. She and Lauren took Chloe home in a cab, and because it was late, and because Lauren's house was closer, Katie spent the night rather than spend even more time and money on a cab home.

It was a heroic tale, culminating in Katie and Lauren's decision not to tell anyone. There was nothing to be gained by getting Chloe into trouble. Katie had been a model of responsible behavior, and she hoped that her actions would inspire Chloe to emulate her.

Much better to forfeit the valedictory than to run the risk of exposing the truth. Katie assumed that Brad was next in line for the honor, which fed nicely into the story. Her parents would assume that old money ruled, that Trey had somehow intervened and stolen the honor from their daughter, and Katie could selflessly instruct them not to challenge the decision.

She already knew what she would say. "My self-image does not require that kind of outside acknowledgment. I'm fine just knowing that I'm the best. If Brad or his mom or dad is feeling needy for some reason, well, fine. He can have it."

If she was wrong, and the valedictorian turned out to be someone else, she would mention the unweighted A in ceramics, and her parents could argue about that instead of hassling her.

She did not want to back down, but there was something about Ted reaching for the phone that unnerved her. He never said or did anything unless he meant it. The gesture had an unfamiliar and reckless edge, and she was not in the mood to take a chance.

He took his hand off the receiver. "Then we're in agreement."

"Sure," she said. "It's not like I want to sit down and write a speech right now."

"Excellent."

Katie stood up to leave. "But just curious—who gets it?"

"Now, Katie, you know I can't say until I've talked to him, or her."

She walked out without another word, closing the door with just a hint of a slam, and Ted slumped in his seat. He did not like playing chicken. Katie had to know that he would not turn her in, and yet she had made him play his part up to the last possible moment. It made his head ache. He reached for a blank pad and sketched a little duckling with drops of water rolling off its back. Under the duck, which he labeled "Katie," he wrote,

Water off a duck's back.

Impermeable.

Imperturbable.

Implacable.

Impossible.

Imposter.

He fed the page into his shredder, turned to his computer, and called up the document labeled OOH, which was code for "out of here," a string of euphemisms that was his draft letter of resignation. He was revising the bit about how he had rendered himself obsolete by building such a dynamic team, when there was a knock on his door.

He closed the document and yelled, "C'mon in."

Brad folded himself into a chair and gave Ted the kind of shambling grin he rarely saw before May 1. "Hey, Mr. Marshall. What can you do to wreck my life today? I don't think my dad has his checkbook with him."

"Brad, c'mon. You're going to come back here next Thanksgiving so embarrassed because wait, what's this, you love Harvard and you want to say thanks for not letting you do something stupid."

Brad looked genuinely pained, and Ted wondered for an instant if any private consulting fee was large enough to compensate him for having to deal with yet another set of indulged teenagers and their invented woes. Ted had assumed that Brad would stop grousing once Harvard recalled the enduring, six-figure value of the Bradley legacy, but there seemed to be no pleasing some people, and Ted was frankly tired of complaints from such a fortunate boy. He was even more tired of knowing that Brad probably had a good reason for feeling the way he did, unlike some of his whinier counterparts, and that Ted had failed to figure it out. More than anything, he was tired of thinking that he ought to. It was Ted's job to get his seniors into great colleges, not to unravel the family dramas that occasionally informed their choices.

Ted waited until he felt himself start to calm down. When he spoke again, it was with his usual matter-of-fact cool.

"Anyhow, look, I have one last assignment for you. Should cheer you up some."

Brad stared.

"You're the valedictorian. You get to give the speech."

"How come you're telling me and not Dr. Mullin?"

"Because I wanted to congratulate you. Because we hang out more than you do with the head of school."

"Katie's valedictorian."

"Nope, you are. Want to see the numbers?" For the second time in an hour, Ted prayed that a student would not call his bluff.

Brad slumped deep in the chair, as though his bones had turned to sand.

"Who's next in line?"

"I don't know." Ted angled his computer screen away from

Brad and called up the senior class GPA list. Katie first, Brad second by .01, and third, Mike, the boy who had taken Katie to prom.

"It's Mike," said Ted, with a conspiratorial smile. "C'mon. You don't want to hear him go on for fifteen minutes. You do it."

Brad clasped his hands on top of his head, as though to keep his brain in place, and stared at his college counselor long enough to make Ted squirm. Then he stood up suddenly and held out his hand. Ted got up as well, without quite knowing why, and shook Brad's outstretched hand.

"Not going to do it, Mr. Marshall," said Brad. "I don't have anything I want to say."

"Your dad's going to be pissed," said Ted. "Not just at you. He's going to call me up and demand an explanation."

Brad smiled. "Yeah," he said. "Sorry about that. Need me to turn a paper in late or something?" He and Liz had spent a chilly hour looking at the empty seats at their table before they finally abandoned prom, and afterward she had politely declined suggestions of everything from a late-night steak at the Pantry to tapas. They had not spoken since. Katie was out of contention, so there was no longer any need to yield valedictorian on that front, and no reason to hang on to it to impress Harvard, because the wait list was something that happened to other people. Brad was sprung, trolling for a little bit of trouble, thinking that if he was not careful he would turn into his older brother.

"No," said Ted. "We're good."

He spent the rest of the morning meeting with junior-class families who had visited schools over spring break, or who wanted to debate the pros and cons of taking the SATs again in May, having fallen slightly short in April, or who tried to tease out who else was thinking of applying to the schools on their preliminary list so that they could plot a strategy that took into account the twelve other potential applicants at Stanford. By noon Ted was ready to make his move for Lauren. He waited until Rita had left for lunch, and then he placed the call from his direct line, left a message, and sat and watched the digital readout on his telephone. Ten minutes later, the phone number he was waiting for appeared.

"Bob, thanks for calling back so fast."

"Ted. How you doing?"

"No pipe bombs, no death threats. Sixteen percent in the Ivy League and only four kids who care about their wait lists, so I'm good. You?"

"I'm okay unless you're going to beg me about that girl, in which case I'm not at my desk."

"But you called me back, so you must be interested. Did you look at her file?"

"Yeah. Wait-listed." Bob chuckled. "You know the odds on wait lists."

Ted squirmed. "And you know I don't push on them. This is a one-shot deal. I need this girl bumped to the front of the line, I need it before the line even forms, and you won't regret it. She's a special kid."

"So's the boy who's camped out in a tent outside my office," said Bob. "And the girl who sent me a ten-minute computer-animated movie, and the kid with a letter from Bill Clinton. That's the wait-list crowd. How much do you think special matters in the endgame?"

"Bob, come on."

There was a long silence before Bob spoke again, and when he did he sounded even more exhausted than Ted. "I'm sorry. I sound like an asshole. I am an asshole at this point. I have this kid camped out on my lawn. I have to sneak in and out the emergency door every day and set off the alarm just to keep from making eye contact with him. His parents put him on a plane from Denver. He's been on the local TV news. Kids from his high school who already go here are wearing T-shirts that say 'Admit the Commerce

City One.' And I have to tell you, we're not going to take him. I'm just hoping he doesn't set himself on fire when he finds out."

Ted was dug in, determined to prove that he could beat the odds. "All the more reason to look at Lauren, who would never pull a stunt like that. Read between the lines. I mean it. Listen to me. She is going to turn out to be a real asset. You ought to pay attention. You know I don't step up for just anyone."

"True. That's why I like you. You take rejection well." He started to scroll through Lauren's online application, looking for a bit of ammunition he might have missed.

"And you know you took kids who got into an Ivy League school," said Ted. "They're going to turn you down. You're going to have spaces."

"Thanks for reminding me. Because I really enjoy being Harvard's safety school."

"So take her off the list now."

"I can't. We don't even know what we've got yet. Maybe not so many got into Harvard this year, you know."

"Somebody did," said Ted. "Take her."

Bob stopped scrolling. "Hey, hey, hey, Ted, before you go to the mat for this kid, are you sure she's as dying to get in as you say?"

Ted was on alert. "I am. Why do you ask?"

"Because I'm looking at a note here that says that Northwestern is not Ms. Chaiken's first-choice school."

"Please. And whose note would that be? The mom or dad of the kid on your lawn?"

"From the alumni interview. Madison Ames. Says our girl didn't apply early because she wanted to have a lot of choice."

Ted squeezed his eyes shut, hard, and watched the little colored lights dance on the inside of his eyelids. "Bob, I'm going to suggest that perhaps I have a slightly better sense of Lauren's preferences than Madison Ames does. She might have misunderstood. I know this kid wants Northwestern more than anything. More than anything." He waited to see if he was going to have to bring up the steak incident.

So did Bob. After a long pause, he said, warily, "I'm not saying there's anything I can do."

"I didn't say you did. But keep me posted."

"I have to wait to see who commits on May 1."

This was still not heading in the direction Ted wanted to go. "No, you don't, and you know it."

"But if I can't make it happen?"

Ted was surprised at how quickly he replied. "If you don't, I won't sell Northwestern when I go private next year. And if you tell anybody what I just said, I'll deny it, and then I really won't sell Northwestern."

"You're quitting Crestview?"

"I've got two dozen kids from all over town whose parents have a spare $25,000 they'd like to spend to have me help them get their kids into the college of their dreams," said Ted, exaggerating his confirmed clientele, as well as his average fee, because there was no way for Bob to know he was lying. Besides, he was not lying, exactly; he was forecasting. Families would be beating down his door once he handed in his resignation and sprang his new clients from their vow of confidentiality.

"I'd like to put Northwestern on some short lists," he said.

Bob might as well have been a dog standing in front of a butcher's case. Two dozen kids whose parents had enough expendable cash to drop $25,000 on a private consultant, which meant that the parents had money, which meant that they were not prone to foolish investment, which implied that the kids must have enough sterling attributes to make them competitive candidates. And these were students who did not need financial aid, always a plus. Beyond that, who knew? If someone was prepared to spend that kind of money for advice, they might be prepared to endow a wing of a building or put the university in their wills. These were premium candidates, and Ted was offering to help elevate Northwestern's image in their eyes, to present it as the single member of the newly formed midwestern chapter of the Ivy League.

"Nice for you," said Bob, carefully. "But y'know, I have to give her a hard look just like everybody else."

"Sure you do," said Ted, feeling instinctively that he had made some progress.

chapter 17

*Dave faltered for a moment when he first saw the finan-*cial aid letters. He had made the mistake of thinking that his stint as the family's voice of doom would end once all the letters arrived. In fact, he had to continue to be the grown-up—the voice of doom label was Deena's—as he tried to make sense of the money offers in the weeks before the May 1 deadline. The consensus among the financial aid people was that Chloe required less help than Dave or the government had calculated. Worse, all of the offers were for loans in combination with work-study stipends that Deena did not want her to take her first year, or ever, for that matter.

"Need-blind?" he said when Deena called to give him the news. "More like need-nearsighted." She did not laugh, and for once Dave could not blame her; clearly, the benefits of living with Mom had not paid off as well as either of them had hoped. Sending Chloe to a private college was going to be like taking out another mortgage with no house to show for it. As long as Deena insisted on staying put and Chloe insisted on going wherever she felt like going, Dave was stumped. He did not see a way out.

Deena did because she had to, because it was either that or move to Palms. She came up with what Dave had to admit was a clever solution: offer Chloe a new Prius if she went to UC Santa Cruz instead of to a private school; spend $23,000 on a car to save over $100,000 they did not happen to have. Chloe embraced the idea immediately. She wanted a red Prius with leather seats, great sound, and Bluetooth, "so I can call you guys when I drive home without getting a ticket for holding my cell phone." Deena wanted the navigation system. Dave wanted the cheaper Package 2 model, which had cloth seats, no tweeters, and no Bluetooth unless he spent $600 more. The dealers, who had squandered their karma drawing up waiting lists and charging $1,500 over sticker back when people could get financing, were ready to sell anything to anyone who could qualify for a loan. It was a buyer's market—but Dave was looking for a low-end model in a market that still skewed toward the high-end customer. It took him three weeks of daily phone calls before he found a dealer a half hour on the wrong side of downtown who swore he had a red Package 2 coming off the truck the very next morning. Dave could have it if he was there at noon.

He and Deena and Chloe left before eleven, which would have been plenty of time back when rush hour implied that there were non–rush hours, dependable windows of opportunity when traffic sped up from a crawl to a flow. Dave pulled onto the dealer's lot a half hour late, ready with a line about time and traffic standing still, and was relieved to see a couple of guys wiping dust off a red Prius.

Chloe saw it, too. "Look! I bet that's it. See the red one with the door open? I bet that's mine."

"It's a nice red," said Deena.

"Okay," said Dave, eager to assume his role as master of the universe. "We do the paperwork, I write them a deposit check, and in an hour or so Chloe gets to drive off the lot in her new car."

"Do you have your license?" asked Deena.

Chloe shot her a withering look.

Dave strode toward a knot of salesmen standing in the doorway, all of them wearing the neckties and white dress shirts they had adopted at the height of the hybrid stampede to lend dignity to thievery, outfits that on the downslope evoked instead a funereal pall. Deena and Chloe waited at a respectful distance, but Deena could tell almost immediately that things were not going as planned. One of the salesmen guided Dave away from the group for a private chat, and as they started to talk a flush crept up the back of Dave's neck. He made a choppy gesture with his right hand to emphasize whatever point he was trying, and failing, to make, a gesture Deena recognized from all the arguments they had ever had. When he turned away and walked back to his family, he did not look happy.

"They sold the damn car," said Dave, who wondered why none of his wistful fantasies of family life ever lasted as long as they were supposed to.

"But we're here," said Deena.

"Someone else was here an hour ago. Every salesman has a list to call. First come, first served. That's how it goes," said Dave.

"I wonder whose red one that is," said Chloe, eyeing the car with its door open.

"Ask him about that one," said Deena, lighting up. "Go ahead, will you?"

"Sure," said Dave, "but I guarantee you it's taken or he would have mentioned it."

He headed back toward the building, and this time his salesman escorted him to a desk inside. Chloe and Deena stood, transfixed, trying to make sense of all the pointing and nodding and shrugging, the scribbling and crossing-out, the appearance of the salesman's pocket calculator. After several computations, Dave headed back to his wife and daughter.

"Do they have one?" asked Chloe.

"Not really," said Dave. "That red one's a Package 5. Loaded. All kinds of stuff you don't need."

"But it's available," said Deena. "Is it available?"

Dave had the same pained expression on his face that Deena

remembered from their aborted dinner at Sisley's. "Somebody's coming in at three to do the paperwork," he said.

"Then we could have it now," said Chloe, "just like somebody else walked in early and got ours. Let's do that, and then we could go have lunch like you said."

"Ladies," said Dave, "that car is about $7,000 more than the Package 2, for lots of stuff we don't need or want."

"I want leather seats," said Chloe. "I bet it has leather seats included."

"And this way Chloe would have the navigation system, which I know you don't think is necessary but can be very helpful, from what I hear from people who have them." Deena had a closet full of rationales. When it came to making instant gratification sound sensible, there was no one better this side of a pre-rehab addict.

"I repeat," said Dave. "This car is $7,000 more."

"I read an article," said Chloe, and Dave froze, wondering how long Chloe had been collecting ammunition for whatever she was about to say, "and it said that these cars are at a premium because the factories can't make them any faster. I bet if we end up having to wait a month, the car you want is only going to end up costing more. So if you look at it that way, this car today might only end up being $5,000 more than the one you want for me by the time it finally shows up. Or maybe they won't get what you want before school starts and we'll have to get this one, which by then will cost even more. Which makes it a bargain today, when you think about it. I mean, if you add up all the extra stuff we get. And don't the leather seats cost extra on the cheaper one?"

Dave had never intended to pay extra for leather seats, but his daughter seemed to have forgotten that in her frenzy to have a red car right this minute. He appealed mutely to his ex-wife, whose smile told him she was allied with her daughter. Deena was probably very proud of Chloe for having figured out how to turn a $30,000 car into a steal.

To Dave's surprise, Deena took his arm and leaned close enough to squish her right breast against what bicep he had left. Her lips were within range for a kiss; it was a remarkable semblance of intimacy.

"Dave. It's her graduation present, and I feel better with her so far away knowing she has a computer to keep her from getting lost. We're still so far ahead it isn't funny. You know there would've been an extra $7,000 for college, someplace," said Deena, gaily, "so isn't it just a wash?"

"A whole lot cheaper than Hampshire, Dad, and it is such a cool car."

Dave felt his will give way. Seven thousand dollars was a small price to pay for not having to argue with his wife and daughter. A real dad, a good dad, a providing dad, would have bought the fancier car in the first place. As for the three o'clock who was going to drive all the way out here to find that his car had been sold, too bad. Someone had pulled the rug out from under Dave, so Dave had no problem disappointing the next buyer in line.

"Yes, it is a cool car," he said, gently disentangling himself from Deena. "I'm going to go buy it." Chloe threw her arms around him for a moment, which was nice, before she grabbed her cell phone to text Lauren the good news.

Less than an hour later, they were done. Dave was in debt another $25,000 after the down payment, Deena was as ebullient as she always was after a big purchase, and Chloe was deep into her artsy urban fantasy self. She was secretly relieved to be going to Santa Cruz in a new red car. She imagined that she would be the coolest girl there by a long shot, with no competition from true city sophisticates, the way there would have been at the East Coast schools. Chloe might have picked one of those schools to show her parents that she could do whatever she felt like doing, but the red car had provided an excuse to pick her first choice without looking like someone who had settled.

Best of all, her mom was going to be late for Pilates unless they left right away, so there was no time for a family lunch. Chloe made great show of adjusting the seat and the mirrors before she pulled out at a ridiculously reasonable rate of speed, which she maintained because she could see her parents in her rearview mirror. Did they intend to drive right behind her all the way home, her own personal crumple zone? Her dad hung on her bumper until he turned into a gas station right before the freeway entrance, and Chloe, set free, hit the gas and headed for Lauren's, or Brad's, or even Katie's. She intended to drive by everyone's house until she found someone to make a fuss about her car.

❧

Satisfying Chloe was a relatively straightforward process, as long as the manufacturers of cars and oversized handbags and ankle boots and makeup reminded her at every opportunity that personal fulfillment was a credit card swipe away. Finding contentment was trickier for Katie, who already owned the original version of every knockoff Chloe lusted after, frequently in multiple units, for any truly great pair of shoes was worth having in more than one color. She was not profligate. She did not have a pair of peep-toe knee-high boots in her closet, as Chloe did, because it did not take much common sense to figure out that peep-toes were for good weather and boots were for bad. She did own everything that met her standards.

Mere stuff was like aspirin, though, strong enough to get past the normal headaches of daily life but no match for the last few weeks, which were the equivalent of a migraine. Katie required a stronger ego boost than any of her current possessions could provide, so she turned her energy to becoming the most breathtaking senior at the Crestview graduation. Anyone could get a manicure and a pedicure, a haircut and a blow-dry, and she would, and everyone was stuck having to wear a plain white dress under her graduation gown, and hers would cost more than the other girls'. These were familiar thrills, even with new shoes thrown in. Katie wanted to set herself apart, so she asked herself, What resource do I have that nobody else has?

Her mom.

Katie went into her bathroom, flipped the makeup mirror to the magnifying side, turned on all the bathroom lights, and looked for trouble, which even an eighteen-year-old could find under wattage more appropriate to an operating room. She convinced herself that there was a furrow between her eyebrows and went downstairs to look for her mother, who was sitting on the patio, trying to compensate for a tanned adolescence with a layer of SPF 45 sunscreen and a wide-brimmed SPF 25 hat, under a patio umbrella big enough to shield her entire office staff. Katie's mother was always on her guard when she was out of doors, but she always sat on the patio for an hour on the weekend, fully dressed, exposed face and hands slathered, because it struck her as something a hard-working professional woman ought to do.

"Mom."

"Hmm."

"I want you to Botox my forehead."

Joy glanced up.

"Why?"

"Can't you see?" said Katie.

"Not really."

"I hate it when you don't take me seriously."

"Let me take a look," said Joy, who lately felt the need to ask permission before she made physical contact with her daughter. She stood up and placed a professional thumb and index finger at the inner tips of Katie's eyebrows, pulled the skin taut, counted to 5, and released it. On a forty-year-old forehead, the pull flattened out the furrow, but the release brought it back. With elastic teenage skin, there was nothing to flatten in the first place, nothing more than the slightest hint of vertical tension between Katie's brows. If the forehead had belonged to anyone other than her own daughter, Joy would have recommended stronger sunglasses to prevent squinting and delayed intervention until the patient was in her late twenties. But Katie already wore sunglasses, and there was nothing wrong with Botox if you knew what you were doing. Joy emphatically knew what she was doing.

"My professional opinion is that you don't need it," she said. "You might not even notice the difference by graduation."

"But if you say 'the difference,' then you must think there's going to be one," said Katie.

Joy smiled. "Got me there. Fine. It certainly never hurts. I'll give you the family discount."

"Right. After school Monday, then."

Katie disappeared before Joy could think of anything more to say, or at least that was what Joy told herself. She decided that this was a positive sign. A mother who no longer had an issue to broach was clearly a mother who had done a good job, and a daughter whose needs had dwindled to erasing a nonexistent wrinkle was a daughter who had benefited from that good job.

Dr. Joy liked to group her forehead appointments in a block whenever possible. She walked into an exam room, appraised a forehead, and double-checked the solution levels in the syringes that Yoonie had laid out in advance, even though there was no reason to do so. She asked the patient to frown, hard, and marked a pattern of injection sites with a blue washable marker. A half-dozen Botox injections, the standard warnings about not lying down for an hour and no rubbing the forehead, and she was on her way to the next exam room to do the same thing. By the time she got done with the patient in room 3, there was a new patient ready to go in room 1. She ran laps all afternoon.

She was rounding the hallway to begin her third circuit when Yoonie stopped her outside the exam room door.

The nurse spoke so softly that Dr. Joy missed what she said the first time. She leaned in closer and asked Yoonie to repeat herself.

"I am sorry, Dr. Joy, but there must be a mistake."

Dr. Joy waited.

Yoonie tipped her head ever so slightly toward exam room 1.

"Katie is in there."

"Yes."

"I put a Botox tray in there."

"Yes."

Yoonie waited for her boss to recognize the obvious error. She had read an article about using Botox for chronic shoulder and back pain, but Dr. Joy was a dermatologist, not a sports doctor. She had no idea how to place those injections, and she was not foolish enough to try an unfamiliar procedure. Katie could not possibly be here for a cosmetic treatment, but she and Dr. Joy were behaving as though she was. When Dr. Joy reached for the exam room door, her bewildered nurse did what she always did— followed the doctor into the exam room, gave the patient an acknowledging but deferential nod, and stood beside the tray, ready to hand over the first needle.

Joy gave her daughter a disposable headband with a Velcro closure to get her hair out of the way, and wiped a cotton ball soaked in an antiseptic cleanser across Katie's forehead. She wiped again in the other direction, for no reason, while she waited for a slight, queasy flush to subside. There were two possible explanations for the way she felt, neither of them welcome—either this was the first wave of hot flashes or the next escalating step in her chronic indigestion. Joy hoped and intended to get the empty nest out of the way before her hormones or digestive tract betrayed her, but she made a quick vow to read up on the latest hormone replacement studies and buy a wedge pillow, just in case.

"Is there something wrong, Dr. Joy?"

Yoonie had the first needle in her outstretched hand.

Joy reached for it and pretended to study the liquid inside. She turned to her daughter, who, with her upturned face and closed eyes, looked like a six-year-old trying not to peek at a birthday-surprise bicycle until her parents said it was all right.

"Katie, I'm sorry, this isn't the right concentration for you." She spun around and handed the syringe back to Yoonie. "This isn't what I wrote down." Dr. Joy grabbed the tray and hustled her nurse out of the room, with a hurried, "Hang on a minute," thrown over her shoulder at Katie on her way out. She ushered Yoonie down the hall to the lab and shut the door behind them.

"It is the right—" Yoonie began.

"Make up a set with normal saline. Just enough to puff up the site for a while so she thinks I did something. That's it. Normal saline."

"No Botox."

"Of course not," said Dr. Joy, an edge of impatience in her voice. "Have you ever seen me use Botox on an eighteen-year-old?"

"No."

"Then it was a mistake, so let's fix it."

She was out the door, heading down the hall, before Yoonie could reply, not that she ever would have asked Dr. Joy, whose mistake it had been. Yoonie filled a new set of syringes as instructed, headed back to the exam room, and stood by while Dr. Joy went through the motions until all six syringes were empty.

Katie giggled and smiled at Yoonie.

"Now you can't tell Liz, remember," she said. "Doctor-patient privilege, right, Mom?"

"Absolutely," said Dr. Joy, flashing her own brand of conspiratorial smile at her nurse. "Everything that happens in this room is a secret."

She and Katie slipped out of the room together while Yoonie discarded the used supplies and prepared for the next patient. All this deceit, and Yoonie made to go along without anyone asking her what she wanted to do. Such stupid happy people. She slammed the supply cabinet too hard, heard bottles fall on their sides, and allowed herself to pretend for a good thirty seconds that she was not going to open the cabinet to straighten things out.

chapter 18

The Chaikens woke up every morning hoping to find that they had arrived at the fifth station of grief, only to realize that acceptance of Lauren's fate as a registered UCSB freshman was still miles down the road. Sundays were the worst, because there was no workday routine to sop up the excess funk, and because everything that had once been fun suddenly was not. Lauren still slept until almost noon, but it felt more like hibernation than coziness. Joel's attention span was shot; instead of poring over the newspaper, pencil and pad at the ready, he drifted through descriptions of bogies and eagles and jump shots and clay court prowess and wished that he cared. Nora went to the farmers' market and shopped by rote, and when she came home she skimmed too many cookbooks looking for new things to do with cauliflower.

They were hiding out and unhappy about it. When the doorbell rang just before eleven, which the doorbell never did on a Sunday unless a Realtor was trolling for listings, neither Nora nor Joel rushed to answer it.

"Did you invite somebody over?" asked Joel.

"No."

"Me neither."

"You get it," said Nora.

She retreated to the stairwell to eavesdrop, for it was always comforting to hear a Realtor explain that any house within three miles of the beach was recession-proof. Instead, she heard Joel utter "Ted," in a tone of surprise and fear—did the UCs ever revoke acceptances?—so she ran her fingers through her hair and tried to look as though the most pressing issue on her mind was whether to scrape a fresh vanilla bean into the batter for the French toast.

"Ted," she said, striving for calm. "We were just going to have a late breakfast. Let me warm up a baguette for you, or would you rather toast. Come sit in the kitchen with us."

"Coffee cake, she's got a new one," Joel said, pretending that the new automatic espresso maker required him to do anything more complicated than drop a premeasured pod into the pod receptacle.

"Guys," said Ted. He settled in at the long table at the back of the kitchen. "I'm not here with bad news. Quite the contrary."

They both stopped dead and stared at him.

"What, I only get fed if you're nervous?"

On cue, they went back to what they were doing. Nora sliced the coffee cake and set it in front of Ted. Joel put down the cup and saucer he had in a death grip and remembered to offer Ted steamed milk and sugar. For a long moment they floated on the promise of "quite the contrary." They experienced great contentment without knowing why.

Ted was perfectly happy to savor the anticipation, so he waited a long moment before he asked, "Is Lauren home?"

"God, of course, we are so stupid," said Nora. "I'll go get her right now."

"It's fine," said Ted, but Nora was already bounding upstairs.

She closed Lauren's door behind her and hissed in her ear, "Honey, get up."

No response.

"Lauren, you have to get up."

Lauren groaned and spoke without opening her eyes. "Mom, why are you doing this to me?"

"Ted is here."

Lauren pulled the pillow over her head.

Nora lifted its corner. "Did you hear me? Ted, from school, is downstairs eating your share of the coffee cake."

Lauren threw the pillow toward the end of the bed and sat up, furious. She did a very good job of pretending to be comfortable with her fate as long as no one took her by surprise. "Well take it back, because what exactly did he do to deserve it? Why is he here anyway?"

"Stop. He says he has good news."

"They moved UCSB to Chicago?"

Nora sighed. "Throw on some clothes and we'll find out."

She went downstairs and puttered until she heard Lauren on the stairs, and then she stationed herself against the kitchen island because it felt good to have something to lean against.

"Mr. Marshall," said Lauren. "What's up?"

Ted got up and came over to shake Lauren's hand.

"Congratulations, deserving person," he said. "You're in at Northwestern. The email comes tomorrow." He turned to Nora and Joel. "Sorry about the UCSB deposit, which you're going to have to eat because they won't refund it, but I figure you won't mind."

"I'm in?" asked Lauren, taking up a secure position next to her mother.

"How can that be?" asked Nora.

"For sure?" asked Joel.

Ted chuckled. "You guys are a hard sell. Listen. I've been working with someone in the admissions office there, really campaigning on Lauren's behalf, and he called me this morning to say that she's in. I didn't tell you what I was up to because I figure you're tired of the roller coaster, but it's over. Happy ending. Like I said, the official word comes tomorrow, but on a perfectly selfish level I wanted to see your faces when you got the news. I figured you wouldn't mind finding out a day early."

"He called you on a Sunday?" asked Joel.

"See, I should've waited for the official notification."

"You got me into Northwestern," said Lauren.

"Now we're making progress. Are you starting to believe me?"

"You got me in. But everybody says the wait lists never move."

Ted shrugged. "We can speculate all morning on how a slot opened up, but the fact is, it opened, and you get to fill it, and suddenly you've got exactly what you've wanted all year."

Lauren giggled. "This is pretty amazing." She stuck out her arm to shake Ted's hand again, and then she hugged her mother and father, in turn. She broke the crumbly top off a piece of coffee cake and ate it, and when she smiled Nora realized that it had been far too long since her daughter had done so without the effort showing.

"So that's it," Lauren said. "That'll be me next September, strolling across campus at Northwestern. Maybe I can still get into that really nice dorm, the one we saw, remember? Or it doesn't matter. Maybe I'll go on the North Face site and see what the coats look like."

Ted glanced down for an instant, and as he did so, Nora realized that he was not yet done delivering the news.

"Ted. What's the punch line?" she asked, quietly.

Ted looked straight at her, not at Lauren, and tried to maintain his tone. "Some of the freshmen get to start off abroad. Lauren's going to get to go to Prague first quarter. It's a terrific opportunity. Very few freshmen get the chance."

"Prague?" asked Joel.

"Do I have to?" asked Lauren. "I think I'd rather start out regular and go junior year like everyone else."

"That's the point," said Nora, who truly believed that a jury of her peers would not convict her if she took her favorite cast-iron skillet to the back of Ted's head. "You're not a freshman like everyone else. Is she, Ted?"

Ted sat down again. "The acceptance is predicated on Lauren taking her first quarter abroad," he said, "and then she'll come back and move into a dorm. The school arranges all of it. It's not like this is the first time this has happened."

"But I don't see why I can't just move into the dorm right away," said Lauren.

"Why is that, Ted?" Nora assumed that she knew the answer, but she was not in the mood to let him off the hook.

He rearranged the coffee cake crumbs on his plate. "Every school knows that some freshmen never make it past the first term. They get mono, they get stressed, they break up with their new boyfriends or girlfriends and fall apart. They flunk out. They think nobody knows what a joint smells like. Or they decide that the perfect school they've been chasing for two years doesn't live up to their fantasy, and they start chasing another fantasy someplace else."

"What does that have to do with me?" asked Lauren.

"One of those people got a regular acceptance at Northwestern, and they're going to bail while you're in Prague, and you're going to get their room when you get back."

"But there's no regular room for me now. I won't even know who my roommate's going to be," said Lauren, beginning to wilt.

"No," said Ted, relieved that they had hit bottom so quickly, and that now he could begin to rebuild.

"So I'm a freshman but not a good-enough freshman. That sucks."

"Lauren." Joel fretted about his daughter's linguistic health as much as Nora did about STDs.

"Well, it does," she replied. "I can just hear me: 'Hi. I'm a marginal freshman. Want to be friends? I'm going to go do homework to try to keep up with the rest of you.'"

"C'mon," said Ted. "Let's stay focused here. All I've heard all year is that Northwestern is it, it, it. Who cares that you get to go to Prague first, which isn't a real hardship post, you know what I'm saying? The end goal was Northwestern, and you got it. Nobody ever said, 'Northwestern, but only if.' It was just Northwestern."

"I think maybe Lauren never considered the possibility of a yes tied to a first quarter abroad," said Nora. "We need a little time to get used to this."

"I don't need any time—" Lauren began, but Ted squared his shoulders and interrupted.

"Thinking you don't need time probably means you do," he said. "Talk it over. Look at it from another angle. The guy I talked to has kids camping out on his lawn, they want to go there so bad. Kids sending him gifts, parents calling him on the phone." He hesitated for effect. "Somebody enrolled him in the fruit of the month club, we're talking desperate measures here. And yet they took you, and all I had to do was point out that they'd made a huge mistake they needed to rectify. You could think of yourself as being at the bottom of the accepted list, but what I'm suggesting is that you think of yourself instead as being at the top of the wait list. Which is a very competitive place to be."

He waited to see if they were going to protest, and when they kept quiet he pressed on, hoping that their silence meant willingness.

"Look, maybe if they didn't have thousands of apps, maybe if they weren't reading essays at three in the morning, maybe if Lauren's app didn't come right after some National Merit scholar who volunteers in the UCLA brain research lab—no, I don't know that's true, but I don't know it isn't. Maybe they would've taken her the first time around and they're trying to fix a mistake, but whatever it is, why not take it? What's wrong with Prague?"

"I'm working on it," said Lauren. "Excuse me, please." She disappeared up the stairs and very quietly shut her door.

Ted pretended to stir his coffee while he made a little pact with the god of his pending autonomy: if Lauren accepted the offer, he would work strictly by the numbers from now on, the counseling equivalent of the test-prep guy who dismissed any student who failed to score over 2250 on his biweekly sample SATs and then crowed about how all of his students scored over 2250. Ted would turn down the next Lauren. He would turn down a $20,000 fee, as tempting as it might be, from anyone whose kid was a percentage point short of stardom. He would embrace natural selection, as though the Brads of the world were not challenge enough, if only Lauren would say yes to Prague.

He could hardly call Bob back to say thanks but no thanks. If he failed to deliver Lauren, he would never again be able to ask for exactly the kind of favor he had to be able to deliver for his private clientele. He studied the painted fruit on his cup and saucer, and he did not look up again until he had the lemons lined up in a way that pleased him.

"I can think of one other way out."

"I can hardly wait," said Nora. "Sorry. We're listening."

"I can't get her in first quarter, I just can't. You can only push so hard for a given student before you get the sense that you've reached the limit. You can't ask for more. You can't even ask if you can ask for more."

"We know you did your best," said Joel, and Nora pinched the back of his thigh to inform him that she knew no such thing. "What's the other way?"

"If she doesn't want to go to Prague I can ask if she can start second quarter. Skip first, wait for the fallout, and start second."

"Which means she graduates when?" asked Nora.

Ted looked genuinely confused. He never thought past admissions. "I don't understand," he said.

Nora took a sip of her espresso. "If she starts a quarter late, she'll end a quarter late. She won't finish up until the other kids in her class have graduated. So what do they do, Ted? Have a little graduation some time in November for the stragglers they took off the wait list?"

Ted recovered quickly. He knew how to work a parent's sarcasm to his advantage; if Nora was going to be rude, he got to be brusque in return. "If you present it that way to Lauren, she's not going to be able to make an honest decision," he said. "I'm sure they don't graduate a quarter late. She can pick up the classes in summer school. Come on. There are all sorts of ways to make this work if you want to make it work."

"So speaking of an extra quarter," said Joel, "which is not a cheap sentence, I assume there's no prayer of money with an acceptance like this." The government had declared that the Chaikens would have received barely $7,000 in aid against a private school bill, had any of them accepted Lauren, and he was reminded by the warning glint in his wife's eye that they had made a pact to send Lauren wherever she wanted to go. But Joel had taken Nora out for dinner to celebrate when the mortgage slipped below six figures, and he enjoyed the notion of owning the house in another five years instead of feeling that the house owned him. The bakery was paying off the line of credit, which was more than enough debt for him, and $7,000 a year would have added up. It did not hurt to ask.

"Pretty much not," said Ted. "They figure a kid who gets in off the wait list is motivated enough to find the money."

He stood up, brushed coffee cake crumbs off the front of his sweater, and mentioned that he needed an answer by the end of the week. He gave them his cell phone number and tried to make it feel like a gift. Joel walked him to the door, muttering insincerities about how hard Ted's job must be, and as soon as they were alone again Nora grabbed him by the arm and pulled him into the front bathroom, where Lauren could not hear them.

"What're we going to do?" Nora asked. "Do you think she ought to go late like that? I don't think so. Prague, why do you think Prague? Maybe there's someplace else she'd actually like to go."

"I think she's going to Northwestern is what I think," said Joel, sounding far more certain than he felt, "and once it sinks in we go back to figuring out the money. It'd be nice to know what a regular kid—"

"Don't call them regular kids," Nora said.

Lauren pounded on the bathroom door.

"If you don't want me to hear, maybe you should wait until I'm not around, what do you think?" she asked. "I'm going to meet Chloe at the Grove, can I take Mom's car?"

Nora opened the door. "Lauren, if every time there's a problem your solution is to go to—"

"*I want to go out.* Please don't ask me any questions," said Lauren. "We're going to look for shoes on sale, okay?"

"Okay," said Nora. "But if you hung around for—"

"I cannot think about this right now. I have to go do something else. And don't tell anyone. Promise me, both of you, that you will not tell anyone. I don't want everybody talking about it all the time. 'What're you doing, Lauren?' 'What're you going to do, honey?' 'I thought you had two *real* acceptances.' I will go crazy. Promise me."

"Lauren, Mom's just trying—"

Lauren put her hands over her ears, closed her eyes, and hopped up and down, and both her parents stepped back as though she might explode. She grimaced, balled up her hands into tight little fists, and batted the sides of her head. They waited to see what she would do next, but just as suddenly she stopped, went limp, and looked at them with an expression they both would have described as abject.

"Don't you understand? If I stay here I just hate myself for letting you down. I mean, I know you're proud of me but it doesn't help when I feel like"—and her voice slowed down, as though the words were quicksand tugging at her heels—"such a failure. And every time you look at me like that, like you feel so sorry for me, it only gets worse. Please. Can't I go do something that doesn't matter and we'll talk about it later?"

"Well, you don't have all the time," said Joel. "Ted says within the week, so—"

"Dad. I don't want to talk about it right now. Can I please have the car?"

She was out the door before they could do anything more articulate than nod.

Nora slumped against the wall.

"Well, now that we have exactly what we want, my question is, does anybody actually enjoy this by the time they get to the end of it all? Because I'm feeling less than elated about her dream come true."

Joel was running numbers in his head. "Absolutely," he said, not quite sure what he had responded to.

Lauren had not taken into account Chloe's new best friend, the Prius, and when she calmed down enough to call to say that she was coming over, Chloe answered from the parking lot at the Camarillo outlet stores. She was happy to shop while Lauren made the hour's drive to meet her, but Lauren was not in the mood to compete for Chloe's attention with a rack of baby-doll tunics. She pulled onto the Santa Monica freeway with no destination in mind and decided to drive until the freeway traffic stopped moving or she got bored, which happened simultaneously at the La Cienega exit.

She turned onto the first residential street and pulled over to text Brad.

"I am nuts. What are you doing?"

"Come see. What's up?"

"Tell you when I get there."

Brad was sitting at the curb when she pulled up. He opened the passenger door and sat down next to her rather than wait for her to get out of the car.

"So what's the big deal?"

"I got in at Northwestern."

"I figured. Is that the one you picked?"

"No, I mean I got in."

"Right. So which school lost out?"

"Look," said Lauren, "can we go inside?"

She followed Brad into the house, down the long center hall-way and into his mother's room at the back. He had taken everything that usually sat on the big wooden table and put it on the floor, against the wall, and in its place stood all the supplies he had purchased at the art store near Liz's house—the cardboard, the knife, the two kinds of glue, the pens. A rectangular piece of plywood sat in the middle of the table, surrounded by shards of discarded cardboard and balsa wood curlicues, and resting on the plywood was a two-foot-long model of a narrow building without a roof.

"You built that?"

"Yeah, but you first."

"I didn't get in at Northwestern."

"You just said outside that you did."

"I did, now. But I didn't at first. I was on the wait list, but now I'm in, except Ted says I can't go in the fall. I have to go to Prague first."

Brad peered into the model and adjusted an interior wall.

"I don't get it. You were on the wait list? Why didn't you tell me?"

"Would you please keep up? I'm in is all that matters, but I have to go to Prague first quarter and then I can move into a dorm."

"Because?"

"Because I'm not really accepted. I'm accepted once somebody else drops out."

"It happens. Prague is probably cool."

"God, you sound like Ted. Like this is no big deal." She stepped back from the table; she was too angry to stand near something as fragile as the model.

"You wanted to go to Northwestern," said Brad. "So you start late. You still get there."

"Everybody's going to look down at me."

"No, they're not."

"What do you know? I mean, God, Brad, you have the easiest life of anybody. You have no clue. Never mind. I shouldn't have told you. I should just go to Santa Barbara. If I go to Northwestern in January, everybody I meet is going to know why. I might as well wear a big sign that says not good enough. Missed the first cut. I don't know what to do."

"Go to Northwestern. There's no difference between you and some kid who starts in September. I really believe that."

"Based on what?"

"Based on you know it's true. It's all bullshit, give or take."

"I don't know it's true. I wasn't good enough to get in with the other kids, and the other kids were good enough to get in in front of me. So how are we the same?"

"Because you don't know exactly why they got in, and it might not be so impressive. Katie's brother got in at Williams because they needed somebody to yell crew."

"And because he's a physics whiz. Not a good example."

"Jim got in because his girlfriend wrote his English papers."

"Except nobody knows that, so it doesn't count."

"Lauren. You know kids in our class who aren't any smarter than you and they got in because of who the hell knows what. You can't really think that they're any better than you are."

"You got into Harvard and lots of people didn't, so don't you think you're better than they are? Come on, it's not bragging, it just is. And you have to believe that, everybody has to believe that, because if Harvard kids aren't better than other kids, then why does everyone kill to get into Harvard? The Ivy League's the Ivy League because"—and she sputtered, looking for the right superlative—"because it's the Ivy League. You can't have it both ways. You can't say everybody's the same if you're going to a school nothing else is the same as."

Brad turned away from the table and opened a large cabinet. Gently, he lifted something out of the cabinet, and when he turned back again Lauren laughed in amazement. It was the rest of the model—the roof, which was a set of balsa wood wings that were joined at a point at the front of the house and spread from there to wrap the length of the building. The section of roof between the wings was wood as well, and a band of blue plastic about four inches high supported the entire piece. As Lauren watched, Brad inserted the plastic rim into a grooved edge at the top of the external walls. The groove was exactly two inches deep, leaving a two-inch band of blue between the walls and the wings. It all fit just so.

"That's beautiful," said Lauren.

"The blue part is the skylight. All around the house," said Brad, without taking his eyes off the model. "And there would be shades to cover the skylight at night. Section by section, with a remote control." He walked around the table once, considering the building from every angle. Satisfied, he lifted the roof off, put it back in the cabinet, and peered at the interior to keep from having to look at Lauren.

"Go to Northwestern," he said.

"Look, I know you're trying—"

"I didn't really get into Harvard."

"Right . . ."

He straightened up. "No, seriously, I didn't get into Harvard. I was on the wait list for three days. You want to know how much it cost my dad to get me in?"

"You were on the wait list."

"Yeah, well, now it's your turn to keep up. Yes, I was. Ask me how much."

"How much?" Lauren asked, hypnotized.

"Three hundred and fifty thousand dollars. More than school is going to cost. And I'm going to move in in September and nobody will know. Except you. And Ted. And me and my dad."

"I won't tell anyone."

Brad shrugged.

"Your dad wrote them a check for $350,000."

"Okay, forget it, Northwestern was right not to take you right away, because you are really slow."

"Brad. Stop it. You got in everyplace else and wait-listed at Harvard?"

"Yeah."

"That's crazy."

"Exactly. Crazy." Brad mugged a big smile. "But that's my problem, not yours. What I'm saying to you is there are people like me who are going to school in the fall, and we're no different from people like you."

"Except maybe that your father has a spare $350,000 sitting around with nothing to do."

"More," said Brad, as the smile faded, "but that's beside the point. Even if you got off the list to start in September, you'd still wander around worried that everybody knew you didn't deserve to be there, because that's what you do, which is as nuts as my father buying my way in. Worse."

"Thank you. Now I feel a whole lot better."

"Look," said Brad, and then he stopped, realizing that he was about to say to Lauren the same thing that Mr. Marshall had said to him about not being ashamed, whether the source of that shame was the inside track, in Brad's case, or the outside chance, in Lauren's. As far as Brad was concerned, he had much more to be embarrassed about than Lauren did, as he had yet to figure out how to untangle himself from the advantage of his family history. He envied Lauren because she could squander an opportunity on her own merits; she could be stupid and turn her back on Prague. He busied himself cleaning the construction scraps off his mother's table while he sorted out whether or not Mr. Marshall's advice had any merit. He decided that it had none, in his case, but that it was just right for Lauren. Intention made all the difference. Mr. Marshall had said what he said to Brad to get him not to take a chance. Brad was about to say it to Lauren to encourage her to do so.

"Are you going to say something?"

"Say you go to Prague," he said, "and you start school and somebody comes up to you in the dorm to say, 'Don't expect me to hang out with you because I know where you were first quarter, and besides, I know why.' What do you care? You've already got Katie. You don't need another friend to make you feel like shit."

"True."

"So you dump that person and find another friend. Easy choice. Go to Northwestern. You'll be happy there."

She leaned over to look inside the model.

"It's Liz's house, isn't it?"

Brad nodded.

"Yeah. It's making my dad nuts. He keeps asking when I'm going to be done with my arts-and-crafts project. Why don't you tell Ted you'll go?"

"Why is it so important to you?"

"I don't know," said Brad. "I just think you should."

They sat there in silence for so long that Alexandra walked briskly past the room and onto the patio for no reason, although

she had concocted one about having to check the water level in
the birdbath, if Brad thought to ask. Not that she expected Lauren or him to do anything foolish with one or both of his parents
on the premises, but checking in seemed to be the sort of thing
that a mother ought to do.

On her way back she paused in the doorway, coughed slightly
to announce herself, as though they might not notice her standing
there, and stepped into the room.

"Lauren, so nice to see you."

"You too, Mrs. Bradley." Knowing what to say to a parent was
always tricky, but Brad's mom was harder to figure out than most.
Lauren had to make a concerted effort not to get caught in an endless loop of *How are you?* and *How's it going?* with her. She cast about
the room for a potential topic and settled on the photographs.

"These are so amazing, Mrs. Bradley," she said, taking one
down off the shelf. "I guess you were really good. All those ribbons."

Alexandra leaned against the door jamb. "He was a lovely
horse," she said. "A real schoolmaster. My parents spent a fortune
on him."

"I'm sorry. A what?"

Alexandra was startled by Lauren's voice, because "schoolmaster," like a hypnotist's pocket watch, had taken her back to
sixteen, with a brand-new Pikur show coat and her first pair of
custom Dehner boots, her hair caught back in a hairnet and tucked
up inside her riding helmet. She had not felt that beautiful on her
wedding day. "A schoolmaster. That's what you call the ones who
know what you want before you do. The ones who do the right
thing even when you ask for the wrong thing."

"C'mon, Mom, you couldn't have been all that bad or you
wouldn't have won anything."

Alexandra reached toward Lauren for the photo and put it
back in its place on the shelf. "Well, I certainly loved that horse.
Would you two like a snack?"

She was gone before they had a chance to turn her down. Lauren sank into one of the overstuffed armchairs and stared into space, as unsettled as she always was when she caught a glimpse of a mom from before she was a mom. The idea that Alexandra Bradley had had a brief tenure as a star horseback rider did not compute with any of Lauren's assumptions about her. In fact, Lauren had no assumptions about Brad's mother, and how sad was that?

"So what do you do next? Hey, Lauren? Hello."

"Sorry," she said. "I have to let them know in a week, I think."

"Just go. Take first quarter off if you don't want to go to Prague."

Lauren took a deep breath, and then another, as though she had to push the next words out.

"I didn't get in anywhere else," she said. "Not anywhere I wanted. Just Santa Barbara and Irvine."

Brad whistled. "You're fucking with me."

"I am not. Don't you tell anybody either, okay?"

"Deal. But then you really have to go to Northwestern. That's so wrong."

"Yeah. Maybe," said Lauren. She walked over to the windows and spoke without turning around. "You going to give it to her?"

Brad bent over to wipe some imaginary dust off the front door of the model.

"Yeah. Maybe."

❧

Liz's prom dress hung in its dry-cleaning bag, the hanger hooked over the closet door, the plastic bag providing a synthetic rendition of leaves rustling in the breeze. She told her mother that it took up too much space in the closet, but in fact she preferred to hang it on the door, where she could see it. At some point between now and packing for college, Liz would have to decide its fate. Chloe had said, "Find a dress you can cut the bottom off, so you can wear it someplace else," not that Liz ever asked for her opinion on anything, but Chloe did tend to spew, particularly when it came to fashion. Liz had picked the most practical dress she could find, a sleeveless, boat-neck dress in what the saleswoman emphasized was cornflower blue raw silk, as though calling it cornflower made it more special than generic medium blue, but it had so far resisted her attempts to revise it into a regular dress.

More than once, she had held a pair of scissors at what would be calf length, what would be knee length, what would be very short, and waited for inspiration to tell her what looked best. It did not come. She might have tried it on for Chloe, might have risked opening the floodgates of wardrobe advice, but Chloe had stopped bothering with calc tutoring once all of her acceptances came in, which was one of the reasons Liz had spare time to speculate on the dress's fate. She visited Yale's website, scoured the photographs, and found not a single girl in a dress, which made her wonder why she would want to take up room in a tiny dorm closet for a dress she would never wear, regardless of length.

Abandoning the dress was trickier. It made no sense to leave the dress in her closet, as she could not imagine any scenario in which she came home and had cause to wear it again. Giving it away to a charity that supplied prom dresses to poor kids meant that her parents had spent $149 for four hours of what hardly could be called fun. So the dress hung, and rustled gently, while Liz scoured the Internet for information she could use in her valedictory address. Yoonie had convinced Steve to join her for a Sunday afternoon walk, and had tried to make it a family outing, but Liz had turned them down in favor of doing research. The three of them had never before gone for a walk on the beach together, and it seemed like a bad idea to create new things for her parents to miss in the fall.

She was halfway through the list of references she wanted to include in the speech, so she took a break, after "fair trade coffee" and before "carbon footprint," and typed "prom dress" into Google's search lozenge. The answer was sitting right there in the sponsored-links column: Liz could sell the prom dress on eBay.

It felt just right. Someone else would get a pretty dress at a relative bargain and Liz would make back some of the money her parents had spent. Her father would be impressed by her initiative, and she would joke with her mother about having rented the dress for the evening, a nicely dismissive close to the whole awkward episode. She went on eBay and looked at the first six dresses, to see what virtues seemed to be the most popular among prom-dress shoppers. When she was done, she opened her desk drawer and felt around in the back until her hand closed on a tiny safety pin, which she extracted and held at eye level, a profitable bounty of authenticity hanging from it on three silken strings.

Forget Chloe's advice about length. The most useful thing she had ever said to Liz was "Keep the tags."

※

With Ted on the speaker phone, Joel taking notes, and Nora taking notes on Joel's notes, Lauren recited a list of questions about her first-quarter options. Ted wrote them down on the back of a flyer about the benefits of variable-stride workouts, abandoned his planned half-hour in the weight room at the sports club, and ran out to his car in the parking lot to call Bob, whose personal cell phone number he had extracted at the end of their previous conversation about Lauren. Bob ticked off the answers, Ted called the Chaikens back, and he was on the phone again with Bob, confirming Lauren's intention to attend Northwestern, before Nora remembered the inadvertently blackened chicken in the oven.

Lauren Chaiken was going to spend what would have been the first quarter of her freshman year working at her mother's bakery, and if she still felt defensive when she arrived for second quarter, she could concoct a story about taking a gap quarter while she debated pursuing life as a pastry chef. It was all up to her; for the first time in months, she was in charge. After a celebratory pizza with her parents, the chicken in the garbage and the torched roasting pan bobbing serenely in a sink full of suds, Lauren went to sleep relieved for the first time in ten months. Her parents stayed up until after midnight, their mutual insomnia fueled by the fact that there seemed to be nothing more they needed to do, beyond writing four years' worth of very large checks.

chapter 19

At exactly 3:59, the Ocean Heights facilities manager nodded to the security guard, who had already closed the left-hand side of the big iron gate that sealed off the athletic fields. Manny returned the nod, swung the right-hand side closed, and secured the gate. He tugged to make sure that the handle had clicked into place, and then he turned his back on the graduation ceremony. The few students who had ever bothered to be pleasant to him had already sought him out to say good-bye. The majority of the 982 graduates had either ignored him or given him varying degrees of trouble for four years, so he had little interest in what they were about to do or say. All he cared about was keeping the families in and disruptions out. He eyed the sweaty, red-faced man who was rushing toward him and instinctively widened his stance. He put his hands on his hips and pulled his shoulders back.

The man kept coming. He rushed up right next to Manny, rather than stand at a respectful distance in front of him, as though it were the guard's job to open the gate and let him in. He waved at the graduates. Manny stared straight ahead.

Dave flashed a big smile and pointed to his watch.

"Just under the wire."

Manny held up his own watch and pointed to it. Exactly how dumb did this guy think he was?

"I'm sorry, sir, but graduation begins promptly at four."

"My daughter's in there," said Dave, knowing that the longer he argued with the guard, the less of a chance he had of success.

He looked the man up and down. Random leather cases attached to his belt, none of them gun-shaped, but one of them large enough to hold a weapon that would hurt if aimed with full force at Dave's arm, and, speaking of arms, that was some scar on the guard's left forearm. Bullying was out of the question, and something about the guard's stance told Dave that bribery was not a good idea, either, despite the ten that Dave always carried in his left front pants pocket to smooth the way with a random service employee.

He had to make the guard feel sorry for him.

"Look, you got a wife?" he asked.

"Ex," said Manny, who was perfectly happy to talk about anything but being late for graduation.

"Me, too," said Dave. "I'm telling you, I didn't know how many things I could do wrong until she started telling me."

"You got that," Manny replied. "I said to her, if I'm so bad how come you were dumb enough to marry me in the first place?"

"I start out half an hour early," said Dave, which was a lie, "I check the computer to see how's the traffic, and by the time I get to the 405, I'm coming up the 101 . . ."

"The Valley, man, that's never good."

"A spilled truck full of tomatoes," also a lie, "three lanes gone. And my ex is going to make it my fault unless I get in there. I know you've got a job to do. I'll stand in the back if somebody's talking. I won't move until there's music . . ." Dave peered through the bars of the gate and pointed to the far right side of the rows of seats.

"Right down there, I don't even have to step in front of anybody."

The guard turned to look.

"See? Way over there. C'mon."

The seniors were singing some song that was not on the program, so no one would notice a latecomer. Manny opened the gate just far enough for Dave to squeeze through.

"Hey, man, thanks."

"No problem," said Manny.

Dave plastered himself against the fence and sidled down to Deena's row. He slipped into the empty seat next to her just as the football coach walked to the podium.

"Nice," said Deena.

"Have they started?" Dave bristled. "I don't think so."

"No," she said. "The ceremony didn't start on time. Your good luck."

He searched for Chloe in the bleachers, mouthed the words, "I'm right here," and blew her a kiss.

Chloe had seen her father at the gate and leaned toward the boy sitting next to her, whose name was either Guillermo or not. The only time she saw him was during graduation rehearsals, when their identical heights, given her graduation pumps, brought them together, or when she was leaving Liz's house. He walked a nasty-looking dog down Liz's block every day at about five o'clock, even in the rain. Chloe figured it was either to keep the dog in fighting trim or to keep it too exhausted to want to kill someone, but whatever the reason, she had never been inclined to talk to Guillermo until this moment.

She studied his inexpressive expression. Chloe told herself that her taste of the real world, during her brief tenure at Ocean Heights, had broadened her horizons beyond what she liked to call Crestview's carefully vetted, handpicked rainbow coalition. She had no idea where her new world view sat on the continuum of world views; knowing enough to needle her Crestview pals might still be less than half of what a truly enlightened person knew. But she prided herself on her willingness to consider the boy a potential confidant, what with the dog and the sullen gaze and the silence, while her old friends would certainly be too quick to categorize and dismiss him. She did not judge. Besides, he was all she had. The girl on her other side was going to Oberlin with her flute, which was all she had ever wanted to do. She was far too fortunate to be sympathetic.

"I think that's my dad," she whispered to Guillermo or not. "Out at the gate. Nice. Misses his only kid's graduation."

"No shit. Want me to go get Manny to let him in?"

"Like you could do that."

"Hey. I'll do it." He started to get up, and Chloe put a restraining hand on his arm.

"No," said Chloe. "He's late. Gates closed at four. But thanks."

"Man, that's tough," he said. "You don't care your own dad doesn't get to see you?"

Chloe cocked her head and shrugged. "He doesn't care enough to get here on time. Fuck him."

"Okay, then."

Chloe smiled and began to sing in a tiny voice, loud enough for her immediate neighbors to hear, a line of melody and a whispered exclamation:

"Let's get it started—Hah.

"Let's get it started—in here.

"Let's get it started—Hah.

"Let's get it started—in here."

That was all it took. The song ran down the bleachers like a flame along a gas spill, and suddenly the 982 members of the graduating class at Ocean Heights High School started singing, stamping their feet to punctuate the rhythm, the shuddering bleachers laying in the bass.

The boys sang, "Let's get it started," stomped their feet, and 982 voices hollered, "*HAH!*"

The girls sang back, "Let's get it started," stomped their feet, and 982 voices hollered, "*IN HERE!*"

"Let's get it started," stomp, "*HAH!*"

"Let's get it started," stomp, "*IN HERE!*"

Before the members of the administration could figure out whose job it was to squelch the revolt, Bill Midden leapt to his feet, turned his back on the crowd to face his classmates, and raised his arms like a conductor. For four years he had been invisible, friendless save for the cafeteria worker who took pity on his spindly frame and gave him an extra scoop of everything. He played chess with a computer, left the math curriculum in the dust, and fully despised every teacher who had ever voiced concern over what they perceived as his shyness, which only proved how clueless they were. He was not shy. He simply had standards, and had yet to find anyone he could stand to talk to for more than fifteen minutes. Bill Midden had a full ride at MIT, an ardent crush on the girl who sang with the Black-Eyed Peas, and the expectation that he would live his entire life without ever meeting anyone even remotely like her. He was as fed up as an eighteen-year-old could be. It was time for graduation to start and high school to be over.

"Everybody," he yelled, and the senior class replied as one, "*YEAH.*"

"Everybody."

"*YEAH.*"

"Let's get into it."

"*YEAH.*"

Now he raised his arms above his head and became a rap master, his wrists torqued, his fingers pointed at the ground. Bill was in the middle of the middle row. He was untouchable and he knew it. He had his congregation, and they knew their reading by heart.

"Get stupid."

"*COME ON.*"

"Get it started."

"*COME ON.*"

"Get it started, get it started, let's get it started."

"*HAH!*"

"Let's get it started."

"*IN HERE!*"

That was where they got stuck. No one remembered the rest of the song, so they started repeating "Let's get it started," followed by a dwindling "Hah!" or "In here!" until finally the football coach, who had Googled the lyrics on his iPhone as soon as the singing started, stepped past his paralyzed colleagues to the podium. He grabbed the microphone, glanced once more at his phone screen, pointed an accusing finger at the seniors, and started to sing.

"'And the bass keeps runnin', runnin', runnin', runnin' . . .' Am I right here? Yes, surprising as it may seem, somebody older than you outspoken young men and women knows the lyrics to this song. But we have heard your message loud and clear, so I ask you, Fergie asks you, the Peas ask you, as the song says, 'simply to follow your intuition, free your inner soul and break away from tradition.' An excellent theme for a commencement exercise, ladies and gentlemen. Let's take our seats, restore silence, and we will, in fact, commence."

The seniors sat down, chastened. There was nothing worse than having one's rebellion co-opted by an adult who must have memorized the lyrics just so that he could be cool at a moment like this. They folded onto the bleachers as one for a final hour of scripted obedience.

The sequence of speakers was the same as it always was, and attentive parents of older siblings found that entire segments of the speeches sounded vaguely familiar. The dean of faculty reflected on the lessons that she and her colleagues had learned from the seniors, "because education is a two-way street." The senior-class president talked about how thankful the members of the

Ocean Heights senior class were for the myriad lessons they had learned, about life as well as academics, and when he uttered the word "myriad" a senior in the back row yelled, "Kiss-ass." The president of the Parents Association congratulated Ocean Heights on sending two-thirds of its graduates to college, a small increase built on the illusion that two dozen seniors who had not yet gotten around to registering at a community college might be seized by the desire to do so. The principal delivered the homily of human potential, his favorite topic because it was absolutely safe. As long as he stuck to what the class might do, he could say whatever he wanted. It was when he was limited to what the class had done that he found it difficult to defend the inspirational superlatives a principal's speech required.

By the time it was Liz's turn, the sun had baked fault lines into the women's makeup and raised sweat crescents under the men's arms, though several of them were no longer awake to notice. The seniors flapped the hems of their gowns to raise a breeze, and more than one unzipped the front, daring anyone to deny them their diplomas for fighting heatstroke. Hidden bottles of water and cans of Red Bull emerged from under the gowns. The crowd, parents and seniors alike, was reduced by the breezeless heat to cranky unrest, except for Liz and Steve and Yoonie, for whom the valedictory had been a beckoning point on the horizon for years.

Liz thanked everyone a valedictorian was supposed to thank, and then she stood at the podium, silent, looking out at the crowd. She was trying to register the way she felt, to slow down a day that was moving far too quickly, but she waited so long that some of the adults began to squirm in apprehension, fearful that the smartest student in the Ocean Heights graduating class was going to blow her big moment.

The principal nudged the assistant principal, and the assistant principal was about to stand, when Liz began to speak.

"I am standing here thinking how proud all of you parents must be today," she began, "and thinking that probably you have felt lots of emotions during our senior year." She paused.

"Not all of them proud," she said, to an amused murmur.

"Not all of them even close," she said, and the murmur broke into a laugh.

"There were days," she said, "and you know it's true, when you couldn't wait for us to go to college, or get a job, whatever we were going to do, because at least you would have some peace and quiet. We have not been our best selves this year, and on behalf of the senior class I would like to apologize to you for every terrible thing we said or did."

The crowd applauded, and Liz flipped her first index card to the back of the stack and waited until they were done.

"But I also thought I should take this opportunity to defend some of our behavior, or at least to explain it. It's hard to be the American Dream. You remember what it was like, don't you? Your parents wanted everything for you that they didn't have, just like you're sitting there wanting everything for us that you don't have. The one thing you have in common—whether you came here as adults, like my parents, or your grandparents were born here—the one thing that's true of all of you is that you've pretty much already made the big decisions you're going to make in life. So you know what you're not going to do.

"There might be a midlife crisis or two. Maybe one of you will give up selling insurance and become a ballroom dancer, or go back to school at forty-five to become a psychologist, but for the most part, you've made your choices. And I bet they're not quite what you imagined when you were our age. That's okay, that's not a criticism, that's real life, not everyone grows up to be Steven Spielberg, and if they do their kids are probably over at Crestview, not here. It's fun for you to imagine things that we might do, because we have more options."

She gestured at the members of the graduating class. "So when it's our turn to sit on folding chairs, and our kids are up here in the bleachers, we'll be hoping that they have a bigger life than we do, just like you're hoping for that now. That's how it works."

The boy next to Chloe whispered, "Jeez, nothing like cheering everybody up."

"But you see, that's part of why we got a little crazy this year," Liz continued. "You parents need to understand. I mean, your parents—our grandparents, that is—could hope that you didn't have to go through a depression or a world war. But most of your lives have been pretty smooth, when you think about it, relatively good, which means that you're under a lot of pressure to figure out what better lives even are, and we're under a lot of pressure to live them. I mean, thanks to AIDS we can't even have a sexual revolution like you did. And thanks to the economy, we probably won't earn as much as you do."

There was no laugh this time.

"So we end up spending an awful lot of time worrying about college. Whether we're going or not, whether we're going to a good one or not, whether we have a chance at a great one or not, it seems like everyone is trying to take a step up in the world. It makes me wonder, is college really the one thing that's going to make a difference in our lives? Everyone probably knows a great senior who didn't get in where they wanted to go, or an awful person who got into a terrific school, but I doubt that four years anywhere is going to undo eighteen years here. We ought to have more faith in ourselves than that, I think, at least in terms of the great seniors.

"I know what some of you are thinking. 'It's easy for Liz to talk, she's going to Yale, she's got it made,'" she said, flipping to her next card, the first of three that listed every major story she had found on CNN.com in the past month. "But look at what I'm facing. I have to remember to wear sunscreen, and take my calcium, and eat plenty of deeply colored fruits and vegetables, and get exercise. I have to reduce my carbon footprint, take my own bag to the grocery, not print up my emails, buy local, buy organic, watch out for irradiated meat, buy fair-trade coffee, and avoid clothes made in third-world countries even though they're the only ones I can afford."

Everyone chuckled again, in relief.

"I have to stop the genocide in Darfur and cure disease everywhere else in Africa, I have to not ignore the poor in my own country, I have to make sure everyone has health insurance, and I have to make sure the insurance companies that cover us actually pay for anything we need to have done. I have to protect women's rights and I have to pretend they don't need protecting, because feminism is so out of date. I have to make sure that the public schools support special programs for children with autism because it's an epidemic, one in every hundred and fifty kids, but I have to spend more on all the other kids in our failing public schools, except that the budget is too tight to stretch that far."

She was picking up speed. "I have to dismantle the nuclear threat in Iran and Pakistan and make sure North Korea is telling the truth, and while I'm at it I need to bring peace to the Middle East, because we've only been trying and failing for sixty years. Oh, and if I just pack light when I go to all these places, I can have a real impact, because did you know that ten pounds extra, per suitcase, per person, equals the same amount of carbon emissions as 2.8 million cars?"

Liz paused to catch her breath and chided herself for failing to include even a short paragraph of heartfelt feeling in her speech, though she had no idea what feeling she would have chosen. Everything she said made her think of all the things she had not said, which made her think of all the things she did not yet know. She wondered if she would have the nerve to dye her hair or oversleep or fall for a guy who ignored her once she got to Yale, or if the members of her family simply lacked the gene for what other people considered to be normal behavior and she too often thought of as excess. Nature or nurture. It might be generations before a Chang had a memorably or unexpectedly good time.

"Sometimes I think that we are the crest of the wave," she said. "Sometimes I think that me wanting more for my kids will mean making sure they still have a working planet to live on. Think about it: we might be the last generation to lose our minds over where to go to college."

She paused again and looked out at the crowd, some of them smiling, some of them not happy at all, a few sending text messages or checking their lipstick or cleaning their sunglasses, a few still asleep. She glanced at her parents. Yoonie smiled and blew her a little kiss, and Steve nodded and gave her a thumbs-up. Liz's throat closed up.

"I don't mean to depress you on this glorious day," she said, a slight huskiness in her voice that the principal attributed to a speech that had gone on too long. "This glorious day. In about five or ten minutes, almost a thousand of us will stop being high school students. We will never, ever be here, in this way, with all of you, again. Isn't that strange? This part of our lives is about to become the past. From one minute to the next, it all changes.

"So please, moms and dads," she said. "Learn how to text, try not to nag. And hey. Let's stay in touch."

As soon as the processional ended, Chloe elbowed her way past a number of seniors in her row to get off the bleachers and into the gym before Liz got away. A visit to the gym to turn in their robes was the final enforced activity for Ocean Heights graduates ever since two years earlier, when the school had had to pay for a dozen graduation robes that disappeared and could not be traced, despite a YouTube video involving billowing navy blue polyester gowns and girls in bikinis and mortarboards who were too smart ever to face the camera from the neck up. Since then, graduates had turned in their gowns at one of four long tables set against the walls of the gym, where a faculty member matched the number on the inside of the gown's collar with a number and name on the master registration list.

Chloe ran over to Liz, who was first in line at her check-in station.

"Listen, nice speech, but you don't know the latest," said Chloe.

"I'm glad you liked it. I got a little carried away."

"No, that's good, but guess what. Lauren got into Northwestern after all."

"Is she happy?"

"Of course. Well, she will be. But yeah."

"Katie's not happy."

"That's Katie. She's only happy if someone else is miserable. Of course Lauren's happy. Well, okay, it's a little weird, she isn't going until second quarter or something because it's so last-minute I guess, but yeah. She's happy. I think she is."

"Good then. Tell her congratulations for me." Liz patted Chloe on the arm. "I have to go find my parents."

"Oh. Sure. And I have to turn in my gown. Well. Congratulations."

"Congratulations," said Liz, and she turned away. Still holding her gown, Chloe wandered over to the door of the gym and watched as Liz crossed the lawn to where her parents were waiting. First Liz hugged her mom, and then her dad, and then Liz's mom and dad hugged each other, and then they started the cycle over again. They lingered, in no hurry to get to the reception in the parking lot. A few rows away, in a more jittery knot, Chloe's mom and dad looked this way and that, impatient for the chance to lose themselves in the crowd, waiting for Chloe to save them from having to be alone together.

She spun around, ran toward the nearest checkout line, and rushed up to the table ahead of a half dozen other kids. She threw her gown at the cafeteria manager who was checking off numbers.

"Oh my God, I think my mom just fainted," she said. She turned to the first girl in line. "Check me out, will you? I have to see if my mom's okay!"

She was gone before anyone could call her bluff, out the door, running full-tilt across the field, her arms outstretched like a bird's wings, calling, "Hey, hey, hey!"

Dave laughed, louder than he had in a while, and the sound of his laugh tripped an identical memory for Chloe and Deena, a little documentary movie that ran simultaneously inside both their heads—the family at a Fourth of July picnic, Dave sprinting across a crowded park, weaving a serpentine with his four-year-old daughter riding his shoulders no-handed and squealing with delight, while Deena cried, "Careful, careful, my God, you're going to drop her," which Dave never did.

"Careful, careful" said Deena, as Chloe got close. "You're going to knock us over running like that."

Chloe slowed down just enough, just in time, to wrap her arms around both of them. She hung on for a long moment, her eyes closed, until Dave squirmed to get an arm free and return the embrace, and Deena, mistaking his gesture for an escape attempt, said she really wanted to get to the reception before all the little cakes were gone.

❧

The box was sitting on the concrete stoop in front of Liz's house when she and her parents got home, a plain brown box with the words "For Liz" and "fragile" written all over it in big, loopy printing.

Her father offered to carry it inside for her, and remarked when he picked it up that it was awfully light. Liz gave her parents a playful look and told them there was no need to pretend that they did not know what it was, as it obviously was her graduation present. They insisted it was not, which only made her more certain that it was.

Her father placed the box on the dining room table, which had not yet been put back to use, even though he had packed up all of the college brochures and dropped them off at Ocean Heights, and put the Yale paperwork in a slim cardboard file that he kept on the nightstand by his side of the bed.

Liz opened the envelope taped to the top of the box.

"Told you I had a good idea. Slice the sides of the box to get it out. Hope you like it," read the note. It was signed, "Congratulations. Brad."

Steve took a small, sharp knife, cut open the top of the box without lifting the flaps to look inside, and, with Liz steadying the carton, cut down the sides, one by one. The box fell away to reveal Brad's model, and for a long moment, no one said a word. Yoonie and Liz walked slowly around the table, considering the house from every side, while Steve positioned himself at the back of the building, rose up on tiptoe, and stared at the roof.

"It is very beautiful," said Yoonie, who knew nothing about what had happened on prom night and regretted the fact that Liz had not spoken of Brad since. For an instant she hoped that she, like any other mother, had purposely been kept in the dark, that what she had taken as silence was in fact romantic teenage secrecy.

"Where am I going to put it?" said Liz, dashing her mother's hopes. The model was beautiful, but if Brad had stopped to think he would have realized there was no room for it in Liz's tiny house. She tried to focus on the impracticality, and not on the model itself, because otherwise she would call him to say she loved it and start a whole new round of foolishness. She had no desire to start anything; she wanted to show up at Yale without a past.

Her father straightened up. "Rainwater will pool in the middle of the roof," he said. "This requires a drainage system which he has not included in the design, but of course, that is not something he would know yet. It is very handsome. It will not work, though, not without some changes."

Liz sighed and peered through one of the windows at a row of miniature cardboard books on the bookshelf in what would have been her room. "Mom, do you mind if we leave it on the table until we can figure out where it should go?"

Yoonie replied quickly, before anyone could come up with a more practical and less enjoyable solution. "As far as I am concerned, it can sit there as long as you like." She went outside and plucked a few sprigs of the pink alyssum, which she placed on the model's base in exactly the spot where they grew in the real world.

chapter 20

Maintaining the illusion of equality at Crestview was tricky, as it required special treatment not only for parents who expected it but also for parents who assumed that there must have been an error if they got it. A $40,000 annual contribution bought Dan and Joy seats in the third row for graduation, two rows behind Trey and Alexandra, alongside one of the scholarship families that were always sprinkled into the front rows to derail accusations of economic favoritism. Everyone understood the agenda, and people who fell between the extremes resented it, but no one was about to complain. The big donors in the first three rows did not care where anyone else sat, and families whose contribution was demographic, not financial, were not about to draw attention to themselves by asking why they had not been assigned to the back row. Parents like Nora and Joel, who contributed exactly one dollar more than the threshold amount for breakfast with the head of school, always felt slightly guilty about their strategy, so they did not make a fuss. They took their seats in the twelfth row and settled for making faces when the people in the eleventh row turned out to be very tall. Nora peered around them to look for a familiar face, waved at Joy, and wondered if this was going to be one of those tremulous days when she found herself feeling happy to see people she did not care for all that much.

Joy had learned on a London vacation that the proper way to sidle down an aisle was facing the already-seated guests, as it was considered rude to display one's ass to a row of strangers. She was

facing the back of the field, waving a little wave to Nora, when a
giggle drifted by behind her, followed by voices held so low she
could barely hear them, let alone recognize their owners.

". . . a reason she didn't get it, don't you think?"

"Has to be. Like she'd give it up without a fight."

Joy strained to hear more, but she could not tell if the next
sentence contained the word "vodka," "wadded," or "vested." She
straightened her back and resisted the urge to turn around. Joy
prided herself on never listening to gossip, and on only sharing
what she knew to be reliable information, which this clearly was
not. For all she knew, the two women were discussing a friend
who had lost out on a particular three-piece suit at the Armani
sale, and not the fact that someone other than Katie was the valedictorian.

She took her seat and devoted all of her attention to the
program.

"Unendurable," said Dan, tapping his copy with his index finger to reinforce whatever point he was about to make. "Let's ask
for our money back."

"What?"

"I should have asked for a recount," he went on. "You cannot
tell me that Mike has a higher grade point average than Katie does.
Computers make errors. Someone misreads a line, enters a standard A instead of a weighted grade, a 4.0 instead of a 5.0, and the
wrong senior steps to the podium. I should have inquired when
Katie first told us that she was not the valedictorian."

Joy leaned in close, so that only her husband could hear, tried
not to speculate about what she had overheard, and failed. "Perhaps there's an untold story here," she said, weakly, hoping that he
would have incontrovertible evidence to the contrary, marveling
at how so much of his vocabulary had seeded itself in her brain.
Incontrovertible evidence? She had become bilingual; she spoke
English and Dan.

"Oh, yes, I can imagine all sorts of misbehavior. Alcohol consumption in public. Fellatio in the school bathroom. Methamphetamines in her locker. That's our Katie. Honestly, Joy."

Chastened, Joy did her best to match Dan's obstinate faith in his daughter. "I'm sure that Katie didn't want to embarrass the boy by pointing out the mistake," she said, even though random empathy was as unlikely an explanation for Katie's behavior as any of the ones her husband had suggested.

"Then what explains Brad?" said Dan. "I'm telling you, Mike is not supposed to be the valedictorian." He got up suddenly. "I will be right back."

He headed for the aisle and made his way toward Trey, who stood up as Dan approached. Joy watched the two of them and started to relax. They shared a common set of mannerisms, Trey's inherited, Dan's acquired by assiduous study: one hand in a pants pocket to show how beautifully an expensive wool jacket draped up and over that hand, the other resting on a friend's elbow or shoulder, or straightening one's own tie. They drew closer and tipped their heads ever so slightly, like birds, to convey that this was a private, not a social, conversation, to ward off intruders.

A more insecure man might have made good on his threat to inquire about the valedictorian, but in the end Dan would not, because such a challenge betrayed a man's need, and he worked hard to convince himself that he had none. He settled instead for sharing his frustration with Trey. As far as Dan could tell, the only people happier than he and Joy were Trey and Alexandra, happier only because they were more used to it, having been successful for generations back. There was no way to rewrite his own history, but Dan took some pleasure from being the kind of guy, now, who could saunter over to Trey for a confidential chat about a shared slight of no lasting consequence.

"Can it be that the same secretary who wrecked Katie's chances had her way with Brad's transcript as well?" Dan wondered, with a smile. "I see a conspiracy here. We might want to subpoena Mike's dad's bank records, don't you think, to look for a pattern of large donations to Crestview."

Trey smiled. He couldn't help but feel a little sorry for Dan, who probably was not aware of how hard he scrabbled for position.

"Well, what can I say?" Trey replied. "I never quite know with Four. He might have thought, Harvard, fourth generation, everything going my way, I can afford a little . . ."

". . . noblesse oblige?"

Trey shrugged, patted Dan on the shoulder, and turned back to his seat. He had not said that Brad had stepped aside to give Mike a treat, but he was perfectly comfortable if Dan drew that conclusion.

Joy, watching, mistook Dan's purposeful stride for restored confidence and the glint in his eyes for clarity. It was only when he sat down next to her that she felt the slight angry vibration of a man who had just been put in his place by a pro.

"Smug bastard," he whispered to her. In predictable situations, Dan was a master of his own carefully crafted image, but in unexpected moments, to his endless frustration, his instincts failed him. Trey assumed. Dan still aspired. The closest he might ever get to a natural sense of entitlement was through his children.

❧

Mike strode purposefully across the stage, mindful of his mother's reproachfully muttered "Don't stand like your father" when he tried on the cap and gown for the first time. He shook hands with the diminutive head of school and stepped around him to the podium. Slowly, very slowly—as his father had instructed him—Mike raised the microphone six inches, paused, raised it another six inches, paused, and tugged at it just a bit more, until it was in range for a six-foot, four-inch valedictorian.

He was amazed at how fast the laughter came. His father had sworn that all Mike had to do was take his sweet time adjusting the microphone, and the crowd would be his. Mike thought his father was a loser on topics ranging from what he wore to what he drove to his choice of a second wife, a woman who wore Juicy Couture as though it were. That last was his mom's line, a funny person in her own right who would probably still be acting if his dad had not replaced her in the second season with the woman who would become wife number two. But no one argued with his dad about funny, not with two sitcoms winning their time slots week in and week out for four years running. Mike was prepared to be lavish in his thanks right after the ceremony ended, particularly because they had not yet resolved the issue of whether he could have his car at school.

He retrieved his speech from the little shelf under the podium and took a deep breath, not to steady himself but to alert people that something important was coming.

"Valedictorian," he said, and then he paused. "Valedictorian." Another pause. "Where does the word come from? People think it means the person with the best grade point average because that's the person who gets to give the valedictory address. But in fact it's derived from the Latin *vale dicere*, which means to say farewell, and I bet Dr. Johnston's proud to hear me say that after all these years of Latin.

"I'm not denying I have the best grade point in this year's Crestview graduating class," he said. "But the more interesting question, I think, is who I got a better grade point *than*." He drew a wide arc with his right arm. "Who are the people on this stage? I'm saying farewell to all of you on behalf of all of them, and so I think it's up to me to tell you a few things about them—about us—that you might not know."

His father had inserted another pause here, so he waited, one, two, three.

"Of course," he continued, "if you want to get the congratulations out of the way right now, for me being the chosen guy and all, I'm happy to wait while you get it out of your systems."

Mike's father led a smattering of applause, primarily from parents whose children had either gotten into their first-choice schools or had not applied to the same schools as Mike. The others sat on their hands. To them, Mike was a spoiler, one of those seniors with impressive records who had racked up acceptances to a dozen schools simply to show that he could, even if it meant knocking their children out of the running.

"Okay," said Mike. "Let's look at this year's graduating class and see what we've managed to accomplish." He turned to his second page, a list of bullet points, and began to recite.

"Let's look at sports other than soccer, so that nobody can accuse me of only thinking about myself. Crestview's varsity tennis team was first in its division, first in the region, and, no surprise, first in the state for the second year in a row. TiVo that U.S. Open in a couple of years, and I think you're going to see Wayne and Jim going head to head in the final. On the women's side, a second-place finish statewide, to a school in central California that's been in first place for seven years. I think they have a breeding program, if you want to know the truth, so let's say we're first among people with normal DNA."

His dad's line.

"First in the southern California conference in football, third statewide for the women swimmers and fourth for the guys but first for both of them in the region, and did I mention soccer?" He smiled. "First in the state, for the first time in Crestview's history. So let's give it up for Crestview athletes, none better."

He rattled off the seniors' accomplishments in national language competitions, in the Scholastic art contest, as Intel science finalists and National Merit semifinalists, finalists, and winners, thanks to the list that what's-her-name in the college counseling office had provided him.

"But being first is not enough," he said, though he hardly believed it. "If it was, I could just rattle off that list and sit down. . . ."

"If it *were*, not if it *was*," muttered Joel. "Some valedictorian."

"Shhh," said Nora, who had not taken her eyes off Lauren's faraway face.

Mike slowed down for emphasis. "The real question is, what does it take to be first? It boils down to this: We never give up. We know what we have to do to excel, we know how hard it is to do it, and we never give up. If you think I'm exaggerating, look at Frannie Rose. We all remember when Frannie's dad died, but was Frannie going to sit around and mope? She knew her dad wouldn't want her to do that, and she knew the people at UCLA, at the med center, from all the time they had to spend there when Frannie was in ninth grade."

"My God," whispered Nora, leaning toward Joel. "It's the heartfelt human-interest story. He's running for president."

"Shhh," hissed a voice behind her. "And can you sit still? I can't see."

"So she went to them and said, 'Let me work in the lab. I'm going to make sure that someday this doesn't happen to another ninth-grader.' And every year since, in the summers, for four years, Frannie's helped out in the lab when she could've been having fun. Maybe that's the key to the Crestview seniors: We don't hang out at the beach or the mall. We know there's important work to be done."

Frannie Rose, who barely knew Mike and had not known he intended to co-opt her life to make a point, stared at her clenched hands and let people assume that she was overcome by grief. She hated every classmate who had avoided her for four years, as though bad news were contagious, and she looked forward to attending Bates College primarily because no one else at Crestview was going there. This was the last day she would be Frannie Rose whose father had dropped dead on the golf course at forty-five. Next fall she would be Frannie Rose, period. She could not wait to leave.

"Crestview teaches us to step up, more than it teaches us AP Calculus BC, though aren't there more of us in that class this year than ever before? It teaches us to step into the world and claim our destiny, whether it be as a heart researcher like Frannie, or a famous director, which may be my fate, or . . ."

Trey never heard the final component of the holy trinity, after altruism and artistry, because he was on his feet, heading toward the building, as soon as Mike launched into the business about that poor girl whose father had died. People who did not know Trey assumed that he had been overcome by emotion. People who did know him gave him a free pass for this kind of behavior, because he was Preston Bradley III, and his responsibilities did not end at family time, not even on graduation day. He slipped through the building and out to the front courtyard, leaned against the nearest pillar, and closed his eyes. When he opened them again, he saw Ted standing three pillars down, in much the same when-will-it-end posture. Trey walked over to him, wordlessly lit a cigarette, and blew as perfect a smoke ring as his grandfather ever had. For eighteen years, ever since Four was born, Trey had limited himself to one cigarette a week, always smoked out of range of his boy's lungs. He enjoyed them far more than he ever had during his chain-smoking college days.

Ted watched the smoke ring dissolve in midair and made an appreciative little snort, even as he wondered if there was a prep school anywhere in the continental United States that allowed its faculty and staff such a public vice.

"Nice," he said.

"Years of practice," Trey replied.

They had struck a cautious truce since resolving the mess about Brad's slot. Ted referred to it that way, as Brad's slot, as though it had mistakenly been assigned to another student before being returned to its rightful owner. Trey might be disappointed that Ted had been unable to close the deal without a $350,000 boost, but he had to know that there had been a couple of dozen college counselors around the country fighting for the space.

Trey nodded in the direction of the ceremony.

"Not an interesting boy, I have to tell you," said Trey. "Brad would have done a better job up there."

Ted nodded. "Mike," he said. "He knows exactly what he needs to do to get what he wants. A pragmatic kid."

"And nothing more."

"Well, that's between him and his god," said Ted.

"Five years from now his dad'll give him a production job," said Trey, dismissively.

Ted smiled. "And Brad?"

Trey blew another smoke ring. "Harvard Law, don't you think?"

He winked, stubbed out the cigarette, and headed back toward the tent. Ted felt every muscle in his body unwind. He should have known. Trey was never going to complain about Ted's abilities as a college counselor. Trey was going to endorse Ted wholeheartedly, because people might start to wonder if he sounded anything less than enthused. Had there been a problem getting Brad into Harvard? Had the illustrious Four required some kind of special help? No, Preston Bradley III had to be very happy, and loud about it, to compensate for the truth. Ted was safer than safe.

A good thing, for the usually compliant head of school, a man who in the past had done everything he could to accommodate and reward his director of college counseling, had taken an odd position in their initial conversation about the coming year, one that Ted was in the midst of sorting out. He had gone in to see Dr.

Mullin a week earlier with what he thought was a very cagey pro-
posal. He had decided to back off from his original notion of resigning, at least for the first year, because the chance to bank every
penny of the private fees was irresistible and because Crestview
gave him such great access to potential clients. Instead, he told
Dr. Mullin that he wanted to take on a few private clients in his
off hours, high-maintenance Crestview students who might otherwise siphon off his workday energies. He saw this as a good solution for everyone—certainly better for Crestview than if Ted had
asked for the kind of raise that would be appropriate to his sixty-
or seventy-hour workweek at the height of the application season.
He saw no need to define how many students constituted his notion of a few.

To his surprise, Dr. Mullin had responded with words like
"clean break" and "conflict of interest," and inquired as to whether
Ted had considered all of the ramifications of being self-employed.
Specifically, had Ted investigated the cost of the excellent health
insurance that Crestview provided its teachers? Had he considered the employee benefits he would lose? Dr. Mullin was sure that
private consulting seemed at first glance like a far more lucrative
field than high school college counseling, even with Ted's ample
annual bonuses, but had he thought about how he would ride out
a tight second year if the first-year acceptances did not go as he
hoped they would?

"Surely, Ted," said Dr. Mullin, "you, of all people, know how
difficult getting into college has become, even for the most qualified of students."

Dr. Mullin found himself in the unusual position of being
able to throw his minimal weight around. He was riding on the
unexpected receipt of resumés from directors of college counseling at two East Coast boarding schools, as well as an indiscreet
comment by Joe's father that Rita had dutifully reported to the
head of school before Ted asked to come by for a chat. As he had

never before had the upper hand with Ted, he quite enjoyed himself. He urged Ted to take a week or two, no more, to think over the pluses and minuses, and he hoped that Ted would abandon this freelance idea and return to his post next year. He made no mention of the shared directorship that one of the East Coast counselors had suggested, or of Rita's promotion to junior counselor.

Everyone at Crestview would miss Ted terribly, said Dr. Mullin, if he decided to strike out on his own.

Ted's initial reaction was to leave the little guy in the dust; let him promote everyone once Ted was gone, including Rita, and hire the woman from Ocean Heights who had sent him her resumé, to answer the phones. He would not give any of them a second thought, because he would be too busy making bank deposits and looking at larger condos. Ted hoped to stick to his resolve for another week, print up his letter of resignation, and pack up his office. All he had to do was squelch the worried voice that had begun to speak to him, usually at about five o'clock in the morning, asking him if he was ready to make such a big move, suggesting that the real risks outweighed the imagined benefits, reminding him that Brad and Lauren and drunken Katie had come this close to not working out, reminding him further that he worked in a world where getting into Penn and Williams and Cornell and Wesleyan and Princeton and Berkeley and even Northwestern by way of Prague somehow qualified as coming this close to not working out.

⚬⚬⚬

For ten months, the seniors and their parents had acted as though all they wanted was to be done with Crestview and college applications. As the afternoon and Mike's speech wore on, they started to drift, to wonder what life might be like in an hour, over the summer, once college started. The unknown, as it turned out, was larger and more mysterious than they had ever realized, back when their days were full of the distractions of process, of paperwork and deposits and questionnaires and essays. What came next was huge and unfamiliar, and many of them wished a small, private wish for time to slow down a bit while they got used to having no idea of what was coming, which only made time toss its head and run faster.

Parents wondered what they would do if an assigned roommate had a live-in boyfriend or a drinking problem or both, whether their own children had the potential to turn into troublemakers, and how they might find out before they got a call from a school official. Children wondered if they had a large enough wardrobe to last from one visit home to the next without having to do laundry, whether college really was easier than Crestview had been, and how to acquire a fake ID. Random thoughts filled the air like radio static. Few people would later be able to recall Mike's anecdote about Crestview's Model United Nations team.

Mike, for his part, did not notice the mood change because he was headed for his big close, the only part of the speech his father had not heard him rehearse, his own original idea—not quite original in concept, as he had heard about the Ocean Heights graduation, but certainly original in execution, which had to count for something.

"Since I speak for every member of the senior class, I gave great thought to what I want to say, in parting, representing everybody up here as we head off for adventures all over the country," he said. He squared his shoulders, gamely searched for the right pitch, missed it, and began to sing anyhow.

"I will, I will *rock you*." He thumped hard on the podium, twice, stamped his foot, twice, and sang again, "I will, I will *rock you*." Thumps, stamps, silence. The goalie on the Ocean Heights soccer team had sworn that the class went crazy for that Black-Eyed Peas song, and Mike figured he had nailed it with Queen, particularly with the funny swap from plural to singular pronoun, as he was the only one singing. He had expected to have everyone on their feet.

Nothing. What Mike had failed to take into account was the difference between a spontaneous outburst by a bunch of impatient Ocean Heights seniors and a constructed joke at the end of a speech that left everybody out except the winners. He had no constituency. Any senior who had ever had an original thought resented the fact that a human tote board had been named valedictorian, and every parent whose child was not on Mike's winner's list had stopped listening before he finished reciting the athletic honors. The handful of parents who straggled to their feet to applaud, now, did so either out of pity or to persuade Mike to make this the end of his speech, whether it was or not.

When Nora started to get up, Joel put an urgent hand on her arm.

"What are you doing?" he asked. "You can't think it was a good speech."

"I can't see her," she said, shaking free. "With people standing up, I can't see her. I just want to see her."

Chastened, Mike mumbled a final farewell and abandoned the podium, and Dr. Mullin quickly took his place, lowered the microphone, and awarded the diplomas with daunting speed. Once the graduates had filed past him, paused for the photographer, and taken their seats again, he gestured to the choir to stand. The choir always ended graduation with "The Wind Beneath My Wings," because the musical director had made the first round of callbacks for the Harlettes in 1982, and because it was an evergreen on the private school graduation circuit, right up there with "Stand by Me." Parents sometimes needed help letting go, and there was nothing better than a ballad about eternal love, preferably love in the face of separation, to get the stalled tears flowing. As the choir sang, a confusing set of synapses began to fire, old, unused connections, distant sparks of all the emotions that had gotten this generation of parents to reproduce in the first place. Even Nora and Joel got misty, testimony to the enduring power of the song, as Lauren had practiced the alto part so often at home that they were frankly sick of it.

When the song was over, the choir director stepped to the baby grand and began to play "Pomp and Circumstance" and the choir, on cue, filed offstage, followed by the new graduates and the Crestview faculty. The members of the audience stood again to bear witness, their digital cameras held aloft, and headed for the reception on the front lawn. Joy forgot aisle etiquette and bashed several sets of knees with her purse in her haste to get to Katie. Boredom was Joy's enemy, and the ceremony had given her far too much time to consider and reconsider the women's whispered exchange, which she was now sure was about the valedictorian. Try as she might—surely there were numerous other members of the graduating class who were capable of having too much to drink—she could not dismiss the notion that Katie had been deprived of the valedictory for cause. Clearly, Joy had been duped by the story about Chloe and projectile vomiting and Katie's Good Samaritan tendencies, and sleeping over at Lauren's for old time's sake should have been the tip-off. There had not been a sentimentalist on either side of the Dodson family tree for generations. The only reason for Katie to end up at the Chaikens was to avoid coming home.

Joy stepped past the puddle of graduation gowns that the seniors traditionally left in a heap at the edge of the stage and found Katie in a Medusa's knot of sniffling, hugging, overheated girls who seemed suddenly to think that being apart next fall was the emotional equivalent of amputation. They clung and sighed, and it was difficult to figure out which intertwined arm belonged to whom, but Joy tapped on the wrist wearing a Tiffany gold cuff, and Katie extricated herself.

"Yeah," she panted. "Can you believe it? Done!"

Joy took her elbow and guided her a few steps away.

"Done, yes," she said. "I just wanted to ask you, though. I was thinking. About your prom dress."

"Except that this would be the moment to congratulate the graduate, don't you think?"

Joy gave Katie a perfunctory hug and held her at arm's length.

"I meant to ask you then and life got in the way," she said, trying to sound as though the answer did not matter as much as it did. "Chloe was drinking what?"

"God, I don't remember. Some mixed drink in a can. Why?"

"I'm just amazed it didn't leave a stain. And it swam back into my mind while I was sitting there."

Katie kissed her on the cheek and darted toward a friend who was assembling a group photograph.

"Well, let it swim back out again," she called, over her shoulder. "Do the backstroke. It's fine."

Joy stood there, immobile, until Dan caught up with her.

"I could have done without the valedictory," he said.

"If Katie hadn't gotten drunk at prom we would have done without it, because she would have given a decent speech. Honestly. You think you know your kid, and all you really know is the lies she chooses to tell you."

"What exactly are you talking about?"

Joy took a deep breath and pushed a flare of anger back into her stomach, which was where it usually lived, tyrannized on a less stressful day by a daily dose of Prevacid.

"Nothing," she said. "Temporary insanity."

"You cannot possibly believe that she was drinking at the prom. Where would she . . ."

Dan continued his defense of their daughter, but Joy had stopped listening. She did not know what she thought, except that she did not perceive herself as the kind of mother who would raise the kind of daughter who would allow herself to be stupid in this kind of way. The closest Joy ever got to flamboyance was the costumes for their Summer of Love theme dinner a few years back, and she expected a similar rigor from her children. She disdained the easygoing moms who swore that all they wanted was their children's happiness, because it sounded like a euphemism for spoiling a child instead of raising her properly. Joy loved Katie ambitiously—which implied the setting of standards and the evaluation of performance.

Katie had no trouble expressing her disappointment in her parents, ranging from the dubious quality of their first offspring to their taste in friends. For the first time, Joy wondered if a parent ought to be allowed to express disappointment in a child. Unconditional love did not seem like much of a parenting strategy.

"Drinking, not drinking, it is what it is what it is," she said, waving at Brad's mom and striding off in her direction. "I've got my college degree already, thank you. She can do what she wants."

Alexandra waved back at Joy from the edge of a phalanx of Bradley men—her father-in-law, who had driven down from San Francisco, two of Trey's brothers and their two sons apiece, three of the boys in law or medical school and the fourth getting both degrees sequentially, and Trey. The Bradleys turned out in force for family events, in case anyone had failed to make the connection between a boy with a roman numeral after his name and the existence of a dynasty. They assembled to impress, which was why Trey's youngest brother, the one who had spawned a lobster fisherman and a party girl, was kind enough always to construct an excuse and stay home. Trey's mother and Alexandra's two sisters-in-law flitted at the periphery of the family circle in water-color prints as vague as their auras, while the menfolk—a term frequently hauled out of mothballs to describe the Bradley men—moved toward the refreshment table like a rugby scrum. Alexandra, suddenly alone, straightened the silver silk lapels on the jacket of her knit suit and stared enviously at Joy's outfit, a champagne silk dress with a deep neckline and a fitted coat that was one, and only one, shade deeper. To Alexandra, Joy seemed like a woman who was capable of having an affair—not that she would, but that she could. Late at night, when Alexandra could not get back to sleep, she sometimes wondered if she could possibly be any lonelier living alone. She was somehow not surprised when Joy veered off to talk to someone else, and she stood there for a long moment, wondering what she ought to do next.

"Hey, Alex," said Trey's eldest brother, waving a skewer of fresh fruit up and down in front of her nose. "Where are you, day-dreamer?"

"Right here," she said, on cue. "But my goodness, don't they all look so grown-up."

"As they should." Trey's voice startled her, for she had not sensed him coming up behind her. What was it about the Bradley men that made them instinctively surround their prey, even when the prize was as insignificant as having the last word? He clapped his brother on the back and addressed him as though Alexandra were not there.

"I don't know what it is with the girls," by which he meant the wives. "Was Ginny like this when Bud and Jack left home? It's as though they don't see it coming. Brad's nineteen in July. I figure if we get him home winter break next year we're ahead of the game. After that, I think it's calls on our birthdays."

His brother managed a tight smile, for the secret question in his household was whether Bud would get it together for the final year of medical school or make good on his threat to move back into his old bedroom to think things over. "You never know," he said, with a false heartiness. "It may not turn out to be that extreme. Bud shows up more than—"

"There he is," Alexandra squealed, in a tone Trey rarely heard and always disliked. "Brad, Brad, we're over here."

"Like I could miss them," said Brad to another boy, as he considered the imperative that was his family. He raised his arm and waved back so that his mother would stop yelping, and made his way across the lawn. Preston Bradley IV was the only member of the Crestview senior class to be going to Harvard, thanks to the girl who had chosen Stanford instead, and as he walked he was aware of attention he did not want, of heads turning and the occasional admiring, envious murmur. He tried to limit his focus to his family, which was why he did not see Katie's dad until he stepped right in front of Brad.

"So," said Dan, that single syllable dripping with a familiarity Brad had never felt for either of Katie's parents. "Some speech. Where were you and Katie when we needed you?"

Brad smiled. Lauren always cut Katie slack because her parents were so impossible, but a good lawyer would say that her parents' behavior was immaterial.

"Oh, I tanked a math test," Brad said, which was almost true. "That's why I wasn't up there. It wasn't the prom with Katie, was it? I told everybody, I bet she didn't even know what was in that bottle. Hey, there's my folks. See you, Mr. Dodson."

He strode off, feeling as better as a boy can feel when he is about to embark on someone else's version of his future. Brad had settled some accounts in the last days of his senior year. He had refused the valedictory on principle and told his father the truth about why they would not see him at the podium. He had confessed the business about the Harvard wait list to Lauren, which made him feel better and helped her decide to take a chance with Northwestern. He had failed to stand up to Katie at prom, but he had finished the model and given it to Liz, which was as close to apology as he knew how to get and made him happy despite her guarded text—"It's lovely. Mom's crazy for it. Thanks. Luck at Harvard." And he had planted a seed of doubt in Mr. Dodson's brain, which held real promise in terms of the erosion of trust over time.

Brad was at his mother's side before it hit him that such glancing pleasures might be the most that a reluctant legacy could hope for. As she wrapped her slender arms around him, and he wondered why a hug from her felt more like a brush than an embrace, he imagined his father telling the story of the valedictory address and the obvious GPA glitch that had robbed his son of the honor—telling it even though it was a lie, as though it would become true by repetition—to a handful of admiring associates, young lawyers not so far removed from their own grade-grubbing days, who were struck by the level of privilege, of presumed success, that enabled Trey to tolerate such an injustice with a bemused grin. Worse, for a moment Brad could imagine telling the story himself. He might tell it forever, rewriting it over time until its edges were as clean and hard as the facets of a diamond, as he settled into the life he had sworn he would never live. The fact that he saw the possibility made him nervous. He sank against his mother for a moment, until she raised her fluttery hands to his chest and Trey grabbed his shoulders from behind.

"Enough!" he said, with what passed among the Bradley men as a playful tone. He pulled Brad backward. "Come on. You're going to wrinkle your mother's suit."

Nora was capable of bad behavior when overcome by motherhood, and she threw a discreet elbow or two, and used her shoulder as a driving wedge, in an attempt to part the sea of people that blocked her access to Lauren. Her daughter was not standing near the pile of discarded graduation gowns, so Nora hurried out to the lawn, where the crowd fanned out in all directions. It was hard to pick out a specific senior—no, a graduate—in a sea of white dresses, and at first she did not see Lauren or any of Lauren's friends.

For a moment, Nora felt an odd sensation that she had felt only twice before in her life, once on the day Lauren was born and once on the day she got fired: faces she knew she ought to recognize were suddenly unfamiliar, not completely so, but skewed just enough to unsettle her. She stared at people and waited for their features to resolve themselves into a familiar layout, even as some of them smiled and reached over for a quick kiss. Her brain was not cooperating. Her brain was on a quest to find Lauren, and until she did so, the rest of the world was reduced to a quivering mass of unprocessed information.

The dance band started up a lounge version of a Bruce Springsteen song, which helped somewhat, because the crowd thinned as hyperactive graduates and parents who had remembered to take a prophylactic Aleve hit the dance floor. Nora scanned the horizon. No Lauren. She pointed Joel toward the far side of the lawn and set off past the photographer's setup, a drop cloth behind a white chair next to a little table and a vase of white roses, for parents who wanted yet one more staged and awkward portrait of their children, looking not like themselves but like generic, hopeful young adults. No Lauren there, either.

Nora circled around toward the refreshments. Lauren was not at either of the long buffet tables, but one of the girls had seen her near the dance floor. A boy near the dance floor had seen her heading toward the bathroom. Alexandra, who monitored her unchanging hair and lipstick on an hourly basis, came out of the bathroom and said she had seen Lauren near the food table, so Nora began again. Joel caught up with her, and together they completed another unsuccessful lap.

"If we keep moving and she keeps moving, we will never find her," said Nora. "I really want to find her."

A simple expression of desire was like a magnet. A moment later, Lauren tapped her mother on the shoulder and kissed Nora, and Joel, and Nora again. On the second embrace, Nora noticed that Lauren was trembling, slightly. She tightened her grasp, and nodded when Joel pantomimed the acquisition of cold drinks.

"You okay?"

"I couldn't find you," said Lauren.

"That's because we were chasing each other," said Nora. "We couldn't find you, either."

"I am so tired of people I barely know asking me what the deal is at Northwestern," Lauren whispered. Rita, who intended to inject into the college counseling department an enthusiasm she felt it sorely lacked, had seen Lauren in the hallway and called out "Go January Wolverine!" which put an end to the family secret. "It's like people who never cared about me for one minute for six years only want to hear the entire story of my life."

"Tell them anything. Don't tell them anything. You don't owe them an explanation. Tell them you're going to be a master baker."

Lauren continued to cling.

"Will you teach me how to make chocolate ganache?"

"Yes."

"And that little cheesecake thing."

"Yes."

"I don't want to make anything with bananas."

"Oh, good. Are you going to be a diva? I'll fire you."

"Buttercream would be fun, I bet."

"Buttercream is fun," said Nora. "You get into a groove."

They worked through red velvet cake and panna cotta and the little apple charlottes, and still Lauren seemed unwilling to let go and not quite able to relax. It was a nice change from the bolt-out-the-door behavior, but it made Nora feel that she had a job to do here, that she ought to say something maternal. Gently, she held Lauren at arm's length.

"Honey," she began, "it's going to be fine."

"Great! Chloe!" shrieked Lauren. She yanked herself free and ran over to Chloe, who had skipped the ceremony but snuck into the reception to see her friends. This, thought Nora, was transitional parenthood: a mom was as essential as ever until something more interesting came along, at which point she was instantly less than peripheral.

Joel returned a moment later with three cups of lemonade, only to find Nora standing alone, staring blankly at the dance floor. He handed her a cup.

"Now what?" she asked. She wandered off without waiting for his reply.

Less than an hour later, the graduates had changed into their street clothes and were on their way to a club at Universal City Walk that Crestview had taken over for the evening. Most of the parents left as soon as their children drove away, but some of them lingered, confused, trying to make sense of the fact that they would never again need to set foot on the Crestview campus. On one side of the main gate, a woman Nora and Joel did not know tried to guide her sobbing husband toward the parking lot. Another couple walked past, the wife whispering much too loudly to her husband about what she intended to do to him once they got back to their blissfully empty house. Everyone except the sobbing husband seemed to be aggressively, emphatically happy to be footloose, and everyone except the sobbing husband was working overtime to convince onlookers that their delight was genuine.

Nora sank onto one of the teak benches that ringed the front lawn, and Joel reluctantly sat down next to her.

"Here's what I hate about graduation," she said.

"Besides the endless speeches."

"Yeah."

"The uncomfortable chairs."

"Yeah."

"The numbskull valedictorian, the slightly off-key choir. Except for Lauren, of course."

"Stop it," she said, smiling. She leaned against him. "What I hate about graduation is that it's so short."

"Nora. It went on forever."

"You know what I mean. You finally get to the great day and it's, I don't know, what do you think? Thirty seconds to walk up and get your diploma? I expected it to feel different. I expected it to feel big. Memorable. In proportion to everything that led up to it. I mean, it was touching, she looked so happy, but maybe it's us, maybe somebody else would have been happier than us."

"Let's go," said Joel, putting his arm around Nora and pulling her to her feet. She got up willingly enough, so he kept his arm around her shoulder and guided her toward the parking lot, past the security guard, who only wished that the other stragglers would leave so that he could close up and go home.

"It's so fast," she said. "I have to think about what to make her special for breakfast tomorrow. Lunch, probably, by the time she wakes up."

Joel opened the passenger-side door for Nora, which he never did, but he had the sense that she would not budge without prodding. He waited until she was settled, muttered, "Seat belt" as though she were a child, and walked around to the driver's side, in a bit of a haze himself.

He turned the key in the ignition, put the car into gear, edged toward the exit, and headed by rote toward the freeway and home. As he approached the on-ramp, Nora reached over and touched his arm.

"Let's not go home yet," she said.

"Okay," he said, no more eager than she was to walk into an

empty house that he knew would feel different from the pre-graduation empty house. "Where should we go?"

Nora did not reply.

"We haven't had dinner," he said.

"I'm really hungry," she said, slowly coming to her senses. "I didn't eat at the reception."

"Let's go get sushi," said Joel.

"Lauren loves sushi," said Nora, as though it would be a betrayal to enjoy it without her.

"I know," said Joel. "Let's go get some."

He felt as loyal to memory as Nora did, but he thought that the right move might be to resist it, given how much they both liked yellowtail.

A boy in Seattle was diagnosed with mononucleosis in August, two weeks before he was supposed to move into his residence hall at Yale. He decided to take a gap year so that he could sleep eighteen hours a day, which opened a spot at Yale for a boy who worried about whether the theater department at Middlebury had decent contacts in New York, which opened a spot at Middlebury for a girl who had been hysterical all summer about drowning at a school as big as Penn, which opened a spot at Penn for a boy who was equally hysterical about being in the middle of nowhere at Oberlin, which opened a spot at Oberlin for a boy who worried despite everything the University of Chicago said about its campus security, which opened a spot at Chicago for a girl who preferred the gritty reality of the south side of Chicago to the suburban sprawl of Northwestern's lakeside campus.

Which opened a first-quarter slot at Northwestern for Lauren Chaiken.

Thanks to a boy who had to take a nap if he got up to brush his teeth, six disgruntled teenagers and their revisionist parents got exactly what they had been trying for weeks to convince themselves they no longer wanted. Nora and Joel had made a pact to plan family distractions for late August, when Lauren's friends started heading off to school, but a single phone call from a solicitous Northwestern admissions officer changed all of that. They had three weeks to plan a move that had occupied most of their friends since July.

Nora and Lauren trolled the aisles at Bed, Bath & Beyond with a scanner, pointing it at every item they thought Lauren might need and several they were skeptical about. There was no time to debate whether she would get a lot of use out of a steel floor-to-ceiling shower caddy with four mesh baskets. It showed up on several must-have lists supplied by parents of older children, so they ordered it. They priced full-length down coats at REI and Patagonia and had a fight on a street corner in downtown Santa Monica about whether a wool coat and a sweater might do as well. They bought rain boots and underwear and socks. When Joel pointed out that there were stores in Chicago, they stormed out of the room in opposite directions, but not before reminding him that the whole point of shopping at Bed, Bath & Beyond was to have the order transmitted and filled by the store in Evanston. He did not have the nerve to explain that he was only talking about clothing. He went to Costco and bought two more suitcases.

They bought three plane tickets, one of them one-way, which caused Nora to take refuge in the kitchen and not emerge until she had put a gâteau basque with cherry filling into the oven. Joel visited the websites of all the hotels within a five-mile radius of Northwestern, only to find that they were full during move-in week, so they settled for a hotel eight miles away from campus and rented a car, which they reconsidered and upgraded to an SUV.

Lauren emailed her newly acquired roommate, who turned out to be a musical-comedy star from Newark who had never imagined ending up west of NYU, and who seemed to feel about Evanston the way Lauren had felt about Santa Barbara.

"No matter," said Nora, blithely. "She'll be out auditioning all the time. You'll be busy making your own friends."

She did not mean a word of it. She was intimidated by the roommate on Lauren's behalf, but there was no time for ambivalence. Nora had time only for cheerleading, the acquisition of

color-coordinated extra-long twin bed linens, and late-night conversations with Joel about the best way to underwrite their dream
come true.

≈≈

Nora thought she was awake. She was about to call downstairs to
ask Joel to turn on the coffeemaker, but when she opened her
mouth to speak, she heard, instead, a little girl's faraway laugh. It
was not Lauren. Nora knew that laugh. This one was different,
higher, younger, and coming toward her. Someone else began to
laugh, and then Nora heard an unfamiliar deep voice, one that she
would recall with a start in eight years, when Lauren brought
home a man who sounded exactly like that for a significant visit.
She heard Joel's voice, too, and her own intake of breath as she
hoisted a little girl, the laughing girl, higher than she thought
she was able.

Nora was on a beach with all these people, along with a dog
who ran down to the ocean and back, down and back, chasing the
waves until the waves chased him. But then Joel turned off the
shower, and the sound of the surf ceased, and she began, slowly,
to surface.

In that sprung moment between sleep and waking, when it
could be any day at all, past or coming, Nora saw her family in what
might be right now or might be the future, because she could not
tell for sure until she was fully awake. Everything she thought she
knew as daily life could be a sleep story; she had dreamt of herself
as a grown-up, after all, when she was only eight. The moments
she believed she had experienced, before, could all be far ahead in
time.

She might not have given the useless floor-to-ceiling bathroom caddy to a friend of Lauren's roommate who seemed to
think she could not live without it. She might not have stood in
the middle of the street and waved good-bye to Lauren's dorm

window. She might not have gone out to dinner with Joel that night and burst into tears when a woman with a baby sat down in the next booth. This might not be the third day without so much as a text message from Lauren, which would require an intervention if they still had not heard from her by dinnertime. All of that might not have happened, not yet.

Joel turned on his electric razor and Nora woke to the sound with a happy, confused jolt, wondering how she had managed to sleep through an alarm clock that in fact would not go off for another ten minutes, wondering how they would ever get Lauren off to Crestview on time—when at that very moment Lauren was settling into her seat for her freshman world literature survey lecture, and the boy who had sat next to her for the last three classes in a row was leaning over to ask if he could borrow a pen. Another blink, another moment, and Nora would realize exactly where she was.

Acknowledgments

After many years of making sure that every detail was fact, I am grateful to the singular Lynn Nesbit for standing by, as supportive as ever, while I made sure that every detail was fiction. Thanks to Ellen Archer and Pam Dorman for inviting me to do so, and to Barbara Jones and Sarah Landis for their attention and enthusiasm.

The people who read this book or advised me along the way include a friend I have yet to meet in person, a friend who has encouraged me to write fiction since we were applying to college, and astute young readers who served as experts on the high school scene. I am indebted to them all: William Whitworth, Harry George, Nicole Allen, Lesly Gregory, and Benjamin Odell. Special thanks to Ginger Curwen for pretty much everything she ever said about this book, including "Just keep writing."

Marcie Rothman has been a great and caring friend for a very long time, and I thank her, simply, for that. I'm also grateful to Lori Rifkin, Jo Ann Consolo, Phyllis Amaral, and Vicky Mann, in this case for maintaining group sanity during our stint as the parents of college applicants, and to Sam Freedman for his long-distance support. Thanks as well to the admirable Patty Williams and Annette Duffy Odell.

Given the topic, I'm grateful to my mother and my late father for insisting that I finish freshman year at the wrong college, which enabled me to transfer as a sophomore to the right one; one of their many smart moves.

Thanks to my friends in Sullivan Canyon for continuing not to care what I do, unless it involves a horse. And doting gratitude to Clark and Cassidy, cofounders of the carbonial dog-share program.

More than thanks to the only person I would ever allow to refer to me as "My little chicken." She knows how much I love her.

My husband and daughter know how much I love them, too, but here are a couple of pertinent reasons why:

Larry Dietz somehow maintains absolute faith in me, even when my own is flagging. I thank him for pretending it's normal—fun, in fact—to have a wife who expects him to listen while she speculates on whether a fictional girl would or would not do a fictional thing, and further expects him to pretend, convincingly, that such questions have definitive answers.

And Sarah, ever the reader, was my new editor on this project; she took notes and flagged pages and reviewed her comments with me, and I have her spiral-bound copy of the manuscript on my desk, as precious a family heirloom as there can be. I am happy every day because of her, and that was true even when she was applying to college.

Patricia Williams

Karen Stabiner is the author of eight books, a regular contributor to The Huffington Post and the *Los Angeles Times* Opinion section, and an adjunct professor at the Columbia University School of Journalism. Her daughter left for college in the fall of 2007.